BECOMING MRS. WRIGHT

This book is a work of fiction. Names, characters, places, and incidents are a product of the author's imagination or are used fictitiously. Any resemblance to actual events, locales, or persons, living or dead, is coincidental.

A Chronicles of a Dancing Heart Novel

Book Two

Becoming

MRS. WRIGHT

OLIVIA BOOTHE

Three Brothers Press

For all the aspiring authors still struggling with self doubt. If you don't write it, no one will read it. So get off your ass and start writing.

Author's Note

Previously published as Wicked Embrace in 2020, Becoming Mrs. Wright is the 2nd book in Olivia Boothe's completed contemporary billionaire romance duet. The the story remains untouched. However, this new edition includes a brand new cover and two bonus chapters (Chapters 40 and 41).

Content Advisory

For audiences 18 years+, explicit sexual scenes, war veteran, PTSD, depression, death, grief, depiction of a miscarriage, mention of substance use, foul language, depictions of sexual assault (not gratuitous and not by the hero), some physical violence. Reader discretion is advised

One

SARA

"YOUR SKIN SMELLS SO GOOD, BABY," Tom whispered in my ear, his breath stirring me awake, the kisses he feathered over my neck sending sweet shivers down my spine.

I sighed and moaned with delight as I stretched under the cool covers of his bed, the warm rays of the August sun shining brightly through the windows of his posh Hoboken apartment. We never bothered to close the blinds before going to bed, and I reveled, smiling at the beauty of the view outside his bedroom. Across the Hudson River, the New York City skyline glimmered under the buttery-yellow light of the sun.

"And your lips feel divine," I murmured, nestling my back into his naked chest as he wrapped his arm tighter around my waist. "I like being woken up like this."

I felt his lips stretch into a smile on my skin as he pressed me against his body, his erection a hard ridge on my backside.

Dear heavens, would I ever get tired of this? Of him?

Snaking his hand up my chest, he began to play with my nipples as he nibbled my ear, his expert touch making a rumble of pleasure vibrate through my body.

Nope. I'd never get tired of this. Ever since the debacle at the dance company eight weeks ago, we'd been inseparable, spending more time naked in bed than anywhere else. And Tom was a ravenous beast unable to go without his daily fix. But more than needing to satisfy his own desires, he was obsessed with my pleasure, unwilling to let me rest unless I orgasmed multiple times. And I couldn't get enough of his chiseled body, or the way he moved inside me without restraint, the searing heat in his eyes claiming every ounce of me.

"Someone's happy," I said, arching my back, my invitation clear.

"And hungry," he growled as he took his hand from my chest and grabbed my chin in his fingers. Missing his touch, my nipples tingled in protest as he turned my mouth toward his.

I pursed my lips closed, denying him the kiss. With the comfort of spending almost every day with him came the truth of life's not so sexy realities. Morning nookie had a no-kissing clause.

His mega-watt smile spread a mile wide, and he said, "Aw, baby. Your dragon breath is not that bad this morning."

My eyes bulged at his confirmation, and he burst into laughter. Even though we'd known each other for three months, I wasn't accustomed to the reality my breath didn't smell like flowers in the morning. It mortified me. He was Thomas Wright, CEO of Wright and Thompson Luxury and Commercial Real Estate—a man who not only exuded power but was drop-dead gorgeous and a magician in bed. I'd dubbed him Mr. Panty-Dropper.

And some days, I worried this fairytale would end. The man who had mystified me that day at the coffeehouse when I first saw him, the man I'd stalked for days trying to figure out how he captivated me, the man who had somehow found the key and opened the door to my heart, woke up next to me nearly every day. It was, indeed, a dream come true. But happiness couldn't last forever, and the thought always found ways to shadow my light.

Climbing on top of me and caging me in his arms, his wolfish intentions made my troubling thoughts whisk away. His massive six-foot-four frame extended down over my body. Chest muscles rippling, and biceps flexing as he held himself up above me, he said, "If you don't want me to kiss you, I can find other places for my lips to explore." A wicked smile pulled on the corners of his lips, his green eyes twinkling with mischief.

My thighs clenched in anticipation of what that savage mouth of his could do to my sex.

There was no reason to utter my approval. Tom knew he was my weakness.

His pleasurable torture began with a tantalizing cascade of kisses on my neck, each touch of his lips setting my skin ablaze. My nipples hardened, and my breath quickened as he glided down my chest and over my abdomen, lavishing every inch of my flesh with his mouth. I trembled when his lips traveled over my hips, his tongue licking the insides of my thighs. We'd spent all night making love—as well as countless other nights—yet every time he touched me, it felt as scorching hot as the first time we'd been together.

Spreading my legs for him, I readied myself for another mind-blowing orgasm, but before his tongue could do its magic, a sickening feeling curdled in my stomach.

Oh, God. Not again.

Overtaken with nausea, I pushed away from him and hastened to the bathroom, a hand over my mouth.

"Sara?" Tom called after me. But I didn't have time to answer him. Shutting the bathroom door behind me, I leaned over the toilet and dry-heaved until my abdominal muscles ached and nothing but bile came out.

This can't be happening again.

After washing my mouth and wiping the sweat beaded on

my forehead, I closed the toilet lid and sat there naked. The thought chasing me for the last couple of days gnawed at me again, snuffing out the sexual fire Tom had kindled. It had been almost two weeks since I'd missed my period. At first, pregnancy didn't cross my mind. Ever since Tom and I decided to make things official, I'd gone on the pill. When my breasts started to feel tender, I thought my body had been off. Confident my period would come soon, I tucked my worries away. Then the nausea began three days ago.

That's when true worry seeped into my bones. I'd called my best friend, Jen, and she convinced me to take a pregnancy test. Apprehensive, but knowing I needed to do it, I agreed to go to the pharmacy. Aside from the one reckless time in Santa Monica when we first started dating, Tom and I hadn't had unprotected sex. How could I be the one percent who got pregnant on the pill? I couldn't believe my luck.

Seemed the universe could never stop screwing with my life.

I couldn't go through with it, though. The test still lay unopened and buried at the bottom of my handbag. I'd hoped all I needed was more time, that perhaps my period would come by the end of the week. Jen said taking the test would give me peace of mind. But the thought of taking the test gave me more anxiety. Too scared to confirm my fears, I did every-thing possible not to think about it, including planning a memorable night out with Tom. Last night he'd been a tonic to my ailing heart and troubled mind. And this morning, I'd woken up in a gooey, happy-sappy haze. Worry-free.

Until the sick feeling rumbling inside me made me remember.

Shivering in the cold bathroom, I held myself tight as the twisting despair churned in my brain. An unplanned preg-nancy wasn't even the crux of my problems. When I quit my job at the Rebecca Fitzgerald Dance Company eight weeks ago, I never guessed I'd still be looking for work. Alexei

Voronov, the head choreographer for the dance company, had stolen my dance-revival routine, planning to use it in the company's show without my consent. The prick assaulted me when I confronted him about it. Unfortunately, when Tom handed in my resignation with a fist through Alexei's face, the asshole vowed I'd never find a job with another dance company in the city. He must have kept his promise.

Since then, I'd been relentless in searching for work and still hadn't received any call-backs. Now my bank account was nearing zero. And without a studio to rehearse in, my plan to revive my dance career was at a complete standstill. I was beginning to lose all hope. My hair was falling out in clumps from all the stress, and my mood was in the pits. Now a baby? How could I handle another hurdle?

Placing a hand over my belly and unable to hold in my grief any longer, my chest heaved as I broke down in silence.

A knock at the door startled me. "Sara, are you okay in there?"

"I… ah…" Wiping tears from my eyes, I choked on my words. I wanted to confide in Tom. But we'd been dating only three months. We hadn't even discussed the prospects of marriage or having children. I didn't know if he ever wanted to get married, for that matter, especially after what happened with his ex-fiancée. And kids? Well, I'd always seen myself having a family one day, but Tom and I were still getting to know each other. I couldn't see us with children, at least not yet. This was all terrible timing. What if he didn't want a baby? Now or ever? Would he leave me if I was pregnant? Would he ask me to…?

I shook my head, unable to even contemplate the thought.

The doorknob jangled. "Baby, is everything all right?" he asked again.

"I'm okay," I replied, my voice shaking.

"Can I come in?" he probed, his voice edged with concern.

All I wanted was to run and hide, but I couldn't avoid the issue any longer. Tom had every right to know. Taking a deep breath, I stood and took one of the cotton robes hanging on a towel hook, draping it over myself before opening the door. My heart constricted at the sight of him. Tom's golden-brown hair was a messy bundle atop his head, and his olive eyes simmered with a deep fire, worry flickering behind the intensity of his gaze. He'd put on sweatpants and a t-shirt. Thank goodness. Right now, I needed to stay focused, and a naked Tom was hard to ignore. Still, our previous night spent making love crashed through me like a tidal wave, flames of desire licking up and down my body. I'd kissed every inch of his skin, losing my entire being in worshiping him.

I loved him so much my chest ached.

And the news I was about to give him could rip him away from me. Forever.

"Tom," I said, "we need to talk."

Two

SARA

Tom sat at the edge of his bed, elbows resting on his knees, hands cradling his face. "How long have you known?" he asked.

"A few days, I guess. I'm never late, but since I was on the pill, I didn't give it much thought. Well, until a few days ago when I started feeling sick."

He turned to me, eyes darkened. "This is it, then? We are having a baby?"

Sitting next to him on the bed, my thigh touching his, I sucked in a deep breath. "I haven't taken the test yet, but there's a good chance."

He continued to stare at me in silence, his face a canvas of confusion.

I wasn't sure how to read him. Confusion didn't tell me if he wanted to embrace this with me or if he wanted to bolt. Plus, the wordless stare made my skin prickle with panic. Losing Tom would feel like the apocalypse.

What if I had to tackle this alone? Could I raise a baby all by myself?

I peered down at my hands resting on my lap. The answer to that was now irrelevant. I'd made my decision. "I understand how unexpected this is, and well…" I paused, trying to postpone his reaction for one more second. Who was I kidding? There was no use in delaying it any longer. The sooner I told him, the sooner this would be over.

I raised my gaze and nearly lost my resolve when I met his eyes. This time I saw his love for me reflected in those eyes, and it cracked my bones to contemplate losing him forever. I dropped my chin as I shut my eyes and let out the longest breath of my life. "I've decided to keep the baby."

The phrase hung in the air. When he said nothing, my heart dropped into my stomach. Hands shaking, my eyes brimmed with unshed tears. His silence told me everything I needed to know.

"If you don't want any part in it—I understand," I said, trying to sound calm, business-like. As if my insides hadn't liquefied. "I won't ask you for money or anything," I choked out, my cold, hard exterior cracking, betraying the turmoil inside.

Tom took my chin in his fingers and placed his lips on mine. "Take the test," he whispered. And for a moment, time stood still. His kiss was warm and tender. It held hope, a promise that perhaps I wouldn't have to do this alone.

Two minutes later, I came out of the bathroom holding the test stick in my hand.

Tom jumped to his feet, his eyes widening. "So?"

I ran toward him, flinging myself into his chest and wrapping my arms around his neck.

He squeezed me tight for a long minute before peeling me off. "Sara?"

I couldn't contain myself. Tears rolled down my face, but my heart beat with joy. Tom continued to stare at me with dumbfounded eyes as I placed the test stick in his palm. He looked at it then back at me. "What's one red line mean?" he asked.

Wiping wetness from my cheeks, I cocked my head to the

side then burst into laughter. "It means I'm not pregnant. We're not having a baby."

Tom plopped back down on his bed, placing the test stick on his nightstand, and burying his face in his hands.

Not the reaction I'd expected. By now, I thought he'd be celebrating with me. Instead, he slouched on his bed like he had received horrible news. I stopped smiling and hurried to kneel in front of him. As I pried his hands from his face, my blood chilled. His gaze was haunted, mournful. "Babe, what's wrong?" I asked.

He remained silent.

"Tom, did you hear what I said? I'm not pregnant. We are not having a baby." I smiled at him, trying to reassure him I'd delivered good news. *Excellent* news.

He simply stared at me.

"It's good news," I said. "Right?"

He released me from his gaze then laid down on his bed.

I followed, snuggling next to him. "Tom, talk to me. What is going on?"

He turned toward me. "Having a family. Children. It's never been in my plans, Sara. I didn't have a good father figure. How can I be a good father to anyone?"

"I'm so sorry… I didn't realize—"

"Sara, for a moment, I saw my life ending."

Oh. I knew having a baby now wasn't a good idea. I mean, I had been scared as hell, too. But to hear him utter those words? It confirmed my fears. Tom didn't want kids. Now or ever. The ache in my heart was debilitating. If I wasn't going to lose him now, I would without a doubt lose him later.

He must have seen the sorrow frosted over my eyes because he reached over and pushed a strand of hair behind my ear, caressing my cheek. "What I meant to say was, I saw my life ending and a new one beginning. One I wanted to share with you more than anything. Those two minutes you spent in the bathroom, felt like a lifetime to me. Our life flashed before me."

My heart almost exploded with relief and with an overwhelming rush of love for this man. My eyes misted over. He wiped them with his thumb, drying up all doubts I ever had of wanting to spend the rest of my life with this man.

"I saw her, you know," he said with a smile. "A little girl with big green eyes and long dark hair, running around in a pink tutu. Stealing my heart." The warmth in his eyes spoke of the love he felt for a child we didn't even have.

"Tom, I…" I didn't know how to respond. I had wanted nothing more than to not be pregnant, yet he had seen a future with us and our daughter.

"It's not the right time for us, I know that," he said, interrupting my thoughts. "But understand, if you'd been pregnant, I would have married you tomorrow, Sara. And I would have given both of you the world."

Forget speechless, I was without thoughts either. All I could do was burrow myself in his chest where he held me in the most powerful and protective embrace I could ever dream of. I felt safe in his arms, and I knew at that moment there was no doubt Tom was the man I was meant to be with. We didn't have sex that morning, but we did make love, nonetheless.

LATER IN THE DAY, cellphone in hand, I updated Jen as I made my rounds around the city looking for work.

"If you're not knocked up, then why were you late? You said you were feeling sick," Jen said.

"I've been stressed about this whole unemployment thing. Maybe that's it."

"Maybe you should go see your doctor, you know? To make sure."

"I'm fine."

"But what if you're not?"

"Hold that thought, I'm getting a second call."

As I waited to cross the street, I pulled the phone from my ear to look at the caller. My chest caved.

Shit.

My ex's sister called me two months ago when I was in Santa Monica, but I never returned her call.

Dammit.

I had zero desire to talk to this woman, but she'd keep calling if I didn't answer.

Trying not to end up on the hood of a taxi, I hurried to the other side of the street along with a horde of New Yorkers rushing back from their lunch break. "Jen, it's Lisa," I said, putting the phone back to my ear. "Can I call you back?"

"Fine, but don't forget."

"Okay," I said, then clicked to receive the incoming call. "Lisa… hi," I crooned with the fakest happy tone I could muster.

"Hey," she replied coolly.

"Listen, I'm sorry for not calling you back sooner."

Lie.

"No worries," she said, the tone of her voice barely masking her annoyance with me. "It's so loud over there. Sounds like you're in Times Square."

"Broadway, actually. I lost my job almost two months ago, so I'm running around submitting resumes."

"Terrible," she replied with zero concern. "Look, the reason I'm calling is because I need a favor."

"Okay…" It was a good thing she couldn't see my wincing face.

"I have this…friend I want you to meet," she said, an air of mischief to her voice.

"I'm not interested in meeting anyone now. I'm seeing somebody."

"Oh, it's not like that. He's a…dancer. You know. Like you."

That caught my attention. I stopped under a scaffolding on Broadway and 19th street, near the Ballet Company where I had an appointment. Covering one year with a finger so I could hear her better, I asked, "A dancer?"

"He's looking for work in the city."

"Like I said before," I told her, "I lost my job, so I don't think there is much I can do. I can't get him an audition if that's what you're asking."

"Bummer. But you can still meet with him, though, can't you?"

"What for?"

"Talk to him, you know. Give him some tips or something."

"Lisa, I'd love to help him, but there isn't anything useful I can do for him. Plus, I'm swamped looking for work myself."

"Can you at least talk to him? Please. He is new to the city and needs someone to show him around."

"You want me to babysit your friend?"

'Sara, can you do it or not?"

It was nearly 1:00 p.m., and if I didn't get off the phone with her, I would be late for my appointment. Resigned, I said, "Doesn't sound like I have a choice, do I? Give him my cell and tell him to call me."

"Um, he doesn't have a phone, yet. We communicate through email, but why don't I tell him when and where you could meet him. How about tomorrow?"

"I have plans with my boyfriend this weekend."

"It's just for an hour."

"We're going to be up in Lake George. His brother is getting married this Sunday."

"How about Monday?" she pressed.

"Tuesday is better. I can do five o'clock. Int'l House of Java at Rockefeller."

"Super. He's going to be so stoked to see you."

"Who is this guy, anyway?"

"Someone I've known forever. It's going to be great. You're gonna love him."

"Okay, well—"

"Anyway," she interrupted, "I gotta go, but thanks again. Talk to you soon, bye." She hung up before I finished my thought.

That's when I realized I didn't even know the dude's name. And that I had two minutes to run to my appointment.

MY DAY TURNED into another jobless afternoon. The Ballet Company wasn't looking to hire any new assistants. I was going to have to change professions if I was ever going to be employed again.

When I pushed through the front door of Tom's apartment, I found the place draped in shadows. As I turned on the foyer lamp, I caught sight of Tom sitting in an armchair. Facing the panoramic view of the evening New York City skyline, he remained still as a statue.

"Tom?"

Still dressed in his suit, and not bothering to say hi, he raised a hand, a slight flick of two fingers was his wave hello.

Hmm. What's that about?

Shedding my shoes and greeting Bax, his chocolate lab, I rushed into Tom's bedroom, eager to get out of my pencil skirt and blouse, and happy to liberate myself from my shirt and bra. I slid into a white tank top and a pair of black yoga pants then walked back out and toward the man in shadows.

I almost tripped on the suitcase sitting on the living-room rug. "Whoa, you finished packing?"

Silence.

I walked closer until I was right behind him, my hands resting on his shoulders. I rubbed them, trying to release some of the evident tension coming off his body. "My bag is in the Jeep," I said. "Maybe you can bring it up for me later? I have some extra things I need to add."

"It's empty," he replied coolly.

"What's empty?"

"The suitcase. I haven't packed."

I came around to face him. "Is something wrong?"

"Nothing's wrong. I'm simply not going to the wedding." Tom leaned back on his chair, spreading out his legs. "I don't know why I ever agreed to go to this thing."

I pulled the ottoman in front of him and sat down. "You agreed to this because James is your brother, and you are his best man. This is your family."

He sat up straighter, arrowing his gaze into mine. "That's exactly why I can't go. I haven't been home in ages. I swore I'd never go back."

"That was then, Tom. Things are different now. *You're* different."

He took a deep breath as he leaned back. "I don't think I'm ready to confront my ghosts."

"You mean your ex?"

He blinked, refocusing his bloodshot gaze on me. "Yes. And my father's memory. My whole past."

Leaning in close, I placed a palm on his cheek. "But you're not alone. I'll be there with you. I can help you get through it."

Tom shook his head, pulling away from my touch, unwilling to accept my reassurance. "Sara, we'd be opening Pandora's box. The town I'm from is extremely small. I'll be running into old acquaintances. People who knew me when everything happened."

I reached for his hands, drawing his tormented eyes back to me. "When you were with *her.* I know. I get it. But that's not you anymore. You're with *me* now."

Letting go of my hands, he brushed his fingers through his hair. "They'll be questioning why I haven't been back in all these years."

"Are you sure you're not projecting your own thoughts of guilt about your mom?"

He tunneled a spiny look into me. I knew about guilt. It gave me the right to be honest and blunt.

"You don't need to be secretive with me," I said. "I know it shames you. You think you abandoned your mother and your family. But you had your reasons. It's time to tell them the truth."

He raised an eyebrow, his eyes doubtful. "At my brother's wedding?"

"Why not?"

Running a palm down his face, his body bristled. "I'm not ready to talk about it. It took every ounce of my being to open-up to you, and now you think I can do it with *them*? This is James's weekend. Not going to make this about me."

"Does that mean you've changed your mind, then?"

He settled a curious gaze over me, his features softening. "Why are you so intent on us going, anyway? Aren't you at least a bit nervous about meeting my mother?"

Well, of course.

"This weekend is not about me either."

He took my hand and pulled me onto his lap. I snaked an arm around his neck while he held on to me.

"I'm bringing a girl home," he said, nudging my nose with his. "It's one hundred percent about you."

Resting my head on his shoulder, I played with his tie. "You think she'll like me?"

"She's gonna love you."

Pulling on his black tie, I brought his lips closer to mine. After the emotional start to the day, followed by another fruitless job hunt, I needed his comfort. "I missed you today."

"Hmm, is that so?" he replied, his voice bouncy with roguishness, reminding me of the sparkle that lit up in his eyes when he wanted to play. "Didn't we just see each other this morning?" he asked.

"Well, I don't like spending a second without you." I leaned in for an innocent kiss, but at the feel of his hot breath on me, my insides lit up like a raging pyre.

His tongue licked the seam of my lips, urging me to let him in. I obliged, allowing him to claim my mouth with his hunger. Without hesitation, I repositioned myself, straddling him, pushing myself into his body as my legs slid through the slits of his armchair. His large hands grabbed my ass and gently guided me closer to him, forcing me to graze his growing erection through his pants. My playful cat was back, and his rumbling moans vibrated on my skin as he descended his untamed mouth over my neck, sending chills down my spine and electric currents straight to my clit.

Heavens, I could never get enough of this man. I was addicted to his scent, his taste.

Moving over his lap, I rubbed my center over his hard cock, ripples of pleasure spreading from my core.

"I see what you're doing," he said in a throaty whisper as he grabbed my ass harder, rocking my hips over his length, the friction making me wetter.

I smirked. "Oh, yeah? And what's that?"

"Using sex to get me to forget about the wedding."

"Me?" I replied with an innocent giggle.

"It's working," he uttered, his voice deeper now. "All I can think about right now is me inside you, baby."

"In that case…" I took his hands off my ass and peeled myself off his body.

His eyes widened, the feral expression of desire flaming hot yet confused. "Whoa, wait. Where are you going?"

"Shush. Just stay right here. I'll be right back."

He didn't reply, but the way he looked at me made me feel like he would punish me if I didn't return to his lap. I knew his kind of punishment, and it involved his tongue and his refusal to let me come until he said so.

I was okay with that.

The thought made me dizzy with arousal. I smirked and turned around, sauntering over to his stereo where I queued up a sexy, jazzy tune. Sauntering back toward him, I made sure our gazes locked, and with one heated look, I let him know everything I wished to do to his body. He growled, and the sound only made me hotter and more determined.

I came to a stop behind his chair, and brushing my lips against his ear, I said, "I think we need to release some of this tension." My voice soft, I moaned as I slid my hands over his chest and further down until I cupped his cock in my hand. I stroked him through the thin fabric, watching with ravenous eyes as he moved his hips upward, begging me to unzip him and take him in my hand. He looked so delicious under my touch; I fought to contain my appetite.

I could have succumbed to him then but tonight was about him. Tom was so accustomed to being in control, always being the one deciding what came next, but this time, I wanted to give him the gift of letting go. Perhaps, it would help him deal with the turmoil churning in his chest. Or I might fuck this up and never again have the nerve. Either way, tonight, I would be the one in the driver seat.

Three

TOM

Fᴜᴄᴋ. If there was someone who knew how to blast through my defenses, it was Sara. Her perfume scent of vanilla and spice enveloped me as she brought her lips close to my skin, her mouth tracing kisses over my neck as her hand glided up and down my cock. I was so hard, I could've ripped straight through my pants. I turned toward her lips and tasted her, my haunting past fading, along with the ghosts still living there. Shoving aside all the torment and pain, I let her lips and hands drug me.

My muscles flared with male need as my tongue swept the inside her mouth. The warmth of her breath and the pulsing thrum of her desire shot a bullet of adrenaline straight through my heart. Sara had no idea how madly I needed her tonight. Her body. Her fire. Her love for me.

To make me forget.

To numb the sickness anchored in my gut—the debilitating addiction whose sharp claws still lay buried in my flesh. My mind flashed with the razor-edged memory of the glass of whiskey I'd poured earlier that day. It sat at the bar, untouched. It had taken every ounce of strength I possessed not to relapse. Sara hadn't noticed, thank God. She'd think it was my PTSD. That the nightmares had returned.

But the truth was, I didn't tell her how bad the pregnancy scare rattled me. I'd wanted to be strong for her. To let her know she had me—no matter what.

But the idea of being a father dredged up the memories of my abusive childhood. Now, in less than twenty-four hours, I would be back there. Where my life turned to shit. A mix of anxiety and anger fermented in my chest. The thought of seeing my family. Of stepping foot inside that house…it completely fucked me up.

But right now, there was no time for any of that nonsense. This was one of the reasons I was in love with Sara—her ability to trap me in a universe where only she and I existed. And I loved the universe she was creating for me now.

I was about to invite her to sit on my lap when she suddenly pulled away from me.

What the…?

My gaze was wild as I tracked every move she made. Sara paraded in front of me, the sway of her hips taunting my animal instincts. My eyes feasted on the way her stretch-pants hugged the curve of her ass and the lean muscles of her long legs. Shit. She had the sexiest legs I'd ever seen. And I wanted them resting on my shoulders.

"Do you want to see me dance?" she asked, calling my attention away from her legs and my indecent thoughts. Biting her bottom lip, she looked over her shoulder, her sultry gaze twinkling with dark amusement.

Do I want to see her dance?

Was she fucking serious? There was nothing more beautiful.

I nodded yes, my heart aching in anticipation.

Sara stood still for a moment, her chest rising and falling, her deep breaths sawing in and out in tune with the rhythm of the music she'd queued up a few minutes before. In awe, I watched the chords imbue themselves into her muscles. Her body came to life like a butterfly emerging from its cocoon. Her arms outstretched as if pulled by invisible tethers. Her legs carried her across my wood floors like a bird gliding through the air.

As the seduction in the song rose, so did her confidence. Sara's innocent beauty matured before my eyes, her body demanding my full attention. Eyes wide and heart racing, the pounding in my chest intensified as her delicate hands slipped into the waistband of her pants.

Sara turned to face the twinkling New York City lights, and in that same playful and fluid motion, she gyrated her hips as she lowered her pants to the floor, exposing the black, lacy thong underneath. She bent down, giving me a tantalizing view of the small of her back and her exquisitely round ass. Fuck. She looked so gorgeous, and the sight of her like that—showing herself off to me—only made me want to ravage her. As if my cock couldn't get any harder, she stepped out of her clothes and dropped to the floor in an impossible split.

Shit.

Her striptease artfully toyed with my imagination.

With that one mischievous trick, she awoke the beast inside me. My dick throbbed at the sight of her spread legs. I was painfully engorged, desiring nothing more than to take her right there on my floor.

To the beats of the music, she rolled onto her back, spreading her legs, arching her spine, and showing me more of her secret places. My own legs urged me to the edge of my seat. There was no way I could sit there any longer. I rose to my feet, set on pouncing on her, but Sara stood and walked over to me, placing a palm on my chest, and pushing me back into my chair. "You stay right there," she said, her voice raspy, coating me like hot wax. "Just watch," she added with a tone of command and authority that left no room for negotiation.

Just watch? She must be fucking joking.

But she wasn't smiling. Sara remained dangerously close, eyeing me with hot intent.

Fuck. Me. She had me by the balls. I swallowed hard. I loved every ounce of it. To have her take control of me like this… it was one hundred percent what I needed.

I smirked and nodded, leaning back in my chair, letting her know I would play by her rules.

For now.

Sara began her torture by slipping my suit jacket off my shoulders and yanking it free. Once finished, she leaned into me, pressing her breasts to my chest. She lowered her lips to my neck, trailing smoking hot kisses from my jawline to my ears, licking until I could no longer contain myself. I slid my hands up her shirt and massaged her braless flesh, rubbing my palms against her perked nipples.

I tried to rip off the damn tank top, but she stopped me.

"Nah-uh," she crooned. "I said, just watch." With that, she grabbed my hands and entwined her fingers through mine.

I gazed up at her beautiful face and found the gleam of success shining in her eyes—a feline about to snatch her prey. Her lips were a magnet. I couldn't stop staring at her fleshy mouth. Couldn't stop thirsting for her kiss. Lost in delirium, I let her take my hands as she tied them behind my back—with my own tie.

"What's this?" I asked in a breathless whisper as I glanced over my shoulder.

"A little fun," she uttered, triumph dancing in her chocolate eyes.

This wasn't my typical type of kink, but she'd aroused me to the point of agony, and the idea of being vulnerable for her made me even hotter for this woman. She grabbed an armless chair from the dining table and placed it in front of me.

Holy fuck. I had a feeling where this was going.

With slow and fluid movements, she straddled it, gyrating her hips in tune to the music. Then she lifted her shirt and rested the fabric on the mounds of her breasts. Through the iron bars of the chair, she gave me a full view of her naked chest.

My breath caught.

Those hard, dark nipples drove me wild. Now, I wasn't so crazy about the control she had over me.

My cock hurt, anxious to rip from the confines of my pants. My muscles flexed as I pulled on the restraints wrapped around my wrists. I looked up at her with wonder. She had me good. Someone had clearly taught her how to tie a knot as good as an Eagle Scout. I wanted her even more. She had the nerve to turn me on like this and then tie me up? Oh, I was gonna kill her. A sweet death of pleasure with my tongue. I was going to make her come so hard she'd be lying motionless in my bed for hours.

Licking and sucking her fingers in unison with the music, her hands found her breasts. She massaged them, rubbing, and pinching her nipples as she moaned and writhed on the chair.

I closed my eyes, imagining those nipples between my teeth.

Yeah. I'm gonna kill her.

When I flipped them back open, our eyes locked onto each other.

"Untie me," I ordered.

"Not yet."

My jaw twitched. "Please. I need you."

I'm fucking begging?

She's so dead.

Her fingers slithered down toward the middle of her parted legs, holding them there until, with one slow move, Sara slid her panties to the side and showed me her freshly waxed mound. I lost it. My animal mind imagined everything

I wished to do to that body. My mouth watered as my drunk-with-lust eyes drowned in her nakedness. Her pink flesh glistened, the swollen nub of her clit poking through her private lips. I couldn't wait to slide my tongue over it. To drive my dick into her slick seam.

"Untie me, Sara." My voice was deep with male heat. Her name lingered on my tongue as I continued to struggle against the restraints. This time it wasn't a request but a damn warning.

She ignored me. Instead, with erotic delight on her face, she proceeded to pleasure herself, spreading the folds of her pussy, exposing more of her wetness, and flicking her clit with her index finger.

Fucking. Hell.

I needed my fingers in there. My tongue. My cock. I gulped, but all I tasted was the desert in my mouth. Watching as she dripped wet with arousal, imagining myself inside her slippery and tight entrance, made every muscle fiber in my body thrum. My tongue yearned to glide up and down that slit until she came, priming her for when I drove my dick deep inside her, filling her to the hilt.

She moaned and whimpered as she neared climax.

Ah, fuck. I loved watching her come.

Ragged breaths sawed in an out from my lungs as I imagined her writhing underneath me, mewling in ecstasy as I moved inside her. My breath seized in my chest, my heart pounding against my ribcage with excess force.

I shut my eyes again.

Christ, this woman is going to kill me.

"Do you want me?" she dared ask.

Her voice brought me back from impending delirium. Flipping my lids open, the sight of her was silk wrapping around my body, her words lava dripping down my skin.

"I want to fuck you," I clamored to her, my soul begging for her mercy.

Sara unsaddled the chair and strode toward me, her mouth sucking on her finger. My body trembled with readiness. With eyes ravaging her delicate skin, my mind continued to flip with images of what I ached to do her. On her back. On all fours. Then she dropped to her knees and unbuttoned my pants.

Fuck.

Skillfully slow, she rolled them down past my waist and thighs, my hard cock springing free as she lowered my boxers. I felt the blood pulsing through the bulging veins in my shaft, my crown growing hotter and firmer. I wanted those rosy lips wrapped around my girth, the tip of her tongue tracing every vein. Before I finished that thought—or breathed—her hot breath and wet mouth were on me.

"Ah, shit…" I moaned.

She licked my shaft, balls to head, saliva dripping, her tongue swirling until she swallowed my crown with famished hunger, guiding me deep into her mouth as she stroked me with her hand in fluid motions. I could feel the back of her throat as she glided up and down with fervor. I was harder than steel, her hot mouth close to summoning an explosion from me. Just when I thought I could no longer hold it back, Sara peered up at me through her long lashes, drawing me out, her tongue lapping at the tip of the head before raking her teeth over the tight skin.

Shit, that alone had my brain glazing over.

When did she learn how to do that?

I grinned at her. She replied with her own devilish smile.

Oh yeah, this was heaven, and she was the goddess.

With a sloppy kiss on my shaft, she buried me inside once more, sucking and slurping me up so fast I was ready to have the best motherfucking orgasm of my life.

I urged her with a growl, demanding she stop torturing me and get me to the fucking finish line. "Yeah, baby, just like that. Ah, fuck." My pleas only made her want to prolong it further. As she felt me tighten, she stopped and pushed up from the floor.

Damn. This woman.

With this game, she was going to murder me. I glared at her. There was going to be hell to pay once she freed my hands. As I was about to order her to untie me, she shut me up with her breasts near my face.

She might have been able to keep my hands from taking her, but there was no way she could stop me from devouring her nipples. I lowered my lips to her flushed skin and licked her flesh. Moans vibrated through her, driving me into a frenzy. She fed me her body, and one by one, I sucked and bit her nipples until they were red and hard as diamonds.

Yeah, I can inflict pain, too.

I still couldn't stop pleading. "Dammit, Sara. I want to be inside you." I needed to release the maddening tension—the buildup of this fucked-up day. She was my comfort, my only peace, and if she didn't give herself to me, I'd go insane. My labored breaths made her skin prickle. I continued to lick, swirling my tongue on those full, heavy breasts, trying to show her what the rest of her body was missing.

Her own heated breaths steamed from her lips. She pushed off me. Then, without wasting any more time, she hooked one finger through the waistband of her lacy thong and slipped out of her underwear.

Now, we're talking.

Seconds later, she straddled me, planting a brutal kiss on my lips as she descended her hot center over my cock, melting over me.

Ah…

Fucking beauty—the sight of her satiating her need with my body. My mind swam with salacious thoughts as I savored the aroma of her arousal. I yanked on the binds around my wrists. They were so tight, I'd most likely drawn blood. Every muscle in my body rippled with desire to hold her and touch her skin. Her hair cascaded down her back then over me as she flipped her head forward and reached for my neck, crashing her mouth into mine in a fevered kiss.

Her fleshy lips tasted like honey, and her tongue was alive with a fire so hot it singed me. I gorged on her until, with a bite to my bottom lip, she pulled away. We were so close our breaths became one. She panted and seeded her gaze into mine as she continued to grind her hips over my erection, squeezing my cock with her silky warmth, driving me to oblivion. I didn't want this to end. This mindless, unimaginable pleasure made my entire body tremble. I tried to think of something else, of some random business deal, of some shit on my to-do list—anything to keep me from coming inside her now.

Her smile was lazy and wicked. She knew exactly what she was doing to me, and she enjoyed every morsel of her torture. "Don't hold back, Tom. Give yourself to me."

"Not… yet," I panted.

"Always so in control. But how much longer can you keep it together, baby?" she moaned that last word as she sped up her pace, burying me so deep inside her, I felt every inch of her inner walls.

"You don't play fair," I told her, yanking on my restraints.

"You don't think so, huh?" Her moans turned to cries as she neared her own climax. Her gaze never leaving mine, she hooded her eyes, her mouth partly opened as each delicious sound she made blasted through me like a bolt of lightning. She was as intoxicated as I was by this little game she'd decided to play. And I loved every second of it.

Loved every inch of her. The connection we shared went beyond the pleasure we gave each other. I felt it building in my chest, in the way my heart squeezed for this woman. In the way I wanted to give myself to her, needing her to own me. But if she wanted to see me come for her, she needed to give me something first.

"You enjoy torturing me like this?" I asked in a growl.

"Yes," she crooned softly.

"Making me beg to fuck you?"

"Fuck, yes," she said, even more breathless.

"Is this what you want?" I asked as I bucked my hips upward to meet the wet silk of her sex. "I'm so fucking hard for you, baby, make me come inside you as you come, too."

At my imploring words, she said, "Not yet." With that, she pulled away from me, leaving me panting, my dick throbbing and slick. She sat on the ottoman across from me, so close I could smell her sweet scent. Then she parted her legs, putting herself on full display as she played with herself. In deliberate slow circles, she rubbed her swollen clit with a finger, using her own juices for lubrication. She moaned like I hadn't heard her before, the kind that's not for show and not for anyone but herself. She was prolonging her orgasm for as long as she could, making her clitoris so engorged it made me mad not to be the one rubbing it and driving her to an ardent release.

Her breath quickened as her cries rolled off her tongue. As she panted in anticipation of her orgasm, I watched her eyes flutter with rapture, then she finally came, her fingers soaked as she put them inside herself, pumping with every clench. My own body tensed, my balls hurting from not being able to come. An animalistic rage built inside me with the need to fuck, the need to make her mine. Then she walked over to me, her eyes still hooded, licking her fingers as she bent down and grabbed the armrests of my chair, caging me in her scent. "Your turn. How do you want it?" she purred, her lips twitching at the corners.

"Untie me," I uttered, my voice heavy.

Sara smiled as she walked behind me to loosen the knot. As she released me, I flexed my hands. My wrists were so red they were practically raw.

Noting the red rings, Sara took my hands and rubbed my wrists. "Oh no, Tom. I'm so sorry—"

I pulled away and grabbed her hands. "You started this game, now I finish it."

"But your wrists…"

"Will be fine," I replied coolly as I stood, my cock still raging hard. "You asked how I wanted it."

She peered up at me, her doe eyes shining with curiosity and simmering with feminine desire.

I lowered my lips to her ear. "Turn around and put your hands behind your back."

Her breath intensified as she obliged. I picked up my now ruined tie from the floor and fastened her hands together. There would be hell to pay. Her body trembled as I made sure her hands were secure. With her back to me, I pressed her into my chest and in gentle touches, feathered my fingers over her skin, touching every inch of her body, focusing on her breasts, circling her areolas until her nipples were hard as pearls.

"You like that, baby?" I asked. "The way my hands make you feel?"

She sighed her approval.

I caressed her hips, my hands closing in on her mound, but never making contact. She writhed, using her legs for friction.

"Did I say you could do that?" I whispered by her ear. "Open your legs and keep them spread."

"Touch me, then. I want your fingers playing with my clit."

"You're no longer calling the shots." I circled around her, drinking in the beauty of her naked body. The swell of her breasts, the curve of her waist, the tone of her long legs. And between them, her wetness. All of that was mine, and when I met her brown eyes, I felt her silent plea. I stepped closer and lifted her chin up with my fingers, nipping at her lips, pushing my tongue inside her, tasting her breath. And as I kissed her, I slid a finger between her legs, touching the soft and silky flesh until I found her swollen nub.

She moaned into my mouth, and it wrecked me. It was that same moan she'd given off when she pleasured herself, and it intoxicated me. I wanted that moan, and I wanted it while I was inside her.

"Get on your knees," I instructed her.

She did as commanded. With her hands bound behind her back, she looked like an erotic dream. I took off my dress shirt then stepped out of my pants and boxers. I grabbed her head in one palm and threaded my fingers through her thick, brown hair. With my other hand, I rubbed the pad of my thumb over her bottom lip. Damn, that mouth. I needed her lips around me one more time. "You want me inside your mouth?"

She nodded, looking up at me with eyes that could drown me. Taking my cock in my hand, I brought it to her lips and slowly penetrated her. It was sublime. I pumped my hips, each thrust pushing my dick further. I caressed her cheek as she sucked on my crown, slow then fast, her eyes locked on mine, the back of her throat making delicious sounds.

It went on forever—me fucking her mouth and she taking every inch of my cock like it was the last time we'd be together. I didn't want it to stop—this feeling of now owning her, of showing her what I'd wanted to do to that fucking perfect mouth of hers since she started this tease.

Ah fuck, I could've come right then, but that's not how I wanted it to end.

I pulled out of her mouth and kissed her before walking behind her and helping her up. "We're going for a walk."

She said nothing as I guided her to the bedroom and had her climb up onto the bed. Back on her knees, I bent her over, the side of her face flat against the mattress, her hands still bound behind her back, her ass at a perfect level.

I stood at the edge of the bed, her legs slightly apart in front of me. "You look so beautiful like this, baby," I said, caressing her skin.

The noises she made ignited me like a blaze, revving up my hunger for her.

"Tom, please."

I glided a finger down her seam. "Is this what you want?"

Her legs quivered.

"You're so wet, baby." I found her clit and mimicked what she'd done to herself earlier. "Is this how you like it?"

She made the sound, the one that drove me insane before. Now, I wanted to be the reason she moaned— only me. Taking her hips in my palms, I spread her ass cheeks and penetrated her slowly, watching as I put my crown in, holding it there then pulling out, repeating it several times until she begged me to come in deeper. All the pent-up sexual energy from earlier raked through me, and I couldn't get enough. With my thumb, I rubbed the entrance to her anus, adding pressure as I drove my cock into her pussy. It made her so wet, she began to glisten.

Fuck me. My mind went wild. This woman was going to be the end of me. We hadn't had anal sex before, but dammit, seeing how needy and wet she was, I wanted to take her there. Badly. I needed to take all of her, and holding back was unbearable. Before losing control, I calmed my thoughts. Tonight was not the right time. When we did it—if we did it —it would be under her terms. When she wanted it.

Still, I couldn't stop ramming into her. The harder I pushed, the louder she cried both in ecstasy and pain, fueling me. But what fueled my primal need to own her body, and what created the tight knot of sexual tension ready to uncoil in my groin, wasn't the sight of her tight ass and her hands bound behind her back. It had been her devotion to me—the fact she'd taken control and given it back. That she'd tried to help me forget—to help me heal. I had no idea how or why allowing her to rule me like this would be liberating in so many ways.

And as I felt my body tighten, my orgasm ready to burst, I

reached for her wrists and undid my tie. Her arms relaxed, and she let out a deep sigh. I traced my lips over her back until I reached her ear. "Turn over, baby."

As she did, I bent down to kiss her. "I love you, Sara."

She smiled sweetly, her eyes lazy, her limbs spent. "I love you more," she replied, her voice a mere breath.

"Can you take another round?"

She nodded, smiling as she spread her legs.

I feathered my fingers over her skin until her entire body flared with goosebumps. Then I kissed her soft breasts, sucking on her nipples, taking pleasure in the way her body reacted to me, the way her back arched. She was ready, but I needed more. Parting her folds with my fingers, I found her clit with the tip of my tongue. I brushed over her hard nub until I felt her legs shake. I was addicted to her taste, to the way her engorged clitoris felt against my tongue as I flicked and sucked on it, to the way her legs clenched as she was about to come. She was so fucking wet, I couldn't wait to be inside her again.

With two fingers, I pumped inside her as my tongue summoned her climax. Her cum was sweet and salty, and her scent fired off every neuron in my brain. I needed her now. Climbing up onto the bed, I drove inside her as she pushed up on her elbows and watched me bury myself in her warmth.

"Tom," she panted.

I reached over and brushed my fingers over her plump mouth as I continued to thrust my dick inside her, my tempo quickening. Her eyes rolled, her legs quivered. This was me owning her, and it was what pushed me to the finish line.

"I'm gonna come again." Her words were barely audible.

"I'm coming too, baby."

In one final thrust, I let myself fill her as she screamed out my name, her walls clenching around me. I pulled out as I continued to pulse, watching as I poured the rest of myself onto the outside of her sex. I couldn't stop gorging on the beauty of it as I reached between us, using my fingers to lather

her folds with my cum. She spread her legs wider, welcoming my touch. She'd taken every ounce of me. Claimed me as I had her. Mind, body, and soul.

She was one-hundred percent a goddess.

My goddess. And I never imagined I could possibly love her more than I already did. Yet, that night, I fell deeper into the bottomless abyss of my love for her.

SARA

THE NEXT MORNING, wanting to beat the weekend traffic, we woke up at dawn, had a light breakfast, and packed up the Rover before jumping on the New York Thruway. Sitting in the passenger seat, I rested my head back and closed my eyes, relishing in the rare but welcoming cool August air. I was more than happy for the reprieve from all the recent heat. Being able to sit on leather seats without singing my legs, and traveling with the windows down and no AC, was refreshing.

Plus, Tom had woken up in a great mood. No brooding and no second thoughts about the wedding. Perhaps it was the fact he let himself be vulnerable with me during a time when he's usually his most dominant. Getting him to drop his guard wasn't easy, but last night, something in him broke—hopefully the remaining wall of his defenses. I only wished I'd known sooner tying him up would be the secret to extinguishing the storm-cloud always hovering above him. Last night hadn't been the only time I'd found him gloomy and moping around the apartment, dragging his man-paws like a crestfallen lion.

Back when we first met, he told me about his dark past. I learned the demons lurking inside were more ill-defined than he'd led on. All along, I thought I was the one with the shell to crack, but as I got to know him better, I realized Tom had a concrete wall built so thick and high around his heart, it was possible not even a wrecking ball would be enough to chip it.

The emotional-beating he endured with his first love ruined him for the many women he encountered long after her betrayal. I didn't know how it happened, and he didn't either, but back in Santa Monica, he told me I was the only woman to find a door to the fortress protecting his heart.

Like an open book, he laid his feelings out for me. No secrets, he'd said. But when it came to his childhood, he'd always left it vague. What I later learned was that Shayna's betrayal and his time in the war were the tips of the iceberg. His true torment, what pushed him to leave his home in the first place, lay buried deep in his childhood. His relationship with his father scarred him for life. Even years after his father's death, his ghost still haunted him.

And when James called one night and asked Tom to be his best man, the man's face completely drained of color. He never thought he'd receive an invite to the wedding, let alone be part of it. After all these years, he was sure his mom and brother had given up on him. In his heart, he felt deserving of their rejection. What he realized when his brother called was that all this time, he had been the one to reject them.

Visiting his childhood home would not fill him with nostalgia. The painful memories of his life in Lake George would crash into him like a tidal wave. But he knew he couldn't keep avoiding his family forever. It was time to face his past, and I was ready to be his lifeline. Tom was there for me when I finally told him about my mother's death and my failed dance career. He defended me against Alexei and Rebecca. He offered to support me until I could get back on my feet. He'd loved me when I couldn't even love myself. I owed him the same devotion. And even though I wouldn't be able to erase his scars, I would make sure to be a salve if those old wounds re-opened.

AFTER THREE AND a half long hours, we finally arrived at the Village of Lake George. A quaint little town, the Village welcomed us with small touristy shops, restaurants, and ice-cream parlors. The strip was not long, and after a short five-minute drive through the center of town, the resort-lined streets morphed into secluded lodges hidden behind tall pines. A few more minutes in, and residential homes adorned the streets.

Tom drove with no urgency, and I enjoyed the scenery, but I knew his true intentions weren't to give me a tour. When the car began to crawl down a long, narrow street leading to a dead end, I knew we'd arrived at our destination. The loose white stone of his mom's driveway crunched under the tires of the Rover. His childhood home was a classic lake house. The large colonial with starkly white siding and black shutters lied nestled at the edge of the water, its expansive grounds welcoming us with open arms. As its backdrop stood the breathtaking views of the evergreen mountains and immense, shimmering lake. The wraparound porch summoned images of lazy summer afternoons lounging on the oversized Adirondack chairs while sipping fresh squeezed lemonade.

As I pictured myself sitting on that porch, enjoying a cool breeze brushing against sun-soaked skin, I noticed Tom's lack of fascination. He'd grown up here. Lake George wasn't a weekend getaway for him. It was a reservoir of tragic events drowning any happiness trying to surface through the murky waters of his past.

Sweat beaded on his forehead as he stared ahead. I reached over and caressed the back of his neck. "Baby, it's going to be fine."

He had no words, but his face was a mask of shadows

highlighting his fear and anxiety. I grabbed his chin and forced him to look at me. Wordlessly, I reassured him I would be his rock. Whether things went smoothly or if everything tipped south, I was not going anywhere.

He nodded, then he turned off the ignition and sucked in a deep breath before releasing it with a puff of resignation.

Sitting on the porch stairs awaiting our arrival was his brother, James. The broad smile and chiseled features were un-mistaken traits of the Wright brothers. Unlike Tom, James's golden-brown hair sat cropped short, and his lips were slightly less full. Still, equally as tall and muscled, there was no doubt these two were carved from the same mold.

Tom exited the car as James approached.

Dressed in faded jeans and a red plaid shirt, his brother was a complete contrast to my lion who had chosen more formal attire—black dress pants and a blue button-down. I stayed in the car and watched in awe as these two men stood mere feet from each other, unmoving and examining one another as if neither could believe what was happening. Then, without a single word, they embraced each other in a tight hug.

Tom signaled for me to join them. As I walked over to the brothers, I extended my hand out to greet James, but his emerald-green eyes widened as if a handshake was an insult. He grinned, stepping forward and reaching out for me. "Around here we hug, Lil' lady." Then he wrapped his huge, muscled arms around me and lifted me up in a bear hug. When he planted me back on my feet, I stuttered with a laugh, "Um… hi. I'm Sara."

He put a hand on his waist and nodded at me. "Tom's girl. I know."

"You think mom will like her?" Tom asked.

James scanned me over. "Um, your guess is as good as mine. You know how she is. She doesn't even like Penny, and she's about to become my wife."

The men stared at my horrified eyes then burst out laughing.

I shook my head and pretzeled my arms over my chest. "Really? This is my welcome committee?"

Tom tucked me under his arm. "Oh, baby. We're just messing with ya."

"Clearly." I didn't smile.

"And a firecracker, too?" James cooed as he walked to the back of the car to open the trunk. "Good. You need a strong woman to put up with your shit."

Tom followed James. "Still think you're quite the comedian, huh? And I can get my own bags. Thanks."

James put a palm against Tom's chest. "Nonsense, Lil' bro. Mom's in the kitchen cooking up her famous dinner feast. She's been so anxious to see you, so you better go on in and say hi to your momma before she comes out here and hits me over the head with her spatula for not helping her guests with the bags."

Tom's brow crinkled. "She still hits you with the spatula?"

"And the fucking wooden spoon."

"Surprised she hasn't used her iron skillet over that hard head of yours." Tom playfully whacked his brother upside the head.

"Shut up."

Tom threw the Rover's keys at his brother. "Don't scratch it." He smirked as we walked toward the house.

"Ha. I'll make sure to take it for a joy ride, Lil' bro!" James called out from behind the Rover.

Tom turned around at his chuckling brother. "You know, being born a measly one minute before me doesn't grant you big brother status."

"Oh, it sure does. Always did and always will."

I grabbed Tom by the elbow. "He's older?"

Tom flipped his brother the bird as he turned to answer

me. "He wears that status like someone crowned him fucking king."

"I heard that, Lil' bro," James shouted back at us.

"I meant for you to hear it, Jack-Ass. And stop calling me that."

"And stop enjoying how much you hate it? Nah."

I shook my head.

This was going to be my weekend—hanging out with a pair of toddlers.

Five

SARA

Stepping foot inside Tom's childhood home felt unreal. It was as if we were passing through a time portal. The white screen door slammed behind us as we ambled through the foyer, the aging hardwood floors creaking beneath our feet. Covered in paisley wallpaper and wood paneling, the cozy lake house was a complete contrast to the hard lines and solid colors of his Hoboken apartment.

Tom stopped with caution in front of the staircase leading up to the second-floor quarters. He looked up and stared in silence, hands in his pockets, his spine tense. I placed a palm to his back, pulling him back from whatever place and time he'd briefly traveled to.

He turned toward me. "Christ, this place hasn't changed since the last time I was here. Same old green carpet on these stairs, no new pictures on the walls." His eyes seemed haunted, darkened with uncertainty.

I reached for his wrist and pulled his hand out of his pocket, lacing my fingers through his. "We don't have to stay here, you know. There's plenty of lodging nearby."

He squeezed my fingers as a warm smile etched across his

face, the nebula in his eyes dissipating. "I'll be okay. Plus, my mother would never allow it."

I tightened my grip. "Are you sure?"

He nodded then leaned down and kissed me. "Positive."

The screen door slamming behind us startled us out of our kiss. "Oh, c'mon, don't tell me I have to put up with you two smooching and being all over each other this whole weekend," James cackled as he pushed through the front entrance, dragging our suitcases.

Tom tried to joke back with his brother, but his gaze brimmed with discomfort, his grin lacking humor. Noticing Tom's weariness, James dropped the drollery and patted his brother on the shoulder. "Just memories, brother. You'll be fine." The genuine smile and tranquil eyes offered Tom the support he desperately needed.

Tom dipped his head in acknowledgment, seeming grateful for his brother's graciousness.

"Smells delicious in this house…" I chimed in, trying to alleviate the heaviness settling over our arrival.

James puffed out his chest. "It's Mom's famous apple pie."

I gaped at him. "Famous, huh?"

His face beamed. "You bet. No one bakes 'em like she does," he said as he picked up my purple suitcase and started up the stairs.

Tom noticed his brother had left the black and bigger suitcase at the bottom of the stairs and went to reach for it to bring it up, but James stopped him. "That one stays down here."

Tom's face scrunched. "My room's upstairs."

James laughed. "You're sleeping in the sunroom, Lil' bro."

Tom balked at his brother's campy demeanor.

"That's bullshit, and you know it."

The twin shrugged. "Penny's not allowed to sleep in my bedroom either."

"Tough shit," Tom spat, as he tried to go up the stairs with his suitcase.

Putting a hand to Tom's chest, James refused to budge and blocked the way up. "Man, seriously. Boss's orders." His jovial tone darkened, snuffing out the daffy gleam in his eyes.

"Mom put you up to this?"

"Her house. Her rules."

Watching as his back muscles flexed, I reached for Tom's hand, hoping my soft touch would calm him. "Tom, it's okay. It's just for two nights."

He turned to face me, anguish flooding his eyes.

"We'll be fine," I assured him.

Tom turned his gaze back toward his brother. "I'll take her bag to my room."

It wasn't a request. James must have noticed the determination in Tom's eyes and gave up the fight. He nodded, and Tom took the suitcase from his brother and led me up the stairs.

"Don't keep her waiting long," James warned as he descended the steps.

Tom's bedroom was not much bigger than my current room in Jen's apartment. Modest and simple, it was comprised of a full-sized bed covered in a gray bedspread. There was one mismatched dresser directly in front of the bed with a small tube TV resting on top. The walls were wood-paneled, and only a few pictures hung over his bed: Tom in his football uniform. Tom at graduation. Tom in his MARPAT fatigues.

He took note of my gaze as I scanned his room.

"What is it?" he asked.

I turned to meet his eyes. "What do you mean?"

"You're very quiet." Shoulders bunched high and eyebrows that seemed permanently stitched together, he stared in petrified silence, waiting for my answer.

I offered a gentle smile. "Never imagined myself here, you know?"

Hands in his pockets, Tom stood like a statue in the middle of his room, his eyes wild with anxiety.

"You look like you're ready to bolt. Can I do anything to help you get through this?" I asked.

He turned around and walked to the only window in the room. He peeled back the white curtains and stared out at the lake. I followed behind him and wrapped my arms around his narrow waist, resting my head on his broad back.

"This helps," he sighed as he placed his hands over mine. "You being here."

I gasped as I peeked around his arm to look through the window. The view was unlike anything I'd ever seen. The vast lake glistened under the afternoon sun, creating a kaleidoscope of colors bouncing off the ripples on the surface. Not a single cloud clogged up the blue sky. All around, the immense evergreen mountains dwarfed the landscape as small boats lazily sailed the waters. The panorama was breathtaking, a real-life painting of splendor and serenity.

"I could wake up to this every morning," I uttered as I pushed forward to stand in front of him.

Tom wrapped his arms around me as I nestled into his chest. "It used to be my solace," he began. "But after a while, you don't even notice it there anymore. It dissolves into the background."

"I can't imagine that being true." I turned from the beauty of the lake and peered into his eyes. He seemed so unaffected by the calmness, his gaze jaded.

He tucked a loose strand of my hair behind my ear. "Try living here for eighteen years, Sara." When I said nothing, his expression softened, and a smile curled at the corners of his lips. "But I can see the appeal for someone who's never been here."

For a moment, the man I knew surfaced from his murky abyss. "So..." I said, trying to change the subject, hoping to spark some happy memories in his mind. "Your mom's baking is making me want to sample her famous apple pie."

"Are you ready?"

"For pie?"

He chuckled. "To meet my mother."

I hiked up a brow. "Is anyone ever ready to meet the parents?

"Let's not keep her waiting any longer, then. I'm sure she's dying to see you."

Six

SARA

WHEN WE ENTERED THE KITCHEN, James was pulling out a roasted turkey out of the oven. He placed the bird on the counter and caught sight of us standing by the kitchen entrance. His gaze lingered over us for a few seconds before he nodded and grabbed his mom by the elbow to pull her away from the sink. As she turned toward James, he tilted his head in our direction. She stilled for a moment before drying her hands on her apron and pivoting her body to face us.

Tall and elegant, Tom's mother was close to her sons in height. Her blonde hair, now dulled by grays, still looked voluminous, styled straight and resting at her shoulders. Her green eyes beamed as soon as she met Tom's gaze, her wide smile trembling with the onset of tears. "My boy…" She rushed toward us, her arms reaching for the son she hadn't seen in years.

Tom dropped my hand as soon as his mother extended her arms and buried her in his chest. After a few moments, they released each other, his broad smile telling her everything he couldn't say with words.

Dabbing at the streaks of tears on her cheeks, she said,

"I've dreamed of this day. You've no idea how happy you've made me."

"It's good to see you too, Mom." He turned to me as he blinked away a hint of wetness from his eyes. "Sara, I'd like you to meet my mother, Adeline. Mom, this is my girlfriend."

I smiled and moved forward to give her a hug, but she offered me her hand instead, a chord of uneasiness springing inside me as I grabbed her hand and noted the firmness of her grip.

"Pleasure to meet you, Sara," she said coolly, her eyes devoid of the warmth I'd seen sparkle in James' gaze when he met me.

"Likewise," I replied, still jarred by the unwelcoming expression on her face. I'd not expected we'd become instant friends, but her coldness was a stark contrast to the sunniness of both her sons.

James cleared his throat from across the kitchen. "Okay, now that introductions are out of the way, let's have some turkey. I'm starving." As he lifted the bird and carried it to the separate dining room, he motioned with his chin for me to grab the dishes on the kitchen counter. "Sara, be a doll and grab the plates and help me set the table, yeah?"

I left Tom and his mother in the kitchen and followed James, relieved to escape the heavy awkwardness suffocating the air around me. "You got it."

As I took care of the place settings, James continued to pop in and out of the kitchen with all the trimmings.

"This looks like a Thanksgiving feast,' I said with a sigh as he placed a dish of corn casserole on the table.

"Don't take it personal," he said, catching on my prickly mood. "She was like that when she first met Penny, also. She's just overly protective of us."

Somehow, his reassurance didn't make me feel any better. But I wasn't about to let this little bump in the road sour Tom's homecoming. After all, this weekend was not about me.

"Your mom always cooks like this?" I asked with a side glance, carefully tiptoeing away from his comment.

He smirked, acknowledging my unwillingness to talk about how his mother's frigid demeanor had affected me. "She wanted to go all out for you guys. It's been a while since she's had real visitors. Well, aside from me and Penny."

My lungs taking in a breath of relief, I perked up at the prospect of having a female ally. "Is Penny coming over for dinner?"

"Definitely. She wouldn't miss it. Should be here soon. Went to get all fancied up for tonight, know what I mean? Hair, makeup, and all."

I stopped mid-placing-fork-down and peered up at him. "Oh. What's happening tonight?"

He closed one eye in an exaggerated wink. "You ladies are taking her out for her last fun night as an unmarried woman."

I blinked hard. "A bachelorette party? The night before the wedding?"

He narrowed his eyes over me as if I had horns coming out of my head. "Well, when else would you have it, luv?"

"Me, your mom, and Penny?"

He laughed. "I doubt my mom will be joining ya, but Penny's friends are all stopping by later tonight to pick you guys up."

I sat down on one of the dining chairs, forks and knives still in my hand.

"Tom didn't tell ya?"

I shook my head no.

"The guys are taking me out tonight. He didn't want to leave you here while he went out gallivanting with me."

My eyes shot up at him. "Gallivanting?"

"Aw..." he crowed as he tilted his head with an impish grin plastered on his face. "I'm just messing with ya. Just beers and some pool, nothing to worry about."

I rolled my eyes at his joke. "You always such a goof?

He shifted his gaze away from me, a roguish smile pulling on his lips. "Sometimes."

"Always," Tom uttered as he walked into the dining room. "What's my brother blabbering about, anyway?" he asked me as he took a seat.

One by one, I handed Tom the utensils for his place setting. "Something about the bachelor-bachelorette parties tonight. Which you apparently forgot to mention." I met his gaze as I handed him the knife.

Tom craned his neck toward his brother. "Already stirring up trouble, and I haven't even been back home for an hour?" He turned back to me. "I had James ask Penny to take you out with them tonight."

"I've been told."

He leaned in closer, and whispered, "I'm sorry I forgot to mention it to you. I've had a lot on my mind."

That was kind of thoughtful of him. At least, I wouldn't be trapped in the mountains with his mother while he went out for beer and pool which I was sure was code for hard liquor and naked boobs.

"It's fine. I'm sure it will be fun."

A short time later, the doorbell rang as Tom and James argued over who could do a better carving job on the turkey. Adeline watched her boys with the merriment only a mother could appreciate.

"That's probably Penny," James uttered. "Sara, Luv, can you get the door for me while I show Tom here how to properly carve this bird."

I chuckled as I walked toward the front door. "No problem. By the way, you guys are ridiculous. Food's gonna be cold by the time you cut that turkey."

Penny's hazel eyes widened when I opened the door, and she saw my unfamiliar face. "Penny? Hi. I'm Sara, Tom's girlfriend."

"Oh, hi," she replied as a warm smile formed on her

heart-shaped lips, tiny dimples half-mooning at the corners. No double-cheek kiss combos here. Nope. Around here they liked to hug, and as she walked in, she pulled me into a genuine embrace, immediately making me feel like one of the family. Her freshly styled short bob gleamed with professional shine and smelled of fancy shampoo.

"So nice to meet you, Penny."

"Same here, girl." She pulled me in closer, and whispered, "Can I be honest? I've been a nervous wreck all day."

"About the bachelorette party?"

She walked to the mirror on the foyer wall and checked her hair. She patted her forehead and nose with a tissue. "That. And dinner with The Mother. And meeting James' brother, of course."

I offered her a half-smile, and whispered, "I know what you mean. Got my first dose of it earlier."

"That woman scares me," she whispered back conspiratorially.

"Well, I've got your back if you've got mine."

Winking at me, she said, "I like you."

I winked back. "And don't worry about Tom. He's been a ball of nerves himself."

"About meeting me?" she asked with surprise.

"About… a lot of things. You'll be fine," I said, placing a hand on her shoulder and escorting her to the dining room.

"Here we go," she intoned with a touch of dread. "Entering the witch's den."

Stifling a laugh, I followed behind, her dark humor already making me feel loads better.

Seven

SARA

Penny's maid of honor dropped us off around 1:00 a.m. Unfortunately, there wasn't much of a nightlife in Lake George, and everything closed shortly after midnight. We'd spent most of the night at a karaoke bar drinking cheap beer and awfully belting out the best of the nineties. Penny and her girlfriends were a riot, but I felt off not being with Tom. It was my first night in Lake George visiting his family, and I was by myself with four strangers. Penny's besties were sweet gals, though, and hanging out with them made the night more bearable, but my head throbbed, and I was more than happy to turn in early.

The guys had apparently gone out of town for their celebration, and I hadn't heard from Tom all night. By the time I crawled into bed, there were still no texts or calls. I jostled with the thought of breaking the silence and calling him, but I didn't want to be *that* girlfriend.

I tossed and turned so long I should have worn a hole through the mattress. It wasn't until a long while later, as I was finally drifting away into a dream, when the sound of a door slamming closed and floors creaking with heavy footsteps jolted me up. I glanced at my phone to check the time.

3:00 a.m. Something felt wrong. I'd figured they'd be out later than this. Plus, Tom and James weren't quiet about their arrival.

An icy claw crawled down my spine.

Pulling my legs from under the covers, I grabbed the silk robe laying at the foot of the bed and wrapped it around myself as I headed out of his room and down the stairs. Darkness filled the house, shadows dancing in the moonlight.

"You should have told me," Tom said to someone, his deep voice resonating through the walls.

"I didn't know he'd be there tonight, Tom," James barked, his tone charged.

"What's going on," I said as I tied the cloth-belt of the floral silk robe and walked down the stairs. "You guys are going to wake up your—oh, dear heavens." I rushed toward Tom. "Is that blood on your shirt? And your lip… your eye." I took in the entirely of his messed-up face with a gasp. "What happened?"

"Nothing," he snapped, looking at his brother.

James averted my gaze and marched into the kitchen, leaving a wake of silence between Tom and me as we stood alone in the foyer.

I met Tom's gaze. "Start talking."

"I don't feel like talking."

I moved closer, my face inches from his. "You don't get to come home all bloodied and not tell me what happened tonight."

"Sara, look at me." His eyes flashed with wildfire, a warning he was about to come unhinged. "Not. Right. Now." The alcohol stench on his breath nearly knocked me off my feet. He walked past me and through the living room until he reached the back entrance, the hiss from the door sliding open echoed through the sleeping house before it hissed again and clicked closed.

I walked into the kitchen, looking for James. He sat at the breakfast table, a glass of water in his hand. I took the chair opposite him. "What happened tonight?"

James scratched his brow and took another gulp of water. "Allen. Asshole was at the bar tonight."

"Shit."

"Place was packed. Music was loud. The guys, were just hanging out by the bar, bullshitting. Tom says he's gotta take a leak. Next thing we know, glass is breaking, chairs toppling over—it's a fucking madhouse. Allen's lying on the floor, bleeding from his nose."

"Oh, man."

"I didn't see what happened, but Tom already had a broken lip. He kneeled over Allen and delivered another blow before security escorted them both out. With all the commotion, by the time I made it outside, Tom was gone. We fucking drove everywhere looking for him for about two hours. We found him walking on the shoulder of the highway, heading back home. Piss drunk."

I glanced toward the backyard. Tom's silhouette was visible through the thin curtains. "I need to talk to him."

"Sara, it's not a good idea right now."

As I turned back to Tom's brother, my face scrunched. "Why? If he's hurt…"

James looked down at his glass of water. "I don't know how much he drank tonight. He's not well."

I pushed up from my chair. "Even more of a reason—"

James grabbed my wrist. "Don't, Sara. He's… riled."

"Riled?"

James stared at me as if that was enough to let me know what was wrong. It wasn't.

"James, what is it for crying out loud? You're scaring me."

He peered deep into me, his eyes plagued with worry, his face marked with apprehension as he ran a palm over his short hair, wrestling, it seemed, with some truth he wasn't sure he should reveal.

"Tell me," I demanded. "What happened tonight?"

He exhaled deeply, his eyes darkening with unease. "He's… uh… had…" James hesitated, the silence heavily punctuated with the dread coating his breath "… a few drinks," he uttered those last words carefully, accentuating a different, more profound meaning I didn't understand at first.

I tilted my head, my gaze narrowing, my mind peeling back the veil. James' breath caught as his eyes flashed with the realization that up until now, I hadn't known what *he's had a few drinks* meant.

"I'm so sorry, Sara. I thought you knew."

His words cut through my flesh. A raw feeling scraped through my insides. I couldn't define it. Was it anger? Disappointment? Pain? I thought Tom and I decided there would be no more secrets between us. We'd mended our wounds with a promise of unbroken trust. Yet, here was another unturned stone.

Hands trembling, my body broke into a cold sweat. I sat back down. It couldn't be this. He wouldn't have kept this from me. It didn't make sense. We'd been together for three months. I'd been practically living with him. There were no signs he still struggled with a drinking problem. No red flags. How could I have missed it?

That's when it hit me. The sickening, disturbing feeling coiling in my gut as I recalled every single moment with crystal clarity. How *had* I not known? The signs had, in fact, always been there. He'd told me about the drinking affliction he had when he was younger, back when he'd first enlisted in the military. Shayna had been the one to pull him out of the hole. I just never grasped how deep it ran.

The drink in his hand that never touched his lips. The always-full glass of wine at dinner. I shook my head. Tom *had* tried to tell me.

I'd been so foolish.

"Sara," James' voice dragged me out of my troubled thoughts. "Go back to bed. You shouldn't see him like this. Let me handle him. This is not the first time he's relapsed."

"It's the first time with me."

"Exactly why you should let me do this. Tom's not himself when he's drunk."

"No one is when they drink."

"That's not my brother out there on that porch. Certainly not the man you fell in love with. I want him to have a chance to explain, but right now... it's not the right time. Things will come out wrong, I know it. I've already dodged getting into a fistfight with him tonight. Insults at me I can handle. At you?" He shook his head. "Look, I don't need Penny getting pissed at me tomorrow because of a bruised eye."

I turned toward the back porch. The lights were off, but the moon was on full display, and through the thin, white curtains, I could see him plopped on one of the Adirondack chairs. My chest heaved. How could I leave him out there like that? Why hadn't he called me?

James put his hand on my shoulder. It was a warm gesture, pulling me from an impending breakdown. "I should be there for him," I whispered, my voice cracking.

"You will be. When the time is right."

I turned to face Tom's brother, and when our eyes met, I lost it. James took me in his arms and let me weep into his chest. "How does running into Allen cause him to relapse?"

James pulled me away from him and escorted me back up the stairs. "I guess you know the whole story?"

I exhaled deeply and sat down on the top stair. "It wasn't easy for him. But he told me about the affair and how it fucked him up when it came to women."

James sat next to me in the dark and rubbed his face with his hand, shaking his head. "It happened so quickly."

"You didn't see what actually caused the fight?"

"Nah. We were too late. Honestly, we found him by chance. His phone was dead, so we couldn't even call him. He's pulled this shit before, Sara. Well before he made all his money. Look, chasing him never ends pretty. I figured, he's a big boy, he'll find a way to get home when he's ready. After circling around several times, we gave up and turned back home. That's when we saw him, on the fucking side of the freeway, walking."

"I can't believe it."

"Not kidding you, luv. He was wobbling all over the side of the road. He's lucky he didn't get swiped by some speeding asshole."

"Where the hell did he go after the fight?"

"He found a bar."

"After all this time, that jerk is who breaks him?"

"Sara, Allen was like a brother to us, more so to Tom than me. What he and Shayna pulled was disgraceful. And after Tom's near death, they fucking flaunted their affair as if nothing had happened, as if my brother hadn't been laid up in bed for months in a coma."

"Did Tom tell you what led to the fight at the bar?"

"All he said was Allen talked shit, and he shut him up."

"What the hell do I do? You're his brother. Tell me."

"I know he's my twin, but I've never been able to reach him either. He's got the toughest shell to crack I've ever known. You have a better chance of getting him to talk."

"Talk? I don't even know what I'm supposed to say. We've been dating for three months, and I had no clue he still had a drinking problem."

"He's got his baggage, Sara, but he's one of the good guys. Shayna fucked him up, but you're piecing him back together. You're the first serious girlfriend he's had since her, at least that I know of, but I'm pretty certain he's not felt for someone what he feels for you."

"And what makes you so certain?"

"The way he looks at you. You're everything to him."

"He is… everything to *me*."

"Then don't let this mess things up. He's made it out of the hole before. He'll get out again."

Eight

TOM

A BURNING ACHE in my back woke me from sleep. As I peeled my lids open, the sharp rays of an early sun pierced my eyes. I raised a hand to block the light and tried to blink away the sleepy haze still holding me prisoner. Every muscle in my body was as sore as if I'd slept all night on a slab of concrete. I stretched, my stiff bones protesting, realizing it wasn't concrete I'd slept on but a wooden chair. After coming home, I'd passed out on the back porch.

I hadn't yet been able to open my eyes fully when a gentle voice sledgehammered through my skull.

"Morning, sleepyhead," Sara whispered, but she might as well have sounded a blow horn to my ears.

My head throbbed with fire. I had to press two fingers to my temples to keep the pressure down.

Shit. What the hell happened?

"How do you feel?" she asked. Her words were innocuous, but her tone suggested she was referring to more than just my headache. I hadn't yet looked over at her, but I could already picture the poignant stare.

I groaned as I straightened on the Adirondack chair, the

previous night crashing through me like a stampede. Fuck. There was a shitload of explaining to do.

"Here," she said as she handed me a cup, the steaming aroma of a dark roast hauling me back to life. Then she placed two aspirin in my other palm.

I took the pills, sipped from the cup, and finally dared a look her way. She sat next to me on a twin Adirondack chair. Sara smiled a sweet, tender smile that warmed my insides more than the coffee.

"What time is it?" I asked.

"Six thirty-five."

"How long have I been out here?"

"You guys stumbled through the front door around three."

"You heard us?"

"You weren't particularly quiet."

"I didn't mean to wake you."

"I wasn't sleeping."

"Strange bed?"

"I guess," she replied coolly, slightly rolling her eyes.

I puffed out a breath. A pissed off girlfriend was not helping the sick feeling in my stomach. "Sara, I… I'm sorry. Last night was a disaster."

"I know," she said. "Nice eye by the way." Her chin tilted toward my face.

I grimaced, remembering the fistfight.

Allen fucking Jacobs.

Back at the bar, I'd run into my childhood best friend turned dickhead. It was all downhill from there.

I leaned on the backrest and took a hearty gulp of my coffee. "What part do you want to hear first?"

Dressed in a pair of pink sweatpants and a black tank, Sara leaned back on her chair and crossed her legs as she sipped her own coffee. "If today weren't your brother's wedding, I'd grill you to death, but you already look like death, and James and Penny are getting hitched in a few hours, so how about the cliff notes?"

Fair enough.

Not that I wanted to do this right now, but the fastest ticket to a soft mattress and a couple more hours of sleep was to come clean. I glanced over at Sara. Her face was cold with determination. She wasn't going to let me slide.

Fuck it.

"We went to O'Kelly's, a bar outside of town, you know, to avoid running into old acquaintances." I wiped a palm down my face. "Fucking good that did. I bumped into Allen coming out of the men's room."

I hadn't been ready to see him. After all my years in the military, facing the worst man had to offer, you'd think nothing would startle me. Well, my mind went blank as my heart almost shot out of my chest the instant I saw him. A sheet of cold sweat coated my face and dripped between my shoulder blades. I hadn't seen Allen since before I left for my last tour. We'd still been friends back then. I never confronted him about his affair with my fiancée Shayna, and he never reached out to me either. Why would he? He'd run off with the woman I loved.

"Well, look what we have here. Army boy is back in town," Allen taunted.

I pushed past him, purposely knocking into his shoulder in the narrow hallway to the men's room.

He swirled around and grabbed me by the arm. "Yo, what the hell is your problem? You can't say hi to an old friend?"

"Get off me," I growled as I pulled my arm back. "We're not friends."

"Still pissed about that white-trash whore. Way I see it, I did you a fucking favor. That good-for-nothin' two-timing bitch is—"

I hooked him in the face, cutting him off before he finished his insult. The punch knocked him off his feet, dropping him backward on his ass. He touched the corner of his mouth, a drop of blood beading on his lower lip.

Peering up at me, he smirked as he licked the blood off his finger. Sinister delight flickered in his eyes. "There he is. Welcome home, asshole." He pushed up to his feet and ambled toward me, standing so close I could smell the beer and cigar stench saturating his breath. He ran his fingers through his thin, oily black hair. "That new little tail you chasin' know you still got feelings for Ol' Shayna?"

The smart thing would have been to walk away.

But I saw a different opportunity and took it. I head-butted him so hard I may have broken his nose. Allen was no trained Marine, but he wasn't a stranger to street brawls either. He recovered quickly, delivering a swift blow to my right eye before I had a chance to block him. Lucky strike. The rest of the fight wasn't so well choreographed. Allen was a drunken mess, and I could have ended the fight with a simple chokehold, but something inside me roared. The rage I didn't know I still harbored all these years flared with deadly fire.

We threw a few more punches before we drew a crowd. Among all the shouting and excited yelps from those cheering us on, James and his buddies called out to me as they wove through the mass of bar-goers, but it was too late. I'd already been escorted out of the club through a back entrance by the time they reached the scene.

"James told me they found you walking on the side of the road," Sara said.

"I was so pissed, I needed to be by myself. It was a stupid decision, I know. And I ruined my brother's night, so I'm not proud of it.

"And getting drunk?" she asked.

"That was never part of the plan."

She sipped her coffee. "I didn't even know you still had a problem."

"I don't."

Her eyes stilled over me. "Tom. You relapsed."

I pushed up off the chair, the damn coffee spilling all over my pants. "Fuck," I said, wiping the liquid off and handing Sara the cup. "Look, it was irresponsible. It won't happen again."

"Where are you going?"

I stopped mid-step. "To get more sleep. Party is not for at least a few more hours."

"We're not done talking about this."

I sighed deeply. I hated being a complete jackass, but the word relapse didn't settle well, plus the sick feeling in my stomach didn't help. I knew I owed Sara a better explanation for all this.

"We'll talk. When we get back home, okay?" I said.

Her silence was reply enough. She accepted, but not happily.

Nine

SARA

As I PEERED out the family-room window, warm contentment bubbled from inside. I smiled at the contrast of the smorgasbord of activity circulating through the Wright house compared to the epitome of tranquility just beyond the glass. The fog blanketing the lake had rolled out by late morning, and the scattered clouds hugging the skies had cleared out along with the mist, freeing the sun to shine its splendor over the mountains. The bright rays glimmered off the surface of the rippling waves as small boats sailed by. Birds chirped, and the breeze rustled leaves. It was a perfect day for an outdoor wedding.

I exhaled, a smile stretching on my lips. Losing myself in that view was the only thing I could do to keep my mind from stewing. While the night hadn't been very pleasant, and leaving Tom out on the porch had left a sickening feeling in my stomach, waking up to the rosy reds and purplish pinks of the morning skies had been pure medicine to my aching soul.

The sounds of women shuffling around in matching robes, fussing about hair and make-up, steaming their dresses free of wrinkles while others feasted on cucumber sandwiches and champagne, drew my attention from the serenity of the lake back into the mayhem of marital preparations. I smiled again, watching their sheer excitement as they noted the time.

Two hours 'til show time.

Tom sat on a tall chair, a bright light shining on his face, grimacing as Penny's make-up artist dabbed cover-up over the tender flesh around his eye. She'd showed up an hour earlier than scheduled to help with Tom's bruised eye. Although he wasn't too thrilled about wearing makeup, it would make the photographer's job a bit easier during the touchup process— plus it would keep guests from asking too many questions.

Questions to which even I still didn't know the answers.

But that was a topic for another day. Today was his brother's wedding.

A waiter carrying mimosas passed by, and I snatched one off his tray before he scurried off to tend to the bride and her maids. Mimosa in one hand, I ran my other hand through Tom's soft hair while the makeup girl did her thing. "I'll be outside," I said, letting my fingers swirl in his silky locks.

Wearing jean shorts and a white tee, I walked out to the back porch and leaned against the railing, watching as the event staff arrived to set up the immense backyard with chairs, banquet tables, dance floor, stage—the whole shebang. I sipped on my sparkling OJ as it all played out like a well-rehearsed dance. Everyone knew their role and executed it timely. Caterers arrived shortly after, milling about, setting up their mobile kitchens while the florist and her staff made everything look whimsical in cream whites and deep purples. Big, extravagant flower arrangements adorned with long, leafless branches and draped with sparkling lights, sat at each table. Votive candles decorated all surfaces, and lanterns lay strewn across the yard, high above the ceremony space and dance floor.

When the sun went down, it would all look like a midsummer night's dream.

HOURS LATER, after the wedding was over and most of the guests had left, I bid the Wright family goodnight and slipped away to my room. It'd been a packed day, and as beautiful as it all had been, I was glad it was over. Earlier that morning, I'd hoped the party would make my worries dissipate, but it only made things worse. Tom felt distant. Focused entirely on the wedding. Which I knew was his job, and I didn't fault him for wanting to be the best best-man he could be. I knew he wanted to make sure everything went smoothly for James. Especially after what happened the night before.

He carried out his best-man's duties perfectly—smiling, shaking hands. All business. It was the skin he was most comfortable in. He delivered a funny and sentimental speech and made sure James didn't get too drunk. He barely mingled with the guests. It shocked me I was able to steal him away for the last dance.

Keeping occupied was his way of avoiding what happened. It meant he didn't have to entertain meaningless *where have you been all these years conversations* with family and friends he hadn't seen since he'd gone back on tour. But his coolness was a façade. Underneath his relaxed demeanor, I saw the storm roiling his calm waters. I felt it every time his hand grazed mine. Every time we stole a glance toward each other. There, beneath his toothy grins and glittering eyes, was the tormented, angry, disappointed, broken man I'd seen the night before. It still plagued him.

Even after the bulk of the people had left, and all who remained were Tom, James, Penny, Adeline, and the bridal party, Tom couldn't stop working. He milled around the house pretending to tend to random tasks. I gave up trying to get him to sit down with me for one second, to share a moment. A kiss. Something.

The bridal party was sprawled all over the living room. Bridesmaids were barefoot, their lilac-colored gowns no longer crisply ironed, their tightly bound curls now loose and messy. Groomsmen had their jackets off, ties were missing, shirts were open at the collar and untucked. This crew was exhausted and already mentally checked out. I scanned around the room for signs of Tom, but not to my surprise, he wasn't among the languid bodies.

"Good night, all," I said to the open room. "Great party. So nice meeting everyone."

There were some grunts, some *nice meeting you, too* replies, and a few waves.

Back in my room, I slipped out of my sunny dress, put on sweatpants and a tank, and plunged under the covers. My eyelids felt heavy, and I thanked the heavens sleep would beat me soon so I wouldn't have to toss and turn for a millennium.

Five minutes later, my bedroom door creaked. "Hey, are you awake?" Tom's voice startled me out of the fog of incoming sleep.

With my back to the door, I said in a croaky voice, "Yeah."

"Mind if I join you in my bed?"

I turned to face him. "Won't your mom be mad if she finds us?"

"She can ground me if she likes." He walked over and slid under the covers next to me. His full-sized bed barely had enough space for both of us. He had to press my back tight against his chest as he wrapped one arm around my waist. "I'm sorry," he whispered in my ear.

"For what?" I asked.

"For being such an ass the last couple of days."

"Well, it's been a rough last couple of days."

"I screwed up. It won't happen again."

I turned in his arms to face him. "Babe, it's more than

that. Allen deserved whatever you did to him. It's what happened afterward that worries me. I didn't know you were still struggling with a drinking problem."

"Sara…" He shook his head, pulled his arm away, and turned to face the ceiling. "It's not something I like to talk about, and up until last night, I'd had it under control. Never thought I'd relapse like that. It won't happen again. Trust me."

I placed my head on his chest and wrapped an arm around him, listening to his heart thunder inside. "How do I know that? What happens when the next blast from the past shows up?"

He inhaled deeply. "There won't be a next time. We leave tomorrow. First thing in the morning. I've had enough of this place."

I sprung up, knowing I'd been the one to push him to come. I felt responsible. "You've barely spent time with your mother. Please, don't let what happened rob you of precious time with your family."

His eyes twinkled. "I invited her to come stay with us for a few days. She accepted. I hope that's okay with you."

I blinked several times. "I'm… so glad to hear it." I tried to smile, but I felt my lips struggle to form a believable curl of happiness. Not that I didn't want him spending time with his mother, but that woman scared me.

"Yeah?" His face lit up as his lips stretched wide. It was the first sign of joy I'd seen all day that didn't drip of masked grief.

"It will be good for you guys to spend time together." I laid back down, placing my head over his chest. His heart beat steadily now, the overwrought energy he'd been giving off dulling off. I was willing to put up with anything if only to see him happy. Even if that anything was his mother.

"I can't wait for you both to get to know each other," he uttered.

I said nothing. He didn't need to know how my insides twisted when her gaze traveled over me with distaste.

All that mattered was his peace of mind. The tension in his body receded. He was content. Even if just for this moment, my lion had come home, and it gave me the serenity I needed.

He twirled a strand of my hair. "How about a backrub to drift you off to sleep?"

A ripple of relief spread through me, latching on to every cell. I needed his touch now like I needed oxygen. "I'd love one," I said, breathing deeply into his chest.

At times throughout the wedding, I wondered if our relationship would survive this. I'd seen him troubled before, been a first-hand witness to the darkness lurking inside, but the shadows in his eyes today had spoken of a different kind of demon still staking its claim.

This relapse made me wonder how much control he truly had over his drinking problem. Tom wasn't one to ask for help. He hated taking the pills for his PTSD. He'd told me about his refusal to see a therapist for the nightmares. How could he bounce back from a drinking problem without professional help? Without the support of those who loved him?

I'd been at the verge of tears all day, thinking about the craziness going on inside his head, about the fact he'd kept it from me, that maybe he thought I wouldn't understand or wouldn't be strong enough to help him through it. Being here now, caged in his arms, was the confirmation I'd needed all day. No matter what, he came back to me. It gave me the confidence to believe we could work through this.

He kissed the top of my head as I curled into him. Head down on his hard pecks and one leg wrapped around his, I hoped the warmth of our bodies laced together like this told him I was his anchor as much as he was mine.

We're going to be okay, baby...

Right as I began to drift to sleep, a hard exhale puffed out of his chest. I knew that sound all too well, and it was enough to drive the sleepy haze away. He'd come in wearing black briefs and a t-shirt, and the hairs on his legs against my bare foot tickled my senses, making me crave his body. It had been two days without his touch. Two *long* days. He must have felt my soft moan because he pressed me tighter against him as he began to feather his fingers over my back.

Heat rising between us, his touch sparked an electric current that coiled in my core and shot through all my extremities. I arched into his fingers, urging him to touch me everywhere, not just my back. Hell, we both needed this and there was no reason to play coy. Sensing my approval to his subtle advance, his fingers rolled over my neck, ears, and scalp. Tom knew exactly how to get every nerve ending in my body screaming for his hands.

Itching to touch his skin, my fingers climbed up his shirt, tugging at his chest hair. His body tightened then relaxed as he let out a deep groan—that intoxicating sound he made when aroused. Wanting proof, I lowered my hand to the heavy bulge between his legs. The feel of his cock in my hand transformed my already heated body to a red-hot volcano ready to erupt. I lowered his briefs, his long, thick rod springing free.

"Do you want me to taste you?" I asked in a whisper, my breath steaming on his neck, my mouth watering to have his cock filling it.

"You need to ask me that?" he replied.

I lowered under the blanket, and trailing kisses down his abdominal muscles, I let my lips blindly search for him. It was sheer delight as the warmth of the silk wrapped around the head of his dick touched my mouth. I licked him, slow and wet, savoring the salty-bitter taste of the dewy drop on his tip. Tom's legs tensed beneath me as I heard him let out a rumbling moan. He reached beneath the covers and tangled his fingers in my hair. I licked even slower, letting saliva coat his shaft as I massaged his balls. The hard grip of his hand in my hair was my signal—he loved what my mouth was doing to him.

I sucked hard on the head of his cock, making sure my tongue teased the rim in a circular motion. His hips pumped upward in tune with my sucking. Wrapping a hand around the shaft, I stroked in round, fluid motions, squeezing upward as I pulled him in and out of my mouth. His ragged breaths intensified. I stole a glance his way, and the exhilaration of triumph filled me. His eyes were heavy-lidded and drowned with lust. He watched me, lips parting as he moaned my name.

I grinned.

He echoed it. "You're so fucking wicked. You're going to make me come in your mouth if you keep sucking me off like that."

I loved the taste of him, but I loved him inside me more. I pulled the covers back and tugged off my sweatpants and panties before crawling over him, lavishing his abdomen with my lips, and carving an ardent path up to the hard planes of his chest. I straddled him, burying my nose in the crook of his neck, inhaling his scent—fading cologne mixed with the musk of his skin. Masculine. Raw. Pure adrenaline-laced sex. He trembled as I nibbled on his ear, his breathing slow and profound.

Oh, he was so mine.

"I missed sleeping in the same bed with you last night," I whispered.

He shivered, his skin hot to my touch. Tom reached for my neck, threading his fingers through my hair, bringing my mouth to his. The instant our lips touched, he consumed me —nibbling, biting, sucking. It was as if he hadn't eaten in days.

"I'm sorry about last night," he breathed the words into my mouth as we kissed.

"I know," I replied, equally breathless.

He stopped kissing me, forcing his gaze into mine. "Sara, hurting you…"

I placed a finger over his lips. "Shush," I intoned as I lowered myself over his erection. "It's over."

We both gasped as he pushed his hips up to meet me, both of us moaning as I rocked over him, his hands gripping my thighs. "Ah, hell. You're so fucking wet," he uttered.

My eyes nearly shot to the back of my head, drawn by the extreme sensation of having him inside me. My blood surged with a current of adrenaline and endorphins, heightening all my senses, each of them focused on him—his hard body, his hot touch, the sweet scent of his sweat, the throaty sounds vibrating through his chest.

Straddled on top of him, his cock so hard it hurt, he guided my hips back and forth. It wasn't just about feeling his body rocking with mine, it was about the love I felt for this man. About being able to squelch our fears and all our sadness whenever we came together. His touch made me forget about everything tormenting me while giving me every-thing I needed to feel whole again.

And right now, I needed his touch everywhere. I lifted my tank top over my head then flung it to the floor. My tits bounc-ing, his eyes widened as he took in my naked chest. When he looked at me like that, I felt so sexual and feminine, it was addicting.

He threaded his fingers in my hair and tugged me down closer over his chest. We kissed as he grabbed my ass, slipping the head of his cock in and out of me, the popping pressure of the ridge of his dick against my opening as he pulled out sending shockwaves straight to my g-spot. Then he pressed a finger to my anus, and I almost lost it. My hunger for him exploded, this raw need to have him filling me everywhere ravaged my body. He'd done this back when I danced for him, and now he was torturing me again by making me want *things…*

He knew exactly how to drive me out of my mind. I wanted to push down onto him, to feel the entire length of his thickness, but he held my ass in place.

"No, baby. *I'm* doing the fucking," he growled. "I like how the tease gets you soaking wet."

"Tom," I panted, "I want to come all over you."

"Show me."

Startled but emboldened by his challenge, I put my hands on his chest. Still facing him, I unsaddled him, his dick slowly sliding out of me. Then I got into a squatting position over him, resting my hands on his thighs. He held his cock in his hands and guided it back inside me as I came down, my legs spread in such a way he had a full view of my sex as he thrust upward into me. My head lolled to the side, drunk in pleasure as he circled the pad of his thumb over my slick and swollen clit. I cried out in ecstasy as I felt my orgasm coil into a tight knot in my abdomen.

I rocked back and forth harder, his dick deep inside and his finger expertly thrumming me to a muscle-clenching release. "Fuck. Yes."

"Just like that, baby. I'm going to come too just watching you. Where do you want it?"

I tilted my head back, legs trembling, muscles aching from the strained position, but not enough to make me stop. "Inside… please. I want to feel you coming inside me."

"I want to look into your eyes as I do."

Shit. I was so near to losing it, but I held on. Raising my head, I slowly opened my eyes. There it was. That moment. That instant when our gazes locked, and we were in another world.

"I love you," he whispered.

"I love you more," I replied as we both came in an explosion that obliterated any coherent thought. Tom groaned a muffled growl, or he may have woken everyone in the house. With every thrust, he emptied himself inside me, and I watched with fascination as his spent smile and languid eyes claimed every ounce of my heart.

SOMETIME DURING THE NIGHT, I awoke with a terrible urge to use the restroom. Tom was sleeping on the outside of the bed, and sandwiched between his huge frame and the wall, I did my best to climb over him with as little commotion as possible. Then, without warning, he forcibly gripped me by the shoulders and thrust me over the bed. I tumbled to the ground with a loud thud. Tom dropped over me, his fingers digging into my upper arms as he pinned me to the floor, eyes open, but not seeing me. His gaze clouded with fury, it burned into me with hatred and disgust.

Panic surged up from my gut, and I wanted to scream, but something stopped me. There were no words coming from him. No sound, only anger. That's when I realized he was still in a dream.

The Nightmare.

I struggled to shake free of his hold, but it only made him grip me harder, the pressure so intense I couldn't hold in the cry that escaped from my lips. I didn't know what to do. Was I supposed to try and wake him, make him come to? Did I need to lay there still until the wakeful dream ended? Tears welled up in my eyes from the physical pain, but also from the anguish I saw reflected in his. I could not fathom what he was reliving, but whatever it was, it transformed him.

His hold on me loosened for a quick moment, and I instinctively reached for his face, placing my palm on his cheek to soothe him. I wanted to bring him back from whatever torturous place he'd travel to. He seemed confused, lost. "Tom, it's me. Sara. Come back to me, baby. Come back."

But his eyes filled with fury once more, and he slapped my hand away, now fisting his hand and coiling his arm back to deliver a punch. This time, I couldn't hold back my screams as I struggled to break free. A frantic knock at the door was my savior.

"Sara! What's going on in there?" James' panicked voice echoed in the hallway as he managed to push through the flimsy lock.

The loud burst startled Tom, and he blinked hard, a petrified expression blanketing his face as James rushed in and pulled him away from me.

"What the hell…" Tom whispered, shaking his head.

"Sara, you okay?" James asked, helping me sit up.

"Yeah, yeah. I'm good."

"What the fuck is wrong with you?" he asked Tom. "What were you about to do?"

"James, no," I said. "It's not his fault. He was having a nightmare."

James shot a worried look at me. "A nightmare?"

"I'll explain later. Get him some water, please."

He cocked his head, his eyes narrowed. "Are you sure you're okay?"

"Yes, I'm fine. Trust me. Please…water."

"I'll be right back."

Tom sat on the floor, his back resting on the side of the bed, his knees propped up, jaw muscles clenching.

I reached for him, but he flinched. "Tom, it's okay. You're awake now."

He clasped his hands together as he brought them to his face, his eyes watering as wetness rolled down his cheeks. His body trembled, breaths running ragged.

I kneeled in front of him, trying to take the hands away from his face. "Oh, Tom. Baby, it's okay. It's over now."

Lashes soaked, he opened his eyes and dropped his hands. The storm in his eyes raged like a dark inferno. I couldn't stand seeing the pain ravaging his body anymore and drew him in for an embrace. He lowered his legs, and once again, I straddled him, but this time, it was a different kind of love we made. I sat there, on his lap, wrapping my arms tightly around his neck.

I don't know how much time lapsed, or when James had come back in and left the glass of water on the nightstand, but at some point, the tears stopped. I had not wanted to let go of him, so we sat on the floor, cradled in each other for a while.

At some point, I said, "Let's get back in bed."

"I can't."

"Baby, please. It won't happen again."

"Sara…"

"Tom. Let me help you through this."

He closed his eyes and shook his head *no*. "I need… time." He slid me off his lap and stood.

"Where are you going?"

"I'll see you in the morning." Without looking back at me, he opened the door and left me in the dark.

Alone.

Ten

SARA

A BLARING alarm coming from outside woke me around 7:00 a.m. I was still on the floor, slumped over in a terrible position, the side of my face plastered against the shaggy, blue rug sitting on the floor next to Tom's bed. I didn't know how or when I fell asleep. Last thing I remembered was Tom walking out on me and leaving me alone in his room. Last thing I wanted to hear at this moment was a loud noise jarring me awake. I pushed to my feet, my body stiff from sleeping on the floor, and looked out the window. A large truck was backing into the driveway—the event staff coming back to pick up the tent and event furniture.

Come on, why so early?

I sighed and crawled into bed, bringing the covers up and over my head. I wasn't ready to get up. Not ready to face the inevitable. The weekend had been a total failure. From running into Allen two nights ago and getting into a fistfight, to relapsing, and now this? Out of all the crap Tom had to face the last couple of days, the nightmare scared me most—because it scared *him* most.

I could have chased after him last night. Made him see reason. He almost punched me in the face during a night terror. It wasn't him. It was his nightmare. His PTSD. It wasn't something he could control, but it was something we could work through with help. I knew if it hadn't been for his brother that my face would have been a broken mess of bones. Thank the universe that's not how it played out. And now, we had a chance to deal with it.

Last time he had an episode was two months ago, when a venomous toad—his ex-personal assistant— tried to seduce him in his sleep.

Thinking about it again made my blood boil. I flipped the covers down and stared up at the white ceiling. Remnants of now-dull neon stars stared back at me from scattered places on the ceiling. A glow-in-thedark solar system.

Thinking about Tom as a child curved a gentle smile across my lips, but it disappeared when I thought back to the memories he'd recently revealed. His childhood hadn't been one of whimsical moments. It'd been one of abuse and neglect.

Heavens. How could I chip at that iceberg? How could I be the one to help him heal? I had no idea where to begin. What to say. His cuts went too deep. But he had to get through this. Needed to. Because I was not willing to accept the alternative.

I would not lose Tom to this nightmare.

A HALF-HOUR LATER, I walked into the kitchen, freshly showered and hair still wet. Tom's mom was at the kitchen window, watching the event staff finish outside.

"Morning, Adeline."

She turned around, a beaming smile on her face. "Hi, Sara. Sleep well?"

I smiled, not wanting to commit to an answer that wasn't true. "Could have done without the early wakeup call," I said as I nodded toward the backyard while I ruffled my hair, hoping to air-dry it into wavy curls.

She shied away. "Sorry about that. Forgot to mention they were coming early. Everything else okay?"

She knew. She must have. If not because she heard, then because James told her.

"Everything is peachy," I told her with a frosty smile.

"I feel like we hardly had any time to talk, you and I."

I sat on one of the barstools by the island. "Tom told me you're coming down to visit us."

"Next week I believe. I'm excited. Gosh, I don't remember the last time I visited New York City."

"We'll make sure to show you a good time."

"Looking forward to spending some time with my son. And you, of course. To catch up."

My eyes crinkled without mirth as I forced my lips into a smile that barely curled. "Of course. I'll make sure he sets aside special uninterrupted mother/son time. Tom's a bit of a workaholic, so his schedule gets hectic, but trust me, for you, he'll cancel all his meetings."

"Thank you. Are you living… with him at his apartment?"

Blood drained from my brain and pooled at my feet. There it was, the question. This could make or break my relationship with this woman. She was still high on certain values if she didn't allow her sons to sleep in the same bed with their girlfriends in her house. But she had to know we didn't follow those same rules back home. Premarital sex was not as taboo anymore, but that didn't mean she wouldn't judge, and her probing eyes were making me feel like a filthy harlot for sleeping with her son.

If she only knew what Tom and I did on his bed last night…

"I actually share an apartment with my best friend, Jen, on

the Upper East Side. I do visit Tom, though. Frequently." I added that last part very pointedly.

"I see…"

As I was about to change the subject for both our sakes, the doorbell rang. "I'll get it," I chimed, claiming my escape.

I let out an exasperated breath as I walked to the front door, trying to shake the uneasy feeling Adeline left caked on my skin from her judgy eyes. The bell rang one more time before I reached for it. "Coming. Hold on." I turned the knob, pulled the door open, and my eyes widened when I found a young woman standing outside, a small boy holding her hand.

Blonde, wavy curls cascaded to her shoulders, those same beach curls I was trying to acquire, but that right now looked more like hay I'd picked from a barn. Her sea-green eyes shone brightly under the morning sun. And her smile was captivating. She was as breathtaking a woman as I had ever seen. The skin under her eyes crinkled a bit as she smiled and said hi. The crinkles didn't fade, perhaps a sign that while she looked youthful, she was a little bit older than I was.

Dressed in a long flowing white skirt and a formfitting pink tank, she looked like she was ready for a day lounging by the lake. Her sun-kissed skin and her hour-glass figure made her look like a beach goddess.

She extended her hand out to me. "Hi, I'm Shayna. Is Tom home?"

Whoa, what?

This had to be a dream. No. A nightmare. This could not be Shayna. Not the Shayna Tom had talked about. Not the ugly, evil harpy I'd envisioned all this time. Not the ogress who tore his heart right out of his chest. Not the Shayna who cheated on him with his childhood best friend while he fought for our country overseas. Not when he almost lost his life, and she never even bothered to visit him at the hospital.

No. This woman in front of me with her gorgeous wavy hair and her shimmery green eyes, her perfect white smile and outrageous figure, standing beside the adorable young boy with brown, messy hair and olive-green eyes—

Wait. Olive green eyes?

With streaks of honey?

Impossible.

The resemblance was uncanny. But Tom said Shayna and Allen eloped and their son had been born shortly after. The boy could not be Tom's.

Yet…

I stretched my hand out and took her slender fingers in mine. Her skin felt soft and delicate. "Hi. I'm Sara. Tom's out back. By the lake."

"Shayna?" James's voice startled me from behind.

She waved at him. "Hi, James."

"What brings you by?" he asked.

"Isn't it obvious?" she said, shrugging, and rolling her eyes.

"No, it isn't." James' clipped tone caught me off guard.

"Your mom mentioned Tom was back in town. I saw her at the ACME."

James narrowed his gaze. "Did she now? Did she happen to mention anything else?" he asked, eying me briefly.

"Just that he was leaving today. Figured I stopped by and say hi." Her voice was soft and innocent. It grated against my skin like a jagged knife.

James scoffed. "Just say hi?"

Her smile fading, she motioned to the child beside her. "James. Please. Not in front of Alex."

James knelt to eye level with the little boy. "Hey, buddy. Alex, is it? How old are you?"

"Six."

"Six? Are you sure you're only six? You're almost as big as me."

The little boy giggled. "See, Mama. Told ya I'm getting big. It's the chocolate milk. I drink lots of it," he replied, puffing his chest.

"Well, keep at it, buddy." James ruffled his hair a little. Then he stood up to eye Shayna. "Like Sara said, Tom's out back. Keep it short." He looked down at Alex. "I might have some chocolate milk in the fridge. Interested?"

The little boy looked up at his mom, eyes bright with hope. "Mama?"

"Yes, Alex. You can go in with Mr. James."

"Have you ever dunked double-stuffed cream cookies in chocolate milk?" James conspiratorially asked the boy.

"No. Mama says they have too much sugar."

"Don't listen to her. Double-stuffed cream cookies were created for dunking. Come on. I'll show you how to dunk like a man."

"James!" Shayna's eyes bulged.

But he was already gone with the little boy.

Shayna walked back down the porch stairs and turned the corner to head toward the backyard. I stood at the doorway and watched as the last of her blonde locks disappeared.

I was afraid to move. Afraid to breathe. Afraid to think.

Tom's mom had spoken to Shayna and not told us. She'd told Shayna Tom was home. Why would she do that? What was she playing at? I knew we weren't the best of friends now, both of us territorial over Tom's affection, but this? This didn't make sense. I mustered the courage to step back inside the house, needing courage, because otherwise, I wouldn't be able to face the little boy sitting and dunking cookies at the kitchen table with James.

What if he was Tom's son? What if all this time there was this beautiful six-year-old with his beautiful golden-brown hair and olive-colored eyes waiting to win his dad's heart? Tom would never turn from him— or her—the woman he'd loved more than life itself.

I walked past James and the boy, where they sat in front of the kitchen table with two tall glasses of chocolate milk and an almost full bag of cookies splayed before them.

"This is amazing. My mom never lets me eat these. Best day ever!"

"She's going to hate you for this," I said as I passed by, hinting at the sugar rush the kid would have soon.

He smirked. "That's the plan."

I stood by the sink, looking out the window into the backyard. Adeline sat on her rocking chair out on the back porch, watching the same scene. Shayna walked toward Tom as he folded chairs and handed them to the event staff down near the lake where the ceremony had taken place. She walked with caution as if the wind would blow her away with each new step. My body trembled, my skin dampening with sweat.

What is he going to do? How's he going to react?

I didn't have to wait long for those answers.

Eleven

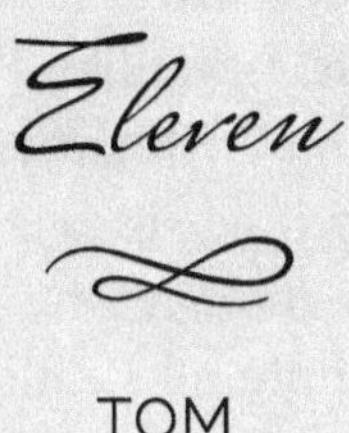

TOM

DURING WHAT WAS SUPPOSED to be my last tour in Afghanistan, I sustained severe injuries when the Humvee I'd been traveling in was knocked over from the shockwave of a roadside bomb. Broken bones. Head trauma. Took weeks under an induced coma for the swelling in my brain to go down and many more months in rehab to finally feel like a man again. Still, at the time, I would have preferred my battle wounds a million times over the agony that ravaged through me when I learned of Shayna and Allen.

What they did to me… That's the kind of pain that drapes over your skin like a toxic coat, seeping through your pores, burrowing into your muscles, carving paths into your bones until it drills so deep it becomes part of your marrow. I begged the doctors to put me back under. To pump me full of every fucking type of narcotic they had. I needed infinite numbness. To feel absolutely nothing.

To *know* absolutely nothing.

That was six years ago.

The scars were barely visible now. And up until I'd met Sara, I thought the emotional lesions inflicted by Allen and Shayna had healed as well, but this trip up to Lake George had been a harsh reminder of how deep their betrayal gashed me.

When you're a soldier, you train, but nothing ever prepares you for the first time you're hit with a bullet, not even over Kevlar. I remembered my first time shot by a rifle square in the chest over my vest. It felt like I'd taken a bat blow from a professional baseball hitter. It thrust me backward so hard, the wind burst from my lungs in one violent exhale, followed by pressure so heavy I thought my ribs had splintered and punctured flesh. Thankfully, all I suffered was a spider web of bruises across my chest and soreness for days.

Like I said. You never forget your first time.

Coming home was no different. When James asked me to be his best man, memories of my abusive childhood and my relationship with Shayna surfaced like a rotting corpse in a lake. You don't forget the first time your father hit you so hard he knocked out a tooth. You don't forget the first time you saw your mother's face so bloodied you couldn't make out her features. You don't forget the first time you fell in love or the first time you thought you'd found where you belonged. You certainly don't forget the first time the woman who saved you was also the woman who ripped out your beating heart.

I knew coming home would dig up old ghosts. I anticipated running into them. In the last few months, I'd done nothing but try to prepare myself for the possibility of having to confront them. But like a soldier shipped off to war, no matter how hard you train, how much you prepare, you're never ready.

When I caught sunlight bounce off the golden hair of the person who now approached, my chest caved as if I'd taken a bullet. My lungs constricted, my breath catching as I turned toward the visitor.

"Tommy," she whispered with a bright smile, her voice sweet and mellow as a flute.

I stumbled backward, almost losing my footing. Aside from

my mom, Shayna was the only one ever to call me *Tommy*. It had been six years since I last saw her smile or since I last heard my name roll off her tongue. All this time, my resentment had morphed her into a woman I thought I despised. But when she smiled, my universe spun. With one simple up-twist of her lips, she sent me back eight years to when I met her—to when she stole my heart with that same radiance shining off her now. The way her mouth curved at the corners, and the way her green irises twinkled brightly in the sun were enough to take any man's breath away.

With one word—my name—she reminded me of the love we'd once shared. Yet, powerful as it had been, now it was a distant, dark memory. Nothing but ashes. At least, that's what I'd taught myself to believe. But standing in front of me now was that living, breathing memory, and I'd never felt so frightened in my entire life.

She should have been some random stranger who'd ambled toward me. Just one more event staffer coming to pick up some chairs. It wasn't. It was Shayna Sanders. My cheating ex-fiancée. The woman I once vowed never to stop loving.

Why in God's name is she here?

Trying to mask the unwieldy emotions simmering underneath my skin, I ran a hand through my hair, then tucked my hands in my jeans' back pockets. I stared at her in terrifying silence, unblinking, unable to produce a coherent phrase. The only audible sound was that of the leaves bristling above us in the trees, but they may as well have been steel blades grating against each other.

The awkwardness of the moment impregnated the air with a heaviness so intense, it forced me to take a couple of deep, long breaths to feed oxygen to my muscles.

"It's so incredible to see you again," she said with a timid smile, her lips trembling and her voice cracking as her fingers twirled the ends of her hair—a habit I'd discovered early on when I met her. She did it when nerves ran a current down her spine. "You… look great," she added.

What the hell was with the absurd pleasantries? Our shit ended with a cataclysmic seismic event. Everything abandoned in a pile of ruins. And she told me I looked great?

How did she even know I was here?

Words vaporized on my tongue as she moved closer. I stepped back. Being this near to her made the veins in my temple throb. Shayna's gaze tracked my feet as I walked away from her. Receiving the silent message, she came to a halt. She looked up at me and answered my silent question with a gentle smile meant to put me at ease. "I talked to your mom at the ACME."

Right. As if slapping on that innocent smile would make the idea of her and my mother meeting at the grocery store seem normal. I continued to stare in silence, my body so tense it could have snapped in half. My mind was in complete pandemonium, my skull ready to crack.

What. The. Fucking. Fuck.

This shit weekend just kept getting shittier. First, the brawl at the bar with Allen, then the nightmare last night. Almost hurting Sara. Now Shayna? I thought I'd get away with at least not seeing her. She was one ghost who could have stayed dead.

"She mentioned you were visiting—"

"Why are you here, Shayna?" I cut her off, her name tasting bitter on my tongue.

She blinked fast and crossed her arms, holding her body tight. My question took her off guard. Smile fading, she lowered her gaze. "I wanted to see you. Thought you might be happy to see me, too."

Happy? I'd been dreading the moment since I learned about the wedding. After everything she did, the last person I wanted to see was her. "You're three hours from where I live. If I needed to see you, I would have."

She looked back up, her brows creased. "You didn't want to see me?"

I'd be lying to myself if I said I never thought about it. There was one fleeting moment while I was in rehab when I thought about coming home and fighting for her. I'd wanted to know what I'd done wrong she felt she needed to be with another man. The moment didn't last long.

"No," I lied.

"I don't believe that."

She could still read me like a book.

"You're here now," she pressed. "You weren't going to say hi before you left?"

"I came for James's wedding, not to dig up graves."

"Is that what I've become?" she asked,

"It's been six years, Shayna." I couldn't believe I was standing there, talking to the woman who made me believe in love only to rip it away from me. She may have looked harmless with her big green eyes and lustrous golden hair, but I could also recognize a snake in human skin.

She bore her gaze into me, her eyes wet with the onset of tears. "I never had the chance to apologize for what happened."

"An apology wouldn't have fixed anything," I quipped.

"I know. But…"

"What, Shay? It would've made you feel better?"

She didn't say anything, her eyes big as saucers, red and moist.

"Well, does it?" I snapped, ignoring the streaks down her face.

She wiped the wetness, but the crying didn't stop. With quaking fingers, she tucked golden locks behind her ears. "Why are you being so harsh?"

I blinked hard. "Harsh? Are you kidding me?" I grimly uttered, perplexed she thought she could show up after all this time and expect I'd greet her with a smile and a hug.

"I wanted you to know that despite what happened, I *did* love you," she said.

I scoffed, laughing harder than I'd intended. "*That* was love?"

Shayna's eyes narrowed over me, the lines on her forehead deepening. "How could you say that? We were together for almost two years before—"

"Before you cheated on me with my best friend," I reminded her with steel in my eyes.

She bit her bottom lip in anger before responding.

"You have no idea what it's like to be with someone who is never home," she barked, shooting her rancorous gaze at me. "To only be able to talk to them for brief moments over the phone, to not know where they are and not be able to ask questions. You don't know what it's like to be home waiting for *that* call." Her chest heaved, engulfed with emotion, earning her the pause she needed before delivering the next sentence. She closed her eyes, and solemnly said, "The one where they say you're a widow long before you're married."

Nice, practiced speech. It didn't move me. "You got the call. But I wasn't dead, was I?"

The swirl of confusion in her eyes as she opened them told me everything. She hadn't expected I'd be so fucking cold. "Dead was only a matter of definition," she spat back. "The doctors said you weren't going to make it out of the coma. That you would be a—"

"Vegetable. Do I look like one?"

She sighed and hung her head. "I screwed up, okay. Is that what you need me to say?"

"I don't need you to say anything. What you should admit to yourself is that you didn't come see me in the hospital because you were already with Allen, and you saw your ticket out."

Her head sprung back up, her eyes wide. "No. No," she whimpered. "That's not it. I couldn't bear the thought of seeing you like that. You must understand. Please. You need to believe that."

"No. I don't. But I didn't come home seeking answers or apologies, Shay."

"Right. You just accepted what happened."

"What did you want from me? To come home and beat the shit out of Allen? To demand you come back to me?"

"Maybe. Why not? Any reasonable man would have fought for his woman. You never even came home."

I gritted my teeth and threw her words right back. "Any reasonable woman wouldn't have cheated."

Pain flickered in her misty eyes as she sucked in a small breath. The more I looked at her, the more I wondered why I was even having this pointless conversation. This wasn't good for either of us. It had been six long years. Time to end it. For good. "There was nothing left for me here," I uttered. "Part of being a man is being able to accept defeat."

"Always a soldier. What about your family? They stopped mattering to you, too?"

"I'm done having this conversation with you, Shay. You're not that person for me anymore. That's all there is to it."

"Oh. And someone else is?"

"You didn't think I'd stay fucked up forever, did you? I mourned you longer than I should have, but what we had is past tense, Shay. I've moved on. You should, too."

"I know I deserve your rejection. I just…I'd hoped… maybe somehow we could—"

"Mend things? Like I said—past tense. Please, let's end this now before it becomes something it doesn't need to."

"You've moved on." Her words were heavy with torment, her eyes darkened, distant.

"I'm. Happy," I said.

Shayna nodded toward the house. "The brunette?"

"Sara."

"Do you love her?"

"Madly so."

"She's a lucky girl, then."

"*I'm* the lucky one."

She crossed her arms and walked past me toward the lake. "I'm not with Allen anymore, by the way."

I turned and stepped closer behind her. "I heard." I wanted to say I was sorry, but I didn't care either way. From the look of things, he'd been a dickhead who didn't deserve her, even if she'd also fucked up. She was better off without him.

She turned back toward me, her eyes wide. "You heard?"

I nodded.

"After what happened to you…" Shayna's gaze dropped away, perhaps shame kept her from being able to look me in the eyes every time she mentioned the past. "Things were not the same between us. It was hard. We struggled financially. He became a drunk, and after we broke up, he drank away any money he made instead of paying child support. Barely bothers to see his son anymore."

I lived that life once. The kid deserved a better father. I knew not seeing his dad was rough on the boy, but it was better than seeing him drunk. "He deserved the broken nose," I mused.

She whirled her head around to face me. "What?"

"Saw him at O'Kelly's Friday night."

"Oh lord," she groaned, brushing her hands through her hair. "Don't tell me, you guys…"

"It's all right. Long time coming."

"I made a mistake," she said after a short silence. "I know that now. I've known that."

"It's over, Shay."

"If I could take it all back…" She struggled with a new deluge of sobs. "God, Tom. I never meant to hurt you. I wish I'd never chosen him. If… I could take it all back now, I would never leave you."

Fucking shit. I battled to understand the chaos suddenly exploding inside me. Those five searing, razor-edged words cleaved my heart in one thundering crush I hadn't expected. It released the fear I'd stored inside, along with the love and hate I'd imprisoned in there. I hadn't been ready for the damn blow. I didn't want—didn't need—to fucking hear her laments. Not now. Not ever. But something came over me, something I could not hold back, and before I was able to summon the courage to keep myself at bay, I reached for her and held her in my arms as she wept.

Part of the reason I never went looking for her six years ago was because I knew the instant I saw her again—the moment I touched her—she would have destroyed me. My love for her had been so fierce, I would have forgiven her. And she wouldn't have deserved it. Not back then. And I wouldn't have cared.

The last few weeks before coming to the lake, I'd felt like such an asshole—a liar—because I told Sara and myself the reason I didn't want to run into my ghosts was because I didn't care to see them. The thought of facing off with the backstabbing son of a bitch curdled in my gut, and seeing Shayna's face again was a new memory I didn't need.

The truth—the damn, repulsive truth—was I had been afraid to see her because a part of me—a broken, lonely, dark part of me—feared somewhere in the deepest shadows of my heart, perhaps there still existed the same bandaged-up soldier who'd cried himself to sleep every night for countless months. That somehow, seeing her would open the vault and release feelings I hadn't been able to kill. I'd stashed them away instead.

The love I had for Sara now was one of the most certain realities in my life. It was pure, it was intense, powerful, all encompassing. I was an ebony sky, and Sara was the moon and the stars that lit up my world. If there was one ounce, one single chance that seeing Shayna would steal the light from my world, I didn't want to take it. It shamed me to think that way. To measure what I felt for Sara against the love that once burned for Shayna.

Perhaps I didn't deserve her. There should have been no fear in my heart. I should have been certain as the sun is bright seeing Shayna wouldn't awaken anything in me. But I'd been so afraid, and this moment became the culmination of all those fears. If seeing her seemed a bad idea, holding her was asinine, especially knowing Sara was likely watching us from the back porch with the sharp eye of a sniper.

I breathed deeply into her hair as she cried, inhaling the fresh aroma of her shampoo—that same spring rain scent. The soft brush of the silky strands through my fingers as I caressed her head, the warmth of her body cradled in mine— it should have overwhelmed me. The love we'd once shared should have risen from the ashes like a motherfucking phoenix. It's how I'd always envisioned this would go down. It's how I had dreaded it would all end.

But it didn't.

And the happiness filling my whole body now, spreading over every single fiber of bone and muscle, proclaimed louder than my lungs could belt out that I could hold this woman in my arms and feel nothing but compassion for her broken soul. This was a blessing I didn't deserve. My life was safe. My love for Sara was intact.

All the sorrow and self-torment had dissolved in one tiny plume of smoke.

Everything I ever felt for Shayna was no more.

She pulled away, her eyes still wet, yet sparkling with a pinch of hope. "I wish you'd come home, Tom. I wish you'd come back for me."

I looked deep into the abyss of those eyes. I tried searching for regret or great sadness. I found only emptiness.

"Things happened the way they were meant to, Shayna. As painful as it was to lose you, I'm a happy man now, and I wouldn't give that up—wouldn't give up Sara—for anything or anyone in this world. I regret nothing."

She nodded, lips trembling. Whatever we once had died the moment she chose him over me. There was nothing left between us but a black hole.

After a moment, she said, "Would you like to meet Alex?"

"Alex?"

"My son."

"You named him…"

"Alexander. After your middle name."

"Allen didn't object to that?"

She let out a meek laugh. "I don't think he even knew it was your middle name."

I didn't know why that made my heart ache, but it did. Maybe she *had* loved me, but like many of us, she wasn't perfect, and she made a bad choice.

The kid had no bad part in our story. And somehow, I knew meeting him would be the last page to this final chapter.

"He's here?" I asked.

She nodded.

I put my arm around her and guided us toward the house. "Let's go inside. I'd love to meet him."

Twelve

SARA

As I watched them through the window, I heard the scrape of a chair against the linoleum floor. A second later, James stood next to me, watching the same scene unfold.

"It doesn't mean anything," he said.

My eyes remained fixed on Tom and Shayna as they approached the house. "I'm trying to convince myself of that."

"Last thing you need is to come off as a jealous girlfriend."

I rolled my eyes and scoffed. "I'm not jealous."

He pivoted to face me and waited until I turned away from the window to look at him. "*I* would be," he admitted, as if trying to reassure me even though what I was feeling was natural, it still wasn't a good idea to show it. Not here. Not right now.

"You're not helping," I said, turning back toward the window.

"I know my brother. He's just being kind."

"There are other ways to show kindness," I said, wrapping my arms around myself. "None that involve him putting his arm around her," I whispered, hoping the little cookie-dunking boy wouldn't hear. "This is not how I envisioned this would go."

"You've envisioned this?"

I breathed deeply, turning, and leaning my backside on the kitchen counter, unable to watch their continued display of… whatever it was they were feeling for each other. "Sorta," I said with a shrug. "I mean, I knew coming up here meant anything was possible. But I thought he'd be more… annoyed. Pissed. Like, get-out-of-my-sight-I-never-want-to-see-youagain. Ever. Type of annoyed. Know what I mean?" I said, looking at James for affirmation.

He grimaced as he turned to the window. "Maybe. If he still loved her. But I've seen the way he looks at you," he said, shifting his gaze toward me, a gentle smile pulling on his lips. "He doesn't feel that for her anymore. Don't think he ever did."

"Are you kidding me right now?"

He chuckled. "No. I'm not kidding. He loved her, yeah. But this thing between you two… It's different. The real shit, if you ask me. And I got married yesterday, so I think I'm a bit of an expert when it comes to love." He polished his nails over his shirt in mock bravado. The little gesture reminded me so much of Tom and his corny ways.

"Expert?" I teased him, my head cocked. "Come back when you've been married ten years, have three kids, and maybe I'll consider you an expert."

His forehead creased. "Three kids? Woman, please. You want to give me an early heart attack? Let's start with one, okay. Like, in a year, at least."

"Speaking of, where is your beautiful bride and the future mother of your brood this morning?"

He laughed. "Sleeping. I may have kept her up late," he said winking."

I slapped his arm. "James, there's a child in the room."

"He's busy with his cookies. And you're trying to deflect and change the subject."

I lowered my gaze, staring at my fingertips as I picked at my nails, smiling at my feeble attempt to shift attention. "Just don't think talking about it is going to make me feel better about it, you know?"

"Sara," he said, his gentle tone pulling my gaze back up. "All I'm saying is… he loves you. *Only* you."

Footsteps thumping on the creaky wood floors of the porch stairs claimed our attention.

Here we go.

What was I supposed to do? I had no idea what had gone down by the lake. One moment Tom looked like he was ready to tell her to fuck-off, the next he was wrapping his arm around her. Did she even know I was his girlfriend? It's not like Adeline said anything to me about what she'd told Shayna at the ACME. By the time I had walked back into the kitchen, she'd been out on the porch watching Shayna walk down to Tom. And as they walked up now, she stood up from her Adirondack chair and greeted Shayna with a long hug as if she was the girl Tom had brought home that weekend.

Angst burned in my chest. I'd wanted nothing more than to have Tom's mom like me, accept me. Maybe I'd hoped to impress her. And up until this morning when I walked downstairs, I thought things could one day improve between us. Looking at her now and watching her smile at them made me question everything.

The glow on Shayna's face as they walked to the door sent my heart into a gallop. She was breathtaking.

I couldn't imagine how Tom ever fell for me. Shayna was attractive on a whole different level. With her lustrous golden hair, her delicate facial features, her feminine figure, all I could picture was her on the cover of Vogue magazine and me on the cover of Nothing magazine.

Dammit.

Why am I letting her get to me like this?

Josh's abandonment had rocked my confidence, but Tom had made me feel beautiful and desired again. I knew I wasn't some runway supermodel, but I was no scrape-of-the-barrel consolation prize either.

"Breathe…" James whispered in my ear as they walked through the door.

His voice had that similar calming effect Tom's possessed.

"Thank you," I whispered back.

"Mommy!" a little voice exclaimed. Cookie-Dunker jumped off his chair, running toward his mom.

His shout startled me, jolting my heart a bit.

"Hey, baby," she said, exuberance filling her voice as she introduced her son to Tom. She didn't bother acknowledging me.

"Hey, buddy." Tom squatted so he could be at eye level with the little boy. "Alex, is it?"

"Alexander David."

A wide smile creased Tom's face. "Well, Alexander David, guess what?"

"What?"

"I think you have the coolest name in the world."

"My mommy says she named me after a superhero, but I know all the superheroes. No one has that name."

"Well, maybe you'll be the first." He looked up at Shayna, and they shared a smile as if only they knew the secret meaning behind Alex's comment.

"I do have a cape. But mommy says I can only wear it at home."

"Okay, little man," Shayna scolded playfully, ruffling her son's golden-brown mane, her cheeks flushed. "That's enough *mommy says.*"

Alex looked up at his mom and smiled. "Mommy, guess what?"

"Yeah?"

"Mr. James taught me to dunk cream sandwich cookies. It's so cool. Please, can we get them? Pretty please?"

Shayna shot James a steely gaze before looking back down at her son. "Um, we'll see, baby."

Alex beamed.

Tom stood back up, his gaze flickering to me. He must have noticed my uneasiness and wanted to reassure me we were okay. He smiled, tilting his head a smidge. We could share silent secrets, too, and the wordless exchange was all the comfort I needed.

"Shayna," he said, calling her attention. "You've met Sara, my girlfriend?"

She glanced my way, a frosty smile on her lips. "Um, yeah. We met. Earlier. Right?" she asked me rhetorically.

I nodded anyway.

She extended her hand out to me in some awkward gesture of friendliness between two people who couldn't care less about being friendly to one another. "I don't think I properly introduced myself, though," she added. "Shayna. Tom's—"

"She knows who you are," Tom cut her off as I took her slender fingers in my hand, his comment

making things even more uncomfortable.

"Ah, okay. Well, happy meeting you, Sara."

I smiled, but all I wanted to do was scoff. She wasn't any happier at meeting me than I was her.

Tom grunted as he peered down at his watch. "Shit. We need to get on the road, Sara."

Shayna's eyes darted between Tom and me, realizing she was no longer part of the conversation. "Um, I guess I should get going."

"Yeah, sorry," Tom uttered. "We need to get back home. Thanks for stopping by. Maybe we'll see you guys again sometime." Classic dismissive Tom. I didn't miss that side of him, but I was ecstatic he was giving her a dose of it.

"Let's go, Alex. We need to get home, too," she said.

"I'll walk you out," Tom offered, his strides wide as he guided to the front door in a gentle rush.

"Well, isn't that nice," Tom's mom began as she watched her son disappear into the foyer. "She named him after Tom."

I shot her a startled gaze. "Excuse me?"

"She means his middle name," James corrected his mother, placing a palm on my shoulder.

Oh. Because that made things better.

SHE NAMED HIM ALEXANDER.

Dammit. I didn't even know Tom had a middle name.

Things stopped computing after that little tidbit of information. Perhaps it was a survival mechanism, something my body did to avoid the bile-inducing stress of meeting his ex-fiancée in the very flesh. It was dumb, I know. It was nothing.

It. Was. Nothing.

Heavens, if it was nothing then why was I sitting in Tom's Rover, two hours into our trip back home, my mind still twisted into a mangled mess?

Maybe this was new-girlfriend syndrome.

Childish? Check.

Silly? For sure.

Stupid? Most definitely.

But there was only so much I could control about how I felt, especially when I hadn't been the only one not saying a word for two hours.

I trusted Tom. I knew he loved me. But seeing Shayna had meant something. It had to. How could a love so strong not leave some trace of the initial attraction they once felt for each other? She had feelings for him. It was evident in the way her smile curved at the ends. She was trying to summon memories of their past. Her eyes sparkled as she tried to meet his gaze. It lingered on him for too long. Those wordless conversations now belonged to us. She had no right to stake a claim.

None.

And that was it. The worst part was I couldn't stop comparing myself—our relationship—to theirs. For Pete's sake, I hadn't even known Tom had a middle name. The hollowness in my gut when I learned she'd named her son Alexander almost made me vomit. She knew more about Tom than I did, and while I knew they shared two years together and had been engaged to be married, I couldn't help comparing my measly three-month relationship to theirs. I was a grain of sand on their beach.

"What if we have a son?" I asked him out of nowhere, finally turning toward him. Not the best way to break the terrible silence, but it was the one question still buzzing in my brain.

"What if we do?" he asked back, without even looking at me.

"Tom, she named him Alex. Doesn't it bother you a little?"

"Why should it?"

"What if we want to name our son Alex?"

"It's just a name, Sara. Plenty of kids named Alex out there."

"Only one who is also Shayna's son. Who she told you she named after you. It's a forever reminder."

"Reminder of what?"

"Of the love you two shared. Of the love she still has for you. She wanted you always to remember there's this little boy running around with your name, who she imagines is your son." I crossed my arms and held myself in a tight embrace, trying to placate the tremors rattling through me.

Tom pulled over on the shoulder, cars flying past us on the freeway. "She named him Alexander, not Thomas."

"Because Allen wouldn't have allowed that. It was her subtle way of doing it."

"Why does it matter?"

"Because she had no right, Tom. Because I didn't know your middle name. Because maybe one day, I would have known, and I would have wanted to name our son Alexander.

"We still can."

"It wouldn't be the same."

"Right. It wouldn't. Because her son is not mine. Yours. Will be."

Whoa. I dropped my gaze, blinking away wetness.

"Baby, what's wrong?" he asked, taking my chin in his fingers, turning my face toward him.

"I'm sorry," I said, my voice trembling. "Seeing you with her… it wasn't easy."

"Wasn't something I planned, Sara."

"Why would your mom do that, invite her over?"

"It's a conversation I'm going to have with her when she comes to visit. Today, I just wanted to get out of that place." He took the car out of park and checked for oncoming traffic before pulling out of the shoulder and crossing over to the left lane.

"When are you planning on talking to me about it?" I asked him as he rested his head back, settling into an easy cruise. His gaze lost.

"Talk to you about what?" he said with a yawn.

"You had a full-blown conversation with Shayna, the woman who fucked you over, and you have nothing to tell me?"

He looked at me briefly then back at the road. "What's there to say? She wanted to apologize. I accepted. Nothing else."

"Nothing else?" I spat back, sitting straighter in my seat,

the seatbelt digging into my hip. "You were out there for twenty minutes. And after what happened between you two, you came back into the house like nothing happened? Please, help me understand."

"Shayna and I were together for two years, Sara," he replied, his tone clipped.

I shook my head in disbelief and leaned back in my seat, slouching, arms crossed. "So what she did gets scrubbed? And I'm quite aware you were together longer than we have," I said, shooting him an icy stare. "Thanks for reminding me how insignificant I am compared to her."

Tom ran a palm down his face as he took a deep breath. "Don't do this, Sara. You know that's not true. I've told you— shown you what you mean to me."

He had, but it wasn't the point. This was about how he felt about her. "Did she think she could just show up, say I'm sorry, flash you a pretty smile, and somehow you'd forgive her and get back together?"

"Even if that had been her plan, it wouldn't happen. I'm with you."

"And if you weren't with me?"

"What are you asking me?"

"If you hadn't met me, would you consider getting back with her?"

He paused, his jaw clenched. "No."

"You don't seem so certain."

He shot a quick look my way, his eyes narrowed and darkened. "I. Am. Certain. Just like I'm certain about you. I don't think I need to keep proving that to you, or do I?"

I didn't answer. I knew he loved me. I just needed to be certain he didn't still love her.

After a brief silence, he said, "Are we okay?"

"Yeah…" I groaned.

He turned back to the road and continued to drive home, both of us in utter silence the rest of the way.

"SARA," Tom said softly, "wake-up."

I jerked at his touch as his fingers brushed my cheek.

"I'm sorry. Didn't mean to startle you," he said.

Rubbing my eyes, I sat up straighter in my seat and looked around. "I thought we were going back to your apartment? Are we staying at my place, instead?

"I'm not staying."

A fog of confusion swirled in my mind. "What do you mean?"

"I'm dropping you off."

He must have *noted* the million questions firing off in my head because he cut me off before I uttered a single word. "It's not what you think. I just need time to process what happened this weekend."

I unbuckled my seatbelt and turned to face him. "It's not what I think? What else am I supposed to think? Shayna shows up, and suddenly now you are asking for space?"

He hung his head back, seemingly annoyed with me. "This has nothing to do with Shayna, I promise you."

"Then what, Tom? Why do you need space?"

Reaching for my hands, he tried to calm my rising anger. "Baby, listen to me, the last thing I want from you is space. Believe me. This weekend was rough for me. I went knowing things could get ugly. I just didn't know how much."

"Should I be worried?"

"Not about my feelings for you."

"What the hell is that supposed to mean?"

"I relapsed. And… I hurt you, Sara."

"You didn't."

"I pinned you down in my sleep. If it hadn't been for my brother, I would have… Look, I need to figure this out on my own."

"You shouldn't do this alone. Let me help you."

He let go of my hands and sat back in his seat. "I have to do this alone. The relapse, the nightmares… it has nothing to do with you."

"It doesn't mean I can't help you."

"I should have done this a long time ago. I took the pills, but I never talked to anyone about what happened, not in any way significant."

"You're going to see a doctor?"

"That's my plan. Baby, give me a few days, okay? To sort through this mess."

"What does that mean? Can we talk on the phone? Can we see each other?"

"It means I will call you as soon as I get home, and as soon as I wake up."

"How about seeing you?"

"I don't want to be in a situation where we are sleeping in the same bed. At least not until I can figure out how to control this."

I stared away from him, my heart splintering. I wasn't prepared to lose him. I knew that's not what he was saying, but it felt like it. What if the nightmares didn't stop?

"Sara, baby. Look at me."

"I… can't. I'm afraid. I did this. It's all my fault for pushing you to go this weekend."

"No. I should have dealt with it sooner. It's no one's fault but mine. Sara, look at me."

I did as he asked.

He leaned in and kissed me, pulling my hair behind my ears, caressing my face. "This is not me saying goodbye. You know that, right?"

I nodded.

"I love you, Sara. We'll get through this. Promise."

I wouldn't be able to leave him if I stayed any longer. "Call me, okay?"

"As soon as I get home."

I kissed him one last time and stepped out of his car. He went to get out, perhaps to help me with my bag, but I stopped him and opened the back-passenger door and retrieved it myself. "I got it. Goodnight. Love you."

"Love you, too."

I walked up to the stoop of my entrance without looking back. A boulder pressed on my heart, telling me if I looked back, it might be the last time I saw Tom. I sucked in a deep breath and prayed I was wrong.

Thirteen

TOM

Leaving her gutted me straight from my chest down through my stomach. It tore me up inside more than my own personal torment. But what else could I do? I needed to keep her safe, and that meant keeping her away from me. At least until I could clear my head and sort through the mangled disaster of the weekend.

My damn drinking problem and the hellish nightmare that almost ended with my fist through Sara's face, that right there, was why I was scared shitless. Why the mere thought of ever physically hurting Sara had me quivering like a fucking scared dog, and it was why I was running away from her.

I turned the car stereo on and hiked up the volume to the track blasting through my speakers. I didn't go straight home, choosing instead to drive as far away from civilization as I could. I had to because the rage and anguish battling inside made me want to seek solace in the bottom of a bottle.

I banged a fist against the steering wheel. I'd been fine. I'd kept this fucking problem under control for so long. Why did I spiral?

Because you're the fucking apple that didn't fall far from the tree. That's why, asshole.

I shook my head. Shit, last time this happened, Shayna had pulled me out of the hole only to plunge me into it again. Took me months to crawl out of that disaster. But I did, and Jake had been there to help patch me up. We made a pact: No relationships. No commitments. Ever. For good fucking reason.

Pain.

Women don't get it. They don't understand how hard men love. How their essence imbues itself into our blood. How their breath is in our lungs, and their scent drapes over our skin. A fierce possessiveness rakes our body we can't even explain. This need to protect them, to keep them safe. This desire to tuck them into our chests, but to also open our hearts to them. To let them into that place no one ever sees. Perhaps it's part of our DNA. Who the fuck knew? All I did know was, it is the kind of love that destroys.

Pain.

I vowed never to feel it again. Not for a woman. Not for anyone.

No love. No pain. Simple as that. And up until I'd met Sara, it had been a cakewalk. Now, look at the shit I was in. Wanting. Needing a woman like I needed fucking oxygen. Thinking about the future. Marriage. Children.

I'd let my guard down, and Sara crawled into that place. Opening the vault left me vulnerable not just to her, but to everything else afflicting me. I didn't regret seeing my mother or being there for my brother at his wedding. I'd missed them and needed them back in my life. But it came at a cost. Had I been the asshole I'd turned myself into prior to meeting Sara, running into Allen might have not brought me back to the day lying in my hospital bed, wrecked, not knowing if I'd ever be the same man again. Knowing my brothers had died, and I'd lived. Back then, I'd wished it'd been me who died in the convoy.

Pitiful. I know it was cowardly to feel that way, but it had been those feelings of despair that led me down the wrong path then, and what led me down the same path on Friday. It dredged up my feelings about the war. Those wounds will never heal. The grief will never cease. But the nightmares had to end, or I'd lose Sara, and you might as well kill me because I didn't possess the strength to lose her.

SOMETIME LATER THAT NIGHT, I arrived home, haggard and ready for sleep. I shot Sara a quick text goodnight. I could have called, but I knew we'd end up talking about the weekend, and I didn't have the energy for it. There was one phone call I couldn't put off, though. I undressed and jumped into bed, scrolling through my contacts, and pulled up a number I thought I'd never need to dial again. Hitting talk, I waited for the call to connect, my hands already clammy.

"This is… unexpected," said the croaky male voice on the other end.

"Glad you haven't changed your number, old man."

"I'm your last lifeline, how could I?" he said.

"I relapsed."

"Hence your midnight call."

Exhaling deeply, I said, "I'm sorry. Should have called earlier."

"Did you dump it?"

"No."

"I've never approved of your methods, kid."

"Having it near me wasn't the problem, old man."

There was a pause on his end. All I heard was his labored breathing. Then, he uttered, "Need me to come over?"

"Not tonight."

"Are you sure?" he asked.

"Yeah… I'm sure."

"Why did you call, Tom?"

"Needed to know you were still there."

"I am."

"Can I call you tomorrow?"

"Yes. There's a meeting at seven. I can take you."

The word meeting alone gave me anxiety. "No meeting. Not yet. I just… need to talk."

"Any time, son. I got no place to be."

"Thanks, Tony. I appreciate it."

Hearing Tony's voice brought me peace, even after all the years of not seeing him.

He became my sponsor shortly after the shit with Shayna. A recovered alcoholic and Vietnam War veteran, he came into my life at a time when I needed him most. He understood my PTSD and helped me dig myself out of the hole. Once I was sober and well enough to re-enlist, I shipped out and didn't reconnect until I finished my last tour and came home.

I reached back out to him, but he didn't approve of my new lifestyle, particularly when it came to my social life. Tony didn't think partying with Jake, having booze in the house as a purposeful temptation, and pretending I wasn't an alcoholic was a good idea. It wasn't, but I thought myself invincible, even against whiskey. I had a booming business and beautiful women at my feet. I convinced myself my old life was over, including my drinking problem. My ideology and behavior went against everything he believed in, against everything the program stood for. We parted ways, but he told me never to lose his number.

I was glad I hadn't.

Fourteen

SARA

BOTTLE OF WATER in my hand, I plopped on my worn brown couch, taking a long gulp of the icy liquid, and thinking about the long-ass day ahead of me. I'd woken up around 6:30 a.m., and unable to go back to sleep, I rolled out of bed, moved the living room furniture, and danced. Well, pranced, because you could hardly call what I did dancing. Nevertheless, after the weekend I'd had, it was the remedy my body needed.

After two hours of twirling and leaping, I took a break.

I wiped sweat from my brow, my body still thrumming with life. I looked around the sunlit room and expunged a deep breath. What was I supposed to do with myself? I didn't have the energy nor the desire to go job hunting, and if I stayed in my apartment all day, I'd drive myself crazy. Jen was working and Tom…

Who knew what he was up to. He was his own boss, so it was possible he hadn't even gone to work. I'd received a text around midnight to say goodnight. It only takes twenty minutes from my apartment to his, so where he went after he dropped me off was beyond me. And frankly, I was tired of mulling over it. I'd tossed and turned all night. There was no need to keep spinning circles inside my head. He'd had a shitty weekend himself, so if a little space was what he needed, I could handle that.

I hoped.

Showered and freshly caffeinated, I headed out the door around 10:00 a.m. There was no real plan. All I wanted was fresh air and the chaotic sounds and sights of the city to drown out the pestering voice inside my head urging me to call Tom. I threw my phone inside my messenger bag, along with other essentials, and went for a walk around Central Park.

I'd been lying on a plaid blanket on top of a soft, grassy patch by Belvedere Castle, enjoying the sun, drinking a latte, reading the book on my To-Be-Read list for ages, when my phone chirped with a familiar text ping. I knew the sender.

But I was reading a hot and steamy sex scene.

I finished my chapter before pulling the phone out of my bag and reading Tom's message.

Tom: Hey

Me: Hey back

Tom: Miss you

Me: What's not to miss?

Tom: lol

Tom: Busy?

Me: Unemployed, remember?

Tom: Hungry?

Me: I could go for a sub.

Tom: Meet me at my office

Me: I'm in yoga pants and sneakers

Tom: Sexy

Me: Maybe. But not exactly office attire

Tom: Twenty minutes?

Me: Gonna take me longer than that.

Tom: Famished. Don't make me wait long.

I sat up and grinned wide and stupid. Dammit. I hated how much control he had over my emotions. I'd been all no-man-is-going-to-dictate-how-I-feel-today since I woke up, yet there I was, giddy and bubbly with excitement about meeting up for lunch with my sex-dripping, high-powered executive-boyfriend in his large corner office, overlooking the city as if he was the king of this fucking world.

Well, my world at least.

And he ruled it. And it scared me half to death to know how much power he had over me.

Last night, I'd feared the worst. Today, I'd pretended I didn't care, and now I couldn't wait to see him. One day, I would end up in an asylum. No doubt.

The building housing his Westside office was a hundred-floor high-rise located right in central Broadway. Impressive. Intimidating. It reminded me of the magnitude of who Tom Wright was. He wasn't just my sexy other half. This man was filthy rich, insanely powerful, and panty-dropping hot.

Once I arrived there, I took the elevator to the ninety-third floor, and as I strolled out, I puffed out a breath, taking in the large, frosted-glass double doors dominating the entry-way. The inscription read—Wright and Thompson Associates: Luxury Residences and Commercial Real Estate.

Hesitant to walk right in, my confidence dwindled. I'd never been inside his actual office. Dressed in yoga pants and a t-shirt, and with my hair up in a messy bun, I didn't quite fit the part of the woman Mr. Iced Double would date. I stood outside by the elevator for a minute before Tom's new assistant opened the doors and greeted me. Young and portly, he was about my age and height, with a short curly mop atop his head.

"Hi, Ms. Hart," he said shaking my hand.

I cocked my head. "Craig, seriously? How many times are we going to go over this? Sara is fine."

He blushed, a nervous hand raking through his hair. "Um, right. Sara. Sorry, we're accustomed to keeping things formal around here."

"Well, I don't work here, and I'm not a client. Stop being formal with me." I smiled as I gently nudged his arm.

He simply nodded and wiped the sweat off his brow.

A bit dorky, and a tad on the nervous side, Craig was a better option over the gorgeous red-head with big boobs.

Craig I could handle. Tiffany? Not so much.

The main floor was a large open space with several glass-walled offices flanking the perimeter. The center of the room had a lounge with black leather couches and cubicles. Craig gestured for me to follow him. "Mr. Wright's office is right this way," he said, leading me toward the back where I spotted a large corner office.

As my eyes slowly skimmed past the opened doors to my left, my legs froze when I saw who was sitting in one of the smaller offices only a few doors down from Tom's.

"Tiffany?" The question was supposed to be silent in my head, but I couldn't hold back my astonishment at her presence. Craig stopped to look back at me as Tiffany lifted her gaze, her lips parting and eyes widening.

Yeah, it's me.

"Mr. Wright is right this way," Craig continued, touching my elbow, urging me to follow him, his voice noticeably nervous.

I ignored him and walked right into Tiffany's office.

"Can I help you?" she asked, indifference spewing from the pores on her overdone face.

I glanced back at Craig. "Tell Tom I'll be right there. Need a minute with Tiffany."

"But—"

"Craig. I said I need a minute." And with that, I closed the door behind me.

"I have nothing to say to you," she began.

"Shocking. A few months ago, you had loads to say to Tom."

"I have nothing to say to *you*." She stood her ground, her eyes raging with brimstone as her skin flushed deep red.

I walked closer. "Good. I don't care to listen to you talk, anyway."

"Feeling threatened much?" she scoffed.

"Good one, but no. You eliminated yourself from the equation long ago. Remember? Or should I refresh your memory?"

She leaned back on her leather chair, legs and arms crossing, an ice-dripping grin carving along her lips. "He invited me to stay. It was Tom who asked me to dinner, honey."

"Because he felt sorry for you, *honey*," I spat her word back with venom. "Don't know where you get these illusions you are going to get him back, Tiffany. You never even had him to begin with."

With calculated movements, she stiffly stood up from her chair and approached me until we were face to face. Sneering, she said, "How sweet. You think Tom loves you. He's got you charmed with all this, huh?" She waved a hand in the air. "The money. His hot body. I'm sure you love the way he fucks you, don't you?" She winked as if trying to tell me she knew how well he fucked. "Let me break it to ya, Sweetheart. Tom doesn't love anybody. Once he gets bored with you—and it won't be long before he does—you'll be another nobody in his life."

I inched in closer. She may have stood taller than me in her mile-high stilettos, but I gave two flying fucks about how ridiculous I looked squaring off against this viper in my yoga pants. "It must kill you to see he's in love with me," I said with a sardonic smile.

Her lips thinned, her eyes crackling with scorn. "You know how many women have been in his sheets?"

I offered no response. I knew the list was long.

She must have noticed the wavering look in my eyes and pursed a smile. "You are nothing special, Sara. I've been around too long to be intimidated by little girls like you. Who do you think he came back to when he finished with his little adventures? Me. It was always me, Sweetie. Because when he is done fucking around with you, he is going to need a real woman, not some stupid little cunt like you."

I slapped her. I didn't know what possessed me, but I slapped her hard across her face. She tried to hit me back, but I grabbed her wrist before she delivered the blow. "Listen to me very carefully," I said, my hot breath on her face. "You keep your sleazy hands off my man, or you'll be trekking your ass back to California. Permanently. Because next time you try something as stupid as seducing him again, I will personally send you packing."

She stared at me, still stunned, and holding her throbbing cheek. I let go of her and tromped out the door in search of Tom.

Craig stood outside waiting for me, wide-eyed and jaw dropping as he peeked inside Tiffany's office. I stormed past him in the direction of Tom's office.

"He's on the phone," he called out behind me.

"I don't care," I replied, my voice vexed. This last office was not walled by glass. Guess the boss liked his privacy. Turning the knob, I allowed myself inside and shut the wooden door behind me.

Cellphone to his ear, Tom paced back and forth by the large windows behind his desk, Midtown as his backdrop. I hadn't seen this version of him, yet, in action at work. Dressed in dark-grey suit pants, a black button down and matching suit vest, he was too obnoxiously gorgeous, which made me even angrier.

"Hold on a sec, Eric." He turned to me. "Sara, I'm going to be a couple of more minutes."

"I can wait." I sat on one of the cushy chairs in front of his desk.

He frowned, probably picking-up on the slight annoyance in my voice.

"So, yeah," he continued to speak to the other person on the phone, "tell his rep this is our final offer. If he doesn't accept, our client is walking away and taking his two hundred million with him. No, Eric. No more negotiating. Fine, have him call our broker when he is ready to make a deal. He's got until three this afternoon, or the money is off the table. Thanks, bye."

He ended the call and looked at me. "Why do you look so pissed?"

I hiked a brow.

He blinked and dropped his chin to his chest. "About that…"

I crossed my legs and scowled.

He sucked in a deep breath. "I was going to tell you."

"Why is that woman here, Tom? I thought you said you had reassigned her as the office manager in California?" I pushed up from my seat, unable to contain my frustration anymore.

"I had, but Jake needed a new assistant, and he re-reassigned her."

Hands on my hips, I stalked toward him. "He can't do that."

Tom sat down on his chair and leaned back. "Yes. He can. He does own half the company."

"Why would he do that after what happened?"

"He doesn't know what happened, and I don't care to tell him."

My breath stopped short. Containing the choler and disappointment raging inside was borderline unfeasible. "Why do you protect her so much?"

"I'm protecting *you*. If he knows about what happened, he is going to start more drama."

"Sounds to me like he is trying to create drama already. Why else would he bring her here?"

"Because he's trying to get into her pants again."

"Lovely."

He stood and walked around his desk to reach me. I crossed my arms in silent protest, but he hugged me anyway. "You are such a firecracker. You know that?"

I pulled away. "This is not funny, Tom. I don't like her here."

"What would you like me to do?"

I shot him a cynical look.

"I can't fire her."

I sighed. Made no sense to me why he couldn't. Or wouldn't.

"Sara, we are not even on speaking terms right now."

"You know, she didn't even try to deny it. She openly said you are going to leave me for her."

"You spoke to her?"

"I walked by her office and barged in. You think I'd pass up an opportunity to let her have it? I even slapped her."

He stuck his hands in his pockets as a hesitant smile pulled at the corners of his mouth. "I'm partially flattered, maybe slightly aroused, but that wasn't necessary, and definitely not in the office."

I arrowed a cold, dark stare into him. "I didn't do it to flatter you. Quite frankly, I can't believe I lowered myself to that level. This is your fault. Entirely."

He walked back to his chair, plopping down with a sigh. "Please tell me you didn't come here to tell me something I already know."

"I came to take you to lunch and ended up running into your little surprise out there," I growled, pointing toward the door.

His eyes widened then softened over me. "You came to take *me* to lunch?"

"Yes. So? And don't change the subject," I warned him, now pointing that same finger at him.

"Women haven't typically taken me to lunch." He smiled so warmly I had a tough time staying mad.

"It's only lunch, and nothing fancy. I'm jobless."

"I don't need a fancy lunch. Come here," he said, motioning for me to sit on his lap.

I sighed, defeated. It had been one night without him, and I missed him more than the desert misses the rain. I needed to be in those arms hours ago. Strolling over to him and sitting over his thighs, I draped an arm around his shoulders, his large frame dwarfing me.

"You know, this is one of my fantasies?" he mused.

"Let me guess… sex on your desk?"

"Sex on my desk with your yoga pants ripped and by your ankles," he uttered, lavishing me with a kiss over my neck, igniting my skin in all the right places, Tiffany's face fizzling out from my memory.

I closed my eyes and let his kiss reach every nerve ending. His fantasy did sound hot. My self-control was no match for his devious intentions. All he had to do was touch me, and the reason I was so mad evaporated. Already wet and wanting him to bend me over his shiny oak desk, I couldn't wait for my naked ass to be on display to the NYC skyline.

I mean, what was the point of being mad? If there was one thing I was sure of, it was Tom's feelings for Tiffany. She broke his trust. And once that happened, there was no earning it back. The viper had zero chance of getting between us. It still made my blood spike with venom knowing she'd tried. But what better way to deal with a bit of female rivalry than by fucking Tom in his office mere doors from her?

TOM

SHE TURNED ON MY LAP, straddling me with her back to my chest. She moaned as I palmed her breasts, her nipples hardening under my touch. As she readied to yank off her shirt, I grabbed her hand and brought it to my cock. "You make me so fucking hard, Sara."

She took as much of me as she could and stroked me, moaning as I moved my pelvis upward to meet her hand. Holy. Hell. When she squeezed my girth, she turned my dick to granite. And as she ground into me, I could feel every curve of her backside, her supple body and the feminine scent of her perfume turning me into a savage beast.

Unable to contain myself, I reached for her waistband and slid a hand inside her yoga pants. When my fingers found the wetness between her legs, she quivered on my lap, her legs spreading wider for me as I brushed her clit.

"Damn, baby," I breathed over her ear as she gyrated on top of me. "I love the way your pussy feels…"

"Yeah?"

I circled her clit, using her juices for lubrication. "You're dripping. And your clit. Ah fuck. It's so swollen and hard."

Waves of heat flared through my muscles as I continued to touch her, the tightness in my groin coiling with arousal.

"You want me to make you come like this?" I asked, lightly rubbing her nub between my fingers.

Writhing on my lap, she nodded yes.

I rubbed it a little harder as I licked the side of her neck by her earlobe. "I know you love it when I do that. Pressing on it, spreading your wetness all over it, getting you so hungry for me."

"Oh, Tom…"

"Fuck. You're such a wet dream, baby. I can do this all day, playing with your sweet little clit. God, I swear I can feel it throbbing between my fingers."

She braced the heels of her feet on my desk as we both watched my hand move inside her pants.

"I know what you want," I whispered, torturing her with the heat of my breath against her skin as I inserted my middle finger inside her pussy. "I'm sorry about last night," I said. "Leaving you at your apartment. Alone. It killed me." Burying my finger deeper, I held it there, without saying a word, the only sound the growl that rumbled through me. "Sara…" Her name was a sweet curse on my tongue as I began pushing on her g-spot, summoning her orgasm. "I hate myself for hurting you. For not being a better man."

"Tom…"

"I fucked up, but I'm going to make it up to you. I promise," I said, my words breathless, my own need pillaging through me.

Last night, I'd discarded her, and I knew it stung her deeper than she would admit. I wanted to soothe that wound. To let her know with my touch that regardless of the swirling chaos of our lives, I needed her now more than ever. There were so many hurdles left to overcome, but this was the beginning of our journey. This was my way of letting her in, of allowing her to soothe my own wounds.

Her body grew heavier, her limbs melting in my arms. This was Sara surrendering to me, and I was more than willing to own her. I put my free hand inside her pants as well and stroked her clit with one finger while I continued to finger-fuck her with my other hand. "I want you coming on my lap, baby," I growled in her ear.

Her pussy thrummed with fire over my fingers, swelling even more as she savored the pleasure I was giving her. Watching her body writhe, her hips bucking as she neared climax, was intoxicating. Her walls were so slick, she soaked my fingers. I pulled them out, licked off her juices, then put my fingers back inside her.

Sara's moans were now needy, unyielding pleas, and I was ready to give her what she wanted. "You want my cock inside you, baby?" I breathed the words over her neck.

She nodded, breathless.

"Tell me."

"Fuck me, please."

Those words on her lips made mine curl into a sinister grin.

"Say. It. Again."

"Tom…" she moaned. "I need your cock, baby."

Fucking hell. When she uttered those words, my dick throbbed. I wanted to be inside her so badly, but I wanted her to come first. I nibbled on her neck and strummed her clit in that circular motion she loved so much. She lost all self-control and cried out my name as she orgasmed, hard and thundering on my lap, just like I wanted.

I chuckled as she came down from her release, her body slack over mine. "My employees are gonna think I murdered you in here. But lord, watching you—hearing you—come under my touch is a fucking drug. I don't care how hard you scream, baby."

Panting, she said, "Yeah, well, we're not done."

"No?"

She turned around to face me, narrowing her gaze over me as she reached between my legs and stroked my rock-hard erection. The golden-brown flecks in her eyes flared like hot embers, making my chest rise and fall with long, deep breaths, my dress shirt and suit vest feeling too tight. "We're not going to make it to lunch," I warned as if that was reason enough to stop her.

"Screw lunch," she breathed the words over my lips. "Rip off my yoga pants, Tom. Bend me over your desk and fuck the hell out of this fantasy."

Well, now that was a proposition if I ever heard one.

SEX in the office is a lot less messy in fantasies. All the documents previously on my desk lay scattered on the floor with Sara kneeling over them, yoga pants and panties by her ankles, shirt lifted above her naked breasts, and her dark nipples hard as pearls. The sight of her bent over my desk while I took her from behind a few minutes before had been sex on fucking steroids. I'd grabbed that fine ass of hers and spread those cheeks, pounding into her so deep I knew I'd hurt her. She didn't show it. Her moans had dripped with ecstasy. Neither one of us cared that just outside my door employees were busy at work.

I'd been ready to blow my load inside her when she demanded I'd come in her mouth instead, wanting to swallow every drop of my cum.

Fuck. Yes.

And as tough as it was to pull my length out of her pussy, I couldn't deny her what she wanted, especially when she begged me to slide my dick inside her sinful mouth. I put her on her knees, my shaft pulsing and tightening as I parted her flushed lips, her hands wrapping around my girth. I didn't want to come yet, but she sucked on me so hard and sloppy I lost all self-control.

Continuing to gorge on the sight of her on her knees, her breasts jiggling, nipples hard as pebbles, and those damn yoga pants still at her ankles, sent my orgasm over the top. I came so hard, I shot straight into the back of her throat. My body still vibrating with aftershocks, she sucked on my cock until she licked me clean, her tongue hungry for more as it slid up my length balls to the crown.

I peered down at her, caressing her cheek, wiping off a milky bead from the corner of her lips. "Fuck. I love the way your mouth feels on me."

She curved a smile.

I helped her to her feet, and she dressed as I zipped up and tucked my dress shirt back inside my pants. Checking my watch, I said, "If this is your idea of a quickie, I think you need a lesson in telling time."

"I'm not the one who took forever."

"Baby, I didn't want to let go of the feeling. I'd fuck you into tomorrow if I could."

"See, not my fault," she said over her shoulder, winking, and bending down to tie her sneakers, giving me a full view of those yoga pants hugging her backside.

I slapped her across an ass cheek, the snap stinging my hand. "Ow!" she squealed. "Definitely all your fault. If you didn't look so damn fuckable bent over like that." She stood and rubbed a palm over her butt, her eyes wide. "That hurt."

"Good. It was meant to."

As she helped me pick up the scattered documents, she said, "I have this thing later today, around five, but I'm free after if you want to do dinner. You know, since we didn't get to do lunch." Her voice was soft and coy, her gaze never meeting mine. Our office rendezvous was everything I loved about us. Hot. Spontaneous. But I hadn't forgotten what happened over the weekend, and what I needed to do. I couldn't let one passionate moment get in the way of my mission to fix this mess.

"I can't," I replied coolly, hating how dismissive I sounded, but knowing I had no other answer.

She looked at me, her eyes dimmed. "Oh."

"I mean, I have a meeting," I tried to recover, but the damage was done. This whole thing was killing her, and I hated myself for having to be such an asshole. What else could I do? I had to get my drinking problem back under control, and I needed to find a way to make the nightmares stop, and not just with meds.

"You're working late tonight?" she asked, probing for info.

"It's not a work meeting."

She waited for me to say more.

I ran a hand through my hair. Talking about my issue was always an *issue*. I'd avoided it like the plague, even with Sara, but after the blow-up in Lake George, I couldn't side step around it anymore. "I'm meeting with my sponsor."

Her eyes widened as she realized why I was being so careful about what I said. "I see. AA."

"Just with him. I don't do meetings."

"But your sponsor…isn't that part of attending AA?"

The intercom went off. Thank God for the interruption. "Mr. Wright, Eric is here with his client," Craig announced.

I pressed the speaker button. "Bring them to the small boardroom. I'll meet you there in a sec." To Sara, I said, "I'm sorry, I have to run. You can stay in my office if you need to. I'm going to be a while, though."

She grabbed her shoulder bag and smoothed out her hair. "It's ok. I'm leaving, too."

"What's this thing you have at five, anyway?" I asked as I escorted her out of my office. Heads turned in our direction, employees curious to snatch a glimpse of my new girlfriend. Up until now, Craig had been the only one to meet Sara.

Other than Tiffany and Jake, who knew her from the Santa Monica trip, all everyone knew was the boss was dating a new girl.

"Just a favor I'm doing for Lisa," she said, walking toward the entrance.

"Who's Lisa?"

"Um…"

"Um?"

She stalled for a brief second. "Lisa is… Josh's sister."

We paused at the double doors. "Josh, as in your ex?" I asked as she turned toward me.

She nodded.

A string pulled at my heart. "You didn't mention you still talked to him."

"I don't. His sister sorta came back into the picture a few months back. She was at Jen's birthday thing. At the club, remember? After our first date."

I smirked, recalling Sara's drunken antics and the almost-sex we had in my truck. "Just remember you writhing on my lap." I winked, then asked the obvious question. "What's this favor she wants?"

"Some friend of hers is in town, and she wants me to play tour guide."

"Why you?" I asked.

"He's a dancer."

I tucked my hands in my pockets and puffed out my chest as my gaze narrowed. "This friend is a guy?"

"A dancer," she corrected me. As if that made a difference.

My back tensed. "And you don't even know who this person is?"

She cocked her head and raised a brow. "No. Why so concerned? I'm just meeting him for coffee."

"After what happened with Alexei, I don't trust people, especially some friend of hers who you've never met."

She rolled her eyes and clicked her tongue. If she didn't

look so adorable with her pouty lips, I'd slap her ass again for being so bratty.

"We're meeting in public at International. I'll be fine," she said, huffing.

Craig called from the back of the office. My clients were anxious.

"Call me after you're done meeting this dancer guy," I whispered to her as I leaned in for a kiss.

"Don't worry about me."

Like that was possible. This whole thing sounded shady, but I needed to tame my instincts to protect her against all the wolves out there. Sara was a big girl, and I needed to trust her. "I'm always going to worry about you. Promise me you'll call." My eyes remained fixed on hers, waiting for a confirmation.

"Ok. I will. Go, before you're late for your meeting."

AFTER CLOSING the deal with Eric's client, I walked back to my office, and when I saw the individual sitting in one of my guest chairs, I contemplated doing a one-eighty, until she turned and caught me mid-step at the door.

"We need to talk," Tiffany said.

Walking past her to my chair, I replied, "Please. Leave."

"I'm not leaving until you hear what I have to say."

My lips curled in a mirthless smile as I sat down and glared at her. "Haven't you had enough drama for today?"

She pretzeled her arms over her chest. "Wow. Must be fun dating a five-year-old. Did she come in here complaining and crying about what happened? She hit me, you know. So, not only are you going out with a five-year-old, but you are also dating a violent psychopath."

I inhaled deeply and snickered, trying to stay composed. Dealing with girl drama was not on my to-do list for the day. "I'm not going to get involved in your catfight, Tiffany."

"You think this is funny?" She cocked her head, waiting for a response. "Of course, you would find two women fighting over you amusing. That's what you like, to watch us suffer for you."

"Okay, I've heard enough. Please, leave."

She stood up and approached my desk. "How can you do this to me, Tom? After everything we went through, after all we shared?"

"Tiff, what you and I had… it was a friendship. Nothing more."

"A friendship? Well, you sure didn't act like a friend when you were fucking me from behind."

I pushed to my feet. Hands clenched, my skin about to burn through my suit, I stalked toward her. "We fucked. Past tense. I never wanted anything more from you, and you knew that. Whatever fantasy you built after, that was all you. There was one good thing between us, Tiff, and that was the friendship I thought we had, but you threw that away when you tried to come between Sara and me."

She squared off with me. "That's how you treat your friends? You fuck them, and then shove them to the curb like they don't matter?"

"I never shoved you to the curb. I dated other women, you dated other men. How was I supposed to know you still had feelings for me?"

"You wouldn't, Tom. You never cared about how any of us felt."

"I cared about you. That's why I ended it. *We* ended it."

"You cared about me? Ending it is what tore me apart, Tom."

"What else do you want from me? If I'm sorry about anything, it's ever letting you in my bed."

"You can't possibly mean that," she said, her eyes flooding. "I'd take it all back if it meant we wouldn't be in this situation right now."

"That's it? You are not even going to consider—"

"Consider what, Tiffany? I'm in love with Sara. After all these years I'm finally happy again."

"And I'm supposed to be happy for you? Watch you fade into the sunset with another woman?"

"As my friend, I thought you would be. I was wrong about you, Tiff."

"I will never be happy you are with someone else. I was able to handle you sleeping with other women, but falling in love? That. I can't deal with."

I dropped my chin to my chest and shook my head. "I'm sorry to hear it."

"I didn't mean—" "You need to leave," I told her.

Her eyes told me she still had so much she wanted to say, but my eyes reaffirmed there was nothing else she could say to make me change my mind. It was over between us.

The end.

Tears streamed down her face as she stormed out of my office, almost knocking into Jake when she yanked the door open. He swerved away from her, a giant grin on his face.

"Bruh," he said, strolling into my office, hands in his pockets, "What the hell? So much for no office drama."

I glared. "Close the door."

He did and walked over, sitting across from me, placing an ankle over a knee. "How did it pan out with the Wilkinson property? Craig said—"

"What the fuck were you thinking? I reassigned her to the L.A. office for a reason."

He put his leg down and sat straighter. "Yeah, well you didn't exactly tell me what happened back there. Ever since you started dating miss little brunette—"

"Sara."

"Whatever, man. I'm kinda fed up with this fucking melodrama myself. This female bullshit you're dealing with is your own goddamn fault. Frankly, you're lucky she's not accusing you of sexual harassment."

"I reassigned her because she broke my trust, not because she didn't sleep with me."

"Right. Coz you'd already fucked her plenty."

"It was a consensual relationship, and her employment was never contingent on it. Do I regret it? Absolutely. Even before Sara came into the picture. Regardless, Tiffany and I ended things a while back. This shit is unacceptable."

"Why not fire her then? Why did you let her keep her job if she's such trouble?"

"Because I'm not a cold-hearted prick. She needs the job. Her brother depends on her income."

"She could get a job somewhere else."

"Not one that pays what we pay her."

"Whatever, man. You made your bed…"

"Save it. Just do me a favor and do your best to keep her busy on work. I don't need another outburst like today."

"Well, maybe not parading your new girlfriend around the office would be a good place to start. Flaunting her in front of Tiff, and fucking her in the middle of a workday loud enough for your employees down the hallway to hear, ain't winning you any brownie points."

"You keep acting as if I owe anyone any explanations. Again, just keep her busy and off my business."

He winked. "I'll do my best."

Sixteen

SARA

I STROLLED into the Int'l House of Java and found an empty seat by the window. It was a quarter to five, and I still had fifteen minutes to kill before Lisa's friend showed up. I took the book I'd been reading at the park earlier today out of my bag and dove right into my juicy romance. Two paragraphs into my novel, a man plopped onto the seat across from me and planted a coffee cup on my table.

"Hope I remembered how you like it," he said.

My mind froze, along with the rest of my body. I couldn't even lift my gaze from the pages of my book. That voice was unmistakable.

"Sara?"

I stared at the words, trying to focus on something that made sense, but the letters appeared jumbled as if I'd forgotten how to read.

'Sara, please look up."

My chest heaved. I tried to gulp air, but anxiety clogged my lungs. My hands shook, followed by a current of tremors running the entire length of my body.

The man reached across the table and tried to take the book from my hands. I pulled it back as if losing the book was forgoing the only shield protecting me from him. "Don't," I muttered, surprising myself I'd been able to speak. Summoning courage from where I knew I had none, I peered up and stared into his clear sky-blue eyes.

Time stood still—maybe there was something about coffee houses and running into ridiculously attractive men that made the universe collapse on itself—except this time, the man sitting across from me wasn't my knight in shining armor, and I wasn't hearing the angels sing. Bells weren't chiming, and my heart wasn't breaking into a dance number. Nope. This time, I heard scraping metal and the cries of tortured souls.

Like a beaten prisoner facing his punisher—the one who'd flogged my back until all flesh peeled off—I now stared at the man who had broken my soul.

"Say something," he uttered, his eyes darkening with worry.

I cocked my head, and suddenly, the Earth began to spin on its axis once more.

After all these years, now he cared what I had to say? Countless times I'd replayed this exact moment in my head. Scripted long and winded repertoires. I'd sat him on the witness stand, and I'd played prosecutor, judge, and jury. I'd sentenced him to a lifetime of unhappiness and relished in his misery only to realize none of it ever brought me happiness.

I'd laughed. I'd cried. I'd killed him, and in the end, I'd even kissed him.

Yet, there I had him. Center stage. And I couldn't think of anything I wanted to say.

"Sara, I'm sorry."

I'm sorry?

For years, I'd dreamed of hearing him say those words. I'd prayed he'd come crawling back to me. Remorseful. Devastated. Pleading for mercy.

That he'd tell me he made a mistake, and he still loved me.

I'm sorry…

I repeated his words inside my head several times, but no matter how many times I heard them, they failed to fill me with relief.

My eyes remained fixed on the man across the small table.

It was Josh.

His curly, golden hair once wild and unruly, sat cropped short on the sides. The loose silky curls on top of his head were the only reminder of his younger, crazier days. For a moment, I missed how I used to tangle my fingers in the mess of bouncy locks when we closed in for a kiss. His face had matured, his boyish good looks had transformed into a canvas of pure masculine beauty—a prominent forehead, angular cheekbones, and a square jaw now hugged by a stubbly beard. His eyes, rimmed by thick tawny lashes, still gleamed, springing memories of the times I would lose myself gazing into those sparkling pools. The harsh African sun had weathered his skin, but it suited him well. It reminded me of the summers we spent together.

He'd always had the perfect golden tan. And his lips… damn those fleshy lips of his. They curled into his familiar crooked grin—the charming smile I'd fallen in love with so many years ago. Right now, it was a reminder he'd also driven a stake through my heart.

Why is he smiling at me? Why is he here?

Then it hit me. Lisa.

I shook my head and sucked in a deep breath.

"I know what you're thinking," he said.

I closed my book with a loud thud. "You couldn't possibly," I replied with a scoff as I opened my bag and put the book away before getting up from my chair.

"Where are you going?" he asked, getting up from his and reaching for my wrist.

I yanked it from his grasp. "Tell your sister never to call me again. This was low. Even for her."

"Sara, wait!"

I turned and walked away, but not before looking over my shoulder and saying the words he never could, "Goodbye, Josh."

I **WALKED** into my apartment and slammed the door, rattling the dishes inside the buffet.

"What the heck is that about?" Jen pushed up from the couch and stormed toward me. "Are you trying to break our door?"

I'd managed to keep my composure the entire walk from Int'l to my apartment. The whole forty-five minutes, I walked in silence. Not shedding a single tear. Not talking to myself or muttering all the things I wished I'd said to Josh. I'd walked in peace.

That composure failed me now.

I dropped to my knees.

Jen crouched beside me. "Sara, oh my God, what's wrong?"

Before I replied, the intercom buzzed. "Go, take it," I said.

Jen stood and pressed on the intercom. "Jen speaking."

"Miss Roberts," Pedro said, "I have a gentleman here for Ms. Hart."

She looked down at me. My wide-eyed expression told her everything. "She's not expecting anybody."

"Well, he says it's urgent, and he is not leaving until she comes down. Should I call the police?"

I shook my head no, which only confused her further. Jen's shoulders bunched as she stared at me, silently demanding answers.

Pursing my lips, I mouthed, "No police."

Jen stumbled through her words, perhaps unsure of what

she was saying. "Um, Pedro… that won't be necessary." She raised an eyebrow at me. "What would you like me to tell him?"

"I don't know," I blurted out.

Jen must have sensed the air of desperation in my voice and sighed. "Pedro, just tell the man to hang tight. I'll call you right back." As she let go of the button, she turned to me, her eyes wide and expectant. "Sara, what's going on?"

I stared up at her, my heart pounding. "Josh. He's back."

Jen's body froze. "What did you say?"

I might as well have told her it was a Yeti. I was still in shock myself.

"He showed up out of nowhere." Then I thought for a brief second. "Well, not exactly out of nowhere."

"What do you mean, not exactly?"

"Lisa plotted this. They both did."

The intercom buzzed again.

Jen whirled toward the intercom and pressed the button. "Pedro, I told you I'd call you back."

"It's Josh," said a deep yet smooth voice.

When he first spoke at the coffee house, I'd felt a shot of electricity course through me. My whole body had hummed with an affinity, a reaction I hadn't been prepared for. For years, I struggled to put away my feelings for Josh, to forget the sound of his voice, the touch of his hands, and the feel of his lips. After meeting Tom, the need to suppress those feelings no longer existed. Tom had swooped in and yanked out the tethered box storing all the dead emotional weight I'd been carrying around for years.

Then why did my body respond like this, jolting at the profound rasp of his voice? Back at the coffee house, it had made sense. I'd been in shock. But now? It was even more unnerving. His voice was disarming, it was enchanting, like being dipped in honey. I let out a trembling breath, the rankling anxiety churning in my chest uncoiling.

Jen's body stiffened at the sound as well. "Josh, it's Jen."

"Jen, I need to talk to Sara."

"Wow, you say that as if you haven't been out of our lives for four years. As if you didn't just up and leave without an explanation. How about a hello at least?"

"I know I screwed up. And not just with her."

There was a pause over the intercom. Jen bit her bottom lip and closed her eyes as her brows furrowed. When Josh had left, he hurt her too. For months they'd grown closer. The three of us had attended the same high school, and Josh and Jen had always competed for my time and attention.

In the months after my mother's death, their mutual concern for my well-being matured their relationship into a true friendship. Jen had come to trust him, and I knew it cleaved her heart in two when he left without saying goodbye to her either.

The intercom buzzed again. "Jen, please. I just want to talk to her. Afterward, you can say whatever it is you've wanted to say to me all this time. I know you think I'm a scumbag for leaving as I did. For not coming back. I deserve your anger and disgust. Yours and Sara's. I know sorry will never be enough. But I am truly sorry."

My heart sank. There was a reason I had loved him so much. It hadn't been the excitement of dating the hot, blond quarterback. It hadn't been the rush of riding in his fast car or the thrill of riding him in the back seat. I'd loved him because of his kind heart and genuineness.

There wasn't a mean bone in his body. At least, not when we'd been together. He was the guy the younger classmen looked up to. The guy who helped his elderly neighbor with her lawn or her garbage or her groceries. He was the friendly face who greeted and helped customers at his father's market. He was the guy who always bought me chocolates and a teddy bear on Valentine's Day, and the guy who stuck a giant heart-shaped card on my locker because he wanted everyone to know—loud and clear—I was his girl. Josh never once missed any of my dance competitions, at least the local ones, even when he had to rush across town from one of his games still dressed in his uniform just to make my number.

Surreal as the whole situation was—him showing up at the coffee house, following me to my apartment, his voice echoing in my living room—there was normalcy about it, too. It's as if the four years we'd been apart had collapsed in on themselves. I heard the remorse in his voice. True and utter regret for his actions. I didn't know why he decided now was the time to come back. Why he felt he needed to talk to me after all this time.

I got up off my feet and walked over to the intercom where Jen still stood solid as a block of ice.

I pressed the button. "I'll be right down."

Jen unfroze and grabbed me by the shoulders, spinning me around to face her. "You're not going anywhere until you tell me what the hell happened."

"The dancer Lisa wanted me to meet up with today wasn't a dancer. It was Josh."

"Why would she do that?"

"I don't know."

"I bet she called him after my birthday party. That was the first time we'd seen her since the breakup. She probably rushed to call her brother to tell him—"

I sucked in a deep breath as I interrupted her. "Tell him what, Jen?"

Her eyes narrowed over me. "That she saw you with a new hunky man at your side, that's what."

Rolling my eyes, I bent down to grab my handbag and keys from the floor where I'd dropped them. "You think he came back home because he's jealous I'm dating someone? Don't be ridiculous."

"Then what?" she asked, folding her arms across her chest.

"That's what I intend to find out," I said, reaching for the doorknob.

She leaned her back against the door, preventing me from leaving. "That's it? You're just going to go talk to him?"

"Jen, what else am I supposed to do? He's clearly not leaving, so unless I talk to him, I'm going to need to call the police."

She shook her head, her shoulders bunched as she stopped leaning against the door. "This whole situation seems so… so… wrong. I mean, did he follow you home?"

"Unless Lisa told him where we live. Look, there's nothing right about leaving someone the way he did then showing up four years later, demanding to speak to me as if he has any right to make demands. I could tell him to fuck off, but something tells me I need to hear him out. He went through all this trouble."

She scoffed. "What? Now your heart is soft again? Don't forget you're with someone new."

I shook my head in disbelief. Why was she being so difficult about this? I was the wronged party here. If I wanted to hear what he had to say, I had every right to do just that, without her throwing Tom in my face. "My feelings for Josh are not suddenly springing back," I snapped at her. "This is closure, and I need it."

She uncrossed her arms, and her expression softened. "This is going to open a big ass can of worms. You don't need that right now."

"I'll be fine," I replied coolly, still annoyed. I opened the door and stepped out, murmuring, "Gonna go for a walk or something. I'll call you if I need you to come and rescue me."

She gave me a faint smile as I closed the door behind me and headed toward the elevator to meet up with Josh Buckley.

Seventeen

SARA

I DIDN'T HAVE much time to prepare a speech or even string together a few words. While I'd been with Tom, memories of Josh had faded. Moving-on had become a possibility, but just when I thought life was starting to settle around me, Josh decided to drop out of the blooming sky.

As soon as the elevator door opened, my gut clenched when I saw him standing there, waiting for me. My heart thumped to the beat of a war drum as heat rose up my neck and into my face. I rotated my shoulders as I shook my arms and hands, trying to calm the nerves.

Hands in his dark denim pockets, his biceps bulged out from the short sleeves of his thin gray t-shirt. Gleaming blue eyes, warm and welcoming, greeted me as his lips parted into a smile. It was a small, gentle smile, shy and uncertain.

As the elevator closed behind me, the breath I'd been holding escaped my lungs in one long, drawn-out sigh.

"I feel exactly the same," he said with an amused chuckle.

"Oh, yeah? Did your girlfriend leave you without saying goodbye, only to fall off the face off the earth and show up four years later like nothing ever happened?"

His smile morphed into a frown. "Not like nothing ever happened. I know I screwed up. That's why I'm here."

"What makes you think I even care about anything you might have to say? Four years is a long time, Josh. I've moved on. I thought you had, too."

"You came downstairs, didn't you?" he said with a shrug.

I narrowed my gaze. "Don't make me regret it, smartass."

"Are we going to do this here?"

"Well, I'm not inviting you up to my apartment." I walked toward the exit, leaving him behind to follow. Once outside, I took a deep inhale of the late August muggy air. It did nothing to cool the heat radiating throughout my body.

Smoothing my frizzy hair back, I stood at the bottom of the steps and waited for him. As he descended the steps, I couldn't help but notice the changes four years had done to his body. Back in high school, he didn't have a shortage of girls pining for his attention. He'd been the captain of the football team and generally worked out in the school's weight room. He'd had considerable muscle on him for his age, and his blond hair and blue eyes were perfectly swoon-worthy.

Now?

Holy hell. The Josh I'd known had been a boy. This guy was a man. Okay, yeah, I was still mad at him, but it didn't mean I couldn't appreciate his physique. He wasn't as tall as Tom, but he was up there. His jeans sat low on his hips and hugged him right below the belt in such a manner my inner vixen purred inside her cage as she flashed me with memories of Josh and me in the backseat of his Firebird.

What is wrong with you? I scolded her. He broke your heart. Remember?

I forced myself to glance up from his crotch just as he took the last step. His thin, tight t-shirt did very little to hide his rippling muscles, and his densely chorded arms were inked with full sleeves of intricate and colorful tattoos. Add the tan skin, the stubbly beard, and the golden hair…

The universe did not play fair.

"Where to?" he asked.

"There's a bar down the block."

"I could use a drink," he said.

"Yeah, me, too."

He settled in next to me as we walked toward the end of the street, heading for The Live Bar. It was a small joint frequented by artsy folks who enjoyed listening to music from aspiring musicians. Tonight, it happened to be jazz night.

I shook my head. Was Josh really at my side?

He was so close I felt the heat coming off his body and smelled the musk of his cologne. For crying aloud, in the sweltering late summer, I could almost taste the sweat on his skin. And I hated everything about it— how nonchalantly he walked next to me and how easily this encounter transported me to the past as if there wasn't a four-year gap between us.

Our breakup had been unconventional. We'd never officially ended things. It was more like he'd left us open-ended. Someday he might return, someday he might not. Well, someday happened, and there he was—in the flesh—about to answer the question. What if the truth was worse than not knowing?

We walked in silence, neither one of us in any type of hurry to get the conversation started. Back in the lobby of my building, I hadn't been able to hold his gaze. Those eyes were mirrors into the past, and I hadn't been ready to step through that time portal. I didn't know if I was ever going to be ready, but I knew if I wanted closure, I needed to walk through the threshold.

For a Monday night, The Live Bar buzzed with activity. Josh and I barely said a word to each other as we waited ten minutes for a table. I stood by the entrance, arms crossed, pretending to be listening to the jazz singer on stage. He stood next to me, hands in his pockets, bobbing his head as if he was enjoying the music while we waited for our host. They sat us at a snug table for two near a corner by the front windows facing the street. My heart sank. It might as well have been a table for one. We were practically sitting on top of our neighbors and on top of each other for that matter.

"Welcome, guys. What can I get for you tonight?" our male waiter asked.

Josh ordered a Guinness. I asked for a Tequila Highball. When our waiter left, Josh raised a brow and said, "Tequila?"

"One of those days," I replied, sighing.

His lips twitched, a nervous smile tracing across them as he looked away.

I hadn't come to play games. I needed answers. "Well? It's been four years, Josh. You got me here. What is it you want to say?"

"I had this whole speech prepared," he said, scratching at his beard. "Now the words are dissolving."

"Why did you come back, Josh?"

"Because I couldn't keep putting it off."

"Putting what off?"

He held my gaze in silence as if weighing his answer.

I looked away and blew out a rankled breath. I'd waited too long for this moment for him to waste my time. "If you're not going to talk, then I guess I can leave." I made a motion to stand, but he took my hand.

"Christ, woman. You haven't changed." Guiding me back down to my seat, he added, "Can you give me a moment to gather my thoughts? Seeing you again after all this time, it's just... a lot to take in. I want to make sure I say the right words."

"What does it matter at this point, Josh? Our lives went separate ways. I'm with someone. You're—"

"I'm not," he replied grimly, his eyes hardening as if insulted by my comment.

"I. Am," I spat, trying to drive the point deep like a dagger.

He smiled, but a strained expression filled his eyes with a hint of bitterness. "Thomas A. Wright, the Real Estate Mogul."

My eyes narrowed, not sure if I should have felt startled, confused, or creeped out.

"I Googled him," he said matter of fact.

"How did you know who to Google?"

"My sister can be resourceful."

I closed my eyes and sucked in a deep breath, trying to calm the anger boiling at the mention of Lisa. "Your sister is quite something…"

He smirked, running a large palm through his short curls. "Don't be mad at her. I put her up to this."

"She's always worshiped you," I said, rolling my eyes. "I doubt you had to bend her arm much."

"Let's not make this about Lisa."

"Well, you're not talking much about anything else," I snapped.

Smiling, he reached up and swiped a loose lock of hair from my eyes, tucking it behind my ear. His touch felt strange against my skin. His body was so close, I could almost feel his breath on me. I didn't remember those goddamn tables being so close, or I wouldn't have brought him there.

"You're still so spunky. And beautiful, angel girl," he said, his fingers lingering too long by my ear.

"Don't call me that," I said pulling away from him, unnerved at the body contact.

"You used to love it when I called you that."

I balked, my patience wearing thin. "Josh, we were kids back then," I reminded him, my voice rough as nails. "Just cut the crap and tell me what you came all the way back to New York to tell me."

As he was about to crack his lips open, thunder exploded with a loud clap, startling some of the patrons, including us. Sitting right by the window, I felt drawn by the sound of rain pelting against the glass, the sky brightening with the flashing light. My eyes quickly caught a glimpse of a man dressed all in black standing across the street with a camera, aiming it at the bar.

Strange.

"What is it?" Josh asked, following my gaze to the man now tucking his camera under his shirt and speed-walking away.

"That guy was in the rain snapping pics of the bar."

"Probably just a photographer taking pictures in the rain, Sara. I used to do that. Still do, sometimes."

"I guess…" I replied slowly, trying to come back to the conversation, but my mind lingered on the man, an uncomfortable prickle at the back of my brain seeding doubt.

Our waiter arrived with our drinks. "Thank you," I said to the young man as he set my glass down.

Josh reached for his beer, nodding his thank you to the waiter. He waited until the guy walked away before raising his foamy pint glass. "To old times," he said with a wink.

Raising my glass, I clinked it against his. Josh's lips curved into a playful smile as he took a hearty gulp of his stout.

Regardless of my annoyance with him, this time, I offered him a smile back. He did have a brilliant set of sparkly white teeth and a grin that could typically blast away anger.

Typically.

I held on to mine just a little longer and sipped my drink, my eyes watering a bit as the fumes burned down my throat. It was strong, but it was what I needed to get through this torture.

"How's your tequila?" he asked.

"Perfect."

"The frown is for me, then?"

I put my drink down and tapped my nails on the glass. "Quit stalling."

Pausing before taking his next drink, he said, "Straight to the point, huh?"

I nodded.

"Fine." He gulped down the rest of his beer and waited a short moment before leaning back on his chair. "After I left, I disconnected from everyone, including Lisa and my mom. I couldn't bare having reminders of home."

My heart squeezed, thinking back to the day I found out he'd left. "Reminders of me, you mean."

"Of why I left you." He drew close, resting his elbows on the table, his hands clasped by his chin. "Despite what I did, I loved you. Never doubt that."

I held his gaze. "I don't doubt you did, I just don't know why you stopped."

"Sara, I didn't stop loving you. Things got complicated. I left because I loved you."

Taking another sip of my drink, I leaned over the table and said, "That's horseshit, and you know it. You left because you loved me?" I scoffed, my eyes ready to spit fire. "That's not how love works, Josh."

He leaned forward as well. "What happened to you—the accident—it tore me apart." Josh's forehead creased with deep lines. "You almost died, Sara. To see you hooked up to machines… your face so swollen. All the bruising and the blood. It was like a scene out of a horror movie."

"I know. I lived it."

"I lived it with you," he snapped, tapping a finger on the table. "Or who do think was at your bedside as you recovered in the hospital? I had to watch as you fought for your life day in and day out. I'm not a religious man, Sara. You know that. But damn if I didn't pray every single day for you. And the day you woke up, the day those eyes of yours finally opened and looked at me, I knew it would be the last time I'd see them shine. I knew I could never comprehend the immense loss you felt for your mom. We all loved her, Sara. It was a tragic loss for all of us, but for you, it was…"

"What, Josh? What are you saying?"

"What I'm saying is… after her death, you weren't the same person anymore. And I don't fault you for it. But I felt lost. I had you, but it was just your body, just your shell. The vibrant girl full of life I'd fallen in love with… I couldn't find her."

I didn't think it would be possible for him to hurt me again but hearing him say those words caused a piece of my heart to shatter once more. "My mother died, Josh. My spine almost broke. What else did you expect? I wasn't whole."

"You don't think I understood that? I told you. I didn't blame or fault you for it. You had every right to feel the way you did, but—"

"How can you sit there and tell me you left me because you felt I was hollow inside and expect me to accept it? That's when I needed you the most, Josh. I needed you to help put me back together. After everything we had shared, everything we had promised each other, and you could not wait for me to heal? Did you think I'd stay broken forever?"

His gaze softened over me. "That's not why I left, Sara."

"You came all this way to tell me, so just fucking say it."

"I left because… because while you were in bed broken and numb, I found comfort in someone else."

Time stopped ticking. "What did you just say?"

"Jen, Sara."

I blinked. Something didn't compute. "What?"

"She's who I relied on."

I stared at him, still confused. Or maybe I refused to understand because what he was insinuating made no fucking sense. "You grew close because of me. You became close friends out of mutual concern for my well-being."

"We did."

"Speak clearly, Josh."

"It… was more than that, Sara."

I thought about those words for a second. He couldn't mean… more than what, friends?

Absurd. And out of line.

"No. I won't let you do this," I gritted, shaking my head in utter disbelief. "I can't believe you came all the way back home to smear my best friend's name. To try and blame her for what happened between us. We're done here." I pushed to my feet, knocking into our table, and rattling my drink glass. I hurried away, squeezing through the crowd, fleeing from this man, from the pain he was still causing me. Emptying out into the torrential downpour, it was like drowning in an ocean of tears.

"Sara, wait! Please, hear me out," Josh called out from behind me.

I turned toward him in a flash, my hair heavy with water and sticking to the side of my face. "No, Josh. I don't want to hear you say it. An affair with my best friend? I can't accept that."

"We didn't have an affair, Sara. We shared one kiss. One."

The confession was like acid poured over my chest. "One kiss still tastes like betrayal, Josh."

"That kiss… it was wrong on so many levels. I know that, Sara. We fucked up. Believe me when I tell you neither one of us intended for it to happen."

I paced on the sidewalk as rain continued to drench us. "This… can't be happening to me right now." I looked at him, shaking my head no. "Jen's my best friend, Josh. She could never… she would never."

His chest caved, knowing his truth was crushing me. "She hated herself for it, Sara. And I hated myself, too. And if you'd known the truth? You had been through so much pain already, losing Jen would have destroyed you completely."

I scoffed. "Losing *you* destroyed me completely."

"You needed her more than you needed me."

"I needed love. I needed my friends. And you both failed me." Sneering, I said, "You know what you are, Josh? A goddamn fucking coward. Both of you were. But you weren't even man enough to face your mistakes. Jen stayed. You packed your bags and left. But all for a kiss? It doesn't add up."

His lips trembled as rain streaked down his face. "You're right. It wasn't just the kiss. I fell in love with her."

Another crack splintered through my heart, the shattering sound echoing in my body. "Did she know you were in love with her?"

"No. I didn't tell her. Didn't tell anyone."

Crazy thoughts swirled in my head while a tornado of emotions pillaged through my soul. "But she must've guessed."

"I don't know. And back then I didn't care. I hated the idea of causing you more pain."

"You didn't think leaving me without saying a word would hurt me?"

"What do you want me to say, Sara? I was a fucking eighteen-year-old, and I fucking made stupid mistakes. We all make mistakes in our lives we later regret. Some more than others, but nevertheless, they fester and, eventually, you deal with those regrets."

How dare he? I stalked closer, my body tense with anger, my fists clenched as rain mixed with my tears. "Why now, Josh?" I demanded. "If you were so worried you'd come between us, why show up four years later to drop this fucking bomb on me?" I spat the words at him as I hit his chest. With arms held loosely at his sides, he took every weak punch, knowing he deserved my anger. "I didn't need to know why you'd left. I didn't need to know…" I whimpered.

He put his arms around me as I wept into his chest. "I made a mistake by leaving you like I did, but staying would have been worse. I left because I didn't deserve you, and I didn't deserve Jen."

My body trembled. I could not contain so much emotional torment. Every inch of me was cracking, piece by painful piece. "Then you should have stayed away," I said, pulling from his embrace. I didn't want him touching me, I didn't even want to breathe the same air.

"I loved you, Sara. I loved you deeply, but when I kissed Jen, I realized there was more beyond loving somebody. There was a bond, an unmistakable draw binding me to her on a different level. The moment I kissed her, something lit up inside me. That fire hasn't stopped burning. I came back because I want—"

"Her," I said flatly, realizing the real reason for his return. "I have to go. I can't hear anymore."

"Sara… please. Just let me finish."

"Enough. You've managed to rip my heart out a second time, Josh. I can't believe I ever loved you. I wish we'd never met." I turned to walk back to my apartment.

"Sara, wait."

Spinning around in fury, I said, "Do not follow me, Josh. Or I swear, this time, I *will* call the cops."

Eighteen

SARA

IT's a term people throw around like a commodity.

BFF…

The acronym is even more popular. But what does it truly mean? How much stock do people put into it when they refer to someone as their BFF? Well, for me, it meant everything. It meant family. It meant trust. It represented my core. The person who would always be there no matter what. Until the end.

Jen and I had been best friends since we were in grammar school. We knew everything about each other. *Everything.*

Well, at least up until twenty minutes ago.

Soaked, I walked back to my apartment. It didn't matter if it felt like one hundred degrees to the average person. To me, the wetness caused a chill to seep into my bones. I shivered in the air-conditioned elevator, my teeth rattling as I rubbed my arms. When the doors opened, my dark resolve to storm into my apartment and demand answers from Jen faded to a pale gray. I put my hand out as the elevator door almost closed then walked out.

What was I supposed to say to her? This betrayal was unconscionable. Not just the whole *kissing my boyfriend while I laid on a hospital bed holding on to life by a mere thread* but hiding it from me. Making me believe all this time Josh had left me because he didn't love me, because there was something wrong with me.

She let me doubt myself. She let me cry to sleep for countless nights. She watched me mourn our relationship, held me in her arms as rivers poured from my eyes. What was I supposed to do with this information? Could our friendship even survive this betrayal?

Cloaked in shadows, the apartment was deathly silent, the only sound came from the humming air conditioner. I flipped on the entry light and wasn't too surprised to find the space empty. Even though Jen would normally be sitting at the dining table studying, Josh showing up had changed everything. He'd thrust our world into a vortex. She had to have known Josh would reveal everything to me. Why else would she not be home? Either that or she went to bed early, which was also out of the ordinary for her.

I slipped out of my shoes and padded over to her bedroom door and stood right outside, holding the knob, but I didn't turn it. I couldn't bring myself to confront her, not yet at least. I couldn't figure out what I felt, whether pain at her betrayal or disillusion at her lies. A part of me also understood why they did it. You can't help who you fall in love with. I could almost even forgive them at some level if they had told me they'd fallen for each other. To hide it, though? To leave me without an explanation? To let me dwell in pain for years? How could she watch me cry and be miserable and never tell me the truth?

No, I couldn't face that version of my friend. I didn't bother finding out if she was in her room or if she'd left to go spend the night elsewhere. I went back to my bedroom, wishing it was all a nightmare and that everything would go back to normal in the morning.

I laid down on my bed and cuddled next to Skiddles. She

was warm and nudged my nose with hers, granting me permission to share my bed with her. My head throbbed. I could not make sense of the day's events. The truth was, I was glad Jen wasn't around for me to confront her. I wanted to pretend what Josh told me never happened.

Jen not being home gave me the time I needed to think about how I would approach her. I didn't want to come out guns blazing, demanding answers. I wanted to give her a chance to rebut his claim and provide me with her version of the events. Deep down I prayed she'd tell me it was all a lie, and she didn't know why Josh had made up such preposterous stories. Deeper down, I knew it was the truth. Josh wouldn't go through the trouble of finding me to spin such a tale.

I shook my head and blew out a long and troubled sigh. The thought of calling Tom to tell him everything weighed heavily on my mind, but he'd been through so much already. Going to Lake George had been a shit-fest. How could I dump this on his shoulders right now, when he was battling his own demons? No, I couldn't do that. At least not tonight when he was supposed to go see his sponsor. Tomorrow would be another day, and hopefully, I'd at least have more answers. Just then, my phone buzzed with a text.

Tom: Can I call you?

Shit. How was I supposed to mask my grief? I didn't want him guessing I was not well. My problems were nothing compared to the true torment he was going through. I needed to stay strong for him. I had to do my best to sound normal.

Me: Yes

A moment later, my phone rang. "Hey," I said low and calm.

"Hi. Everything okay?" he asked.

"Yes. Why do you ask?"

"Intuition."

"Tired from a long day, is all," I replied.

"How did it go with the guy?"

"Um… fine, I guess."

He grunted. "You don't sound so certain."

"It went okay."

"You don't want to talk about it?"

"There's not much to say."

"You'll be meeting up again?" he asked.

"Don't think so. There's not much more I can do for him. So, how did it go with your meeting?" I said, hoping to change the subject.

"It wasn't a meeting. Just went to see an old friend."

"And how did it go?"

"He put some things into perspective for me. Relapses aren't easy, but it doesn't mean I can't get back up."

"What about your nightmares? Are you going to see a doctor about that?"

"I don't want to."

I knew Tom was stubborn and proud, but his choices affected both of us, and this was something he needed to address. "You can't live like this," I reiterated.

"Being on the meds… the thought of having to be dependent on pills again…"

"It's scary, and it sucks," I said. "You know what else sucks? Not being able to live a normal life."

"Life will never be normal for me, Sara."

I sat up in a jolt, my already rankled mood getting the best of me. "What about me? Us? Aren't wea reason to seek help?"

"Of course, it is," he answered with similar fervor. "I didn't say I wasn't going to go. I just wish I didn't have to."

The assurance he wasn't backing out on his decision to seek help eased my temper. It had upset me because I cared so much about him, and all I wanted was to see him well. He didn't have to suffer those debilitating nightmares. "You don't have to do this alone," I said. "I'm here for you, Tom."

"I know you are, Sara. Thank you."

"When are you going to make the appointment?"

He chuckled. "Pushy-pushy."

"I'm not playing. I can get pretty annoying."

"Okay, okay. I'll give my doc a call tomorrow."

"Promise?"

"I swear."

After a few minutes of catching up on the rest of our day and exchanging *miss you's* and *love you's*, we both called it a night. Hearing his voice had been a salve to my bleeding heart. Still, getting rest wasn't easy. My mind was a swirling tornado, plus the menstrual cramps had finally started. Terrible timing, but I was happy to get my period and put the pregnancy scare completely behind me.

After taking a sleeping aid and some painkillers, I was able to get some sleep.

Nineteen

TOM

I MUST HAVE HIT the snooze button ten times, maybe more, before pulling the plug from the wall. I seldom needed the alarm to wake me. Most of the time I was up before six and out the door by seven and in the office by eight. Today, it was half past seven, and I was still lying under my sheets, Bax sprawled next to me, keeping Sara's side warm. Why was I dreading going to work? I mean, I was my own boss. I could've called out sick and given myself the day off.

The problem was clear. My whole cycle was off. Not having Sara sleeping by my side had screwed with my rhythm. I liked sleeping with her head on my chest. I loved waking up with my arms wrapped around her waist, my nose buried in her hair or neck. Her sweet vanilla scent was better than the coffee aroma emanating from my kitchen when my automated coffee maker went off. Opening my eyes in the morning and seeing her tucked into me made me feel whole and ready to conquer the world.

She'd turned me into a rambling idiot.

Dammit. I missed her in my bed, in my home, in my life.

I needed to call my doctor soon and get my life in order, or I'd go out of my mind.

My skin bristled thinking about the call. Why the fuck had the dreams returned with such a vengeance? I hated the goddamn pills, what they represented—that I couldn't handle my shit. That I couldn't let go of the past, of my mistakes. The doc wouldn't just prescribe me meds. He'd want to sit me down for a chat.

Fucking chats never did much for me. Who wants to relive their worst nightmare? Who wants to dredge up all the muck from the bottom of the ocean of their greatest regrets? But if I wanted any semblance of a normal life with Sara, I needed to do this. I needed to numb myself. Doc would say heal, but there's no healing from my past. There's taking the pills and pretending everything is ok. Truth was, the pills would simply douse the wounds with their own special kind of morphine.

I turned to Bax and rubbed his neck. "We're gonna get her back soon, buddy," I said. "Momma will be back home before you know it."

Bax groaned as if doubting my words. "Have faith in me, buddy. I'm gonna get my shit together. I'm not screwing this up for us. I promise." This time, he perked up and jumped off the bed, barking his orders to go for his morning walk.

LIKE AN ASSHOLE BOSS who walks in late while demanding all his employees be in on time, I strolled into my office around 10:30 a.m., a hand in my pocket, the other carrying an iced Americano. Everyone seemed to be busy at their computers, I even noticed Jake handling a video conference call in the boardroom. Some people waved at me as I passed their cubicles and offices, others nodded their hello. Others averted my eyes. Craig was waiting at the entrance to my corner office, a stack of papers and envelopes in his arms.

"Morning, Craig."

"Morning, Mr. Wright."

"Busy day already?" I asked, opening the door to my office.

Craig followed and placed the large stack on my desk as I took off my suit jacket and plopped on my chair.

He sat across from me. "Mr. Thompson has been on that video call with the Highland property brokers since nine," Craig said.

"Must be some major deal he's working."

"He's been trying to schmooze them all morning, but personally, I think they don't like Mr. Thompson and are giving him a hard time to bust his chops."

I fired up my computer. "Jake's not easy to like, but he's a good businessman. He'll close the deal. Even if it costs him some serious brown-nosing." I chuckled and turned to Craig for my morning debrief. "What's my schedule look like for today?"

"Well, you had a 9:30 call with the Brookland Brothers, but since you weren't in, I rescheduled."

I slammed a fist on my desk, the bang making Craig jump in his seat. The Brookland Brothers were developers who were looking to sell all twenty high-end units in their new luxury apartment complex across from Central Park. It was a big contract with a hefty commission. I'd been trying to get them to agree to work with us since before they started construction, and they'd finally agreed to take my call. And I'd blown them off.

"Fuck!" I pushed up from my chair. "How the hell did I forget about this?" I fixed my gaze on Craig. "Why didn't you call me?"

He sucked in a startled breath. "I... I did, but you didn't pick up, sir. I left you a message."

I paced behind my desk, hands on my waist. "Shit. This is

not good. Can you get them on the phone? I don't want to lose out on this contract because I fucking overslept."

"I called their secretary earlier and rescheduled for next week," Craig replied.

"That's too late. By then, they will have hired a different firm. Get them on the phone today."

Forehead coated in sweat, he said, "Secretary said their schedule was booked. I tried. Trust me."

I clenched my jaw, and muttered, "Are you saying you can't do this?"

Craig stood from his chair and wrung his hands. "No. Not at all, sir. I'll try to get them on the phone. Right away."

"Don't just try, Craig. Do it."

As he walked away, I noticed an unaddressed manila envelope sitting atop the stack of documents I needed to review. Thomas Wright blazoned across in black sharpie. "Wait, Craig. What's this?"

"I'm sorry, sir. What's what?" he asked, turning around.

"What's with this envelope? It doesn't have a return address. Where did it come from?"

"I… um… it was laying at the bottom of all the other incoming mail this morning. Given its informality, I figured it was personal, so I didn't open it."

I stared at the manila envelope confused as to what it could be. Whoever dropped it off, did it in person—before the office even opened if it got here before the mail carrier made his drop.

What the fuck?

"Should I check its contents, sir?" Craig asked.

"No. That won't be necessary. Thanks, Craig. Let me know as soon as you get the Brookland Brothers on the phone."

"Will do."

"Close the door on your way out."

As the door shut behind Craig, I continued to stare at the

envelope. Something odd spiked in my blood, an uncomfortable tingle that put me on edge. Just as I was about to reach for the envelope, my phone alarm went off. I needed to call Dr. Feldman. I took a deep breath as I dialed his number. Waiting for the receptionist to see if the doc was free, I tucked my cell between my ear and shoulder, reached for the envelope, and picked up my letter opener.

"Tom, long time since I've heard from you," the doctor said.

"Hey, Doc. Sorry to pull you from your patients, but this is important."

"I have a few minutes before my next session. What's going on?"

I stuck the blade through the envelope and cut through the paper. "Well… the nightmares, Doc. They are back."

"I'm sorry to hear it. You need an appointment?"

"Um…" I paused a second as I reached into the envelope and pulled out its contents. "I wish I didn't, but…" my thoughts cut off as soon as I laid eyes on the contents. The phone fell from my shoulder, landing on my desk with a loud clank before bouncing to the floor. My blood iced and my hands trembled as I gripped the photographs clasped in my hands.

The real nightmare had just begun.

Twenty

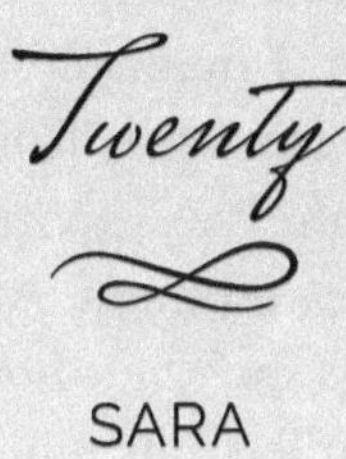

SARA

EVEN WITH THE sleep aid and ibuprofen, I was restless most of
the night, waking up sporadically because I was hot, sweating,
or needing to go to the bathroom. At one point, I woke up
panting from a bad dream I couldn't remember. However, as
bad a night as I had, I woke up feeling less stressed, as if
everything didn't weigh as heavily on my shoulders anymore. I
was still angry with Jen, but it wasn't something I couldn't
handle.

Perhaps today would be a better day.

I rubbed the sleep from my eyes and rolled out of bed. My
abdomen still felt a little sore, and when I went to the bathroom, I realized I'd spotted through my underwear. It seemed
I was getting my period after all. Changing into a clean pair
of pink pajama shorts and a white tank-top, I trudged to the
kitchen half asleep, startled to find Jen finishing a bowl of
cereal. A tight spring coiled in my stomach when I saw her.

So much for being able to handle this.

I still had no idea if she'd been out all night, or if she'd
gone to bed early. Looking at her was like staring at a stranger.
She seemed so different now, as if a veil had lifted from my
eyes. I didn't greet her and instead reached for the breadbas-

ket, opened a new loaf, and pulled out two pieces of whole-grain bread. I slid them into the toaster then pulled an egg crate from the fridge, trying to act as normal as possible.

Just breakfast as usual.

For some reason, even though I carefully pulled a skillet from the bottom cabinet, I managed to smack it against every single other pot before freeing it from the back corner. The clanks echoing through the apartment accentuated the awkwardness of this tense moment. After firing up the range, I cracked two brown eggs over the hot skillet and stirred very gingerly as the eggs fluffed, all while keeping track of Jen through my peripheral vision. She'd been watching me the whole time, as if waiting for me to break the silence.

Good luck with that. I'd been glad I hadn't seen her the night before because I didn't have a clue how to begin the conversation, and not much had changed since. Those five minutes it took me to make toast and scrambled eggs felt like the longest five minutes of my life.

"We should talk," she said out of nowhere, causing the skin on my body to prickle.

"About?" I asked nonchalantly as if I had no clue what she meant, wanting her to be the one to breach the topic.

She finished her cereal and put her white bowl aside. "I take it he told you everything?" she asked so matter of fact it stunned me. The jig was up, and it was time to fess up, but it felt so cold and unremorseful, I had a hard time believing this person was the same Jen I'd known all my life.

My blood stilled as I contemplated her words. She'd just confirmed Josh's claims, and it burned hotter than I imagined it would, but I didn't want her to know how gravely those seven words rattled me. I looked up from my skillet and cast her an unemotional stare before looking back down and pouring the steaming eggs onto a small plate.

Keeping quiet, I reached for the butter, slathered it over my toast, and took a bite before punching a button on the automatic coffee maker and waiting two minutes for my coffee to fill. All in agonizing silence.

Glancing at her from the corner of my eye, I noticed her jaw clench. Good. The awkward wait and my nonchalance made her anxious. And I wanted her like that. Off her game. Unable to tame me. She'd always been like my mother, soothing my pain, calming my anger, and keeping my emotions in check. Today, I was not letting anyone hold me back, not even her.

Once finished, I poured in a little French vanilla creamer. "How did it feel?" I asked, returning the butter, eggs, and creamer back to the fridge and grabbing my mug and plate as I strolled to the dining area, sitting my ass down across from her.

Her brows pinched as she fixed her gaze on me. "How did what feel?"

Taking a mouthful of eggs, I swallowed, then said, "Kissing my boyfriend while I lay injured in bed?" I cocked my head and bit into my toast again as I waited for her response.

She blew out a puff of air. "Is this how we're going to do this?"

I dropped my toast. "I guess you expected I'd run in here, tears streaming down my face, sobbing like the idiot I've been all these years, thinking you were my best friend. Meanwhile, you've had this little gem in your dark closet of secrets."

"I don't have a closet of secrets."

I sipped my coffee. "Right. Who needs a closet full of them when you have the mother of all secrets stashed away?"

Her facial features softened, the hard edge she'd tried to maintain since I walked in the kitchen faded. Her bloodshot eyes watered and I knew she'd been trying to keep her emotions in check, but now her composure failed her. "Sara, I'm sorry."

Watching her hold back tears triggered mine, but I held

them back as well. I'd cried my share of tears the night before. I didn't need to shed any more.

"I'm truly, truly sorry," she reiterated, lips quivering.

"Sorry? That's a word I keep hearing a lot lately. You know what? I'm quite tired of it. You know why? Because it doesn't fix anything." My words sounded crueler than I intended, but it was the truth, and tears or not, she needed to know how deeply she'd cut me. "It doesn't take away the pain I suffered at the hands of both you and Josh. What you guys did... I can't even." I shook my head and took a hearty gulp of coffee, letting the heat singe my insides.

"What we did was a mistake."

That made me fume, and I smacked my hand down on the table. "A mistake is something you do while meaning to do something else, Jen. What you did was—"

"A bad decision," she interrupted. "I should've never let him kiss me."

I scoffed. "Now it's Josh who started it all?"

"Fine," she snapped, matching my tone. "We kissed each other, and I am no less guilty than he is, but trust me when I tell you I regretted it the instant it happened."

"He seems to think it was the most magical moment in the world," I mocked. "Were you in love with him?" It was the question that hadn't stopped bouncing inside my head since the moment Josh confessed.

"Sara, I..."

I stuffed eggs into my mouth, but I may as well have chewed on cardboard. I'd lost all appetite for breakfast. I chased it with more coffee. "Josh is incredibly charming, and you'd be crazy to deny you weren't attracted to him. Every girl in a twenty-mile radius practically wanted him. They would have given anything for us to break up."

"I never wanted you two to breakup," she said, her voice cracking with the onset of more tears.

I didn't let that distract me. I needed to know. "Jen, you didn't answer my question."

She looked down at her fingers as they twirled a napkin on top of the table. "Prior to your accident, I never gave it much thought. Yes, he was insanely attractive. That's just stating the obvious, but I never thought anything beyond it. I didn't daydream of Josh and me together. You two were madly in love and incredibly happy. I would never want to see you heartbroken over him." Her eyes remained fixed on her fingers. She couldn't meet mine, and it told me everything.

"But it all changed when I was lying broken on a hospital bed."

She snapped her gaze back up at me. "No. That's not how it happened."

"Then when did the magical moment occur?" I pressed, my even keel demeanor cracking at the edges.

"It was after you were back home and refusing to get better. When you were popping pills, and we were worried about you."

I pushed the remains of my breakfast away. "You just had to throw the pills comment in there, didn't you?"

"I know it hurts, but it's the truth. You were self-medicating and it—"

"And it what, Jen? Go on and say what you've been wanting to say all these years."

She stood up and walked to the living room. "I'm not going there with you."

I pushed up from my chair and followed her. "We're already there so we might as well air out all our shit."

As she reached the couch, she turned to face me. "I don't want to make this about you or what you were going through."

Drawing closer, I said, "But it *is* about me. You seduced my boyfriend."

Taken aback, she pressed a hand to her chest. "Seduced? Are you kidding me? You think I wanted a guy I couldn't have? Why would I want to put myself through the torture of pining for my best friend's boyfriend? I never had any intentions of taking him from you. That was the furthest thing from my mind. It never even occurred to me he might have feelings for me."

A mirthless smile curved at the corners of my mouth. "So, when you realized he did have feelings, you took your chance?"

As she plopped on the couch, she shut her eyes and let out an exasperated breath. "It wasn't like that. We grew close, yes, but never like that. We went out to lunch, and we talked about you." She looked up at me and made sure to drive the point home. "Always you, Sara. Because you were the most important person in our lives. Because we wanted nothing more than to see you pull yourself out of the dark hole you'd fallen through. But at the same time, we wanted to give you the time you needed to grieve, to put yourself back together. Josh tried to get close to you, but you pushed him away."

Ouch.

Her comment stung because it was true. And it pissed me off further. "This is now my fault?"

When she realized she'd hit an old wound her face softened. "No. Definitely not. I'm not saying that. Never. But you gotta understand what he was going through. He'd lost you, too, Sara. And he was hurting."

I paced, hands on my hips as I recalled all the times I'd refused to see or talk to Josh because I was doped-up and wanted zero company. "You... were there for him when I couldn't."

"Sara, it didn't make what happened between us right. I've regretted what I did every single day since the day it happened. You have to believe that."

My resolve to not shed a tiny tear dissolved into nothingness. "Why didn't you just tell me, Jen?" I asked.

"Because the kiss was pointless, Sara," she said wiping my eyes. "We were on his couch having pizza. His mom was in the kitchen washing dishes for crying aloud. It was the most unsexy moment I could ever imagine," she chuckled. "But he kinda leaned in, and we kissed. I instantly realized my small attraction to him went deeper than his incredible physique. I felt the kiss everywhere, and it's why I knew it was a mistake. A bad decision."

"It doesn't sound like a pointless kiss."

"It was pointless because we could never have anything beyond that kiss. He knew it, and I knew it."

"Can't believe I was so blind."

She took my hand in hers. "Stop seeing it like that. I didn't say anything because I didn't want to stand in the way of your happiness. I figured he was emotionally drained, and he needed to feel close to someone. I happened to be there at that moment. I never thought he might have feelings for me. I ended our night right away and left his house. It was the last time I ever saw him. A week later he up and left."

"Did you love him?" I had to ask again. After what Josh told me, that'd he'd come back for her, I needed to know.

"I think… I didn't allow myself to. If that makes sense. The kiss was reckless and stupid, and I wish it never happened, Sara. In another world, perhaps. Where you two weren't together, I could have loved him, but it wasn't the case. I was ready to stop seeing him. In fact, I had planned to tell him the day I found out he had left. I never had the chance."

"All the years I spent wondering. It's confirmed. He didn't love me anymore."

She squeezed my arms. "But he did love you, Sara."

"But he wasn't in love with me. He fell for you. He said so last night."

Her eyes widened as if she still believed Josh had only kissed her because she filled a void in a moment of loneliness. "Believe me when I tell you I never gave him reason to fall for me. Sara, I never seduced him. I never made a move on him." Jen's hands shook as she held my arms, perhaps fearful I wouldn't believe her.

"I know you're telling me the truth. Just wished you'd told me back then."

"Would you have believed me I hadn't intended for it to happen? Would we still be friends?"

"I don't know. Maybe, maybe not. But that's the price of friendship."

She let go of me and sat back, crossing her arms. "All these years, I thought about telling you, but what good would it have done?"

"Knowing the truth might have closed the wound sooner."

"And it would have opened a new one. It would have torn us apart. I didn't want to lose you, Sara. I don't want to lose you now." She sat up straighter and rooted her gaze into mine. "You're my best friend. My only true friend, and I would have done anything not to jeopardize that."

"Including lying to me."

"Yes. And I'm sorry. I was selfish, but I didn't do it just for me, I did it for us. I didn't want you losing him and me, especially after losing your mom. You have no idea how much I wish that kiss never happened."

"He might not have left, Jen. Josh and I might still be together, ever think about that?"

She swayed her head. "Yeah, that's true. Or it might have ended later, who knows. I can't say for sure because the reality is, he did leave, and I can't change that. But if you were with him still, you wouldn't be with Tom."

I rolled my eyes. "Tom has nothing to do with this."

"He has everything to do with this. You are in love with the one man you say is your true soul mate. The one man you can't live without. Things happen for a reason, Sara. I believe that, and I know deep down you know it, too. The universe is always meddling, that's what you always say. This was her meddling, Sara."

I tucked loose hair behind my ears and sighed. "And I will cry a million tears over it because that was a very tragic time in my life, and it sucks the universe would be so cruel to put me through hell first before giving me the most incredible man years later. I'll never understand her ways, but I understand that regardless of how bad it hurts, the truth is always better."

I looked at her, and my heart ached because I understood exactly why they'd kept quiet. "You were both trying to protect me from more pain, and back then, I wouldn't have seen it that way. Josh and I would have broken up, and you and I may have stopped being friends. I know what you guys were trying to do by not telling me, but it doesn't stop the sting of it all. It doesn't make the pain of knowing my best friend and the man I loved had fallen for each other."

"What can I do for you to forgive me?"

I squeezed her hands and stood up. "There's nothing for you to do. Now that I understand the true power of love and how we pretty much have no say in the matter, I can't fault you for falling for him. Up until that major fuck-up, he'd been amazing. Everyone loved him."

"I wish you hadn't found out this way."

"It sucks," I said, laughing, and walking back to the dining table to pick up my dishes. "I've been trying to piece this all together since last night, trying to make sense of it all, but I've given up. Sometimes things aren't meant to fit together. I could stop being friends with you, but could I? I would never throw away a lifelong friendship over a stupid kiss that happened years ago. Things do happen for a reason, and you're one hundred percent right, if I were still with Josh, I wouldn't be with Tom, and Tom is everything to me."

"Are we… still friends?"

"We will always be friends, Jen." Putting the dishes in the

sink, I added, "Gonna need a little space while I deal with this mess, that's all. Josh is back, and he has no plans of leaving."

She blinked. "What do you mean?"

As if on cue, the buzzer went off. I walked toward the front door and pressed the intercom. "Yes?"

"Ms. Hart, there's a gentleman at the door."

"Who is it?"

"Same man from last night, ma'am."

Oh, great. Here we go.

I turned to Jen, but she had disappeared into her room, shutting the door behind her.

Twenty-One

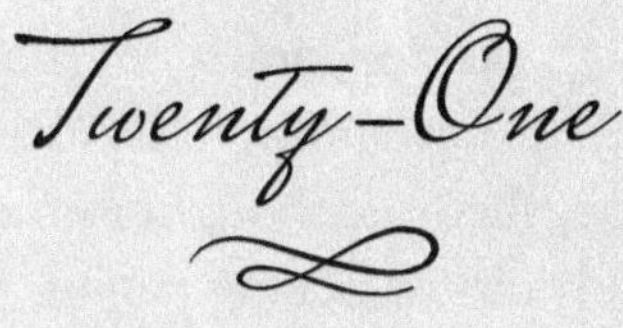

TOM

WHAT IN GOD'S name is this?

Staring at me in full color were stills of Sara and a blond man sitting close to one another having drinks. In one shot the man was so close, he might as well had been her lover. He appeared to be caressing her cheek or touching her hair. My blood ran so boiling hot through my veins, I had to loosen my tie and unbutton the top of my shirt to cool down, but it did nothing to calm the rage surging through me.

Photos of him entering her apartment.

Photos of them walking together.

Photos of them seemingly arguing in the middle of the sidewalk.

Who sent these? When was this? Who the fuck was the man she was with?

None of it made sense. More photos revealed they were sitting at the Live Bar a block away from Sara's apartment. A place we frequented. The shirt she was wearing was the same shirt she'd been wearing the day before when she'd visited me at the office. It couldn't be, but it had to. Could that have been the dancer she had met up with?

No. No. She met him at Int'l. At least that's what Sara told me. "Fuck!" I ran a hand through my hair in a frantic attempt to calm the electrified nerves bulldozing through my brain. There had to be a perfectly logical explanation for this. There had to. Otherwise…

Otherwise, I was going to lose my shit.

I paced as sweat beaded down my back and soaked my shirt. Was that why she seemed off last night? Had she been with him? Shit. I squashed the thought immediately or my body would have erupted into a fucking raging volcano. What was wrong with me? My mind was headed on a one-way trip down a dark path. Very quickly. Nothing good would come of it.

A knock at the door drew my attention. "Come in."

Craig strolled through, a question ready to spurt from his lips, but I cut him off before he had a chance to utter a single word.

"Who the fuck sent these?" I asked him, holding the photos in my hand.

"I don't know what you mean, sir."

"The fucking manila envelope you brought me this morning."

"I told you, I found it under all our other mail," he sputtered.

I ran a palm down my face. "But who dropped it off? Who the hell was here first thing this morning?"

"I… um… well, me. I opened and found everything."

Slamming down a fist on my desk, I said, "There was no one else here? Tiffany? Jake?"

"No, they came later."

I walked around my desk, grabbed my car keys, and stormed past him and out my door. "Anyone know who the hell dropped off this envelope?" I called out to the sea of cubicles, holding the envelope high above my head for everyone to see. Some people poked their heads up, their eyes wide and confused.

"Well? Anyone?" I demanded.

People met each other's gaze, shaking their heads no, their faces scrunched in confusion. I stalked down the aisles. "Any idea who might have dropped this off?" I asked a female employee, then I turned to her neighbor across the way and asked her the same thing.

More headshakes and narrowed eyes.

"Listen, people, someone came into the building this morning before the office opened and dropped off this envelope. I need to know who," I shouted into the room like a crazed man.

Jake came strolling out from the conference room scratching his head. "What's with all the shouting?"

I approached him and nudged his shoulder, encouraging him to follow me. "Someone's fucking with me, and I intend to get to the bottom of it."

"What are you talking about, man?"

"I need to talk to security. I want to see the surveillance videos from last night and this morning. I need to know who dropped these off."

Craig trailed behind Jake and me. "Mr. Wright. Mr. Wright!"

When I didn't turn around, he shouted louder. "Tom!"

I turned on him, heat beaming through my eyes. "What, Craig?"

"The Brookland Brothers. They're on the phone."

"I can't take the call right now."

Craig's eyes widened. "Sir? But..." He tried to hand me a cell phone.

I shook my head and turned from him, stalking toward the exit. "Not. Now."

Jake grabbed me by the shoulders and spun me around. "Tom, the Brookland Brothers? You have to take the call, man," he said, his voice grim.

"Fuck the Brookland Brothers," I replied, shaking his hands off my shoulders. "I'll handle them later."

"Later? Are you out of your fucking mind? You already missed the call this morning, and now you're going to blow them off again? Might as well kick this potential contract goodbye. We're talking millions, Tom. Down the goddamn shit hole."

After all the work I put into our company every day, his reproach was a gut punch I didn't deserve. I stepped closer, nearly chest-to-chest with him, and gritting my teeth said, "You're supposed to be my partner, why didn't you cover for me this morning when I wasn't here for the call?"

"Because I was working on another deal. Or did you not see me in the conference room when you strolled in after ten?"

"Listen to me, brother. I don't need this shit from you right now."

"What's in the envelope, Tom?"

I shoved the sickening photos into his chest. "Look for yourself." I turned to Craig. "Get in touch with security. Tell them I want all the footage from last night and this morning. And I want to know how this person got in the building without a keycard."

"Right away, sir,' he responded, taking off in some random direction.

I kept walking toward the front entrance. As I pushed through the glass doors and reached the elevators, Jake called after me. "Where the fuck are you going?"

"To get answers."

"This," he said, holding up the pictures, "is not worth losing a contract with the biggest developer in New York City." He shoved the pictures back into my chest.

I said nothing and waited for the elevator to open.

"Tom, they are going to hire a different firm."

Remaining silent, I took the pictures and put them back

inside the envelope then walked into the elevator as soon as the doors glided open.

"For Christ's sakes, Tom. We can't afford to lose this contract. Not over some fucking chick. This is not right. Dammit, Tom…" His voice trailed as the doors closed and the elevators took me down to the parking garage.

In my haste to leave, I'd forgotten my phone back in my office where it fell to the floor. Fuck it.

I had no time to go back. Once I jumped in the car, I reached into the locked glove compartment of my Range Rover and grabbed the one object I prayed to God I wouldn't have to pull out today. Taking a few deep breaths, I kicked my car into drive and sped through the streets of Manhattan.

Twenty-Two

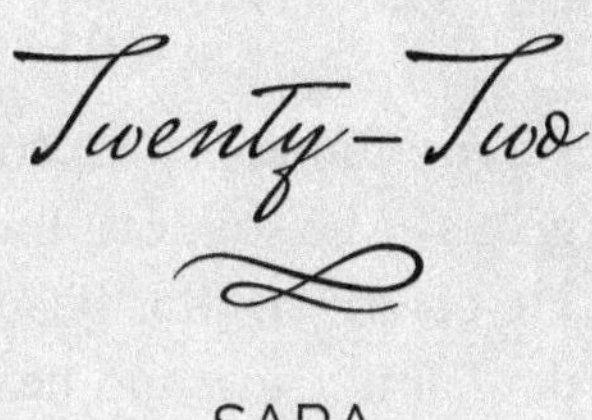

SARA

MY BESTIE LOCKED herself in her room and my ex-boyfriend, who apparently was still in love with her, was downstairs in my lobby. These two blondes were going to drive me nuts. What was I supposed to do, leave him down there? And why was Jen so afraid to confront him? If anything, I should have been the one locked up in my room refusing to talk to anyone. I had enough reason to be upset at them both, yet there I was, about to play peacemaker.

I pressed on the comm. "Pedro, let him up."

A minute later, he knocked on my door. My body tightened as nerves coiled around me. Last night I'd told him off and now I had invited him to my apartment? For what? There couldn't be anything else left to say. Yet, something inside me couldn't let go. Despite everything, I'd loved him once, and even though our love no longer existed, I couldn't erase him from my past. He'd been my first boyfriend. My first everything. As much as I wanted to hate him, I couldn't.

It took me longer than it should have to walk up to the door and open it. I drew a silent breath as I took in the sight of him. He stood in the same unthreatening pose so signature to Josh—shoulders bunched, hands stuck in his jeans' pockets, a wry grin etched across his face.

His blue eyes sparkled like diamonds as his smile widened. He ran a nervous hand through his short blonde curls, and said, "Thanks. I wasn't sure if you'd give me another chance to explain."

I peeled my eyes from him and stepped aside to let him in, thankful that as gorgeous as he still was, I was no longer a prisoner to his charm. He could flash his beautiful smile, strut his fine ass in those dark denim jeans, and flex his muscled upper body through his thin white t-shirt all he wanted. None of it could change how I felt about his betrayal.

As he walked through my foyer, he asked, "Is Jen here? I wasn't sure if she'd left for the hospital already or if she was working an overnight."

His comment halted me mid-step. "Exactly how long have you been keeping tabs on us?" I asked, the hairs on the back of my neck standing on end.

"Oh no, it's not like that," he replied, turning to meet my eyes, a sheepish smile curling on his lips. "I've not been stalking you guys." He paused, mulling over his answer. "Well, maybe just a little social media stalking." His crooked smile widened, but I didn't find him amusing.

"Glad you've matured into an experienced creeper," I said, delivering a suspicious glance.

He cocked his head and challenged me. "C'mon, like you've never googled anyone? Not even your billionaire boyfriend?"

I simply stared.

"Did you Google him?" he pressed.

"Of course, I Googled him," I confessed, remembering the numerous times I'd searched for Tom all over the internet, trying to catch glimpses of who he was before me. "Any sane person would Google the person they're dating." I shot him an icy stare. "There's a ton of crazies out there."

"See," he said as if I'd just proven his point.

I rolled my eyes. "I was hinting at you, genius," I said as I plopped down on my couch and invited him to take a seat across from me on the love seat. "Any more secrets you want to share with me?"

"Secrets?" He sat at the edge of the seat, seeming to wipe sweaty palms on his jeans. "No. I came to see how you were doing. After the bomb I dropped on you last night, I wasn't sure what would happen once you got back to your apartment. I thought about it afterward and realized how stupid it was of me to just dump all that shit on you without considering what would happen with Jen."

"You think?"

He rested his elbows on his knees and fixed his eyes on me. "Sara, I'm sorry. I wasn't thinking. For the past four years, I've imagined the moment I would tell you everything, how I would confess, how I could come back into your lives, how I—"

Sitting with my legs tucked beneath me and arms crossed, I said, "You thought it would be possible? You coming back into our lives as if nothing ever happened? And what exactly does that even mean anyway— coming back into our lives?"

"I guess, what I meant to say was, come back home. When I left, I didn't just leave because of the kiss or because I realized I had fallen for someone else. For years, I'd thought about what I would do after college. What would become of my life? I had no answer. You were it. You were all. I had no dreams of my own. Right before your car accident, I'd been thinking about taking some photography classes, something to make me feel like there was more to my life. When I saw our future begin to fade, I knew I would lose you, but I'd also never be able to pursue Jen. There was nothing left for me here."

"You never told me you liked photography."

He chuckled. "Honestly, neither did I. Kinda picked it up on a whim. I had a friend who lived abroad. He offered me a place to crash while I figured things out. I bought a camera and shipped out. Turned out to be one of the best decisions I ever made."

"Why come back, then?"

"I met a girl, Sara. She was lovely. We got married, and a year later, we were divorced. You know why?"

I nodded for him to continue.

"Because I'd left my heart back here. I traveled, I met people, but it didn't matter how many beautiful places I visited or how many captivating people I met, I couldn't stop thinking of home. I missed you. I missed Jen. I missed my family."

"It took you four years to realize that?"

"No. It took me four years to build up the courage to face the mess I left behind. But I couldn't come home without trying to mend the pieces. When she said you were with someone new, that it seemed you were in love and happy, that's when I realized now was when I needed to come home. You'd healed. I asked my sister to get me in touch with you. But I also knew you'd turn me away."

"So you chose to deceive me instead," I said coolly.

"I know it was shitty of me. I can't stop screwing up. But would you've agreed to talk to me?"

"Don't think so."

"If it was the only opportunity I'd have to talk to you, I had to take it."

"What now, Josh? Where do we go from here?"

"Sara, I know you're happy and in love, despite the pain I caused you."

"I am. So?"

He smiled. "The way your eyes sparkle when you say his name—that's real. The good stuff. And it's why I came back, Sara. I've not been able to find true love. And I'm tired of searching when all along I've known where it is."

I thought about his comment for a second. For a time, I wished he'd never find true love. It was awful and it shamed me. But could the universe have listened? "Last night, I wanted to kill you. I'm not going to lie," I said. "You coming back without notice… Not to mention telling me you and Jen shared a kiss, and that you left because you'd fallen for her. It messed me up."

"I'm sorry about everything," he reiterated.

"After talking to Jen," I said, "I realized there's no point in holding a grudge. At least not anymore. Up until I met Tom, I was still carrying the baggage from my relationship with you. That break up, the way it happened, tore me to pieces, Josh. Do you have any idea how much I loved you? How you leaving me without an explanation—without a goodbye— literally scarred me for years? I couldn't trust anyone. I couldn't fall in love."

He closed his eyes and hung his head. "I don't know how else to say I'm sorry." Looking back up at me, he said, "You gotta believe me when I say this, Sara. It tore me up, too. I know it sounds like bullshit to you, but it's the truth. Not one single day has gone by in the last four years that I don't think about you. About us. About Jen. I think about how it could have all been different."

"Different how, Josh?"

"I don't know. I guess it doesn't matter, right? I screwed up, and I can never take my actions back."

"Or maybe it was always supposed to happen. You know, three months ago, I may have not believed my own words. Three months ago, those wounds still felt fresh, but after meeting Tom, I can't imagine a world where I'm not with him. Things happen for a reason—"

"I know. The universe always meddles. Wasn't that your go-to saying whenever something extraordinary happened? It's what you said when we started dating."

"I still believe that. The timing wasn't right for any of us back then. I see it now. And if we had stayed together, I wouldn't be with Tom."

"So… it's a good thing I left?"

I offered him a gentle smile, realizing I no longer felt the pain of his rejection. "All I can say is, we are at a new cross-roads, and what we decide now will define our future. I forgive you, Josh. I mean it whole-heartily. It doesn't make the news any easier to swallow, but I have peace about it."

He took a deep breath, his chest expanding as he leaned back on the seat and relaxed his shoulders. "Thank you. Your words mean everything to me."

"I also know you didn't come just for my forgiveness. You came for Jen."

He smiled but didn't meet my eyes.

"Josh, are you still in love with her?"

He hesitated. Not because he doubted himself. No. The love he had for her was evident in the way his face lit up at the mention of her name. His hesitation flared because he didn't want to hurt me.

"Don't worry about me, Josh. Just answer the question. Do you still love her?"

Closing his eyes and taking a gulp of air, he said, "One hundred percent. I want a chance to mend things between us and between Jen and me. Your friendship means everything and if there's a chance I could have an ounce of your friend-ship back—"

"It will take time for me to trust you again. If ever. But it's not me you should be worried about."

"Does she not want to see me?'

I grimaced. "You could say that. She's in her room. You're welcomed to go knock on her door if you like, but I'm doubtful she'll open it."

"That angry with me, huh?"

"I can't begin to comprehend how she feels about you. What happened between you two back then is between you guys. How you mend it is your business, but if you have hopes of rekindling those feelings…"

"I just want to mend our friendship first. What happens later…"

"She has a boyfriend, Josh. Who she's been dating for years, and who practically worships the ground she walks on. I wouldn't be surprised if he proposes to her soon."

"I can respect that, but I still want to talk to her."

I walked over to Jen's room and knocked. "Hey, sweetie. Can I come in?"

The door unlocked and her hand snaked out, grabbing me by the wrist and yanking me into her room before slamming the door back shut.

"What the heck?" I spurted out.

"I'm not going out there."

"You've been listening?"

"I heard everything. He thinks he can just waltz back into our lives like nothing ever happened? That everything is going to be all hunky dory? That I'm just going to welcome him into my circle with open arms? No fucking way. I mean, I can't believe you're buying into his bullshit."

I ran a hand through my hair. "I'm just done with all of this, Jen. Can we move on?"

"I moved on eons ago. I've been doing fine these last four years. I don't need him back in my life. A life consumed by school, work, and a boyfriend I love very, very much."

Who was she trying to convince, me or her?

"Look," I said, my skin prickly at how she was handling all of this. "I'm not going to try to force you into anything. I still don't know how I'm keeping it together. Last night I was a bit of a mess, but today… I guess I realized life is too short to live it with regrets."

"It's not about regrets. I'm with Marko."

"So? I'm just suggesting you go talk to him."

"That's Josh out in our living room, Sara. Joshua Buckley.

The guy who tore your heart out. The guy who kissed your best friend. The guy who disappeared without a goodbye for four fucking years. Aren't you a little bit pissed?"

"Jen, I think all this time you might have taken his absence a little harder than me. You've just been better at hiding it."

"For you, Sara. Because I was trying to protect you from what happened. If I showed you how much his departure affected me, you would have guessed something was off."

"You've hidden your pain and anger all these years for me?"

"I had no choice."

"Oh, Jen."

"I'd do it again, Sara. I deserved the pain."

"You need to stop this martyr shit. It's not you. I forgave you, so now you need to forgive yourself."

"I… don't think I can face him."

"You're still in love with him, aren't you?"

Tears streamed down her face.

"Jen, it's ok."

"Sara, I've kept this secret buried inside me for four years. I've tried to move on from it. I love Marko now."

"You love him, but you're not in love with him. It's why you're so reluctant to talk about marriage. Why you're not ready to take that next step."

"Sara… please. Stop."

"I can't. If you think there's a chance you and Josh—"

"No," she snapped, "there's zero chance of anything ever happening between us. I would never do that to Marko and secondly… it wouldn't feel right. After what you went through and what he and I did… No. Josh is the past, Sara. I'm not going to allow myself to be dragged back into that hell."

"What should I tell him?"

"Tell him I forgive him for leaving without saying goodbye. Tell him I'm sorry I let him kiss me, and tell him… despite all that, I don't think we could ever be friends again."

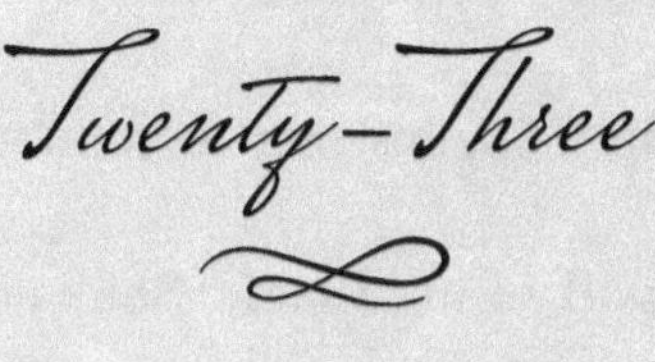

Twenty-Three

SARA

IT ALL FELT SURREAL. I couldn't have made it up even if I tried. I'd attempted to convince my best friend to make up with my ex-boyfriend and consider breaking up with her current boyfriend so she could date Josh. Something was not right with my head, but maybe I couldn't think straight because of the persisting pain in my abdomen worsening within the last hour since Josh showed up.

I grimaced as I walked to the door.

"Sara, are you okay?" Jen asked.

Turning toward her, I said, "I'm not sure."

"What's wrong? I mean, aside from the obvious."

"Haven't been feeling well since last night. Cramping."

"Ah, it could be your period. You were late and with everything you've been through the last few days…"

"Maybe." Placing a hand right below my belly, I winced again. "Listen, if you're not going to talk to him, I'm gonna go tell him to leave and maybe you guys can figure this out another time. I need to lie down."

"I'm sorry for making you do this."

"Don't worry about it. Just gonna walk him out."

She hugged me. "Thank you so much. For being such an incredible friend."

I hugged her back, taking in the scent of her pomegranate shampoo as her blonde curls brushed my face. "I love you."

"I love you most," she replied with one last squeeze before letting me go.

Josh sprang up from his seat as soon as he saw me exit Jen's room. "So?"

Letting out a puff of air, I said, "She's not coming out."

His chest sank. This wouldn't be an easy battle.

I managed a smile through the pain radiating from my neck, down my shoulders, and ending in my lower back. It felt as if pressure was building up inside my body. I needed to get to bed soon, or I was going to pass out. "You didn't expect I'd be the easier of the two, huh?"

He clamped the back of his neck with a palm. "To be honest with you, I didn't know what to expect, but I'd prepared myself for the worst."

I walked toward the front door, grabbing him by the arm for support and dragging him with me. "Tell me, Joshie. Exactly what was your worst-case scenario?"

He stopped and peered at me, raising an eyebrow. "Joshie? Last time you called me that was... God, I can't even remember."

"It was right before the accident. I called you to tell you I was driving to New York with my mom. For the audition. You told me to drive carefully."

He reached for a loose strand of hair that had fallen over my face and tugged it behind my ear. "I wish I'd told you to stay. That I'd tried harder to stop you from going—"

I put a finger to his lips. "No. We're not going to do that. It wasn't your fault. Let's move on. Okay?"

He smiled and nodded in agreement.

I took him by the arm once more. "Come on, I'll walk you downstairs."

As we stood in the elevator, I had to lean on the back wall to brace myself as the pain grew more intense.

"Sara, you don't look so great. What's the matter?" he asked as he reached to offer me support. He held me under his arm as I steadied myself and rode another wave of cramps.

"Sara, let me take you back upstairs, I can walk myself out."

"It's just my time of the month. Nothing to be worried about." The elevator opened and while still under his arm, we walked out into the lobby.

And that's when it happened. The moment my past and present collided.

When it all went to shit.

Frozen at the entrance, Tom stood like a sentinel guarding the exit. Wearing a white dress shirt and black suit pants, his tall stance was menacing. Chest heaving, nostrils flaring, Tom looked every bit the riled lion I knew him to be when he was angry.

On instinct, I uncurled from under Josh's arm.

Regardless of why he'd come, seeing me coming out of the elevator in my short pajamas under the arm of another man could not have looked good, and I needed to reassure him he wasn't seeing something he wasn't. Not to mention he'd flip when he learned the guy who'd just had his arm around me was none other than my ex-boyfriend, the guy he'd once told me, kidding or not, he wanted to kill for hurting me.

"Hey, baby,' I said with a smile as I went to hug him.

He put a hand up to stop me from getting closer. "It's true, then?" he gritted through his teeth.

I halted mid-step, my brows pinched. "What's true?"

He stalked forward. "How long has it been going on?"

I stared at him, unable to make sense of what he was saying. Before I had a chance to reply, I felt Josh's presence behind me. He pushed forward, perhaps trying to save us from the impending disaster palpable in the air. He presented his hand to Tom. "Hey, man. I'm—"

But Tom cut him off before he had a chance to finish introducing himself. Ignoring Josh's hand, he growled, "I know who you are. You're the asshole who's been fucking my girlfriend."

"Whoa, what?" Josh and I said simultaneously. At the same moment, a cramp shot up through my whole body, and I almost keeled backward. Josh rushed to help me. Tom stood still.

"This is how it ends, huh?" Tom asked me, his eyes cold as ice.

Leaning on Josh and nearly out of breath, I said, "Tom… what… what are you talking about. I… Josh… we're not—"

Tom took what appeared to be photos from a manila envelope he'd been holding and flung them at me, but I wasn't prepared for it, and they all scattered across the lobby floor as other residents walked by and stared at the unfolding scene.

"To think I wanted… more with you. That I…" He took something out from his pants pocket and clutched it so hard, I thought he'd crush whatever it was. "I've been carrying this damned thing around for weeks now, waiting for the perfect moment. How ironic. This… right here… turned out to be it."

As I let go of Josh and leaned down to pick up a picture, my eyesight faded in and out of focus. I could not believe what I was seeing. The pictures were all of Josh and me the night before. I peered up at Tom. "You've been following me?"

Josh picked up another photo. "What the…?" He looked at Tom. "This is not what it seems, man. You've got this all wrong."

"Shut the fuck up," Tom sneered.

"Miss Hart," Pedro called out from the front desk. "Everything ok? You need me to get security?"

Tom turned toward the front desk. "That won't be necessary, Pedro. I was just leaving." Without a glance or another word to me, he walked out, but not before placing a small black box on top of Pedro's desk.

A small black box...

My heart sank, my entire body vibrating with panic at the mere implication of what this meant. I scrambled after him, grabbing the box on my way to the exit and hoping for a chance to explain everything was a big misunderstanding, but as I scrambled to the revolving door, I stumbled to the floor in agony as another crushing cramp rocked through me. I lost my balance and hit my head hard on the tile as I landed, my mind momentarily fading to dark. Next thing I remembered, Josh was leaning over me, trying to get me to wake up.

"Call an ambulance," he shouted to someone. "Sara, stay with me," he soothed, running his fingers through my hair, my head resting on his lap.

I groaned, my mind trapped in a hazy swirl, my ears ringing from the pain in my skull. "I... don't feel so great."

"You fell and hit your head pretty badly."

"Is the floor wet? I mumbled, feeling something soaking through me.

"Sara, it's... blood. You're bleeding a lot."

"Did I crack my head open?"

"No, Angel. Blood is dripping down your legs."

I lifted my head to see, but Josh held me down. "Sara, just lie back. Ambulance is on its way."

"Jen... call Jen. Please. Tell Pedro. Front desk," I moaned, my abdomen still cramping.

Josh turned and shouted, "Pedro, get Jen."

"I already called her, sir. She's on her way down."

"You're going to be okay," Josh said to me as he continued to run his fingers through my hair.

I shut my eyes as another jolt of sharp pain shot through

my skull. When I opened them back up, I saw two sets of sparkling blue eyes staring down at me. I smiled, thinking about how angelic my two blondies looked leaning over me. The two who had cared for me last time I laid broken.

"Hey, honey," Jen said, "I rushed down as soon as Pedro told me you fell. EMTs will be here shortly. How do you feel?"

I didn't feel like going to a hospital, that's for sure. The fluorescent lights, the antiseptic smells, the sounds of beeping medical equipment—I hated all of it. Every memory I had of being in a hospital was tainted by my accident. "Forget the hospital. I'm fine. I just need to lie down on my bed."

"Oh, honey. You need to get to an emergency room ASAP. You're bleeding profusely, and I don't think it's from your period. Here, let me look at your head."

"Wait, what…" But as I tried to finish my thought, my heart squeezed in my chest at the implications of her words. "Jen…"

"Honey, don't move, okay. I'm wrapping a couple of blankets I brought down around you. We'll get through this. You're going to be fine."

Turning to Josh, she said, "Pedro said Tom was here?"

"It wasn't pretty," Josh replied. "Pedro had security pick up the pictures, and I gave him the box Tom left."

Her forehead creased. "Pictures? Box?"

Josh leaned into Jen's ear and whispered something that made Jen's face flush crimson. "That son of a fucking bitch!" she yelled. "Does he know? Did he see what happened?" she asked Josh.

He shook his head. "He ran out before we could explain."

"Jen…" My breath trembled. "It hurts… so bad."

"I know, hon. EMTs just pulled up. We're gonna get you all better soon."

In a flash, a team of EMTs lifted me onto a stretcher then put me into the ambulance. As they checked my vitals, Jen rambled out a whole bunch of medical jargon I couldn't decipher. Amidst the medical conversation, the word that would forever change my world cut through my core like a hot, jagged knife.

"…miscarriage…" Jen uttered, and the rest of her sentence died when my mind faded to black.

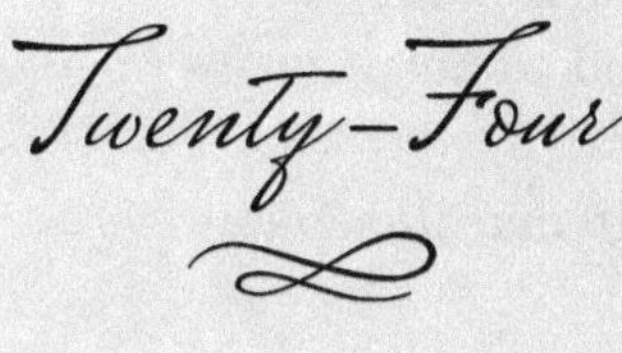

TOM

I woke up sometime in the middle of the night, slouched on the couch and still in my work clothes, my mind in a dense fog, limbs heavy as bricks. Struggling to sit upright, I squinted in my moonlit living room, trying to adjust my vision. Resting on my coffee table next to a bottle of aspirin and a half-filled tumbler was a nearly empty bottle of a Dalmore twenty-five-year Single Malt Scotch Whiskey.

Shit. A vintage. That can't be good.

I rubbed a heavy palm down my face as the images of Sara with that other man crushed my skull again. Unable to tolerate the fierce pounding in my brain, I reached for the bottle of aspirin and downed a couple of pills chased by the remaining whiskey in my glass.

Sleep. Please. I just need to sleep.

Minutes after, the fog took me once more and I fell back on my couch, welcoming the numbness tingling throughout my body and embracing the darkness drowning my thoughts.

THE HOUSE PHONE rang somewhere in my apartment. Rousing me from heavy sleep, my eyes stung from the bright sunlight blasting through my windows. Reluctant to face the world, I covered my head with a couch pillow.

Leave me the fuck alone.

I simply wanted to keep on sleeping—to keep on feeling dead.

The answering machine picked up. *This is Tom, leave a message.*

"Mr. Wright, it's Craig. Sorry to bother you, sir, but I've tried to call and text you all morning. Then I remembered you'd left your cell at the office. Wanted to inform you security found the footage you requested. Please give me a call as soon as you get this message. Hope everything is all right."

"Fucking peachy, Craig," I muttered to myself as the phone beeped. "I'm doing just fucking great."

Quite frankly, I didn't even care about the security video anymore. Whoever the fucking asshole was who delivered those pictures did me a favor. I was done with believing in women. Love was a farce and the biggest pain in the ass. Fuck it all to hell. Whiskey. Now, *that* was something I could believe in. There was truth in the bottom of a bottle. Lead-heavy, I sat up and poured myself another drink. Before I could bring it to my lips, a hard knock at the door pulled my attention. Bax lay sprawled on the floor, looking up at me as if questioning whether I planned to answer the door.

"Maybe they'll just walk away," I whispered to Bax.

He barked.

"Seriously? You're gonna give us up?"

More frantic knocking ensued.

"I'm not home. Please, leave," I yelled.

"Open the fucking door, Tom." Jake's muffled voice crackled. "I'll keep banging 'til you open up."

I needed this like I needed a fucking hole in the head. If I knew Jake, he wasn't kidding. Pushing to my feet, I trudged to the entrance and cracked open the door. "You're an asshole," I said, turning back toward my couch.

He entered and closed the door. "You look like hell," he said, following behind me.

Sitting down, I picked up my drink, and with a mock grin on my face, raised my glass. "To hell."

"I warned you," he reminded me. "And now here you are. Drinking." He paused and picked up the bottle of liquor. "Dalmore twenty-five? This is fifteen-hundred-dollars-worth of liquid gold."

Downing the liquor, I said, "I couldn't agree more."

He sat across from me on the ottoman, elbows resting on his knees, branding me with a fuming stare. "I'm not going to let you do this to yourself."

"Too late." I leaned back on my couch and crossed an ankle over a knee, challenging him to walk me down from the ledge.

"Sara is not worth you throwing away four years of sobriety."

My insides twisted at the mention of her name, and I pushed up to the edge of my seat. Jaw muscles clenching, I gritted, "Don't. Say. That. Name." I reached for the bottle and poured the last remaining two ounces.

"Tom, don't."

"Isn't this what you wanted?" I taunted, raising my glass once more. "You should be drinking with me, celebrating my fuck-up," I said, downing my drink, a sardonic smile plastered on my face as I placed the glass back down on the table.

"*She* fucked-up," he uttered grimly, painfully reminding me he'd been right from the beginning.

I swallowed hard. "She's fucking history. Let's talk about something else, or nothing at all."

He stood and walked to my liquor cabinet and poured himself a glass of my less expensive bottle of whiskey. "I've never understood why you keep alcohol around. Isn't this against the program?" he asked, turning to look at me.

"Having it near and being able to resist it made it easier for me to be around it at parties, business lunches, dinners. Eventually, I didn't even notice it being here. Made me less conscious of it out there." I nodded toward the New York City panorama out my window.

"Also made it easier for you to relapse," he intoned under his breath as he sipped his drink, muttering his words loud enough for me to hear.

The slight tone of disappointment ringing in his voice was disheartening and a bit insulting. He'd not been any kind of a real friend to me lately. Who was he to judge? "Know what, man? I don't need your bullshit right now. If you came here to throw this mess in my face, just do me a favor and leave. And I relapsed back in Lake George. Not here."

"I wouldn't know. Ever since you started dating—"

"Jake. Seriously, man. Not right now."

His jaw muscles tightened. Jake hadn't liked Sara from day one. Not because of anything she'd done back then, but simply because he didn't like women. Well, he liked to fuck them, he just didn't care to love them. To see me head over heels for her, well, let's just say he felt replaced. The bromance was over. In his eyes, at least. And I could understand his tantrum—to an extent. I knew he was itching to rip into me about how he tried to warn me. How he'd called it from day one. How Sara would end up being just like every other lying—

Fuck. I could never call her that. And I wasn't about to let him badmouth her either. But hell, thinking back to the pictures and finding her with that other man made my heart constrict with a squeeze so iron-tight, my body shuddered in pain. A heaviness settled over my chest, and I struggled to breathe. I slouched back on my couch and rubbed my temples, trying to ease my mind, realizing in defeat that ripping her from my soul and stopping the pain would require sudden death.

Or just more fucking whiskey. If I was going to get this woman out of my system, I needed to flood it with something else.

Bitter he couldn't cleave Sara in half, Jake plopped next to me, briefly pulling me out of the dark abyss of my desperation. I eyed Jake's drink as he got comfortable. Legs spread, he placed an arm over the backrest as he brought the tumbler to his lips. "I closed the Brookland Brothers deal," he said triumphantly before taking a sip, a bold grin stretching across his face.

Shit. That cleared my head. I'd forgotten all about the developers. I picked up my empty glass and brought it to his, clinking it in celebration. "Well done, brother."

He cackled. "Yeah, because I saved your fucking ass."

He had, but most importantly, he'd pulled through for the company. I smiled and patted him on the shoulder. "You did good. Thank you."

Satisfied with himself, he winked, the shit-eating grin on his face widening. "How about you? What's the plan here?" Drink in hand, he gestured around to my apartment.

Knowing what he meant, I couldn't meet his gaze. This was where he'd found me the last time—the first time. In a pile of my own shit. It was shortly after I reenlisted, and I was still devastated about Shayna. Women mess with our heads… They turn us into idiots… Those were his words then, and they still rang true. Loud and crystal fucking clear.

"I'm fine," I said, glancing his way, lying through my teeth.

"No, you aren't." He was no moron, but he'd never be able to fathom the extent of what I was going through. Jake didn't believe in love, and he believed in a broken heart even less.

Taking a deep breath, I fixed my eyes on him and offered him the only truth I had. "One day, I will be."

"Fuck her out of your system." Tactless. Crude. That's how he handled things. His words lacked emotion because to Jake, feelings were useless. To his credit, I'd never seen him miserable because of a woman. Which made him a happier man than me. Or just smarter. Either way, I'd take not feeling anything right now over the never-ending ache in my chest. I should have listened to him—allowed myself to remember feelings were overrated.

Still, his lack of emotion couldn't mean he'd never loved a woman, or that a woman had never caused him pain. Jake would never admit it, and he'd never tell me, but I was certain he'd known love once. He'd have to have experienced it, otherwise, why else would he be against it so harshly? If I had to guess, a woman tore him to shreds, and picking up the pieces left of himself, he rebuilt a different man.

"Fucking is your solution to everything," I said, laughing at his piss-poor motto.

He didn't echo my amusement. "That's because *it is* the solution to everything," he replied matter of fact, his blue eyes frigid. "You just need to find yourself a pretty little thing and fuck her brains out until Sara becomes a blur."

My eyes widened. "That simple, huh?" I played along, for his sake, not mine.

He sat up straighter, perked up by the prospect of a good time. "Seriously. Just say the word, man. I got 'em on speed dial. I can have a couple of chicks eager for some double action over here in no time."

I shook my head and laughed. He should've known me better by now. But at least he got me to smile. "Nah, man. That's not me. Trust me. I'm good. Gonna take the rest of the week off to get my head on straight. I'll be back to the office by Monday."

Taken aback, he stood and straightened his dark dress

pants. Face tense, he peered down at me, and said, "Fuck me. You need that long?" He didn't wait for my reply. "Whatever, man. Suit yourself, but do us both a favor, let this be the last time you let some chick grab you by the balls like that. Love is for the birds, Tom. That shit ain't real. Women are good for one thing and one thing alone."

I stood and met his gaze. "You've told me." I gestured with my hand it was time for him to go.

He nodded, accepting my request, and started toward the entrance. "Am I going to need to check in on you daily?" he asked, looking at me over his shoulder as I followed behind.

"No."

He stopped at the door and faced me. "I don't trust you. You're too sentimental for your own damn good."

I crossed my arms, annoyed this visit had gone on too long. "What the hell is that supposed to mean?"

"Means you better not go looking for her," he replied, poking my chest with his index finger.

Staring at his finger, unamused, I scoffed. "No need to worry about that."

"What about all the booze?" he continued to pester.

"What about it?"

"I ain't gonna find you dead, am I?"

Uncrossing my arms, I opened the door and pushed him out. "You need to go."

"Not for nothing, but I think you should consider going. To the program."

I remained quiet.

"At least talk to Tony. He's still around, right?"

"Jake," I said, my gaze hardening, "thanks for stopping by. I appreciate you checking in on me, but it's not necessary." I attempted to close the door, but he put his hand out and blocked it.

"Craig said you left your phone at the office. I can drop it off later tonight."

My jaw tensed, the skin on my face flushing as my brow creased with anger. "Dude, don't even worry about it."

"That look. You really want me to leave, huh?"

"I'm sorry, man. I just want to be left alone."

"I get it. People prefer to wallow by themselves."

"Jake," I growled.

"Okay, okay. I'm going. One last thing, though. Take a shower. You stink."

I COULDN'T GET him out of my apartment fast enough. I knew he was trying to be a good friend, but if I was honest, he was crappy at it. A part of me—the part too weak to acknowledge it—had hoped Jake would have taken all the liquor in my bar and dumped it down the drain. He should have dragged my ass to AA. Forced me to call Tony. Reminded me of the promises I'd made to myself years ago when I'd stared death in the face and almost let it take me. But all he offered me was the possibility of a cheap thrill. Last thing I wanted was to be close to another woman. My heart, my mind, my body still belonged to someone else. Getting her out of my system would require more than a fucking-spree.

I took his advice and showered. Letting the hot water scald my skin, I lingered under the showerhead until the water ran cold and my body shivered. It had been one day. One fucking day without her and I needed her like my lungs needed oxygen. Missing her—the idea of her—the idea of us—was going to eat me alive.

Allowing myself to dream of a life together? Foolish. I was going to marry her. Our children were going to have her skin, my eyes. All nonsense. And the ring? I laughed at myself as I recalled the day I bought it. I knew it'd been too soon. Hadn't known when I was even going to propose. Next week? The following month? The following year? It didn't matter. I'd just wanted to be ready when the moment felt right. I hadn't even asked her opinion. Like some asshole, I just went for big and brilliant. Well, that's two-hundred and fifty thousand in the shredder.

I couldn't care less about the money. I'd gladly shred all my millions, every single penny, if I could erase the images from my brain. Seeing her in his arms had mauled me. His hand on her cheek. The intimate smile between them. I shook my head, but the images didn't fade. They were etched on my mind as if carved with a blade.

I'd let my guard down.

I made the mistake of opening my heart, and I'd lost more than I could have ever bargained for. I'd lost my dignity. My sanity. My love. My life. She'd been everything, and now I had nothing but the gnawing emptiness in my gut.

Pinching my eyes, I tried to staunch the anguish burning through, but it was useless. My chest caved with a dreadful and suffocating weight I couldn't withstand, and the tears silently rolled down my cheeks, hot and fierce, reminding me of why I sought solace in a bottle. Reminding me I loved too hard and hurt even harder.

"Fuck this!" I banged a fist on the glass wall of my shower, wishing it had shattered into a million pieces. Had I overreacted? Had I read things wrong? I mean, I hadn't even given her a chance to explain.

Explain what, though? Why she hadn't told me about him? Why he was coming out of her apartment in the morning, Sara dressed in her pajamas? What more did I need?

No. I didn't need explanations. Didn't want them.

What I needed was to rip her out of my mind and out of my chest. Forever.

Twenty-Five

SARA

THE SMELL of sterilizing cleansers and freshly laundered linens brought in by the orderlies as they changed my garbage and gave me a fresh blanket, coupled with the wafts of my uneaten hospital cafeteria breakfast—eggs, toast, and a fruit cup—made my nostrils flare with disgust. It was the familiar stench of a hospital room, and it triggered an onslaught of bad memories—waking up unable to move, covered in tubes and hooked up to machines. Then the news of my mother's death. The last time I'd been in a hospital had been the worst day of my entire life.

My hands shook thinking about that day. It felt too fresh. Not to mention the irritating sounds of everything that made the hospital run like a perfectly well-oiled machine amplified the nerve-twisting anxiety crawling up my skin. The nurses' incoherent chatter from outside my room, the squeaky shrills of stretchers wheeling by, the snapping of medical gloves as the changing-shift nurse came in to take my vitals, draw more blood, and to make me pee into a cup—all of it made me want to run out of there faster than a bat out of hell.

As soon as the nurse left with a fresh batch of bodily fluids, I begrudgingly turned on my side on my hospital bed and faced the window, the pain from the incision in my abdomen making we wince. She'd introduced herself, but I couldn't remember her name. To me, she was the early morning shift who came to give me another dose of pain-numbing meds. I wondered how much longer I would need to endure this torture. It had been one day, but it'd felt like a life sentence.

Once I'd arrived at the hospital yesterday, they'd rushed me through the ER and, after several examinations from different medical personnel, they whisked me to an operating room. I felt utterly cold and alone as they passed me around to various strangers, each prepping me for surgery. Wetness streamed down my face, and no one asked me if I was okay or who was with me. No one even asked about the baby's father. Did they just assume I'd been single? To them, I was the patient. Meanwhile, I had a name. A name they asked once when checking my tag and forgot immediately after. I was grateful for everything they did to save my life. But unless you've been on that operating table, you can't begin to understand what it feels like to entrust your life to someone who doesn't even know who you are.

On my ride to the hospital, Jen, who was familiar with the EMTs, accompanied me in the ambulance. She'd held my hand as she told me that based on my symptoms, I had likely miscarried. The news shocked my system. I wasn't sure if the chill in my blood had been from the hemorrhaging and loss of blood, or from hearing what I thought to be impossible. How could I have miscarried? I'd taken a test. It'd come back negative. Then it hit me. Like a tsunami. A little person had died inside me, and I hadn't even known it had been living in me at all.

They told me the pain in my chest had been from the pressure of the blood filling inside my abdominal cavity. But what did they know? Had they ever experienced waiting to have some doctor they'd never met scrape the remains of their baby from their body? The turmoil and desolation pillaging through my body that day had been more intense than any physical agony caused by the internal bleeding and pressure in my chest and shoulders. That's why I couldn't deal with hospitals. Everything was so procedural. So sterile. So clinical. There was no other description. It was dead cold.

As I stared at the closed blinds with the sun's rays filtering through, the previous day replayed—ugly, vivid, and unmerciful. The pain of it all was still fresh in my heart.

Josh and Jen had watched over me after the surgery. They were able to stay after visiting hours were over, but at some point, the nurses asked them to leave. Jen knew the staff, she could have pushed to stay, but she understood there was nothing else she could have done for me. And I was relieved to be alone with my anguish.

I was thankful for their concern and attention. Still, I knew they were both exhausted, especially Jen, who had been exceptionally worried about me, her face scrunched in a permanent frown, her hands occasionally reaching for mine to provide the ongoing reminder of I'm here for you... The constant "How do you feel?" or "Can I get you anything?" questions creating more unease in me than any kind of comfort. I pretended to be asleep or too doped up on the meds to hear her. How else could I continue to answer the same question? I felt fucking shitty, and I wanted nothing more than to crawl under a rock and die. There was no other way to put it. Simple as that.

The tragedy of what happened felt so surreal, I was still in disbelief. I hadn't experienced a miscarriage but a ruptured fallopian tube due to an ectopic pregnancy. Any later, and I might have died before making it to the hospital. That thought plagued me. My second brush with death, and it failed to claim me again. Why? What was so special about me the universe felt compelled to punish me like this?

The saddest part about the whole thing? An ectopic pregnancy steals a baby's chance at life. Talk about cruel and heartbreaking. There was nothing they could have done regardless of if I had known earlier or if I had sought help sooner. The outcome would've always been the same. I barely had time to process the news I'd been pregnant before the doctor was telling me he would need to remove the tissue, and that he would try to salvage my fallopian tube. Salvage my fallopian tube? I was still trying to process the fact I'd just lost a living part of me.

"You're young," he'd said. "You should be able to get pregnant again." He'd punctuated that sentence with a smile.

I'd looked at him in disbelief. I'd lost a pregnancy. A baby. My body was going to be scarred forever, and he smiled?

Because it was easy to make yourself feel better about this? It was okay to have lost this baby because I could just make another? I wanted to yell at him, to make him understand I was not one more patient on his operating table. I was Sara Angelina Hart, and my world had been torn from me.

Again.

Punctuate that, doctor!

But he couldn't. Because I never uttered a single word. Because I broke in silence as they stripped me naked, poked my flesh, drew blood, pumped fluids into me, stuck tubes up my nose, and placed nodes and patches on my chest and fingers to monitor my heartbeat and oxygen saturation. They kept my body alive while my spirit died.

Thinking back to that moment, lying on that operating room, so alone and staring up at the blinding fluorescent lights, waiting for the anesthesia to take me to oblivion, I realized I couldn't take this anymore. I couldn't take the universe, or God, or whatever fucking entity kept messing with my life. This was too sadistic, too hard to comprehend.

I'd wanted a comforting hand, a loving word, something, or someone to tell me everything would be ok. That *I* would be ok. But as I'd faded into darkness, my body welcoming the numbness, there was only the sound of laughter as the doctor joked about what happened to him while on vacation that weekend.

And then I was gone.

"Sara?" Jen's voice gently crooned into my room, knocking me out of my shadowed thoughts.

I wiped the wetness from my eyes but didn't turn around.

"Can I come in?"

I did not want her company. Since I'd woken up, I'd wanted nothing more than to be alone with the silence and emptiness in my soul. It was all that remained of me anyway, and being numb was better than waiting to lose everything all over again.

When she noticed my quiet demeanor was not a sign I was resting, she tried the clinical approach. "There was nothing you could have done to prevent this, hon." She walked to my bed, her sneakers squeaking on the tiled floor, and placed a hand on my back. "The fetus wouldn't have been able to survive outside the uterus—"

I sniffed. "Please don't be my doctor right now, Jen. I need you to be my friend."

"I'm trying, Sara."

I turned to face her. "Then understand that nothing anyone can say, medical or otherwise, is going to make me feel better about it. Referring to it as a fetus… now that I know I was seven weeks pregnant, that it had a heartbeat? It was a baby, Jen. My baby."

"But this wasn't your fault."

I pursed my lips, my grief escalating into anger. "Jen, I'd wanted nothing more than to not be pregnant, and now I wish nothing more than to have that baby be a part of me again. I didn't even take a test until last Thursday. I hadn't taken care of myself before that. And after it came back negative, well, how was I supposed to know I should have been more careful?"

Jen sucked in a deep breath and closed her eyes as if she

was tired of saying the same thing repeatedly— because she had. "You wouldn't have known. And that's what I keep telling you. Even if you had taken care of yourself, this would have still happened. Ectopic pregnancies—"

"Can't be prevented," I cut her off, turning away from her. "Same thing you said last night. Same thing the doctor said, too. The fetus wasn't viable. Well, you know what, fuck you and fuck him. It doesn't hurt any less. And what's the point of those stupid early pregnancy tests, anyway? You're the one with the medical background, why did the test come back negative? At least if I'd known I might have been able to…"

But I couldn't finish my sentence, and she didn't bother to offer a reply. She knew I was venting and not necessarily wanting to lash out, but she let me dump my anger on her. I knew the answer. The doctor had told me last night. It'd been a false negative based on a whole slew of possible variables I could never control. Starting with the fact I hadn't even known when I became pregnant. Thinking back to the last couple of months, with all the stress of losing my job and having to look for employment, I may have forgotten to take my pill a few times. I'd been so irresponsible with my body, I was ashamed to admit how lax I had been about it.

I'd even ignored my symptoms for a while before I decided to take the test. And maybe I took the test too soon, and my hCG levels were too high or too low. Maybe I drank too much water that day and my urine had diluted. Or I'd bought an expired pregnancy test. Who knew why the test came back negative, and at this point, why did it even matter?

It mattered because I couldn't stop thinking about my baby. About the little person who had been growing inside me, yet I had never known. I could have loved it even if just for a few days. I could have shared that joy and this pain with—

As if reading my thoughts, Jen asked, "Are you going to tell him?"

"No," I snapped, remembering the scene at my apartment lobby. "He doesn't deserve to know."

"Sara—"

"I did nothing wrong, and he humiliated me," I gritted, turning my heard toward her. The scathing bile rising in my throat at the memory of what happened made me sit up abruptly, shooting a jolt of pain through my abdomen. I winced and cried out in agony.

"Christ, Sara," Jen exclaimed, coming to my aid. She placed a pillow behind my back and helped me recline. "I'm sorry for bringing him up."

I hadn't talked about the incident—about him— since the day before. Truth was, as soon as I learned about the baby, nothing else mattered. It wasn't until I woke up when everything took shape again. The reality of what he did and how he treated me crystallized into a perfect reminder of how deceitful the universe was.

Love?

Love is but a lie meant to charm you into believing in happiness. I guess I'd hoped with Tom the illusion would last longer.

"He had me followed," I muttered, shaking my head. "Why?" I asked, peering at Jen as if she held the answer. She sighed as she sat at the foot of the bed, helplessness clouding her eyes.

"I did nothing to make him think I was cheating on him." Holding back a deluge of tears, I sucked in a strong breath, refusing to shed them for him.

"I don't know what to tell you, Sara. Who knows what was going through this mind? Why he didn't trust you. But I think —*I know*—it had nothing to do with anything you did, hon. Tom, he's got trust issues. He's not much different than you, to be honest."

"Yeah, but I never had him followed. I could have flipped on him when he told me the story about him and Tiffany back in Santa Monica, but I didn't. I gave him an opportunity to explain." I winced again, the anger boiling up from inside blasting right through the pain meds.

Jen scooted closer and took my hand in hers. "Sara, listen. I want to apologize. Josh and I both want to."

"What are you talking about?"

"I feel like all this shit compiled all at once, and it's not fair. It's not fair to you to be going through all this pain."

I scoffed. "Story of my life."

"Sara, I'm serious," she exclaimed, her hand squeezing mine harder. "Josh… he… feels responsible and so do I. If he hadn't come over. If I'd come out to talk to him, you wouldn't have run into Tom in the lobby."

Gazing into her stormy eyes, I spoke calmly and with resolve, "No, Jen. You can't blame yourselves. Do you know what life is? It's a mile-high shit-pile of What Ifs. What didn't happen or could have happened means nothing. What matters is that Tom had me followed, Jen. He destroyed our trust. And our baby…" I paused, my voice cracking as another piece of my heart died. "My baby. Was already gone."

Lowering her chin to her chest, Jen whimpered, slow and barely audible. I pulled her hand toward me and gestured for her to snuggle by my side. We cuddled, laying in silence until the night came, like we used to do as little girls when we had sleepovers.

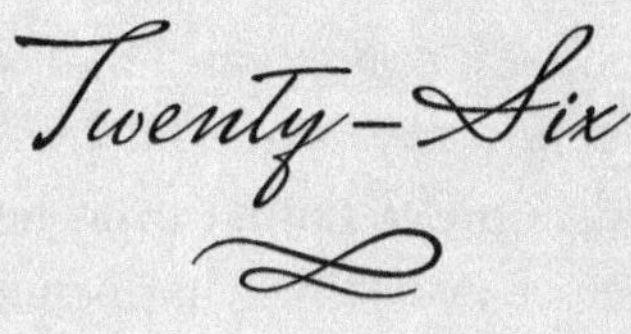

SARA

THREE DAYS LATER, the hospital discharged me. The doctor was supposed to have discharged me when Jen had visited on Thursday, but unfortunately, I developed an infection and remained hospitalized for two more days. By Saturday, if the doctor hadn't given me the green light, I would've left against his orders. Thankfully, tests came back normal, and I went home.

Jen tried her best to make me feel as comfortable as possible. She'd bought flowers and welcome-home balloons. When I walked in, her famous meatballs with spaghetti dinner simmered in pots, saturating the apartment in mouthwatering aromas. I'd had no appetite but ate anyway, commenting on the delicious food, beautiful flowers, and how amazing it felt to be back home.

I lied.

Coming home had felt exactly how I imagined— lonely.

I hadn't wanted to stay in the hospital, but I hadn't been anxious to get back to the apartment either. We didn't talk much during dinner, and once we finished with our meal, she offered to clean up and sent me to my room to rest.

Rest…

I'd been resting for the last four days on a hospital bed. The last thing I wanted was to be stuck inside another four walls tormented by my own wretched thoughts. With a grunt, I plopped on the edge of my unmade bed and glanced around my room. The suitcase from my trip to Lake George still laid on the floor by the closet, opened and half unpacked.

It'd only been a few days since I'd returned from my trip to Tom's childhood home. I hadn't even had a chance to put my clothes away before everything happened. Before…

The memory of the last day I'd been in my room punched through my brain with brutality. Waking up with pain in my abdomen. Talking to Jen about the kiss. Josh showing up to apologize. Running into Tom. Losing the…

My chest heaved, the sting of burning tears welling in my eyes. I reached up and grabbed my hair by the roots, tugging and hoping to numb one pain with another. It was a temporary reprieve, but numbing was the only way I knew how to survive.

When I managed to halt the onslaught of grief, I continued to look around, the stale smell of my fourday-un-lived-room suffocating me. Everywhere I looked, more snapshots of my short-lived happiness assaulted me. Life's cruel humor. Stuck into the groove of the dresser-mirror frame was the picture Tom took of me when we'd gone on our trip to Cornwall. Strapped to his back, I had held on for dear life as we rode on his motorcycle through the picturesque landscapes of upstate New York.

Unable to prevent the warmth of that memory, a slight smile pulled at the corners of my mouth. It'd been the first time I confided in him—in any man since Josh. Tom had kissed away my tears and promised me he would be my safe place. Then, back at his apartment, after trying and failing to convince myself falling in love with Tom would be a bad idea, I gave him the rest of me.

I closed my eyes as the moment took life. The memory of

his hands all over my body still ran hot, capable of igniting desire and unleashing my unrelenting need for him. Lifting a finger to my lips, the flesh there tingled, recalling the sweet savagery in which he claimed me with his mouth—his tongue.

Damn.

"I can't do this," I scolded myself, standing and stalking to my dresser. I picked up the photo of me sitting on his bike, my hair wild in the wind. He'd captured the moment as we stopped at an overlook of the Hudson Valley. "I can't keep doing this. It's over. We're over," I whispered as if the words hurt to be spoken. My breath sawing in an out of my lungs, I ripped the photo in half and dumped it in the small trashcan beside the dresser.

It felt like I'd shredded a piece of myself, a piece that no longer burdened me. Suppressing the angst in my chest, I reached for my jewelry box. Sitting inside were the diamond stud earrings he'd given me back in Santa Monica. I ran a finger over their shimmering brightness. What a night that had been. Jake's Hollywood party. Meeting the red viper. The first fight that almost ended it all before it even started. Tom's confession about his past. The incredible lovemaking followed by syrup-drenched breakfasts.

It had been a fairytale weekend. But the real stories from which fairytales are born don't have happy endings.

And neither did mine.

Taking the earrings in my palm, I looked through my drawer for a small jewelry pouch. I couldn't keep them but throwing them out didn't seem right either. When I finally found the red, velvety pouch I'd been searching for, I stuck the earrings inside and left them on top of my dresser, their new fate sealed. As I turned toward my bed, I noticed Tom's black leather jacket sitting on the floor by my closet. My breath stilled. It had fallen off its hanger in my haste to pack for the Lake George weekend.

I shouldn't have reached for it. Shouldn't have put it on.

Shouldn't have smelled the collar to see if his heady cologne still lingered on the fabric—it didn't. Thank heavens. What did remain was the image of his crooked grin and the glint of mischief in his eyes when he'd given me the jacket. I could still feel the kiss we never shared. I'd imagined it, and it was as perfect as when I first pictured what it would be like to have Thomas Wright threading his fingers through my hair as he brought his lips to mine.

Damn him.

Jerking the jacket off me, I ran to the bathroom to wash my face and neck. I scrubbed until my skin burned, the sting expunging thoughts of Tom from my mind. I needed a change in scenery. Everywhere I looked, all I saw were reminders. And after the loss of my baby, being there would keep reopening the wounds. The black hole in my chest would never close, and the bottomless pit in my stomach would never stop eating me from the inside.

My face dripping wet, I sat on my toilet seat cover and contemplated my future.

Ha. What future?

As if to highlight that dismal thought, I noticed the full hamper of dirty laundry I'd planned to wash. Sitting on top were my bloodied pajama pants I'd changed from that Wednesday morning before heading to the kitchen and running into Jen.

It didn't take long to make up my mind. I couldn't stay in my apartment. I couldn't stay in New York City. That night, I packed my bags in silence and wrote Jen a note. I told her how sorry I was for leaving without saying goodbye in person, but if I'd told her, she would have tried to stop me. I made sure she knew how much I loved her. I didn't blame her for anything. Even told her to let Josh know I had no hard feelings toward him either, and if the two of them ever ended up together, I'd be okay with that. I meant it. I wasn't sure how long I would be gone, or if I'd ever be back to the city, and I didn't want her putting her life on hold for me. Didn't want her trying to find me, although eventually, I knew she'd figure out where I went.

The following morning after she left for work, I packed up my Jeep with two suitcases, a box filled with old CDs, and road trip snacks. After making sure I had everything I needed, I placed the note on the dining table, adding that she shouldn't bother trying to call me. My cellphone was dead and tucked inside my sock drawer. I placed the jewelry pouch next to the note and the leather jacket on the backrest of one of the dining table chairs. She'd know what to do with them.

With a final glance around my apartment, I picked up Skiddles' carrier and whispered goodbye before closing the door and starting my new journey.

SEVEN HOURS LATER, I was still stuck on the New York Thruway. I should've already been at my destination, dressed in PJs and stuffing my face with comfort food. But what should have been a late August morning, four-hour easy commute to the Cape had turned into seven hours through the seven levels of traffic hell. Grams' house was literally two exits away. I could've been there in less than ten minutes. Instead, I sat cemented in the middle lane, the nose of my Jeep sniffing the ass of a sixteen-wheeler as it spewed toxic fumes right into my lungs. And with a toasty ninety-eight degrees outside and no air-conditioning—the perks of owning an old car—the atmosphere in my car was noxious enough to kill me.

Except the universe had a wicked sense of humor, and she preferred to tease.

As I recalled how my life had been so perfectly boring and

uneventful up until he stumbled into my life and screwed everything up, my radio blasted in the background to the crooning sounds of an 80's ballad. I shook my head and smirked—unamused. This drive played out like the opening of a cheesy, sappy romance movie. My body had been pushed through a meat grinder, and I was indulging its suffering with more torture by listening to dragged out, extremely depressing, broken-hearted love songs.

The whole thing was almost comical—if it hadn't been real life.

My life.

As I shut the radio off, right as the song was about to break into the chorus, a gentle purr turned my attention. On the passenger seat of my Jeep, Skiddles sat motionless, staring at me through the slits of her carrier, perhaps wondering what in the world was wrong with me. Taking that moment to gaze into her beautiful green eyes had been a mistake. Tom had the same color eyes, and memories of the day we first met came flooding back.

Friggin' Hell. Is this ever going to stop?

Better to have lost at love than never to have loved at all…

The person who coined that phrase obviously never had their heart ripped out of their ribcage and fed to rabid dogs. I couldn't take the constant barrage of memories anymore. I needed to get to Grams' soon. I needed to be sitting on her back porch, eating pie, and watching the cold New England waters crash against the surf, letting my grief drown in its beautiful dark-blue abyss.

I gripped the steering wheel with iron fists and screamed at the top of my lungs, stupidly hoping somehow my bellows would not only block all thoughts of Tom, but maybe part the sea of cars. Who was I kidding? Like everything else in my life destined to go wrong, I was stuck in the dead of traffic on one of the most depressing days of my life. I couldn't sit there any longer, doing nothing, watching as more time ticked by and we moved forward by a measly two inches an hour.

To add insult to injury, I'd worn shorts, and my legs were fused with the cheap leather seats. Sweat beaded on my forehead and rolled down the sides of my face. As I wiped it with my forearm, I noticed the two kids sitting in the backseat of the shiny Volvo next to my Jeep sniggering at me.

Brats.

I stuck my tongue out at them.

With a resounding sigh, I looked ahead, the back of the truck had the words WASH ME streaked across its filthy doors. Fitting. It was exactly what I needed to do—wash the filth off myself. And by the time I made it to Grams'—if I ever found a way out of this traffic inferno—I would. I'd wash Tom from my system—his touch off my body, his kiss off my lips, his smell off my skin—even if it killed me. As much as I missed him, as much at it tore me to shreds to know our relationship was over, I no longer wanted anything to do with that man. He'd humiliated me. He'd broken his promise to be my safe place, and his promise to never let his anger cloud his judgment. After the Alexei incident, he'd vowed never to give up on us. Ever again.

Lies. All. Lies.

My life would never have a happily ever after. I would make sure to never forget it.

Twenty-minutes later, as if by some miracle, the lanes began to move. There had been a car accident, and by the time I passed the scene, emergency crews had cleaned everything up. All that remained were the skid marks and some debris. I kept on driving.

Sitting on a short cliff facing the ocean, my grandmother's home was part of a beach community nestled on the shore immediately after crossing the bridge to Cape Cod. I couldn't think of a more suitable place to ride out the storm churning in my heart. The salty air and cool New England winds beckoned. Grams was surely waiting for me with a tall glass of milk and a slice of homemade lemon pie.

Summers up here had been some of the happiest moments in my life. Those memories, I cherished. My mother's spirit still lived here. It's where she grew up. Yet, after my accident, you'd think out of all the places I'd want to visit, this would be last on my list. My grandmother had never been a fan of my obsession with dance, and she'd been upset with my mother and me the day of the fatal accident because I was being unreasonable, and my mother hadn't tried hard enough to stop me from going to the audition. Instead, she'd hopped in the car with me.

Grams' house was the closest thing I had to a real home. And when I called to ask her if I could come stay with her indefinitely, she'd cried and said, "Child, you know you are always welcomed in my home."

I couldn't wait to stay in my mother's old room, lie in her bed, and wrap myself in her blankets. Grams had kept the room pristine as if she'd always expected my mom to return home.

Well, perhaps in one way or another, she had.

Twenty-Seven

TOM

IT HAD BEEN three weeks since my break-up with Sara. Well, maybe less, or perhaps more. I couldn't remember. Fuck. I'd lost track of the days. I'd spiraled out of control and had hit bottom. At a ludicrous speed. I didn't want to admit it. At least not the reason for it. Kept telling myself… Just one more day. One last drink. I'll get out of this. One woman won't break me. Now, I couldn't even remember the last time I'd been to the office or the last time I'd been sober.

An unofficial sabbatical, that's what I called it. Be back by the end of September, I'd told Jake. He'd hung up on me. He was such an asshole, but I couldn't blame him. I'd left him completely alone to manage the firm. I scoffed thinking about that decision. I'd likely come back to find Jake had embezzled all our money before running off to some foreign country never to be heard from ever again. Come to think of it, that plan didn't sound too bad. Sometimes I wondered how the fuck we ever became friends. I couldn't stand him half the time.

Regardless, the drive to get shit done wasn't there. I couldn't care less if I ever sold another property. I had plenty of money in the bank. I'd never have to work another day in my life, so what was the point of putting on a monkey suit? I'd be useless as a boss right now, and my crew didn't need to see me like that.

This was temporary. I'd get my mojo back. At some point. Right now, I wanted to sleep.

Bax grunted beside me, nudging me to get out of bed. "C'mon, dude. Five more minutes," I said, my face plastered to the pillow, my eyes shut as I tried to fade back to sleep.

He barked.

I unglued one eye and stared at him, unable to tell if it was day or night. My blackout-blinds never went up anymore. "Seriously?" I asked. "Didn't I take you out like…?" Shit. I couldn't remember that, either. Only thing I did remember was I was out of whiskey. And that would not do.

Stretching and climbing out of bed, I checked my phone —for the time, not like I was checking to see if Sara had called or texted. I mean, why would she? It wasn't like I expected her to come running after me, offering an explanation. Even if she had, I wouldn't have listened. I'd caught her red-handed. There was nothing she could have said to make me see things differently. Nothing.

I glanced at the screen.

No missed calls. No texts.

A balloon of disappointment bubbled out of me.

Dammit. *Maybe I should get rid of my phone.*

Not like I needed people checking in on me anyway. Not like I cared if Sara ever— Running a hand through my hair, I cut myself off from thinking about the one woman I never wanted to think of again. I looked down at the time on my phone.

8:53 p.m. Damn.

I could have sworn at least the sun was still up. As I pulled on a pair of sweatpants and a t-shirt, my doorbell rang.

Who the Fuck?

I'd specifically told the front desk not to let a single soul up to my apartment unless it was Mike delivering Benny's Pizza or Chaoxiang from Jade's Kitchen. Heads were going to roll. My jaw clenched as I guessed who my uninvited guest might be. Aside from Jake, I had zero friends—which was incredibly pathetic—but I'd always been a bit of a loner. Whoever could possibly visit me right now was either him—who I had no desire to entertain—or some neighbor who was entirely out of his fucking mind for ringing my bell at this hour.

Or…

With a sudden rush of adrenaline, I sped to the front and yanked opened the door.

Nobody.

I looked in both directions. Not a single soul in sight. Shaking my head, I walked back inside my apartment. Then I noticed a manila envelope by my feet.

Last time someone delivered a package like this, my life nose-dived into hell. With shaking fingers, I bent down and grabbed it, looking down the hall a couple of more times before closing the door. I placed the envelope on my kitchen counter and stared at it. Thomas Wright sat written across the center in black Sharpie. Like the first envelope.

Whoever was doing this had a sick sense of humor. Then it dawned on me. Rushing to my houseline, I picked up the phone and dialed the front desk.

"Good evening, Mr. Wright," Derick said. "How may I be of service?"

"Derick, who did you let up to my apartment?"

"No one, sir. Why do you ask?"

"Did anyone come up at all in the last five minutes?"

"Well, there was a gentleman—"

"Who was it?"

"He was accompanied by a tenant from the fourth floor, I didn't ask for a name."

"Fuck."

"Something the matter, sir?"

"Nothing. Don't worry about it." I hung up and continued to stare at the envelope, a prickly sensation spider-walking up my spine. Whoever dropped this off had been in my building and hadn't used the front entrance. They knew exactly where I lived and that I'd be home. Something wasn't adding up. Picking up the envelope, I ripped it open. There were four photos inside, each one of Sara at different locations—at the grocery store, bike riding, lounging by the beach, sitting on some porch reading a book. I didn't understand. Then I saw the typed note still stuffed inside.

One million dollars cash. Tomorrow 1 pm. Abandoned warehouse on Wessex.

No money and the next pictures you get will be of her dismembered body.

Call the police—she dies.

I read the note a dozen times, looking over my shoulder and feeling paranoid as if the individual who wrote it was lurking in the shadows. I couldn't process what I'd read. Was this some type of joke or was Sara truly in danger? My first instinct was to call her, but her phone didn't even ring, an automated voice announced the number was disconnected. No wonder I hadn't received any calls or texts from her since the breakup. My hands began to tremble as my body broke out in a cold sweat. Phone tightly gripped in my hand, I paced in my foyer, trying to make sense of this, but dark dread seeped into my bones. Something wasn't right. I pulled up my phone again and fumbled through my contacts, trying to steady my shaky hand as I scrolled through and found Jen's number. I called. It went straight to voicemail.

"Fuck!" I shouted, squeezing my phone so tight I cracked the screen.

What was I supposed to do? Call the police? And tell them what? I had no idea where Sara was. I had no clue who sent the pictures. And if the threat was real, calling the police could...

No. I didn't even want to think about it. I wasn't going to risk it. Regardless of what occurred between Sara and me, if anything happened to her...

God, if anything happened to her, blood would spill. I swore it.

With no time to waste, I ran to the closet in my room. Located inside was a safe I seldom opened. In fact, the last time I had was to lock up my gear. Even though I'd left the military, and I had no intention of ever going back, there was a time when I entertained the idea of doing overseas contract work.

That was after I finished my last tour and before the business launched. I'd needed cash, and killing had been my only true skill. No one ever wants to say it, at least not openly, but assassinating for the government is still murder. Hired hands but with a license to do it, that's the truth of it. It's no less brutal and no less filthy.

Thankfully, it'd only been a fleeting idea in a time of desperation. It would have been a terrible mistake. After the mission failure that led to the death of five of my platoon brothers, I couldn't fire another rifle. Not with the accuracy I was accustomed to. I was not about to put my safety and that of others on my shoddy marksmanship.

Still, I'd had weapons practically all my life. From hunting deer as a boy and a teen, to killing terrorists later in the Marines, guns were as much a part of my identity as my name. I'd kept them in my safe as a precaution. Intruders, perhaps. Never something like this. God, *never* something like this. My fingers froze over the keypad. I couldn't believe I was about to do this. The last thing I'd considered was that someday I'd be going all Rambo trying to rescue Sara from some crazed animal who'd smelled blood.

I needed to find out where Sara was, and I needed to get to her before the drop-time. Shaking the nerves off my shoulders, I punched in the code. Folded neatly inside were tactical clothes I'd kept just in case. Pulling out the pair of black army fatigues and a black t-shirt, I quickly changed before reaching for my Sig Sauer P226 pistol. Locked and loaded, I tucked the gun into the waistband of my pants. As I reached for the case to my M24 SWS sniper rifle, I paused, my fingers trembling over the handle as I grabbed it. This type of weapon had once been an extension of me, now I couldn't even touch it without it plucking a string of nerves.

You said you'd never use that weapon again.

My body tensed at the reminder. I might not have been able to fire my sniper rifle with accuracy anymore, but at least I could still use my pistol without a problem. I hoped. This whole moment was surreal, but I had no time for bad memories or nerves. I put the case down and grabbed extra ammo for my handgun.

You're going to get yourself killed—and her— trying to be a fucking hero. The voice inside my head wanted to make me see sense.

I ignored it.

Peering inside the safe, I reached for my knife calf-holster and slid out the fixed-blade tactical knife. Holding it up and examining its beautiful workmanship, I took a moment to appreciate the decorative, but sturdy Kirinite handle and the long, jagged high-carbon plain-tool steel making the weapon look as deadly as it appeared. I strapped it on and concealed it under my fatigues. Would I need it? Hopefully not, but I couldn't lie the thought of driving it through the heart of the asshole who did this crossed my mind.

Also, inside the back of the safe lay several neat stacks of money amounting to two and a half million dollars in cash. After the shit I'd lived through, being prepared for the *What Ifs* was a must.

Taking out the black duffle bag that was stuffed beside the money, I put ten packages of pre-bundled, hundred-thousand-dollar bricks into the container, closed the safe, grabbed the duffle, and returned to the living area.

I placed the money bag on top of the island and called Jake, quickly briefing him about what happened. He told me my plan was crazy, but I didn't give him a chance to talk me out of it.

"Your place," I commanded. "Twenty minutes."

Twenty-Eight

TOM

JAKE TRIED to tell me to pay the money and forget about trying to find her. He didn't get it. There was no guarantee this man wouldn't hurt her. That he wouldn't try to extort me for more cash later. If he lived, Sara would always be in danger. Especially, if I just went ahead and paid him without any consequences. No. Whoever this asshole was, he'd messed with the wrong man. I wasn't about to let him threaten Sara and get away with it. Yes. Even after what happened, I planned to defend her. Because the truth was, I was still madly fucking in love with that woman. I pretty much drank until I could no longer think just so my mind could block all thoughts of her. But then I'd end up dreaming of her anyway.

No matter what I did, she was in my system. Permanently. I'd love her until the day I died. Yeah, leaving her was like taking a sledgehammer to my heart, but I couldn't take the images of that other man touching her. Call it me being *possessive*. Call it, *she's mine, and no one else can touch her.* Call it, *I'm still a fucking caveman, and I can't stand the idea of her loving another man.* I didn't give a damn. I was one hundred percent alpha male to the bone, and the instant another man trudged on my turf…

Who the fuck was I kidding? A fucking coward, that's what I was. A real man would have fought for her. A real man would have gone after her and given her a chance to explain, to tell me where things had gone wrong. A real man might have punched that asshole in the face.

I… I'd walked away and left her there. Alone. And where was this new knight in shining armor, anyway? Why wasn't he with her? Would he be able to protect her if this asshole decided to hurt her? I couldn't take that chance. I needed to get to Sara no matter what. I had to warn her somehow. Problem was, I had no idea where to begin. But given the pictures—if I trusted they were current—she was not in the city.

Where could she have gone? Why did she leave? Had she gone away with this new man in her life while I drank myself to death? The thought made my insides twist. Was she staying with him wherever she was when those photos were shot? My chest tightened, and I thought about my handgun, cold and seeking justice, pressed against my lower back. I wouldn't let thoughts of Sara with that guy cloud my judgment. This was about her safety. Nothing else.

I had one Hail Mary left. I prayed it wouldn't fail.

Before leaving Jake's apartment, I went over the plan again.

"Bruh, I don't know about this," he said.

"Jake, it's decided. I'm going to find Sara. If you don't hear from me by noon tomorrow, I need you to deliver this money. You're the only one I can trust with this."

He grunted.

"Brother, I need to know you have my back."

He took the duffle bag from me.

"No police," I reminded him, my gaze stern. I couldn't afford to take any chances. If they knew where I lived and where Sara was, and if they were orchestrating this whole fucking ransom, it was possible whoever was responsible wasn't working alone. I didn't know if Sara had been kidnapped, or if they only had a tail on her. Either way, I wasn't risking her safety by going to the police.

PULLING ON A BLACK LEATHER JACKET, I jumped back on my white Ducati and sped off to Sara's Eastside apartment. If anyone knew where Sara was, it had to be Jen. I just hoped she'd talk to me or at least give me enough time to tell her Sara was in danger.

After pulling into the garage of their building, I hightailed it to the front desk. Pedro said Jennifer had been gone for several days and she wasn't due back until the next day.

Fuck. "The next day? Are you sure, Pedro?"

"Yes, sir," he replied. "You can try her tomorrow."

Running an exasperated hand through my hair, I yelled, "I don't have until tomorrow. I need to talk to her now."

"Not sure what to tell you, sir. She said she'd be back tomorrow."

Every moment I wasn't speeding toward wherever Sara was, was another minute lost. What else could I do? "I'm going to wait for her."

Pedro's eyes widened. "Here, sir? In the lobby?"

"I was thinking you'd let me camp outside her apartment."

DIDN'T THINK he'd let me do it, but he took one good look at me. With my black get-up and unshaven face, I either appeared like a man on a kill mission, or a sorry-ass broken-hearted drunk. Perhaps both. I sat on the cold tile outside the door to Sara and Jen's apartment and waited.

And waited.

Time crawled at a snail's pace. My stomach painfully twisted into a knot. I craved a drink more than I craved food. Took every single cell in my body to fight the urge to run to the liquor store. I peered down the empty hallway in each direction and laughed. You couldn't script this shit even if you tried. When did all this happen? In love again. Broken again. Sitting on the floor in an empty hallway, a gun in my waistband planning the rescue of the woman who showed me heaven only to cast me into hell.

I'm a poet, now?

Another chuckle bubbled out of me.

If I wasn't going to get drunk, then I would need to sleep. It was the only other way I knew how to quiet the thoughts.

Several hours later, I jolted awake as something hit my boot.

"I can't believe this. Tom?"

Rubbing my eyes and peering up at the person who'd roused me from sleep, I sighed in relief. "Jen. Thought you'd never show up."

"How long have you been sitting out here?" she asked, her cheeks sunken, her eyes bloodshot.

"All night."

She shook her head. "And no one said anything? Fucking neighbors could see a person breaking in, and they would keep walking by while staring at their phones. Ugh."

"What time is it?"

"Seven-thirty."

Every bone in my body ached from the awkward way I'd slept. Standing, I said, "I need your help."

The pity in her eyes was devastating. I must have looked

worse than I thought. "Let me save you some time, Tom. She's not here, and I don't know where she is."

She might as well have dug the knife strapped to my calf straight through my heart.

Twenty-Nine

TOM

"Took you long enough to come looking for her," Jen chided as she opened the door and strode forward, her words dripping with vinegar.

Her reproach cut, but it was uncalled for. "Why would I come looking for her at all? She's the one who fucked up," I shot back as I followed behind her.

At my comment, she threw the apartment keys on the kitchen counter and whirled on me, hands on her hips, eyes red with contempt. "You're so sure about that, huh?"

I glared back. "I saw the pictures, Jen."

She smirked. It was a mocking grin that iced my blood and raked my skin, making me wonder if there was something I didn't know.

"Men," she started with a sneer, "you always think you have everything figured out. You saw a few pictures, and suddenly you had the whole story." She sucked in a deep breath, seemingly trying to reel in the anger ready to burst from her pores. Shaking her head and looking away, she added, "You were so sure you'd caught her red-handed. God, like you even needed to have her followed." With a sidelong glance, she muttered, "If you weren't so fucking insecure—"

"Hold up," I cut her off. "I didn't have her followed. I don't know who did it or why, but an envelope was left at my office with those photos."

Jen scoffed, walking toward a small computer desk. "Well, you can thank the birdbrain who took those pictures for making an idiot out of you. Those photos you like to reference so much were pure bullshit." Pulling out a manila envelope from one of the drawers, she walked back and threw it at me. "Go ahead, look through them again. Tell me what you see this time."

Gripping the envelope with an iron grasp, my chest caved. The thought of seeing them together again made me seethe. I glared at Jen for starting this shit with me. She was wasting precious time. "I've seen them plenty."

"Look. Again. You came here for something. I'm giving it to you."

I pulled out the photos and scanned through them. They hadn't changed. And neither had the intensity of the stabbing pain in my gut at the sight of them together.

"That man you think Sara was cheating on you with is Josh Buckley," she uttered, interrupting my thoughts. She waited for that tidbit of information to sink in. As my eyes widened, she continued, "Yeah, *that* Josh Buckley. And she wasn't cheating on you with him. She was set up by his sister under the pretense Sara would be helping out her dancer friend." She paused, her face tensing as her skin flushed. Bristling, she growled, "If Lisa were here right now… Ooh, I'd slap that bitch."

My head spun. "Wait, the guy in these pictures is Josh, her ex-boyfriend?"

"In the flesh, honey," she quipped, not bothering to hide her enmity toward me. "And no, he's not a dancer. He and his sister plotted the whole little meet up to trap Sara into talking to him."

Overwrought, I pressed on the bridge of my nose, trying to make sense of it all. "Why?"

Jen's eyes flickered with vexation as she spat her reply, "Because he decided that after four fucking years he would show up out of the fucking blue and drop a bomb on my best friend."

This time her anger didn't seem directed at me, but at Josh or the reason he'd shown up. Regardless, I needed time to process what she was saying and the implications of it all. My mind still swirling in confusion, I wobbled to her sofa, dropping the photos on the floor. Shit. I couldn't remember when the last time was that I'd eaten, but my stomach felt like it wanted to hurl. Plopping on the seat, I leaned back and closed my eyes, taking several deep breaths.

Jen followed and sat across from me. "That all sink in yet? Because it gets worse."

Eyeing her with trepidation, I sat up straighter and waited for her to enlighten me with more awful news.

"Jesus, Tom," she uttered as she crossed her legs. "If you'd only taken a second to carefully look through those photos. I mean, did you even bother to see, to question what you were looking at? There was nothing incriminating in the pictures. Nothing."

I clenched my jaw, almost biting my tongue in the process. She was right. I hadn't bothered to ask the questions. I'd simply assumed. But I'd seen them together in the morning, coming out of the elevator. Sara in her pajamas, under his arm. My mind connected the dots. Trying to ignore the sick feeling in my stomach, I asked, "Why did he arrange the meeting?"

"He came to apologize for his mistakes. To make amends," she intoned with chagrin, rolling her eyes and shaking her head. "Another idiot. He thought Sara would welcome him with a bright smile and open arms. He caught her completely off guard. Poor girl almost had a panic attack. But you know what, she left his ass at the café the instant she realized he'd duped her. Didn't even give him a chance to utter a single word. But of course, he couldn't let her be, let her catch her breath. He followed her home, and once here, he convinced her to listen to him, to let him explain. Needing closure, she accepted."

Listening to Jen recount the events captured in those photos made my blood ripple. Had I been wrong all this time? Had I accused her of cheating when all along Sara had been innocent? "But that was all Tuesday night. When I came on Wednesday—"

"Right. Huffing and puffing like some alpha maniac."

She had it out for me, for sure. I guess I deserved it, but Christ. My accusations weren't completely unjustified. I shot her a steely gaze. "Yes, Jen. Huffing and puffing. But wouldn't you? After seeing pictures that yes, weren't outright incriminating, but clearly suspicious enough to warrant a confrontation? Only to watch as she walked out of the elevator in her pajamas, under his arm, all cozied up and…"

She smiled brightly, displaying another mocking grin that made my neck tingle with worry for what she could reveal next. "Ah, yes," she said, opening her arms wide in an exaggerated gesture. "The grand moment when you realized you had it all figured out. When you humiliated my friend in front of our neighbors. When you treated her like some floozy before turning on your heel and walking out on her—leaving her to bleed out on our lobby floor."

My breath caught in my chest. "Bleeding out? What are you talking about?"

Her face relaxed, darkness shadowing her eyes. "That's right. She never told you," she replied, her voice sullen and distant.

"Jen, what didn't she tell me?" The words trembled from my lips.

"The baby, Tom. Sara lost the baby."

I must have blacked out for a minute, maybe more. I couldn't remember what I said, or thought, or did immediately after Jen delivered the blow. All I could remember was the immense sorrow piercing through my soul.

A baby…

My baby. *Our* baby.

Placing my elbows on my knees and cradling my chin in my hands, I trembled, struggling to hold back the wretchedness burning through my chest. "I didn't know she was pregnant, Jen. She took the test. It came back negative."

Her gaze deepened, perhaps realizing I'd taken the final blow and there was no more grief to fire at me. "It was a false negative. She didn't know either until…" she sighed. "Until she almost died from the ruptured fallopian tube. The baby had attached there instead of the uterus."

Dear God. My insides boiled as I tried to contain my rage, the hatred now flaring in my veins toward the person who took those pictures and started the chain of events leading me to Sara's doorstep that morning. Fury at myself for allowing those photos to deceive me. For allowing myself to seek answers by storming into her apartment like a savage animal and ripping Sara to shreds with my words, with my cowardliness. My despair at realizing I might have been responsible. "Jen, did I… with my confrontation, did I cause her to lose the baby?"

"No. A baby implanted outside the uterus can't survive. It would've happened regardless. That morning, she woke up ill, and we'd had an argument right before Josh showed up again. He'd wanted to talk to me, but I turned him away. Sara was walking him out when you showed up. He was holding her because she had collapsed in pain from the rupture. She could barely stand."

"I saw her stumble and did nothing. I stood there, angry and lashing out while she was dying. While our baby died." I pushed up from the couch and paced, my strides so hard and heavy I could've carved tracks in the floor. "Why didn't she call me after running into him?" I asked no one in particular. "Things might've been different if she'd told me."

Pushing up from her seat, Jen pointed a finger at me, pinning me with a stare sharp as daggers, forcing me to stop. "Don't you even dare try to put this on her. She is completely blameless in this. You want to know why she didn't run to call you right away? Because she is not a fucking child. Because she doesn't need to call you for every little thing that happens in her life. Because she is compassionate and thoughtful, and after all the shit you had been through that weekend at Lake George—all the shit *she* went through—she didn't want to burden you with any more crap. You get it? You may look at Sara and see some broken girl in need of saving, but I see a woman who despite all the hardships the world has thrown her way, she doesn't need a man to make it through life. She didn't need you, Tom. She wanted you. And you screwed up the best thing to ever happen to you. You won't ever find another woman like her. And you know, the funny thing is, I don't even think you're the reason she left. Because on top of everything she had ever lost in her life, the loss of the baby... *that's* what truly broke her."

I grabbed Jen by the arms and bore my gaze into hers. There was no force behind my actions, I just needed her to see me. I wanted her to know I understood how I'd fucked up. I was aware of my reprehensible behavior. I needed to fix this. I needed to find a way to get Sara back. "I need to make things right, Jen."

She didn't bother to wiggle out of my grasp but stared harder into my eyes. "Sara will bounce back. And it won't be because I was there for her, or because you stormed in wearing your not-so-shiny-armor and swooped her into your arms. No. She will bounce back because, despite her tears and all her suffering, she's the strongest woman I know."

I pulled her in closer. "No, Jen. You don't understand. Sara is in danger, and I need to find her before it's too late."

I SPENT the next ten minutes seated at the dining table with her, bringing Jen up to speed on the new photos and the ransom demands. Unfortunately, she said Sara had left her phone behind, not wanting anyone to reach her, and if she'd bought a new phone, she hadn't told anyone. At least not Jen. She flipped through the latest photos, trying to see if anything jogged a memory of where Sara might be.

"I don't know, Tom. Nothing is ringing a bell…" After another agonizing moment, she perked up in her seat. "Wait. This… this photo right here."

I leaned in closer as she pointed to the picture.

"This porch. Oh, my God. I can't believe I didn't see it sooner," she said, leaning back in her chair.

"What? What is it?"

Jen stood and paced, mumbling to herself. "But how could I have guessed? It's the last place I ever thought she'd be."

I joined her, touching her elbow, trying to call back her attention. "Jen, talk to me. Where is she?"

She looked at me, her eyes shining. "Cape Cod. Her grandmother's house."

"Cape Cod? Are you certain?"

"Yes. We spent every summer up there. Never crossed my mind she'd ever go back."

I looked away, remembering the harrowing story. "That's where she was the night of the accident."

"Exactly," Jen breathed the word with relief as if she'd solved a puzzle.

I reached for my phone and handed it to her. "Okay, well, call her. Now."

"Who?"

"Sara. Don't you have her grandmother's number?"

"Tom, that was ages ago. I never kept her number."

"Okay, what's her address?"

"Tom, it's a four-hour drive."

"I know. And I'm running out of time. I need to get on the road."

"I…I don't know the address. I'm so sorry."

My heart sank. This couldn't be it. There had to be a way to get to her. "A village, a street, something?"

"No. But… I went up there every summer. I may not know the address, but I think I can get us there. Her grandmother lives right across the bridge."

I didn't like the idea of bringing Jen along for this trip. She didn't know what lay hidden in my waistband. But I had no other options. I'd figure things out once we arrived there.

"Let's go," I said, ushering her out the door. Glancing at my watch, 8:30 a.m. flashed on the digital face. I had exactly four hours to get to the Cape. There was no margin for error, no room for delays. But no matter what, I was going to get to Sara.

Whatever it took.

Hang on, baby. I'm coming for you.

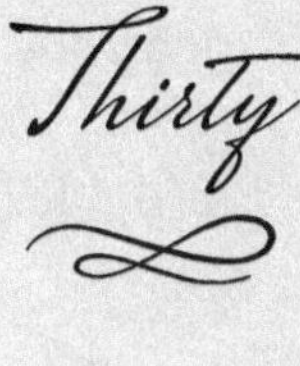

SARA

9:00 a.m.

"Grams?" I shouted as I ran down the steps from my mother's old room.

"In the kitchen," she yelled back.

As I rounded the corner, I caught a glimpse of the breakfast feast sprawled on the island—eggs, bacon, an assortment of pastries and fruits. And coffee.

Ugh. Coffee.

I'd not had a single cup since I'd arrived four weeks ago. It was a silent protest of some sort. "Grams…" I chided with a bit of amusement as I placed my hands on my hips and gazed at her with narrowed eyes. I'd told her plenty of times she didn't have to cook for me.

Her blue eyes twinkling, she peered at me through the top of her red-rimmed glasses as she took a sip of her tea, and said, "Sara, breakfast is the most important meal of the day."

I walked to the fridge and pulled out a smoothie. "I *have* breakfast. See?" I lifted it up, gesturing for her to notice as I shook the veggie and fruit blend I'd been drinking to help detox my body.

"Nonsense," she replied, nodding to the island. "Sit down,

child. At least have some eggs." Her icy stare didn't allow room for negotiation.

Scooping some eggs onto a small plate and adding fruit to a cup of yogurt, I sat on an island stool and scarfed my food down.

"Slowly, Sara. It's not good for your digestion to eat so fast."

Sipping my smoothie, I said, "Just want to get to the beach early, that's all."

"Which beach are you going to?" she asked, walking around to stand next to me. She took a strand of loose hair from my ponytail and tucked it behind my ear. The gesture reminded me so much of my mom. She used to complain my hair was always out of place. Looking up at Grams, I realized how much my mother had resembled her own mother.

Grams was tall and lean, her once golden-brown hair was now all white, but her skin was still silky smooth, with barely any wrinkles—except when she laughed, and the corners of her lips creased with half-moon lines. She hadn't lost her beauty to age, and her ocean-blue eyes continued to shimmer with the youth of her spirit.

"Sandy Neck," I replied, unable to take my eyes off her, her features so reminiscent to my mother's it made my heart pound with longing. "Summer is over, and it's tranquil at this hour," I continued, finally looking away and sliding off my seat. "I get the beach all to myself." I smiled and sighed with contentment. It was my favorite part of the day.

"Wouldn't it make more sense to dance in a proper studio?"

"Sure. But this is different. It's harder to dance on the sand, but it's helping me recondition my muscles. Plus, it's liberating. Just the waves and the music and me. Not to mention I can't afford to pay to use a studio."

Placing a palm to my cheek, she intoned, "Be careful out there. You blast that music so hard in those earphones you don't hear anything else. That's how those girls get abducted, you know. They don't hear their attackers until it's too late."

Shaking my head and smiling, I replied, "Grams, nothing ever happens here."

Eyes narrowed into slits, she tensed her face and uttered grimly, "Until it does."

There was no need for all the gloom, but I knew she worried about me. "I promise to be careful," I said as I leaned in and kissed her cheek. "See you later."

I TOOK the mint-green vintage beach cruiser bicycle out of from the garage and rode it all the way to Sandy Neck, enjoying the curves of Old King's Highway, the scenic route weaving through villages, hugging marshes and private beaches. Memories of my childhood swam through the salty breeze brushing against my skin. Instead of filling me with melancholy, it made my heart swell with joy as I remembered summers spent up there with my mom. I passed our old mini-golf spot, the famous grill we visited after each game, and the ice cream parlor that served the best homemade strawberry ice cream on the East Coast. Ever since coming back, I'd visited it almost every night after supper. It was still as delicious as I remembered. Sitting outside on their bench, watching the sunset as I savored every lick, was medicine to my aching heart.

I should have visited Grams sooner. I'd thought coming up here would dredge up the one lousy memory I thought had tainted the rest. In truth, all the good memories remained intact. It was a gift I planned to treasure for as long as I could. Maybe I'd end up staying up in the Cape for good. Being away from the city had proven to be the best decision I could've ever made.

Once I arrived at Sandy Neck, I parked my bike and trotted to the wet sand near the water. Sweaty from the long bike ride, I stripped off my yoga pants, sweatshirt, and a t-shirt. Underneath my clothes, I'd worn a pair of dance shorts and a midriff shirt.

The air was chilly near the shoreline, but with the sun shining bright, my skin tingled with streaks of heat. Plus, I was warmed up from the ride there and barely needed to stretch. Taking out my iPad from the knapsack I'd brought, I queued up my playlist and put on my wireless earphones. My heart knocked against my chest in rhythm to the start of the deep drumbeats.

I swayed as my muscles absorbed the notes, my lungs breathing the music, and my soul embracing the lyrics.

Pain. It had been a constant in my life for the last four years, consuming and paralyzing, claiming all aspects of my life.

It wouldn't rule my existence any longer. Things needed to change, and this was the start. Purging my life of all the negativity surrounding me began with one song—*this* song. I let the melody direct my movement. Fast and angry at first, my body spoke its truth. Frustration, disappointment, sadness, and even love. I refused to keep giving my all and the universe taking more than I had to offer. The blood sang in my veins as I leaped and twirled, as I fell to the ground in desperation, tired of the nonsense, my knees digging into the sandy grains, my soul pouring out of me.

Every string of fiber in my body strummed in synchrony to every single note plucked by the guitar strings. I was a living, breathing instrument. And as the music tore me down, every ounce of pain falling away from me, the same music pieced me back together. I rose above myself, reached beyond my limits, and with one final breath, I conquered the mountain.

Dancing was living, and I would no longer die.

12:30 p.m.

I danced for two hours and took a quick dip in the cold sea before putting my clothes back on. Now, I sat on the sand, knees up to my chest, arms hugging my legs. Staring out into the vast ocean, I wished to never leave. This place was my sanity, my salvation. Each new day I spent on this beach the waves washed a small chunk of my grief away.

Thoughts of Tom were always there, but the distance between us had helped me see more clearly. I missed him, especially during moments like these, when I thought back to the day at his beach house in Santa Monica when he showed me the most beautiful sunset I had ever seen. The memory stung, but not with resentment. Now, I could think back to those times and appreciate every moment with sweet longing. Oh, how I wished things hadn't ended, that we could have had our happily ever after.

It wasn't meant to be, but thinking back to my drive up the Cape, when I'd regretted falling in love with him, I realized how wrong I had been. I'd lost, but I'd also gained a whole lot —memories of what true love is supposed to be. I could never love with such intensity ever again, and I was okay with that. Our love would always be the kind of love people wrote books about. At least in fiction, we could sail off into the sunset.

Around 12:45 p.m., I picked up my things and headed back up to where I'd left my bike. As I prepared to mount, I caught a glimpse of a black Lincoln Town Car stationed in the small parking lot about thirty yards from where I stood near the bike trail. The hairs on the back of my neck rose like tiny needles. I couldn't be one hundred percent sure, but I could have sworn I'd seen the car before, several times. What would be the chances this would be the same car I'd seen near Grams' house, or at the supermarket the other day, or near the ice cream place I went to every night?

Chances were slim, yet rooted in my gut, I knew it was the same car. And I couldn't make sense of why it would be here, in the middle of the day, as if it had followed me. I thought about going up to the car and finding out who the driver was. Maybe he was someone's chauffeur, and he simply drove around mindlessly waiting for his wealthy client to call on him.

Or…

Nah.

I jumped on my bike and rode away. There was no chance he was following me. Traumatized by what happened in the city, I now lived in terror someone was always lurking in the shadows. At least, that was how I'd felt lately, as if someone was constantly watching me. I blamed my nerves. Tom and I were over. There was no reason for him to send someone after me.

Giving one last glance over my shoulder, I pulled up onto the road and peddled back home—the urgency in my legs had nothing to do with the fact the car pulled out from its parking spot just as I left—at least that's what I told myself. Deep inside, I couldn't wait until I arrived home.

1:15 p.m.

As I rode onto the driveway of my grandmother's house, I dismounted and quickly looked up and down the road. The Town Car was nowhere.

Thank goodness.

I shook my head, feeling silly for thinking the worst. Once inside, I called after Grams but received no reply. Then I remembered it was her book club day, and she was at one of her girlfriend's houses for the afternoon. Sipping Rosé while chatting about their newest literary novel was her favorite pastime.

As I strode through the foyer, I peeled off layers of sweaty clothing, dropping my sweatshirt and t-shirt on the stairs so I could carry them up when I went to my room. I walked into the kitchen in search of cold water, and dropping my house keys inside the glass fishbowl sitting on the kitchen island, I reached inside the fridge for a bottle.

As I closed the fridge door, my body stiffened, and my breath stilled with a gasp. Standing beside me was a strange man dressed in black. Iced blood spread through my body with every hastened beat of my heart. In a blink, instinct kicked in. This man was likely a home invader. I flung the water bottle in his direction and tried to run away from him, but he had been too close, and he gripped my hair before I could get away.

He yanked, and I fell backward into his chest as he put his black-gloved hand over my mouth. Holding me in place by the hair, he whispered in my ear, "We can do this the hard way, or the easy way. Though, I confess, I do enjoy the hard way."

Thirty-One

SARA

My body trembled, and my skull ached with pain at the harshness of his grip on my hair. I struggled to breathe through his gloved hand and reached up to pry it off my mouth, but my attempts made him drop it only to let his forearm slip under my neck into a chokehold. I opened my mouth to scream, but he snuffed out my voice as he pressed hard against my windpipe.

"Tsk, tsk, sweetheart. Screaming and squirming will only make this worse."

I could barely hear him speak, my mind fading to black as he squeezed harder.

No… no. I won't pass out. I can't. Think, Sara.

Think!

Fighting his attempt to knock me unconscious, I remembered the one defense class Jen made us take when we first moved to the city. This man was strong, and trying to fight him would be pointless, but there was one thing I could do.

With every ounce of strength still left in my body, I slowly turned my neck to the side, making it harder for him to press on my windpipe. That little bit of reprieve gave me the short breath I needed to drive life back into my body. My initial instinct as he'd tried to choke me was to grip the arm snaked around my neck, but that was utterly futile—a waste of energy. As soon as I received the first wave of air, I dropped my arms, and in one swift and hard swing, I slammed my hand backward, aiming for the delicate spot between his legs. It took me two, maybe three tries, but before he realized what I was aiming for, I'd hit pay dirt.

One hit was all I needed, and he immediately loosened his hold around my neck. As soon as I felt his arm give way, I spun away from him.

"Bitch," he screeched as he reached between his legs, palming his injured dick over his pants. "I'm gonna make you pay for that,' he growled, eyes feral and dark.

Those eyes made me believe he would do more than hurt me. My heart galloping, I reached for the heavy glass fishbowl in the middle of the island and flung it at him. Bastard ducked just in time. The bowl hit the fridge door behind him, and the glass shattered into a million pieces. He peered back at me, this time his face contorted into pure, wretched malice.

Flinging the glass fishbowl had been a mistake. The moment it took me to grab it and throw it had been all the time he needed to recover from my blow to his junk. He took off after me like a beast after its prey.

Screaming, I ran into the dining room, but he caught up with me in a few strides, grabbing me by the shoulders and flinging me against the dining table. My ribs cracked as I hit the wooden table, the air forced from my lungs. I fell to the ground, my side throbbing from the impact. As I tried to slide away from him, he reached for my legs, but I managed to kick him in the face right before I slithered from his grasp.

He let out a bellowing cry as he palmed his bloodied nose, now dripping blood. I managed to climb back to my feet, but he came hauling toward me, a maddening growl bursting from his throat. My ribs still ached from the hard-hit against the table, and I struggled to stay upright. He reached and grabbed me by the hair again, his grip hard against my skull. I yelped in pain, clawing at his hands, begging for him to let me go.

"I told you to play nice, but you had to go and get all tough," he barked, his voice hoarse and sharp with rage. "I'm all worked up now, Sara. And there is only one way to release this tension. You get what I'm saying, you dumb bitch?" he asked as he pulled harder on my hair. I screamed as I held on to his hand.

Before I could let out another howl, he spun me around, throwing me on the ground and landing my back flat against the floor, bones cracking, pain shooting up my spine. He strad- dled my body, a sinister grin stretching across his lips.

Slapping at him, and clawing at his arms, I yelled, "Let go of me you—"

The back of his hand came hard across my cheek, cutting off my screams and nearly knocking me out. My jaw rattled as a jolt of pain spider webbed through my face, and a high pitch noise rang through my ears, muffling all other sounds.

"Shut the fuck up," he roared as he reached down and clamped a hand around my throat. My airways immediately constricted, sending my body into panic as I lost oxygen. I kicked under his weight and clawed at his arm and his hand, but he was too strong, his body on top of mine growing heav- ier, and every second without air making me weaker.

I thought about my mother in that instant, how if she were alive, this would have been her worst nightmare. I thanked the heavens she'd never have to experience losing her daughter to a violent attack like this. Then I thought about Grams. I prayed her book club gathering went longer so she wouldn't inadvertently stumble upon this scene and have this asshole hurt her too.

My body felt numb now, I no longer had the strength to even raise my hands or move my legs. My vision blurry and fading, I managed to narrow my eyes and briefly focus on my attacker's face. He hadn't even bothered to wear a mask, which meant he'd planned to kill me all along. All I saw were the bottomless pits of his dark eyes and the hard line of his lips as he snarled.

Was he impatient, angry perhaps, at how long I was taking to die?

I closed my eyes, not wanting this man to be the last thing I saw before I gave my last breath. As my vision faded to black, Tom's face bled through my consciousness. I stared into the memory of his beautiful green eyes, remembering the love we'd shared, and the never-ending longing still buried deep inside my soul.

My heart splintered.

He's not here to protect me, to make this nightmare go away.

I'm going to die.

Alone.

MY FACE THROBBED as I slowly peeled my eyes open. It took me several moments to gain my bearings, to realize I was lying down somewhere on a soft surface. A bed, possibly. The pain on the side of my face was intense, drilling into my skull and grating on every nerve. Groaning, I pivoted my neck for a glimpse of my surroundings, but my vision was still hazy, and I couldn't make out where I was.

What happened?

Last thing I remembered… I was lying on my back as a man attacked me, as he choked me to death.

Death…

Am I dead?

Wanting to rub the haze away from my eyes, I went to reach for my face, but panic surged through me the instant I realized I couldn't. My hands were bound, tethered to opposite ends of wherever it was I laid. The next realization came when I attempted to move the rest of my body. My feet were also tethered. Whoever tied me up had prostrated me spread eagle on top of a bed. I yanked on the manacles, the rough fibers of the rope tied around my wrists and ankles digging into my skin, scraping with every twist.

I screamed as the last realization dawned on me.

I was alive. But the nightmare wasn't over.

My pleas never escaped. A cloth pulled tight between my lips nearly tore the corners of my mouth. Unable to speak or scream, I thrashed, yanking against my restraints, but nothing budged. My heart couldn't have beat any faster.

This couldn't be happening.

Chest heaving, I tried to focus on my surroundings. Staring straight up, I recognized the ceiling fan. It was the one from my mother's room.

I'm still in Grams' house. Heavens, how long have I've been out?

Steadying my breath, I focused on sound, trying to decipher if I was alone. The house was utterly silent, a terrifying dread permeating the air.

"Calm down, Sara," a hoarse voice said out of nowhere, shattering the eerie silence.

Him.

I couldn't control my need to scream.

He chuckled at my muffled cries. He was out of my field of vision, but his voice was so near, he may as well have been lying next to me. Tears trickled from my eyes as my mind ran wild with thoughts, fear surging from my gut at what this man planned to do to me. Why else would he have tied me up? Rape? Torture? Murder?

My body trembled, a cold sweat beading on the surface of my skin.

This wasn't a home invasion, and he clearly knew my name. This had to be a targeted attack. But who sent him?

A hand gently caressed my cheek, the smell of old leather assaulting my nostrils as he dabbed my tears with his gloved fingers. "No crying, sweetheart," he said. "This will be over soon. But you do have your dumbass boyfriend to thank for this. For fucking with my money." The steadiness of his voice was facetious and unnerving. A trace of irritation threatened to crack the deceitful calm dancing on the surface of his demeanor. The unrelenting rage I knew simmered beneath his calm exterior was ready to burst out of him.

Eyes widening, a new dark and icy tremor filled my body.

Boyfriend? Did he mean Tom? What was going on?

A weight settled beside me on my right. I was afraid to look, not wanting to make eye contact with this monster. From the corner of my eye, I watched as he checked his wristwatch.

Jaw muscles clenching, he wiped sweat off his brow. "Pretty-boy didn't deliver the cash. I'd say that means he cares more about his millions than he does you. Pity. You are a lovely little thing." His head pivoted toward me.

I shut my eyes, but I felt the penetrating coldness of his stare. His mouth made a smacking noise as if he was wetting his chops, ready to rip into his prey. "Red fucked me over when she paid me a measly five thousand for those pictures of you with blondie. Had I known from the start who those photos were for, I would have asked for more money. Hey, a man's gotta eat, right?" He laughed, a guttural, disgusting laugh that made my insides clench.

But then the laugh suddenly halted, and he snarled at me. "Your boyfriend fucked me over. And that's just not gonna do for me." He leaned down and licked my injured cheek, the hot wetness of his tongue and the rancid smell of his breath making my stomach churn with disgust. "Time to have some fun." Running his fingers slowly down my neck and tracing them down the middle of my chest, he chuckled as he watched my body tremble.

He'd stripped me down to my midriff shirt and spandex dance shorts. At least I wasn't completely naked, but ripping these clothes would be no effort, and with my limbs tied up, he'd have unfettered access to my body. Every time his leathered fingers touched my skin, I whimpered, hot tears streaming down my face, unable to hold back the terror coursing through my veins.

His fingers traced the waistband of my shorts. "Fuck. You *are* pretty, aren't you?" he said. "I'm sure you have a pretty little cunt, too." His fingers trailed between my legs as he touched my sex. This time I couldn't hold back my screams, and I thrashed, violently, nearly ripping the skin off my wrists and ankles, but he'd tied me to the brass posts of my mother's old bed, and there was no give.

He laughed. Cold and unapologetic.

A phone chimed, and he withdrew his hand. "What?" he answered, the ire in his voice ready to burn through the phone. His breaths ran ragged, and his nostrils flared. "Are you sure?" he asked the person on the other line as he looked at me. Vile hatred filled his eyes as he listened to their reply. Gritting, he said, "You know what to do. I'll wrap up over here. No worries. I'll make sure he regrets this for the rest of his life."

He stood up from the bed and walked over to the night-stand on my right, the one nearest the window facing the street, and placed his phone down. I tracked every movement, unsure of what he meant to do next. Whatever he'd heard over the phone wasn't good news, and I worried he would unleash his full wrath on me. The man walked to the window and peered outside. "Quiet neighborhood. Few people walking around this time of day."

I tried to swallow, but the cloth gag in my mouth had absorbed all my saliva.

"Old lady won't be back for at least another two hours. She always drinks too much at those stupid old-lady gatherings, if you ask me." He walked back toward me, his strides short and calculated.

He knows about Grams. About the book club…

"We'll be done by then. All she'll have to worry about is the mess." He pressed a button on his phone and loud, mechanical, inharmonious music piped through his device. His lips curved into a taunting sneer. Leaning down toward my ear, he whispered, "I'm going to fuck you until you bleed, and when I'm done shoving my dick into all your holes, I'm going to slice your throat and watch as you choke on your own blood. But first…" He reached over and propped his phone on its side, the screen facing toward us. "We're going to make sure your rich asshole boyfriend has front row seats to our little show."

He stood, his dark eyes staring into mine before he reached into his back pocket and pulled out a black ski mask.

I screamed—inside my head. Shattering, deafening screams that would have cracked the walls. He noticed the panic flashing in my eyes and grinned. As he slid the mask over his head, climbing onto the bed and straddling me, hot tears poured from my eyes. It was when he undid the buckle of his pants and reached for the waistband of my shorts when I lost it, jerking my body, and gurgling my screams.

As he readied to rip off my clothing, a sudden clash of breaking glass echoed from outside the bedroom. My attacker swiveled his neck toward the door. "What the fuck?" Jumping off me, he shut off his phone and reached for something sitting on a chair nearby. When he raised his hands, I noticed the handgun.

My heart raced, the thuds knocking hard against my chest.

If that was Grams downstairs…

I tried to yell through my gag, to warn her, but nothing coherent or audible came out.

The man stalked to the bedroom door and cracked it open, peeking through, listening for any other noise. Then he slithered out, leaving me tied up in the room.

A second later, gunfire erupted.

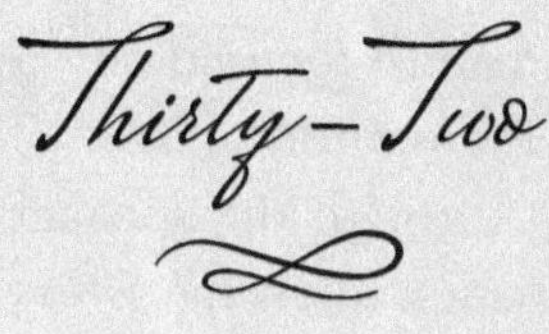

TOM

12:15 P.M.—ABOUT an hour earlier

I sped down route 195 on my Ducati, weaving through traffic, aware Jen was strapped to my back, but unable to slow down or I'd risk not making the deadline. Her arms tightened around my waist as she held on. Through the Bluetooth connection in my helmet, the GPS display on the right corner of my visor signaled we would be arriving at the Cape in thirty minutes, after that, we'd have to rely on Jen's memory to get us to Sara's grandmother's home.

Fifteen minutes was a tight margin. I'd wanted to make it to Sara before the drop-time, but I wasn't certain we could, and I couldn't take a chance with the money being late. I pressed the call button on the side of my helmet and waited for the automated voice.

Please say the name of the person you wish to reach.

"Jake."

Calling Jake.

The phone rang several times before going to voicemail. I shook my head.

What the fuck?

I'd told him to wait for my call. I voice-called again, and again it went to voicemail. Something was wrong. A shudder ran the length of my spine, dark foreboding embedding in my heart. If I failed to get to Sara by the drop-time, and Jake didn't deliver the money…

Taking a deep breath, I focused on the road, on the task at hand. Get to Sara. Get to Sara.

Jen's voice piped through the speakers in my helmet, our Bluetooth communication allowing us to talk in transit. "Tom, is something the matter?"

"Jake is not picking up. I'm worried something happened. We need to get to Sara, Jen. Before the drop-time."

"I think we're close."

"ETA is about twenty minutes now, give or take a few. But it doesn't give us a ton of time to find the house."

"I'll get us there. I promise." With that last word, she squeezed her arms tightly around me once more, perhaps offering me reassurance, maybe giving me permission to jack up our speed. Fiercely gripping the handles, I revved the engine. Fuck whatever the GPS said. I didn't have twenty minutes.

WE MADE it to the Cape in half the remaining time. Luckily, I didn't get pulled over by a cop—or get us killed.

I called Jake one more time, but he didn't pick up. I prayed he was on his way to deliver the money. I didn't care about losing the million dollars. All I wanted was to make sure Sara was safe.

We crossed the Sagamore Bridge and once over the Cape Cod Canal, I pulled over to the side of the road to give Jen an opportunity to ground herself and figure out how to get us to

Sara. It took her longer than she anticipated, and me constantly checking my watch didn't help.

Driving around in infinite circles, each minute closer to 1:00 p.m. without locating the house felt like purgatory. After countless turns and dead-ends, we were now at twelve-fifty-nine and any hopes of making it to Sara evaporated. I tried Jake one last time, but still nothing.

Shit. *If Sara gets hurt…*

My chest tightened thinking about the wretched things that could happen. The rage surging inside me erupted. Come fucking hell or high water, I would shred whoever did this to ribbons.

Vexed and with less than a minute left, I pulled over on some side street and jumped off my bike, ripping the helmet off my head and stripping off my jacket, dropping them both on the perfectly manicured lawn of some beachside mansion.

Dismounting the bike and sliding off her helmet, Jen approached and placed a hand on my shoulder. "Tom, I'm so sorry. I thought I'd remember, but everything looks so different. New construction. Many of these houses look remodeled since last time I visited."

Plopping on the grass, I huffed out a curse. "I failed her," I said, holding my head in desperation, feeling helpless and defeated. "I fucking failed her again, Jen. If something bad happens to Sara…"

"Stop. We're going to find her."

Find her? How?

I looked up at Jen, ready to snap, but she was busy looking up and down the street, her eyes narrowed, hands on her hips as she pursed her lips, trying to figure this puzzle out. Then her gaze widened.

"What is it?" I asked.

"I think… I think I recognize this street."

Jumping to my feet, I slowly stepped closer to her, trying not to interrupt her train of thought.

"Yes. That's the Connor's house down the street. Holy fuck, I know where we are. Come with me."

Leaving the bike and helmets, we jogged down the street and around the corner.

"There," she said, pointing to a large house with blue siding and white trim. "That's the one. Let's go."

Sara's old Jeep sat parked in the driveway. I blew out a sigh of relief and could have kneeled and thanked the gods. As we approached the front entrance ready to ring the bell, I peeked through the glass window of the front door. The inside was an open floor plan, and through the door, a person had a glimpse of the whole downstairs—living room, dining room, and kitchen. The chairs from the dining table lay strewn across the floor as if someone had knocked them over in haste. A nervous alarm rang through my body, spreading like wildfire through my veins as I noticed shattered glass from a vase that had fallen from an accent table. Women's clothes laid on the ground near the stairs to the second floor.

My gaze froze over the smeared blood on the hardwood floor that trailed from the dining room to the staircase. Something was wrong. I reached for the weapon concealed in my waistband.

"Oh, my God, that thing was on you the whole time?" Jen's voice trembled from her lips. "What's going on? What did you see? What are you planning to do with that thing?" she asked, her eyes darting from me to the door.

I blocked her view with my body, not wanting her to see the blood. "Jen, call the police," I whispered, my voice staid and commanding.

"What, why? Is it Sara? What did you see, Tom?"

"Jen, call the police. Tell them someone's hurt and we're going to need an ambulance. My eyes told her all the things I couldn't bring myself to utter aloud.

She nodded, her hands shaking as she reached for her cellphone.

"And, Jen," I added as she dialed, "whatever you see or hear, do not, under any circumstances, come inside the house. You understand?"

Turning toward me, her gaze flashed with terror.

"Jen?"

"If she's hurt…" she choked out, "promise me you'll kill the sonofabitch who did it."

My jaw clenched. I wouldn't rest until he no longer breathed.

Using my Sig Sauer, I broke the door window and knocked shards of broken glass away as I reached in and unlocked the door from the inside. Weapon drawn and my senses hyper-focused, I swiftly moved through the entrance, sweeping the entire downstairs in less than a minute for any other signs of struggle or indication of where Sara might be. I found more broken glass on the kitchen floor by the fridge and grunted out a curse. The attack hadn't been clean. Sara must have fought back.

Good girl.

Still holding my gun out in front of me, I opened the sliding glass door to the back porch and stepped out, looking in all directions.

Clear.

As I walked back inside, a muffled sound came from some-where in the house, followed by the stomps of rushed footsteps right above the kitchen.

Someone was home all right. I rushed to the staircase, weapon drawn, certain Sara was in the house and not alone. Leaning my back against the wall, I ascended, my pistol aimed and ready to fire.

Just as I was about to walk up the last step, a man in black exited from behind a closed door before he drew his own weapon and fired.

The shot hit the wall right above my head, missing me by inches.

Fucker.

I crouched and fired in his direction. As soon as I heard a grunt followed by a loud thud, I knew the bullet had either hit its mark or come damn close. Pushing to my feet, but staying low, I crested onto the second-floor landing and took cover behind a large, wooden hallway chest.

"Asshole," the man screamed. "You just signed your girlfriend's death certificate." Scrambling to his feet and not bothering to look over his shoulder, the man aimed backward and fired two rounds. The shots hit somewhere behind me.

That was my chance. Taking a quick peek around the chest, I watched as he tried to dash toward an open door. Idiot. Taking aim from my post, I pulled the trigger, the bullet hitting the back of his shoulder. The man spun around and fell to the ground, blood splattering on the wall and pooling on the floor. When he saw me pull out from behind the chest, he crawled through the entrance and shut the door, but not before my gaze centered on the image of the woman tied to a bed in the middle of the room.

Sara…

A chill spread through my veins. If I didn't get in there now, there was no doubt he'd leverage his life against hers. With no time to waste, I ran toward the bedroom—weapon drawn—and kicked open the door. The sight of Sara froze my limbs. Tied to the bed posts with ropes, her body lay prostrated, her face bruised, and mouth gagged. Sara lifted her head off the mattress, and her sodden, wide-eyed expression struck me like a bolt of lightning.

I'd made a grave mistake.

A shot fired from behind me, the bullet hitting the back of my upper thigh. The force thrust me forward and dropped me down to the floor. A guttural scream spurted from my chest as I turned over on my back and clutched my thigh in agony. There was no exit wound which meant the bullet had lodged in my femur and given the amount of blood pouring from my leg, it most likely severed my femoral artery, or at a minimum, nicked it. Either way, it meant I didn't have a ton of time. Knowing I needed a tourniquet, I went to reach for my belt, but my heart sank when I realized in my haste to leave my apartment, I hadn't bothered to put one on. Fuck. Without immediate medical attention, I had two, maybe five minutes tops, before passing out.

I couldn't die here. At least not before making sure Sara was safe. I needed to stay conscious long enough to keep the assailant focused on me, and long enough to give first responders time to arrive. As I gripped my shirt and pulled, hoping to tear a strip of fabric to wrap around my thigh, a low chuckle drew my attention.

"Well, this is romantic," a man uttered with a groan. "Wonder what the news anchors will say about this scene." His face pale and clammy, he sat on the floor next to the door with his back to the wall. His right arm lay limp from the shot to his shoulder. He aimed at me with his other hand, the loss of blood already taking a toll on him. "Pretty boy millionaire dies trying to save his cheating girlfriend," he taunted, his voice strained.

I eyed my gun. I'd placed it on the floor next to me while I tried to staunch the bleeding.

"Don't bother. I'll shoot you in the head before you even reach for it," he muttered.

Lifting my gaze from the gun, I glared at him. "I'm going to kill you for what you did to her."

"Pathetic. You should've just paid the money," he quipped, chuckling as he slowly pushed up to his feet, grimacing as he used the wall for support.

Jake never delivered the money?

Shaking, the man continued to aim his weapon at me. "The only one…" he paused as he took a deep, labored breath and glowered at me. "…doing any killing around here… is me," he said, gritting his teeth as he walked toward me, his right arm dripping blood as he kicked my gun away from me. "I'm going to enjoy putting a hole in your head," he snarled.

Looming right above me, he leaned down, barrel aimed at my head. I pressed my forehead against the muzzle, challenging him to shoot. He grinned, ready to pull the trigger, but he'd lost this battle before it even started. In an instant, I lifted my uninjured leg and placed my boot into his abdomen as I grabbed the sleeve of his injured arm with my right arm and his right ankle with my left hand. I yanked forward, while my foot pushed him down in the opposite direction, knocking him off balance in one swift sweep.

Gaining the advantage, I came up on top of him in a side mount. He managed to fire a round into the ceiling as he fell. I fought through the searing pain of my wounded thigh as I knocked away the gun from his hand and pinned down his good arm. Then, without hesitation, I reached for the knife in my ankle holster and plunged it deep into his heart, leaning all my weight into the blade, slowly pushing it down between his ribs, until the only thing visible was the hilt.

He groaned with one deep exhale as my gaze locked onto his. Slowly robbing him of his life, I watched in silence, my hands tightly fisting the handle of my knife as gurgled gasps of air became his last breaths. When the light in his eyes dulled, and his pupils dilated, I pulled the knife out from his lifeless body and stumbled backward, my heart constricting hard inside my own chest as it strained to pump blood through my body. With ragged breaths and my head dizzy from blood loss, I managed to pull myself up onto the bed and finally wrapped the torn piece of shirt around my thigh. But I'd already lost too much blood, and my body was feeling it.

Sara's eyes were soaked with tears.

"I got you, baby," I sputtered out. With my bloodied knife, I cut the ropes tied around her ankles and wrists, then I collapsed onto my back, the soft mattress a reprieve from the pain surging through my body.

The asshole was dead. Sara was alive.

I could sleep.

As I tried to close my eyes, Sara's voice cracked through my mind, hauling me back into the world. "Tom? Oh, my God. Tom." She gripped my head in her hands, her beautiful chocolate-colored eyes bringing me peace as a haze dulled my vision. "Stay with me."

I managed a short smile, thankful for the opportunity to see her face again, for the knowledge she was alive. That I didn't fail her.

"Please, Tom. You need to stay awake. The EMTs are here. Look at me."

My body tightened, and I growled in agony as hands grabbed my injured thigh.

"We got it from here, ma'am," an unfamiliar male voice uttered.

Through slit eyes, I saw Sara's face slip away from sight. "Sara…" I whispered, as my hand reached for her face, her touch.

For her.

"I'm not leaving you," she called out, her voice faint as the fog clawing at my consciousness finally took me, and I was gone.

Thirty-Three

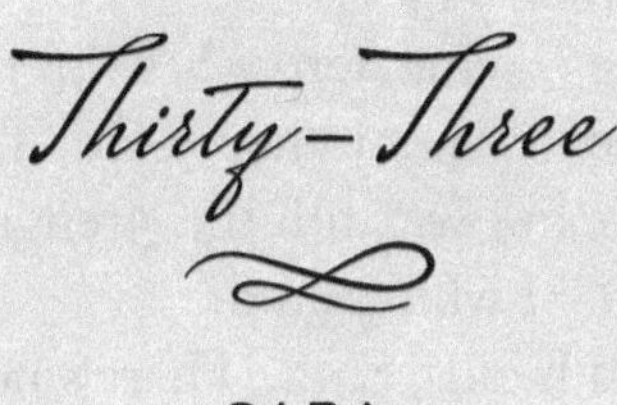

SARA

WHEN THE EMTs arrived at the house, they whisked Tom away into the ambulance before I had a chance to ask which hospital they planned to take him to. The thought of losing him, that he might die from a gunshot wound he suffered trying to save me…

I panicked and jumped out of my bed, trying to go after them, tripping over the body on the floor by the side of the bed as I rushed to the door—screaming, crying. As I ran out of the bedroom barefoot, I slipped on a pool of blood and fell. Razor-focused on Tom, I didn't notice what had become of my grandmother's beautiful beach home. Blood lay splattered everywhere, and bullet holes pierced the walls.

Police and emergency technicians milled through the house as someone grabbed me by the arms and helped me to my feet. "You've been attacked," a man said, "and you're injured."

"She's in shock," a familiar female voice added. But I couldn't process anything. Tom was hurt, and he might not make it. I needed to get to my Jeep and drive to the hospital.

"I… need to go," I said, my voice faint as I attempted to

walk away, but the woman with the familiar voice took me by the shoulders and held me firmly.

"Sara. Look at me, honey."

Tilting my head up, my eyes soggy with tears, her face finally brought me back. "Jen?"

The short smile tracing across her lips tugged at my heart. She didn't need to utter another word. I reached over and sank into her arms, her warmth the strength I needed. "Jen, I need to get to Tom," I whimpered.

"Tom's in good hands, Sara. There's nothing else you can do for him now."

"But he could die."

"Right now, we need to focus on you."

I pulled away from her, shaking my head. "No. I'm okay. I'm fine."

Jen reached for me and cupped my face in her hands. "You were attacked. You are not fine."

"Tom was shot and bled out on the bed," I sputtered.

"And he's getting the help he needs," she reassured me, her voice calm and soothing. Dropping her hands from my face, she remained still and held me with her gaze. "You're covered in blood. How about we get you cleaned up first?"

I couldn't make sense of how or why Jen was there, but her presence brought me peace and centered me in the middle of all the mayhem. I couldn't argue with her and silently let her guide me to my grandmother's bedroom. Once there, we went into the ensuite bathroom where she drew me a bath and helped undress me. I winced as she lifted my shirt over my head.

"Christ, Sara. Your ribs. We need to take you to a hospital. You might have a fracture."

Still dazed, I looked down at my naked body and noticed the dark red bruises across the whole left side of my torso.

"That man did this to you?" Jen asked.

"I… ah…" I struggled through the fog of memories. "He

pushed me into the dining table. Then he…" But as I put the pieces back together, the memory of the attack assailed my heart. I broke into tears as I recalled him straddling me and punching me in the face before he choked me.

"It's okay, Sara. You don't have to talk about it. Right now, we need to get you cleaned up and taken to the hospital." As she helped me into the soapy water, she caressed my cheek, the area bruised from his violent hit. "You're safe now." A knock at the door drew her attention. "I'll be right back," she said as she walked out of the bathroom and opened the bedroom door. I didn't bother to look to see who it was, but I could hear their conversation.

"I need to speak to Ms. Hart," a gruff male voice said.

"I know, Detective. Give me a few minutes to get her cleaned up. She's been through a lot."

"Ms. Roberts, I have a dead body, a wounded man in the hospital, and that woman in there is my only witness."

"And she will answer all of your questions. But she's in shock right now. Please give me a few minutes. Please."

"She refused medical treatment."

"I know. She's not thinking straight. Just give me a few minutes."

"You have five, Ms. Roberts. After that, I'm going in there, whether she's ready or not. Don't make me charge you with obstruction of justice or tampering with a witness."

"We'll be ready in five minutes," she replied, the door clicking closed.

My chest felt heavy as I realized the severity of my situation. As the key witness in a homicide investigation, the police weren't going to let me go until they had answers.

What answers could I give them after everything I'd been through? The images of Tom covered in blood—his breaths shallow, his blank eyes—wouldn't stop replaying in my mind. Pressing my eyes closed, I prayed for this nightmare to be over, to wake up in my bed safe from the ugliness of this day. But when I flipped my lids open, all I saw was the canary-yellow tiles of my grandmother's bathroom, and I shivered. The water was still warm, but my body wouldn't stop shaking, my head a swirl of chaos.

Jen walked in the bathroom and sat on the lip of the bathtub. "Sara. Honey——"

Without looking up at her, I said, "Jen, how did you wind up here?"

She sighed. "We don't have time."

With firm indignation, I shifted my gaze toward her. "I need to know what happened."

She averted my eyes. "You heard the man, we have five minutes."

I reached for her hand and wrapped my wet palm around her wrist. "I won't answer any of his questions until you answer mine."

Letting out a troubled breath, she pursed her lips and pulled her hand from my grasp as she crossed her arms. "It should be Tom who tells you this, but given the situation…" pausing, her face tense, she seemed to struggle with her words. "Tom knows the truth, Sara."

My brows pinched. "The truth about what?"

"That you didn't cheat on him with Josh."

I stared in silence, wondering what happened in the weeks I'd been gone.

"He wasn't even the one who had you followed," she continued.

Still in a state of awe, all I could do was stare in disbelief. "What are you talking about?"

Jen drew closer. "Someone else had you followed. We're not sure why, but it seems that man, the guy who attacked you today, had been following you for weeks after you left New York. Yesterday, Tom received another envelope with more pictures of you. Looks like he followed you all the way up here. He threatened if Tom didn't pay him a million dollars, he'd kill you."

My heart raced at her words, each beat pounding harder in my chest. I didn't even know how to react or what to say. I simply kept thinking back to the moment when I saw the man in my kitchen, to the dark fear creeping up my spine, to the pain at my side as I hit the dining table, to the moment I woke up tied to my bed. The water in the tub suddenly felt frigid.

"He…" I uttered. "He said Tom never paid the money."

"I don't have time to give you all the details," she said, awakening me from the nightmarish thoughts. "But something deeper is going on here. Jake was supposed to deliver the money, but up to the point when we arrived, Tom had been trying to get in touch with Jake with no avail. Jake never made it to the drop site on time. And we don't know why."

"Jake's involved?"

"Honey, all you need to know is that as soon as Tom got that letter and those pictures, he came looking for you at the apartment. That's when I told him. Everything."

My heart sank like an anchor to the bottom of the sea. She couldn't have. "Everything?" I asked, my voice shaky, my eyes wide with shock.

Nodding, she looked away. "I'm sorry for telling him about the baby, but he needed to know, Sara." Turning back toward me, her eyes frosted with sadness, she continued, "Look, you can be mad at me forever about this, but right now what matters is that he came looking for you. He found you. He saved you. And now he needs you. The only way we are going to get to that hospital is if you answer Detective Smith's questions. Okay?"

Tom. Knew. Everything. The secret eating me alive for weeks was out. The pain of it shot through me like a cannonball.

"You need to finish up," Jen said as she stood and left the bathroom, giving me privacy to scrub my skin and rinse off the blood caked in my hair. A few minutes later, I rummaged through my grandmother's bedroom on autopilot, until I found a pair of gray sweatpants and a t-shirt. Once dressed, I combed my hair and stepped out into the police-filled hallway. I peeked in the direction of my mother's room. The man still lay on the floor, covered under a white sheet.

I shuddered and turned from the morbid sight, and as I walked down the stairs to the living room, I told Jen to find my new cell phone which I'd dropped in the kitchen during the attack and call my grandmother to find out where she was—to make sure she was okay. Detective Smith waited at the bottom of the stairs, a small notepad in his hands.

"Ma'am," he said, gesturing to the couch.

Following the silent command, I walked to the sofa and sat. Wearing dark jeans, a white button-down shirt, and blue blazer, he took the seat across from me. As he sat down on my grandmother's pale-yellow armchair, the gold emblem of the police badge hooked to his belt glinted in the afternoon sun shining through the windows. The moment was surreal. I swallowed hard, trying to reel myself back in, but the commotion in the house held my attention prisoner. My grandmother's house looked like a crime scene straight out of a TV police drama. Forensic technicians cordoned off areas of the house with yellow tape. Cameras snapped photos, and swabs of blood were collected in small plastic bags.

This didn't feel like my life.

"Ms. Hart," Detective Smith said, pulling me out of the haze.

"Yes?"

"I know you've been through a big ordeal today, but I need you to walk me through what happened."

Crossing my arms, I asked, "What do you want to know?"

"I need a timeline of events. What led to a dead man in your bedroom?"

I looked over his shoulder and into the kitchen, remembering the morning with Grams. "After breakfast, I rode my bike to the beach. Like I do every morning."

"What time?"

Shifting my gaze toward him, I paused for a second. "Nine or ten," I replied, unsure if that was even a close approximation. "I... don't remember exactly. All I remember is hopping on my bicycle right after finishing my eggs and yogurt and riding to Sandy Neck Beach. I parked my bike and walked to the shore."

Detective Smith scribbled furiously on his notepad, his gold wedding band glimmering in the sunlight. As he looked back up at me, I took notice of the gray hairs peppering his sideburns. He looked to be in his forties, the fine lines under his blue eyes an indication of his years working long hours in the force. "What next?" he asked.

"I danced for a couple of hours. Then, right before I left, I noticed a black Lincoln parked in the lot. It seemed odd. There were no other cars. Typically, there aren't any at that hour during the offseason. Plus, something told me I'd seen that same car before."

His gaze stiffened. "Did you notice anything else, Ms. Hart?"

I scratched my head, trying to think back. "No. Just had a sick feeling in the pit of my stomach, so I jumped on my bike and sped home. Once I got here, I looked down the block a few times. What can I say? I was paranoid. It's only been a month since..." I paused, recalling the moment Tom threw the pictures at my face.

"Yes, Ms. Hart? Since?"

"I was followed once before."

"Followed? By whom?"

Hesitant to answer, I paused for a long moment before replying. "I thought it had been my boyfriend, but now it seems it was all a huge misunderstanding."

"Hmm." He tilted his head and grimaced as if he'd

already solved this crime, and the outcome wasn't anything I'd like.

Narrowing my gaze, I uttered with distaste, "You seem incredulous."

"Just trying to get the facts. Let's get back to the moment you got home. You said you didn't notice the black Lincoln?"

I fixed my gaze into his questioning eyes, and ignoring his question, said, "That dead man upstairs broke into my grandmother's house, tied me to a bed, tried to rape me, and threatened to kill me, Detective. If it hadn't been for Tom, it would be my murder you'd be trying to solve. Tom was shot trying to save me."

"Why did that man want to hurt you?" he asked.

I shook my head. "I can't be certain, but my friend Jen said something about a ransom. And the man told me Tom didn't pay the money, and that I should blame him for what was happening to me."

Leaning forward in his seat, Detective Smith continued to throw questions at me. "Ransom? Mr. Wright is a wealthy man?"

I nodded.

"This man knew about his wealth and that you two were together?" he asked.

I'd never seen the man in my life. Had no clue he'd been following me up until Jen told me. "I… don't know. I mean… I guess. Maybe?" I stuttered as I tried to think of a logical response. "Tom is a successful real estate broker, he knows a lot of people. His wealth is not a big secret. And neither was our relationship."

"Did your attacker act alone? Did you hear or see anyone else?" he pressed, his pen hovering over the notepad.

"No," I replied quickly, but then I took a moment to think. "Actually, someone called him. He seemed angry at whatever was said."

Detective Smith looked away, seemingly lost in thought.

"More people were definitely involved," he muttered, as if making the statement to himself. Then he looked at me. "There's no record of Mr. Wright notifying the authorities. If he knew you were kidnapped or were in any danger, he should have called the police right away. It's a crime—"

"How dare you!" I shot back, interrupting his accusation. "Tom came here looking for me and took a bullet trying to protect me. The only crime committed here was the one committed by the man lying dead in my mother's room upstairs. Tom is innocent of any wrongdoing."

"Did you catch a name?" he asked, unaffected by my outburst and brushing my comments aside.

"No." I pushed up to my feet. I'd had enough of his questions. No more wasting time. "I've told you everything I know, Detective. Unless you have another reason to keep me here, I'm leaving for the hospital."

Detective Smith's jaw clenched as he tucked his pen away in the inside pocket of his blazer and stood to meet my gaze. "I'm sorry about what happened to you today, Ms. Hart. But the man found dead in your room is connected to one of the biggest crime families in the Northeast. I'd like to bring you to the precinct for proper questioning. We need your statement on record."

That bit of information was alarming. If he meant to rattle me, he accomplished it. Why and how I'd been the target of such a criminal boggled my mind. None of it made sense.

"Any information you may have that could lead us to why he targeted you would be greatly appreciated. I am sure you would want to see those responsible for the heinous acts perpetrated against you prosecuted and put in jail."

Yes, he was correct. I wanted those responsible to pay, but I had no other information to offer. My mind was drawing a blank. The only thing I wanted was to find out how Tom was doing. "I'm sorry, Detective. I have no further comments."

"It's not an option, Ms. Hart."

"Sara can't come to the precinct with you, Detective Smith," Jen interjected. It seemed she'd been eavesdropping on our conversation from the stairs. "She needs medical treatment right away for possible fractured ribs."

"She refused medical treatment," he told her with a sideglance.

"That was before I examined her."

"You examined her?" he asked bemused as he turned to look at her.

"I'm a trauma doctor at Columbia Presbyterian," she replied with an air confidence so convincing, if I didn't know her, I wouldn't have known she was lying. Jen wasn't a doctor yet, but I wasn't about to blow her cover. And hopefully, he wouldn't see through her bluff.

His jaw muscles clenched.

"You can't deny her medical treatment, Detective," Jen reminded him.

Detective Smith clenched his jaw and the fire in his eyes nearly burned through the walls. He took out a business card from inside his blazer and handed it to me. "If you do think of anything else, please don't hesitate to give me a call."

Taking the card from him, I said, "If I think of anything else, I'll make sure to do that."

"I could have one of my officers drive you to the hospital," he offered. "In fact, I will be headed there shortly myself if you don't mind waiting a few minutes while I wrap up around here." The questions swirling in my head must have been written on my face because he added, "Don't worry, Ms. Hart. I'm not planning on arresting your boyfriend."

Not yet.

"I need to ask him a few questions if he's awake. Standard procedure. You understand," he said with a wink.

I offered him a short smile. Standard procedure my ass. Detective Smith had a dead, high-profile killer in his hands. I had a feeling he was willing to break a few rules to get the information he wanted, even if it meant interrogating a wounded man in a hospital. "Thank you for the offer, but I can't wait. Jen's going to take me."

"Suit yourself. See you there."

On our way, I called Tom's brother and filled him in. Thankfully, I'd saved his number in my contacts. "James, if something happens to him. If he…" I couldn't finish the sentence.

"Sara, listen to me. He's going to be fine," James tried to convince me, although his voice trembled.

"You don't understand. I saw him. He was in bad shape."

"Sweetheart, Tom's been through worse. If there is one thing I know about my brother, it's that he's a

fighter. He ain't gonna go that easy."

"I don't even know how he's doing right now. It's been over an hour since the ambulance took him. I'm afraid they won't tell me anything since I'm not family."

"You *are* family."

"I'm not, James. They won't tell me anything."

"Which hospital?"

"Police said they rushed him to Beth Israel Deaconess in Plymouth."

"It's about a four-hour drive from Lake George to Plymouth. I'm going to do my best to get there as soon as I can. I'm leaving now."

"Four hours?" The pit in my stomach grew deeper. "Four hours without any news or without being able to see him?"

"I'm going to give them a call, see if I can get anyone to tell me something—anything—over the phone."

"Okay."

"I'll give you a callback. He's going to be okay, Sara. You will too."

I hung up the phone as we approached the hospital. Body

trembling, a cold sweat broke throughout my body. I took a few deep breaths, attempting to calm my nerves.

Jen reached over from the driver seat and squeezed my hand. "Whatever happens, we'll get through this. I promise."

Glancing her way, my heart throbbed. I'd missed her. There was no one else I would've rather had at my side at that moment than her. I squeezed her hand back. "Thank you. For being here now. And always."

"No need to mention it, hon. I'm just happy I was able to be here."

"I'm so sorry for leaving like I did. For not calling. For not reaching out."

"Stop it. That's a conversation for another day. What matters is I am here."

As we walked through the large doors of the ER, I closed my eyes and sent a silent prayer up above.

Please, let him be okay. Please.

My only hope was that the universe was listening.

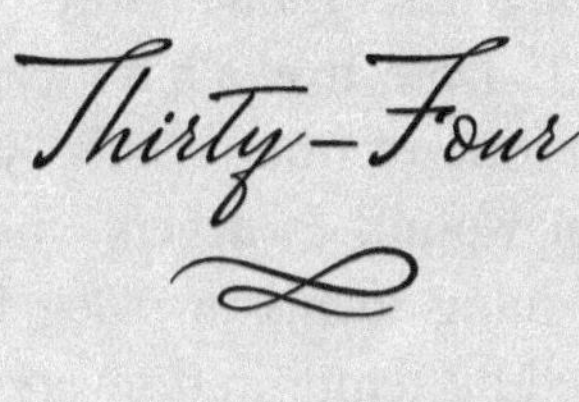

SARA

As I EXPECTED, the hospital wouldn't give me any information regarding Tom's condition, and James was only able to get confirmation Tom was in surgery. Having nothing else to do but wait, Jen convinced me to let the medical staff examine me. The X-rays revealed I didn't have any broken ribs. However, I was extremely bruised and would be in a lot of pain for a while. No broken bones in my face either, but my left cheek was scarily swollen. They gave me ibuprofen and an icepack. They also told me I should go home and rest.

Like hell I would. There was no chance I'd leave the hospital without knowing anything about Tom's status.

Interestingly, Detective Smith was the one who came to the rescue. He'd somehow beat Jen and me to the hospital, and as Tom was part of a murder investigation, he was able to get a bit more information.

I was sitting in the waiting area, leaning my head on Jen's shoulder when he strode toward us and sat next to me. "Ms. Hart."

"Detective."

"He's still in surgery."

I propped up, my eyes wide with hope. "They gave you an update?"

"One I'm not supposed to share with you. HIPPA laws and all, but…"

I could have hugged him, but I stayed rooted in my seat. "Thank you so much, Detective. That means he's okay, then?"

"Well, he's not out of the woods, yet. Your boyfriend sustained a gunshot wound to a very vulnerable area in his leg," he said, motioning to his own leg for added measure. "The bullet fractured his femur and severed his femoral artery. He lost a lot of blood. If the paramedics had been a minute later, he'd be dead." He nodded toward Jen. "Lucky for him your friend here called us when she did."

I looked over to Jen. Lucky indeed. She was more than my best friend. She was a guardian angel. Turning back to the detective, I said, "He's been in there for over two hours now. What's taking so long?"

"Patience, Ms. Hart. Surgeon's gotta patch him up. Plus, he needed a transfusion for all the blood loss. I'm not kidding. He's lucky to be alive."

Rubbing my brow, I pressed on my temples. "It's tough sitting here. Waiting."

"Which is why I'm going for some Dunks. Want anything?"

I hiked an eyebrow. "I beg your pardon?"

"Dunks."

Shrugging, I offered him another confused look.

He shook his head, rolling his eyes as if I was the idiot for not knowing what he was talking about. "Dunkin Donuts," he finally clarified. "Coffee."

"Oh…"

"New Yorker," he uttered as if that explained my lack of understanding. "Let me guess, Starbucks girl?"

Eyes widening, I crossed my arms. "Hey, what's that supposed to mean?"

"You want coffee or not?" he asked, rubbing a palm down his face as he stood.

"A cappuccino with—"

He sighed, cutting me off. "I said coffee, Ms. Hart."

If he was paying, I guess I had no choice. "Cream and sugar."

"And your friend?"

I turned to Jen. Her head drooped to the side. "Rough day for all of us."

"One regular coffee it is. Be back in a jiffy."

AFTER DROPPING OFF MY COFFEE, Detective Smith did his rounds through the hospital. I caught him chatting up the nurses and bullshitting with the EMTs as more patients wheeled through. It was clear he wasn't leaving until Tom was out of surgery and in recovery. I had a feeling he wouldn't let me see him until he had a chance to question him about the incident.

Another two hours later, my sour mood lifted as I saw James bolt through the double doors. I stood and rushed to him, wrapping my arms around him as he buried me in his massive chest, the lapels of his plaid jacket rubbing against my cheek. "Anything new?" he asked as we separated.

I tucked loose hair behind my ears and gave him an unsettled look. "Nothing they can tell me. Now that you're here…"

"You must be James," Detective Smith said behind me as if appearing out of thin air.

Eying the police badge clipped to the officer's belt, James narrowed his gaze and extended his hand out in a professional manner. "Detective."

Detective Smith shook it firmly. "Glad you made it. Your brother is out of surgery now. Nurses said he's in recovery."

A sigh of relief escaped my lips.

"Where's recovery?" James asked.

"He's still unconscious from the anesthesia," the detective replied. "Once he's awake, they will let us know."

"I told you he's a fighter," James said, placing a hand on my shoulder. "Hopefully, we'll get to see him soon."

"I don't know how much longer I can wait," I said.

"I know, me too."

"Well, you two will have to wait until after I'm done asking him a few questions," Detective Smith announced.

We both turned our gazes toward him. James's eyes crackled with irritation, mine had to be blazing.

"Standard procedure," he affirmed, placing his hands on his waist. "Murder investigation and all."

Again, with the standard procedure shit. Thank goodness Jen had seen enough trauma patients during her time at the hospital to know it wasn't standard procedure. She'd told me as much on our way to the hospital. As James was family, he could refuse access to Tom if Tom was still under the influence of medication. Which he was if he'd just gotten out of surgery.

"My brother did nothing wrong," James gritted through his teeth as he took a step forward. "He was trying to protect her."

I put a palm on his chest, trying to calm him as I eyed the detective with a resigned stare. "You can't do this, Detective."

"Your brother shot and stabbed a man," Detective Smith said to James, ignoring me. "Killing him. Normally, I'd have guards outside his room."

James's eyes flickered with fire. And just as he was about to open his mouth to continue protesting, a young doctor wearing green scrubs approached.

"I need to speak with Mr. Wright's next of kin," the doctor said.

James stepped forward. "I'm his brother."

"I'm doctor Issenberg. Your brother is out of surgery. He had a narrow escape, but we were able to get to him in time. He's in recovery now and should be waking up soon. If you want to see him—"

"Excuse me, Doctor. I'm Detective Smith. If the patient is conscious, I'd like to have a word with him first."

Dr. Issenberg grimaced. "I'm sorry, Detective. My patient has been through quite an ordeal. Unless you are planning to arrest him, for the benefit of his health, I advise the first people he sees are his loved ones. It wouldn't suit him well to be questioned until after he's been out of recovery, and all vitals are stable. Plus, he is still under the effects of the anesthesia. It is up to his brother if he wants him questioned."

James and I both turned to the detective. He knew he'd lost this battle. The man took a few deep breaths before nodding and gesturing for us to follow the doctor.

"Let's go," I said to James, wrapping my arm around his. As I pivoted on my heel to follow the doctor, I caught sight of Jen talking with some ER staff. She winked at me, and I knew that somehow, she had helped. I mouthed thank you to her.

WHEN WE WALKED into Tom's recovery room, my bones locked, rooting me to the floor. He lay propped up on his bed, leaning slightly back, wires and nodes hooked up to all parts of his body. His right leg was in a cast and lay elevated. Nurses were in the middle of taking vitals and unhooking his oxygen mask. Closing my eyes and inhaling deeply, I tried not to focus on how bad he looked, and sent a silent thank you to the universe instead—for the paramedics, for the doctors, for these nurses.

One walked up to me, her eyes softening over my face. My bruises were likely even more visible now. "He's waking up," she uttered as she nodded toward him. "Go. He's going to want to see you, sweetie."

I offered her a smile as I approached his bed. Drawing nearer, I took his hand, gently squeezing his fingers. He squeezed back and my heart throbbed with relief, thawing the ice in my veins. Reaching for his face, I palmed his bearded cheek. "Tom?"

His eyes glided open, the familiar olive-green sea of his gaze made my body swell with love. My chest heaved as tears bubbled at the corners. Heaven only knew how much I'd missed those eyes and the way they used to look at me. The way *Tom* used to look at me. I never thought I'd get to see those green eyes ever again. And now, I could lose myself in them forever once more.

"Sara…" he whispered hoarsely, as he extended a shaky hand, dabbing away the wetness from my eyes with his thumb. "No tears, baby."

I leaned in and kissed his lips. "I thought I'd lost you…" I whispered back, my breath coalescing with his.

His smile trembled. "You can't get rid of me. Not even death can keep us apart."

I giggled. "Still my corny romantic."

He shut his eyes and sighed. "Sara, about what happened…"

"Hush," I said, putting a finger to his lips. "Jen told me everything."

"I'm so sorry."

"Stop. There will be plenty of time to talk about all that. Right now, you need to rest and finish getting better."

He smiled, but as he took a moment to focus on my face, something dark flashed in his eyes. Lifting his hand to caress my cheek, his jaw clenched as he realized I still bore the evidence of my attack. "He… he did this to you?" he asked.

Reaching up, I took his hand away from the bruise covering the side of my face. "It's nothing. I'm okay."

"It's not nothing," he gritted, chest heaving as he tried to sit up straighter. "That sonofabitch hurt you."

"And he's dead now," I reminded him, grabbing him by the shoulders and easing him back onto the bed. "Please, you just got out of surgery. You need to rest."

Leaning back, he turned his face from me. "I should have been there to protect you. This would've never happened if I…"

"Tom, listen." I took his chin in my fingers and turned his face back toward me. "It's over. I'm safe. And it's because of you."

He cupped my bruised cheek. "It's because of me you were hurt." He closed his eyes, staunching tears. "I'm so ashamed of what I did to you. Of what happened after I thought you…"

Taking his face in my palms, I said, "Not here. Not right now. The only thing that matters at this moment is you're alive. Everything else is just everything else."

Opening his eyes, he let out a trembling breath. "The fear of losing you, of never seeing you again… it's what kept me fighting."

"I'm here with you now, and I'm not going anywhere."

"I know I don't deserve you," he said.

He'd fucked up royally. And if today hadn't happened, I would have gone on with my life—with a hole in my heart, but nevertheless, I would have moved on. Watching him lying there, broken both physically and emotionally, I couldn't hold on to the grief of what he'd done to me anymore. People were not perfect. People made mistakes. I had a good share of them myself. It would take time to pick up the pieces, but that didn't mean I couldn't forgive. It didn't mean I couldn't start right now.

"We deserve each other," I corrected him as I dabbed at the corners of his eyes.

"Sara, what I deserve is your rejection."

As I parted my lips to utter more reassurances, he put his finger to my lips. "I broke my promise. I know how badly I fucked up. But I never stopped loving you," he said, bringing my hand over his heart, his mouth quivering. "Not for a single breath."

I leaned in and kissed him once again, this time with more fervor and longing. Fixing my gaze into his, I let him know forgiveness wove into every single kiss. There was no need for any more apologies.

"Ahem," James coughed behind me, startling the both of us. I'd completely forgotten we were not alone. "Seriously, you two?" he continued, shaking his head and rolling his eyes. "You guys are too much."

Tom chuckled, looking over my shoulder and finally acknowledging his brother. "I'm sorry. I forgot affection offends you." They shared a smile, and Tom added, "It's great to see you, brother."

"Likewise. Can you do me a favor, though?"

"Anything."

"Quit it with the near-death shenanigans, okay? You're going to give your mama a heart attack."

Tom's eyes widened. "She's here?"

"She was visiting friends in Florida and is on the next flight from Orlando. She's a nervous wreck, you know."

"Tell her she doesn't need to come. I'm fine."

"I doubt she'll listen, but I'll give her a call."

"Tell her I'll call her later. Seriously. She doesn't need to come."

James walked around to the other side of the bed and leaned in to hug his brother. "You gave us quite a scare."

"Thank you so much for coming. For being here for me. And Sara."

"Just glad you're still with us." After pulling away from their hug, James took out his cellphone and walked out of the room to call their mother.

Once alone, I turned to Tom. "There's a detective who needs to speak with you about what happened."

Tom shrugged. "I killed a man. It's expected."

"But it was self-defense. He shot you. And you were protecting me."

"For the record, I shot him first, but like you said, I was trying to protect you. Look, I'm not worried. The man I killed… the world is better off without him. I'll tell that detective whatever he needs to know. I got nothing to hide."

"What about Jake?"

His eyes flickered, perhaps surprised I knew. "I take it he never delivered the money or something worse happened. I don't know. But once I'm out of here, I intend to get answers." He sat up straighter, wincing as he tried to reposition his leg. "Let's get this over with."

Thirty-Five

SARA

THE NEXT FEW days were a blur. I had to file a formal report at the precinct about what happened. Once the feds became involved, they re-interviewed me at least a couple of more times. Each time, they threw new questions at me. And each time, I gave them the same answers. I had nothing new, and neither did Tom, but that didn't stop them from coming. The death also drew media coverage. Such an incident caused an uproar in my grandmother's small community. And of course, then there were all the legal shenanigans we had to deal with. It's a good thing Tom had a highly respected lawyer.

Even though the forensic team had taken all the evidence they could, and the house stopped being a crime scene, my grandmother didn't feel safe. Couldn't blame her. I didn't feel comfortable sleeping in the house either. The police were kind enough to remove all my personal belongings, so I had no reason to go into the room. They also sent in a forensic clean-up crew—upon my request. All the blood was gone from the walls and floor, but the memory of it all remained vivid in my brain. It was something that would stay with me forever.

We took up residence at a nearby hotel. Tom insisted he pay for our stay. He knew it would be indefinite—until I could figure out what would become of my grandmother's home. It was the least he could do he'd said. I knew better than to argue with him. Tom would've figured out a way to pay for it anyway, even if I'd refused. My grandmother had been very understanding about the whole thing.

Grams confessed she'd been thinking about selling the house. She was now in her seventies, and taking care of such a big property was taking a toll on her. I'd found a brochure for a senior community laying in the trash once, but I hadn't asked her about it. Figured if it was in the trash, then she wasn't interested. It relieved me to hear her say she had made up her mind about selling the house. I had noticed her struggle to get up the stairs, and she was constantly worried about the upkeep. It was time to downsize.

Sitting at the dining table in the common room of our luxury presidential suite, I turned to her, and said, "Grams, you're sure you want to do this?"

She closed her eyes and inhaled deeply, her face a painting of melancholy. Opening her eyes up again and sighing, her gaze lost in a distant memory, she said, "Your grandfather bought the house the summer after we were married. His parents loaned him the money. We were so happy then." She smiled. "So in love." Pausing, she shifted her glossy eyes toward me. "Your mother was born in that house. Did you know that?"

I blinked. "I didn't."

"Elizabeth was such a beautiful child. Kind. Thoughtful. Imaginative. And a daddy's girl, of course." She laughed.

Hearing her talk about my mother like that made the memories bittersweet. It made me miss her with a longing so deep, I had to hold back tears.

"We wanted more children, but it was not the Lord's will." Grams reached for my hand and squeezed my fingers. "I know your loss, child. It is the kind of pain you will never forget, but I promise you it does get better. And God will bless you with more children. I'm certain of it."

I squeezed her hand back. When I'd told Grams about my ectopic pregnancy, she'd simply held me in her arms. She was never a woman of many words, but her gesture had been all I needed. Hearing her talk now about her own early loss made me realize there was so much I didn't know about her. And there was so much I wanted to learn. "Thank you, Grams. It means a lot to hear you say that."

Crossing her hands and looking at me intently, she said, "When your mother passed…"

I shook my head no, reluctant to talk about the accident. "Grams, you don't have to."

"Sara, let me speak. Please. I've needed to get this off my chest for many years."

The wounds in my heart always felt fresh whenever the accident was mentioned, and a wall automatically went up. But I figured this wasn't about me, and if there was something she needed to tell me, who was I to deny her that? I nodded, letting her know it was ok to go on.

"When Elizabeth died…" She paused, fixing her gaze to mine as she placed a palm over her chest. "I blamed you for that loss. For that awful pain a parent should never feel. In my heart, you were responsible for taking away my only child."

My pulse quickened, my heart aching with every beat. Although I always knew deep in my soul Grams blamed me for my mother's death, to hear her speak those words nearly tore me in half. I inhaled deeply, trying to keep myself from falling apart.

Noticing the sweat on my brow or the onset of tears, she reached over and grabbed my arm. "Who I was truly mad at wasn't you. It was myself. You see, what you and your mother had—that mother-daughter bond—was something I never had with her."

I couldn't hold back the tears anymore. "I'm so sorry,

Grams. I know the pain I caused you—the pain I caused our family—is irreparable."

Taking my hand in hers, she said, "No, don't cry, my child. Your mother didn't die because she loved you. She died loving you. She died doing what she did best. Being your mother. And that is something I should have celebrated, not resented."

"But you tried to stop her. If she'd listened to you—"

"If she'd listened to me? I knew how much she loved dance. It was the only thing that could truly make her happy. There's no doubt in my mind she would have moved mountains to see you reach the top."

Taking my hand from hers, I lowered my gaze and picked at my nails. "You said it. It's why I blame myself. Because I knew how important it was for her. I took advantage of her dedication to me. I took her for granted."

With her fingers, she lifted my chin. "You know, all she ever wanted as a little girl was to be a ballet dancer. And I never nurtured it. I extinguished it."

Peering into my grandmother's eyes, my heart stung remembering how my mother would lament about her mother's strict rules.

"I am a very practical woman, you see," she went on. "I didn't see much value in dance. Women, they are supposed to get married and raise a family, not waste time pursuing a dream that would never amount to anything. At least, I used to think so. And your mother was a people pleaser. She never wanted to disappoint me. She got married and had children, just like I told her. But when you were born, she did the exact opposite of what I did. I'd been cold and rigid. She was loving and fun."

"She was amazing," I said, nodding, and smiling, wiping tears as I thought back to the wonderful life I had being her daughter.

"The love you had for each other was the love I had secretly longed for all my life. I failed as a mother, Sara." Her eyes watered. The only other time I'd seen her so emotional was at my mother's funeral. "And I was jealous of you both. I've never told anyone. Been too ashamed to admit it. Seeing you in my home these last few weeks reminded me of my daughter, of the relationship I should have had with her all those years. Of all the time I wasted simply being a parent, instead of being her mother."

Reaching over, I took her into my arms. "Oh, Grams."

"I don't want to fail as a grandmother, too," she said, sobbing into my shoulder. "Perhaps you think it's too late for me now. I'm a seventy-nine-year-old lady who wasted my better years being a bitter woman." She pulled away, dabbing at her eyes. "But I'm tired of being alone. That house has been my home for almost sixty years. But all I'll be taking to the grave are the memories. And all I want now are new ones before I go. And I want them with you."

"What are you saying?" I asked, unblinking.

"If it's all right with you, I'd like to move to an assisted living community by you. In New York. Someplace I can be close. Where I can visit and be part of holidays, and bake cookies, and knit your future baby a blanket. All the things grandmothers are supposed to do."

My chest ballooned with so much emotion, it nearly burst. I reached over again and hugged her. "I would love to have you near me. I wasn't planning to leave you here by yourself, Grams. I was considering moving up here permanently if necessary."

"Nonsense, child," she said, pulling back. "Your home is New York City. That's where your dreams are."

"It's going to take time to sell the house, especially after what happened."

She smiled as if she had a secret up her sleeve. "That fellow of yours promised to take care of it. Said he'd have it sold in less than thirty days."

My eyebrows hiked up my forehead. "You've been talking to Tom?"

She grinned wider.

"Let me guess, he said it was the least he could do, right?"

"He did shoot a man in my house," she said with a wink.

"Grams!"

"Oh, sweetheart. Let the man do what he does best."

TOM PUT his top agents on my grandmother's home. Given what happened there, he said it wouldn't be an easy sell, but apparently, although small, there was a market for homes like hers, and he assured us his team would have it sold in thirty days, nonetheless. I had no doubts they'd get the job done. That also meant I had very little time to make all the arrangements for Grams' move to the city. I'd gone up to spend time with Tom in the hospital, but with all the craziness of looking for an assisted living program, selling most of her belongings, and not wanting to leave my grandmother alone, I'd not spent as much time as I would've liked with him.

In the days after the attack, the police shared some details of the investigation, and most of it wasn't good. Turned out the reason Tom had not been able to get in touch with Jake the day of the incident was because Jake never tried to deliver the money. He absconded— that's what the police told us. They found text messages between him and Vincent Dente, the man who tried to kill me. Jake needed the money and had orchestrated the whole thing thinking Tom would simply pay the million dollars. But the story didn't end there.

Everything started because of Tiffany. The video footage from Tom's office showed her delivering the first envelope. She'd tried to disguise herself, but the police were able to identify her. It was enough to draw a confession from her. Eager for some dirt on me, she went to Jake for help. Through his shady contacts, he put her in touch with Vincent. He took the job and gave her the pictures of me and Josh. After Tom learned of her part in the whole scheme, he had her fired.

During one of my visits to the hospital, Tom also told me how after he learned Jake had fallen off the face of the earth, he had his people check their business accounts. While not fully surprised, yet much to Tom's chagrin, he found out Jake had been embezzling money out of the company during Tom's absence. He owed the Moretti crime family a ton of money, and desperate to get out of the hole, instead of trying to pay it back, he figured he'd just run off to some other country, but first he needed enough cash to get out and be able to stay out. He was supposed to split the million dollars with Vincent, but Jake clearly fucked him over. He must have known Vincent would try to kill me if the money wasn't delivered. That sent an icy chill up my spine. He'd known and not cared.

That same night after finishing my conversation with Grams about selling her home and moving to New York, I was lying in my hotel bed reading a book when my phone rang.

"Hello?"

"Hey…" Tom said, his voice somber.

That wasn't him. Something was off. "What's the matter?" I asked.

"They found Jake. Dead."

I perked off my pillow as ice dripped down my back. I didn't like the guy, but he'd been Tom's friend. And as shitty a friend as he had been, I knew the news was tough for Tom. "Oh, my God. I'm so sorry."

"They… ah… found him in a ditch. Naked. Hogtied. Beaten to a pulp. Assholes finished him off with a bullet to his brain."

I gasped, a hand rising to my neck. "That's… awful. When did they find him?"

"This morning. Just got off the phone with Detective Smith. Coroner said he'd been dead for a few days."

"Heavens. I… I don't know what to say. I can't even imagine how hard this is for you."

"I warned him, you know," Tom said, blowing out an exasperated breath. "Told him he was gonna wind up in a ditch somewhere. If he'd just asked me for the money, there wouldn't have been a need for him to have you followed. I would have given it to him. I guess I never realized how deep he'd been in with the Moretti family."

"This wasn't your fault."

"I know. He betrayed me. He almost got you killed. I resent him for that. I can't help being angry and wishing he were alive so I could beat the shit out of him. Yet, a part of me can't help the sting in my heart, either. I've lost another brother, Sara." His voice trailed off, and I could only imagine the emotional toll Jake's death must have taken on him. Clearing his throat, he uttered, "I'm gonna need to head back to the city earlier than anticipated." His business-as-usual tone was an indication he was trying to mask the pain he was feeling. "I need to reach out to his mother. Help make funeral arrangements. Get a handle on things back at the office. Everything is a shitstorm back home."

"Did the doctor say it was ok for you to leave?"

"He was planning to discharge me in a couple of days. To a rehabilitation center. I'll be fine. I can do rehab back home."

"We haven't even had a chance to talk about us." I signed, long and hard. This was not how I'd envisioned our reconciliation. "Tom, how can we make this work when you're not even going to be here?"

"I know I fucked up, Sara. I know there's still so much we need to talk about. But I promise you we will make this work."

"Baby, I want to believe you, but after what happened, trusting you… It's not easy."

"And I deserve your doubt," he said. "But believe me, this time things will be different. I've learned from my mistakes. I'm going to get my shit together."

I hesitated on the phone. Him leaving right now was terrible timing. I'd forgiven him, but the memory of what he did, how he treated me, it still made my heart quiver. "I'm scared as hell about diving back into this relationship with you," I said, "without first talking through this, without figuring out a way to mend all the broken pieces. Now you're leaving, and I don't know when I'll be able to see you again, or when we'll be able to sit down and have a serious conversation."

There was a long and deep inhale from his end. "Sara, I know there's a lot of unfinished business between us. I want to talk about all of it. About Josh, about the baby, about my drinking problem, and—"

"Taking care of my grandmother's affairs is going to take me at least four weeks before I can return to New York. That's a long time to put this on hold."

"When it's time to talk about us, I want it to be about us, not about the investigation, or about Jake, or about your grandmother's move. In a month, hopefully, everything else will be settled, and we can move on with our lives."

"I'll be honest with you, I'm not thrilled about it. It sucks that you're leaving now, but I guess there's no other choice. You need to get your life back in order. And I need to stay here to take care of my grandmother."

"Sara, stop talking as if this is the end. Baby, I'm never leaving you. Ever. You get that? This is temporary. Once all this shit is over, you're stuck with me."

Believing in him was tough, but as difficult as it was, I chose to trust in him.

If there was anything I'd learned since meeting him was that love never came easy. But if we'd survived hell already, we could make it through another four weeks of torture.

With resignation, I agreed to give us more time.

Thirty-Six

SARA

"I THINK WE HAVE EVERYTHING, GRAMS," I said as I loaded up the last box into the trunk of my Jeep. As I closed the liftgate, I caught sight of Grams' snowy white hair. She stood in the driveway, her back to me as she faced her home. "Grams, everything okay?"

"Just saying goodbye."

I walked up beside her and took her hand in mine. "You're going to love Audra's Village. You'll be less than a ten-minute drive from me."

She looked at me and smiled. "I'm ready."

"Then let's get going," I said with excitement. "We have a four-hour drive ahead of us."

I should have been sadder to be leaving Cape Cod, but I didn't even look back. My head felt clearer, my heart lighter. For the first time since my mother's death, there was a sense of peace in my soul, like a massive weight had lifted off my body.

Reconnecting with my grandmother had soothed my grief like nothing ever had. It's as if having her back in my life had been a gift from my mother. There was this warm, tingly feeling in my core as if I knew my mom was watching us. I could feel her love wrapping itself around me, and it radiated through me like a brilliant light of happiness and hope.

As we drove down to New York City, and the skies began to darken, I peered into the ebony sea above us. Deep down in my heart, I knew my mom was not disappointed in me, that she was happy and living her dream. I imagined her up there, somewhere in the expanse, dancing amongst the infinite twinkly stars peppering the heavens.

I smiled. Yes, she was out there and here with me just the same.

And this new clarity also gave me a sense of direction—in love and in my career. In life. In everything. I knew now what I wanted to do with myself, and I had this invigorated drive to take charge of my future. I was going to be with Tom, and nothing was going to get in my way ever again. And I had a mission. I would make my mother's dream a reality and start a dance school. How or where, it didn't matter. But I would make it happen, and nothing filled me with more joy than to know one day other little girls and boys would live their dream because of her.

The excitement made me press harder on the gas pedal. I couldn't wait to be back in New York—to jump start this new journey.

DROPPING off Grams was harder than I'd imagined. Even though she was a quick ten-minute drive from my apartment, it felt awkward leaving her there. We'd grown so close in the last couple of months, a piece of my heart broke off when I said goodbye. Thankfully, as she was only a short drive away, we'd already made plans to get together in the coming weeks.

After parking my Jeep in the apartment's garage, I sat in

my car for a few minutes. The last time I'd been home had been during one of the darkest times in my life. I couldn't believe everything that happened since or how different I felt. This new me was someone I didn't recognize.

And I liked her.

I was not the same girl who walked out of there two months ago. Broken. Defeated. Dressed in shadows and carrying her cat. No. I'd healed and was now full of determination.

Holding Skiddles in her carrier, I exited my car and headed up to the fifth floor. As I jiggled my keys out of my hooded-sweater pocket, I heard shuffling inside the apartment as someone whispered, "I think she's here."

I shook my head and smiled. Of course, why wouldn't Jen throw me a surprise birthday party the Friday before my birthday? I was turning twenty-five that Monday, but was leaving for Paris on Sunday— Tom's birthday present to me—and had told her I only wanted something small. Knowing she'd one-hundred percent ignore my request, I should have worn something a little more appropriate for the occasion, instead of black yoga pants and a white hoodie.

Slowly peeling the door open, I frowned at the dark room as my body tensed, anticipating a big—

"SURPRISE!" a collection of voices shouted as the lights flashed on.

My eyes widened, and my smile grew bigger as I took in the sight. Dead center and flocked by a rainbow of balloons was Jen, wearing a cute Fall-themed skirt and sweater outfit. Her blonde curls were up in a messy-on-purpose bun. She looked stunning, and her blue eyes sparkled like stars as she opened her arms and rushed toward me to give me a hug. "Happy birthday!" she squealed with utter joy as she wrapped me in a warm embrace. "Welcome home, hon. I'm so happy to have you back!"

"I'm so happy to be back," I said, putting Skiddles down.

"You didn't have to throw me a party," I whispered in her ear as I wrapped my arms around her.

She pulled back and winked. "You should know me better."

I smiled and nodded, and as I took in the rest of the room, my heart jolted out of my chest. "Tom!" Without thinking, I ran to him and flung myself into his strong arms. He lifted me into his chest with ease, the feel of his muscles a reminder of the sculpted planes of his body. With a soft yet ardent kiss, he promised there would be more of those lips later. I couldn't wait.

Four weeks had felt like four years. Inhaling deeply, I relished in the scent of his heady cologne, my insides warming with desire. As happy as I was to be home celebrating my birthday, the only true thing I wanted was to be alone with Tom.

"Happy early birthday, Sara," he said, planting another gentle kiss on my lips.

Those lips were soft and warm, stoking a fire in my core. If my living room weren't full of people, we wouldn't make it to the bedroom. Needing to tame my feline, I pulled away from him. "You knew about the party and didn't tell me?" I playfully scolded, nudging his arm with my fist as he settled me down.

Shrugging and with a wolfish grin, he said, "Wouldn't have been a surprise if I told you. And Jen would've killed me."

I turned to look at her.

"Once you swear secrecy to me," she said, tracing a cross over her heart with a finger, "it's a blood oath."

"Wow. You two are now plotting against me?" I shook my head, amused, and worried. Tom and Jen together could be trouble.

"Plotting with your best interests in mind," Tom added, tugging a loose lock of my hair behind my ear.

Rolling my eyes, I exhaled, defeated. I'd never win with them. As I scanned the rest of the room, my breath stilled when I spotted the person standing a few feet behind Tom. "Martha?"

She grinned and waved at me, her mocha-colored skin glowing, her tight, dark curls cascading to her shoulders. "Happy birthday, girl."

I rushed to her. "Martha. Oh, my God. I'm so happy to see you." We hugged, and when I finally released her, she saw the unspoken question in my eyes.

"I'd been trying to reach you for a few days, but since your phone kept coming up as disconnected, I figured I'd try stopping by. Jen said you would be back home this weekend from your trip to Cape Cod and invited me to come celebrate your birthday."

"Is everything alright?"

With her gaze narrowed, she pulled me in closer, and whispered, "Girl, there's so much I need to tell you. Shit is going down at the company."

I gasped as I stared into her eyes. "Tell me everything."

Her impish smile twitched at the corners. She loved gossip like no one else I knew, but I had a feeling whatever news she had, it was more than just your daily buzz feed. This was serious. "Go. Finish saying hi to your guests," she said. "We'll talk later. After cake." Winking, she took a sip from her wine and gestured for me to keep making my rounds.

Standing a few steps away from Martha was Pedro. I smiled in surprise. Outside of his work uniform, he looked like a different man. "Pedro, how lovely of you to be here."

He patted at his short, dark hair and smiled nervously. "You've been missed, Ms. Hart."

I walked closer and gave him a sweet hug. "Please, call me Sara."

"Happy birthday, Ms. Sara." His cheeks reddened, and his eyes shied away.

Placing my hand on his arm, I said, "I'm happy to be back home."

He put his Corona bottle up in a cheers gesture, but as I didn't have a drink in my hand, I nodded my appreciation. Then, peering behind him, my eyes widened. I could not believe the sight. In the back of the room, hands in his jeans' pockets, and shoulders bunched in that signature pose, was Josh.

We made eye contact, and my skin chilled as if coated in a sheet of ice.

Shit.

Tom, Jen, and Josh were all in the same room. I'd not been ready to deal with this little package. I turned around, looking for Jen or Tom, but they were both in the kitchen fussing with the cake.

I turned back to find Josh walking toward me, his hands still in his pockets, and his face mushed into his also famous apologetic frown that asked for forgiveness before he even opened his mouth. My body tensed and my heart galloped hard against my chest.

"Fret not, Angel," Josh said with a smirk. "Your boy and I are good."

I tilted my head and scrunched my brow. "What exactly does that mean?"

"It means you have nothing to worry about."

Crossing my arms, I speared my gaze into his. "Explain."

He leaned in and gave me a light kiss on the cheek. "First, happy birthday. It's great to see you again."

The touch of his lips on my skin made my body go rigid. It felt weird being in the same room with him and Tom. Especially after our last encounter together. I didn't harbor any ill feelings toward Josh anymore, and under different circumstances, I would have been more welcoming, but I didn't know how Tom would react, and I was not prepared to do proper introductions between these two.

"Thanks, Josh. Now, spill it."

He smirked again. "Spunky as ever."

"Josh…" My jaw clenched, unamused.

Putting his palms up, he said, "Okay, okay. We got together earlier today. Spoke man to man."

"Today?"

"Jen called and said she was having a little something for your birthday. She thought it would be a good idea for me to stop by."

"In what universe would that be a good idea?"

He shrugged. "She's the one who invited me."

"So now you guys are friends?"

His blue eyes softened, a hint of disappointment flickering inside. "Just talking, that's all."

"That's all?"

He sighed, sticking his hands back in his pockets.

Realizing I'd made him uncomfortable, I said, "I'm just nervous about you and Tom being in the same room. We're working things out between us, and I don't want things getting messy. You being here…"

"Look, I understand. But, well, Jen suggested Tom and I meet before the party. Kinda get that awkwardness out of the way first. And we're cool."

Frowning, I asked, "You're cool? Just like that?"

"Spoke man to man."

"I don't know what the hell that's supposed to mean."

"It means we're cool," Tom said, wrapping his arms around my waist from behind, startling the beejeebies out of me.

Placing a hand over my racing heart, I leaned into his chest and blew out a breath. "You two have been talking?"

Tom and Josh shared a look I didn't quite understand, but it seemed to indicate that while they weren't about to go for beers together, they had agreed to be civil around each other.

And it was all I was going to get out of them.

Then, as if things couldn't get any more awkward…

Marko abruptly came out of Jen's bedroom door, his shaggy, brown hair still wet from a shower. "Did I miss anything?"

Everyone turned toward him and laughed. He smiled sheepishly, and when he noticed me, he hurried to greet me. "Sara, welcome home," he said with a kiss to my cheek. "Happy birthday."

As I said thank you, I noticed the look he and Josh exchanged. Theirs wasn't as friendly as the one Josh and Tom had shared, but it looked like at least for tonight, they had agreed to tolerate each other.

Yeah, Jen had a whole lot of explaining to do.

Then, as if on cue, she shouted, "Cake!" And everyone flocked to the dining area where she presented the round and obnoxiously bright pink cake.

Before blowing out the candles, I made one wish.

The universe better be listening.

Thirty-Seven

SARA

Pedro was the first to leave the party. Said he had to relieve Frank as the older man had only agreed to cover for a little bit while Pedro came up to spend some time with us. "I think he still has a crush on you," Jen said as I closed the front door and met her in the kitchen.

"That was sweet of him to come," I said, grabbing dirty dishes, and putting them in the dishwasher.

Jen took a plate from me. "Stop cleaning up. It's your birthday."

"Technically, it's not my birthday until Monday."

"Technically, it is your birthday weekend, so it counts."

Sighing in defeat, I put the rest of the plates on the counter and dried my hands, letting her continue to fill the dishwasher. "Fine, I won't clean up. But you owe me some explanations."

She turned to face me as she used her hip to close the machine. "I knew this was coming."

Leaning against the fridge, I said, "First, I want to thank you for putting this little birthday thing together. I know I told you I didn't want anything, but you managed to make this special without going over the top. Thank you."

She smiled as she tucked loose curls back into her bun. "It was going to be me, Marko, Tom, and you for an intimate dinner, but then I ran into Martha, and she said she had something big to tell you. Then Pedro got wind of things. And well, he drools every time he sees you, so I figured, why not?"

I hiked an eyebrow. "You figured?"

"You know me," she replied coolly.

That I did. "What about Josh?"

Wincing, she whispered, "Josh… is a bit more complicated."

"You think?" I drew nearer so no one could eavesdrop on our conversation. "What in heaven's name possessed you to put my ex-boyfriend and Tom in the same room? Not to mention, in the same room with Marko? By the look he shoved at Josh, I'm guessing he knows."

"He knows," she confessed, unapologetically.

"And?"

"And nothing," she said, turning toward the sink to wash the stemware that couldn't go in the dishwasher. "Look, Josh… he's my past, your past. For a time, I thought I had been living this lie, harboring a terrible secret, but now that everything is out in the light, things are different." She paused, a soapy, yellow sponge sitting in her hand as she turned to me. "I realized my feelings for Josh were skin deep. I thought I had betrayed our friendship by falling in love with him, but what I felt for him—that wasn't love. That was… It was…" Returning to her task, she began scrubbing a wine goblet. "I don't know what it was, but it wasn't what you need to form a relationship. Especially after everything I've lived through these past four years with Marko. Plus, you're my best friend." She pivoted her head in my direction. "Well, you're more like my sister. There was no way I would ever even consider dating your ex."

"And Marko was okay with you staying in touch with Josh, even after you told him what happened, why he came back?"

Placing the last goblet on the drying rack, she continued, "I wouldn't say he was okay with it, but it's not like Josh and I are talking every day, like we're suddenly best friends. He sends me a hello text occasionally, and I say hi back, but that's about it. He's leaving for California next week sometime. Who knows when he'll be back, so I figured this was an opportunity for you to say a proper goodbye."

"And Tom? How did he feel about seeing Josh?"

Untying her apron and placing it on the counter, she said, "Well, Tom already knew you and Josh never, you know, that there wasn't anything between you guys. Tom was more embarrassed than anything. I mean, given his behavior last time you were all in the same room and all. He actually wanted to apologize to Josh."

Cocking my head in surprise, I crossed my arms and leaned against the island. "Yeah?"

"Well, that's what he said. Deep inside I'm sure he still wants to punch his lights out. From what I've been able to see, Tom's freakishly territorial, not like he's a Neanderthal or anything, just saying. You know what I mean."

I chortled. "Yeah, don't I know it."

"Even if he knows Josh is not competition, I've seen the looks he's been giving him."

I nodded in agreement. "I noticed the look too, earlier. It's as if he's letting Josh know he's still alive because Tom wills it." I laughed, secretly enjoying how Tom was making Josh squirm.

"Be flattered, honey. That man would do anything for you. Seriously. Anything."

I smiled at her, my cheeks feeling warm. "So… you and Marko?"

"We're good," she said, leaning against the counter, her hands pulling at the hem of her sweater. "We've put the marriage talk on hold for now. He's going to wait for me to finish med school, and then we'll see what happens after."

I reached for her hand and gave her a light squeeze. "I'm happy for you, babe. Truly. You deserve all the happiness in the world."

"Thank you, hon. You, too. You're gonna see. This is going to be your year."

We hugged, her pomegranate scented perfume a reminder of why she was my comfort place. "I think so, too."

As we separated, Martha came into the kitchen, her coat and purse in hand. "Hey, ladies. Sorry for interrupting, but I wanted to say happy birthday again to my girl Sara before I leave."

"So soon?" I said.

She shrugged. "Yeah, I only have a sitter until nine."

"Aw, how's little Bella doing?"

"Good. Gonna be three this January."

"Wow, I can't believe it," I said, shaking my head. I could still remember when she was pregnant with her. "Time flies."

"Tell me about it. Anyway, I need to get going before I miss the train."

"Oh, shoot," I said placing a hand on her shoulder. "We didn't get to talk about the company."

"Girl, well, let me tell you real quick."

"Are you sure? I can call you a ride if you're worried about the train."

"It's okay. But listen," she whispered, closing the gap between us even tighter. "I'll give you the cliff notes. Right after you quit, Alexei disappeared for like four weeks. Guy just didn't show up for work. No one knew what happened, but clearly some shit went down. Rebecca lost it. I mean, she had to cancel all the sold-out shows."

My eyes widened, and my lips twitched, holding back a grin. Gloating was never appropriate, but I couldn't help it. "Can I be honest?"

She nodded.

"As much as I feel bad for the dancers, I do not feel bad for that witch."

"Girl, that's not even the worst of it. Rebecca had a full-blown breakdown. She had to be admitted."

I gasped. "What? You're kidding."

"Nope. Everyone was scrambling. No one knew if the place was going to close, if we would all be out of a job. The dancers started quitting. It was a shit show."

"Then what happened?"

"Asshole came back," she replied with a grunt. "We all thought Rebecca would have fired his ass after he stopped coming to work, but you know how it is. He's holding the strings in that place. Rumor has it the reason he'd been out was because he'd been in a brawl and got his face all messed up."

I looked away and pursed my lips, again trying not to smile. "For real?"

"Girl, his nose was all wrong," she replied waving a hand over her face. "Something definitely happened to him."

I simply shrugged, pretending this was all news to me.

"Look, I'm gonna be real with you," Martha said, giving me the eye. "We kinda all know why you left. Kassandra told us what happened the night at the studio. You should have called the cops on him."

I dropped the act and placed my hands on my hips. "For stealing my routine?"

"No, honey," she said, shifting on her feet. "For hurting you. Kassandra said she saw Alexei grab you by the arm and drag you to his office. Said she heard him say some awful things to you."

Looking away, I thought back to that night. "I didn't realize anyone heard."

"Honestly, Kassandra and that partner of hers should have done something. They just stood outside Alexei's door and let him demean you."

I looked back at her, a tinge of anger bubbling from inside at the memory of that day. "I handled myself. I didn't let him bully me."

"They should've done something. But I'll tell you one thing, whoever punched his face in, deserves a medal." She nodded toward the back of the room, where Tom and Marko stood by the window talking. "Was it him? Did that fine man of yours defend your honor?"

"Martha…"

"It's okay. Your secret is safe with me. But girl, that is some sexy-as-fuck chivalrous shit."

"That's an… interesting way to put it."

"Seriously, though. He deserved it. Unfortunately, it didn't put the fear of God in that motherfucker. Asshole went back to his old ways."

I puffed out a breath. "No."

"Started harassing the new girls. But he screwed with the wrong woman. Let me tell you what happened, honey. That Estella chick, she wasn't taking shit from nobody. Alexei demoted her from principal dancer. Gave the main role to one of the new girls. Well, before we knew it, the police were crashing through our doors and arresting the sonofabitch for sexual assault."

"What?"

"Yeah, she reported him to the authorities. After that, the accusations kept coming. More girls started coming forward with their stories. This asshole is going to jail. Hopefully for a long time. But we need your help to do that."

"What do you mean?"

"We need you to testify. To come forward with what happened to you. If you can corroborate Kassandra's account of what happened, it's more evidence against him."

This time, I didn't hold back my grin. "There is nothing that would give me more pleasure than to see that scumbag behind bars. Karma is a bitch. Count me in. I will happily recount my story. It's time we speak up."

Not long after Martha left, Josh came looking for me. He'd been sitting on the couch by himself the whole time, looking through his phone. Talking to Marko or Tom had been out of the question. I could only imagine how awkward and difficult it must have been to endure the party, but I gave him kudos for sticking around for as long as he did.

Donning his black leather jacket, he stood by the entrance and waited for me to join him.

"Josh, thank you for coming by. I know being here wasn't easy."

"Ah, don't mention it. Getting to spend one more birthday with you is worth a million death looks," he quipped.

"That bad, huh?" I grimaced, knowing Tom and Marko had been shooting daggers at Josh all night.

"Yeah, I think they are both plotting my death and the disposition of my body."

I laughed. "Stop it."

He reached over and took me into a strong embrace. At first, I was hesitant to return the hug, but I didn't know when I'd ever get to see him again, and I truly did not have any hard feelings. Not anymore. I wrapped my arms around him and sighed, finally letting go of my past.

"I don't care if he's watching," he said, somewhat protectively. "You were my girl first, and I will always have a special place in my heart for you."

Pulling away and gazing deep into his blue eyes, I said, "There will always be a special place in my heart for you, too. I wish you all the happiness in the world, Josh. I hope you find the love you deserve."

Brushing his knuckles over my cheek, he said, "I hope the universe hears you, Angel."

"What's next for you?" I asked, looking away and cutting the tether holding us together.

Josh ran a hand through his crown of blond curls. "I'm heading to Cali next week. Gonna stay with my sister for a bit, maybe find a job freelancing photography. Who knows? Maybe find that love you mentioned." He winked, his lips curling into a playful grin.

"Good. I have a feeling you will fit right in with them Californians. Tom has a house out there. Maybe we can meet up sometime."

"I'll always make time for you. Just keep your Tom Cat in a cage, though."

"Stop it," I said giggling. "Go on, get out of here before he hears you." I kissed him on the cheek as he waved goodbye to Jen and signaled he'd call her later.

She frowned and went back to pretending she was cleaning the counters. As I walked back inside toward the living room, Tom approached and met me halfway. "What did he say?"

"That he's shocked he's still breathing. With the way you two were looking at him."

"Not me," Marko announced from across the room."

"Both of you," I uttered pointedly. "You guys are truly something."

"Just making sure he knows you are off limits," Tom said, tugging at my ear.

I slapped his hand away. "He knows."

"Come here," he said, pulling me into a hug. "I've missed you."

"I've missed *you*," I replied, snaking my arms around his waist, and hooking my fingers into his jeans' back pockets.

"Can I have you all to myself now?" he asked.

"Definitely. What do you have in mind?"

Mischief twinkled in his eyes. "Well… I do have another surprise for you," he said cautiously, gauging my reaction.

Jen chuckled from the kitchen as she walked toward us. "Because a surprise getaway to Paris is apparently not enough," she mused in my ear as she pinched Tom's side when she passed by, winking at me as she trotted to the couch where Marko sat waiting for her to join him.

"You know about this?" I asked her, following her legs.

A shit-eating grin spread across her face as she plopped on the couch and slid under Marko's arm.

"Wow. You guys just keep plotting."

"C'mon," Tom urged as he threw a leather jacket over his gray cashmere sweater. "I'm anxious to show it to you."

My blood bubbled with curiosity. "What is it?"

"I can't tell you. You have to see it."

I groaned. "Well, where is it, then?"

"Downtown," he replied curtly, grabbing my purse, and handing it to me. "Let's go."

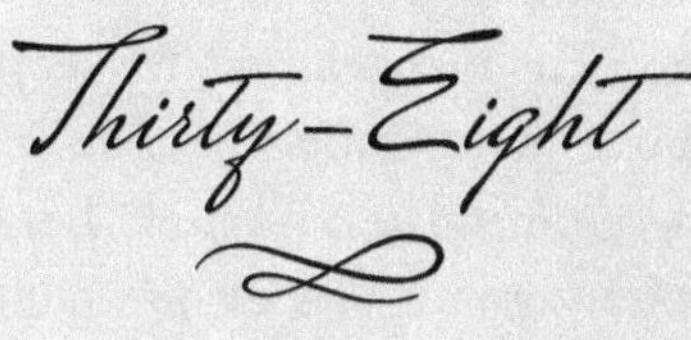

SARA

Without any traffic, Tom was able to drive us into Tribeca in about twenty minutes. He'd utterly refused to give me any clues about my new surprise.

"You're seriously not going to tell me?" I asked as he began to slow down near Church and Walker Street. Spotting The Roxy, I tried my luck again, "Are we spending the night at a fancy hotel or something?"

"You can keep asking all the questions you want, baby. I'm not telling you."

"This is quite infuriating, you know. I've been sitting in this seat for twenty minutes."

"Two more minutes, my antsy kitty-cat," he said as he parked the Rover on a side street.

"We're here?" Looking around, all I saw were a bunch of closed boutiques and a fancy coffee shop. "Where the heck is here anyway?" I asked softly, mostly to myself.

"You're not going to like this next part," Tom warned, "but it's all part of the surprise, okay?"

"Oh, geez. What now?"

He took a tie out from his jacket pocket.

"Wait," I said, sitting back in my seat. "We've not seen

each other for a whole month, barely had any time together since I got home, and already we're jumping into kinky sex?"

His face flattened. "No. But I guess kinky sex is off the table?"

I narrowed my gaze. Kinky sex was never off the table, but he knew that. He just wanted to keep teasing me. "I… didn't say that. I was just wondering. That's all."

"Well, keep wondering. Come here. Let me put this on."

With a sigh of resignation, I let him blindfold me.

"Okay, Sara. I'm gonna come open the passenger door." He helped me out, and a brisk fall breeze hit my face, sending a chill through my body. I still had no clue what was going on, but I finally gave in and let him guide me to my surprise. We walked a few paces before coming to a full stop as the sound of jiggling keys hit my ears followed by the creak of a wooden door.

We walked through a threshold, and I no longer felt the cold from outside. The door creaked closed, and I guessed we were now inside a building. With my sight temporarily gone, I found my other senses had slightly heightened. Every sound my feet made, even the sound of my breath, seemed louder.

"Where are we?" I asked, my voice echoing in the space. Clearly, wherever we were, the room was empty. "Can I take off the blindfold?"

"Not yet. Hold on." Tom let go of my hand and instructed me to stay in place.

"For the record, this is totally creeping me out," I said.

After about five long minutes, he finally said, "Okay, you can take off the blindfold."

As I pulled the tie from my eyes, I blinked several times, trying to adjust to the flickering lights of the multiple lanterns lit throughout the long and empty room. The space seemed industrial, with exposed ceilings, brick walls, and unfinished hardwood floors.

I brought a finger to my lips as I scanned my surroundings, trying to make sense of where we were. I spun in place until I stopped and looked at Tom. His face was unreadable amongst the shadows cast by the candle lights.

"Well? What do you think?" he asked.

I sighed, an apologetic frown creasing on my face. "Um… I don't know what it is. Where are we?"

Tom stepped closer and handed me a small key, a smile curving his lips. "We're in your future dance studio."

My heart halted, the gears in my brain coming to a full stop. Staring at the key resting in my palm, I stood still, too stunned to even breathe.

"I wanted to wait until it was finished," he uttered glee-fully, "but then I realized you'd want to design it with your own tastes, to make sure everything was done to your specifi-cations."

"You bought me a dance studio?" I interrupted, my voice a mere breath, my gaze still glued to the key. I'd barely heard anything he'd said. Incredulity wove through my body like a web.

"Sara, are you okay?" Tom asked, pulling my chin up with his fingers. "What is it? Don't you like it?"

The tears beaded at the corners of my eyes and rolled down my cheeks before I had a chance to staunch them.

"Oh, no. Why are you crying?"

But I couldn't utter a single word. The silent tears kept cascading down my face.

He dabbed at my eyes, trying to wipe the wetness away. "Happy tears, I hope?" he asked, his eyes pleading for a reply from me.

"Tom," I choked out. "I don't know what to say. This…" With the sleeve of my sweater, I wiped my face. "Heavens. This…" but I still couldn't manage to get the words out. What he'd done for me—giving me a dance studio, a place to start building my dream, my mother's dream—there weren't any words that could possibly express the overwhelming gratitude welling in my heart.

"You've been talking about wanting to start a dance school," he said, continuing to dab at my eyes. "About wanting to give kids an opportunity to fall in love with dance, to feel that joy you feel when you let the music take over your body. Baby, when I saw this place, I knew it was it. That this was your studio."

"Tom, how could I ever repay you?" I uttered, looking at the candlelight flickering in his eyes.

"Repay me?" Tom's face tensed. "No, baby. I'm the one making amends here. This studio is me asking for forgiveness." He lowered himself to the floor, the slight wince and grunt an indication his leg hadn't healed entirely yet. Tom sat back on his knees, ignoring his discomfort, hands resting at his sides.

My pulse quickened "Tom, you don't need to do this."

"But I do. For the last month I've done nothing but think back to the pain I caused you. What I did to you..." he paused, his chest heaving. "I can never forgive myself for the way I acted."

I rushed to him, getting down on my own knees.

"Sara," he said, wetness glistening in his eyes. "I should have been there for you. For our baby. I'm so sorry for not trusting in you, for leaving you in that lobby."

"You didn't know, Tom."

Red with sorrow, his eyes stilled over me. "You were in agony. And I left you bleeding. While you and the baby were dying."

"There was nothing you, or I, or anybody could have done to save the baby. It was an ectopic pregnancy."

"You almost died," he gritted, the ire seemingly directed at himself. "I should have been there. You shouldn't have gone through that alone. Sara, if you had died..." he bemoaned, his voice trailing off. "If you had died, I would have gone mad."

Taking his face in my palms, I anchored my gaze into his. "Losing the baby destroyed me. A part of me died that day, and it's a part I will never get back. I suffered alone, and the agony of it all drove me insane. Did I wish you'd been there? Tom, that longing was part of the pain I suffered. And I had to beg the heavens to rip you from my heart or I might not survive losing you as well. But no one heard my prayer. And you know why? Because you're fused with my soul. And after all that pain and all that despair, in the end, you came for me, and you saved me from that monster. You need to believe me when I tell you all is forgiven."

Tom lowered his gaze, his breath ragged.

Still holding onto his face, I pulled his gaze up. "Look at me."

He blinked slowly, and with wet lashes, he opened the windows to his soul. "I'm going to do everything I can to win your trust back."

"Tom, look around. You bought me a studio."

"This?" He gestured with his arms. "This doesn't even begin to patch up the massive crater I created. But I promise you I will. This past month I've had plenty of time to reflect on things. To look at my life and make some hard choices."

"What do you mean?"

"Well, for starters, I've been going to group. And I started seeing a doctor—for the nightmares. Haven't even needed the pills."

A breath of relief filled my lungs. I'd not breached the topic of his drinking problem or the nightmares, afraid to start off on a bad foot, but to hear he'd sought help. It was one of the best gifts he could have given me. "That's… incredible, Tom. I'm so happy."

"It's a start. The road to recovery is long, but for you…" Raising his hand to my chin, he said, "For you, I will do anything."

"You have to do it for yourself."

"I'm doing it for us."

"For us," I repeated, as I leaned in to kiss him.

"I love you," he breathed into my mouth as our tongues touched.

"I love you back," I echoed as the heat from his body radiated through me, making me hot with a desire I hadn't felt in a long while.

A very long while.

Perhaps it wasn't the most romantic setting or the most opportune moment, but maybe that's what made our kiss so perfect. All our love and all our pain came pouring through us in a wicked embrace. And as we voraciously feasted on our mouths, Tom lost his balance and fell backward onto the hardwood floor, taking me with him. I landed on top of his chest, my legs sprawled over his. We both laughed as his head hit hard against the floor and he let out a tiny yelp.

When we stopped laughing, he reached up and cupped the back of my neck with his palm, weaving his fingers through the hair hanging at my nape. We peered into each other's eyes as if searching for one specific star twinkling amongst the trillions of stars living in the galaxies. And when we found each other's light, our souls rejoiced.

"I need you," he said with eyes so feral, they made me shiver. His voice dropped to a rumbling sound that vibrated through my core, and it strummed the wire leading directly to the apex between my legs.

Drawing my lips down to his, he kissed me once more, and I moaned in pleasure, the sound rousing the beast sleeping inside him. His chest heaved and he bit my bottom lip before pulling away one more time and staring at me. His mouth parted as he took in every inch of my face. "You're so beautiful, Sara," he said as he rubbed the pad of his thumb over my lips. He slayed me every time he did that. It was a subtle gesture of possession, one of the most simple and intimate ways he let me know I was his.

And as his hunger for me grew, so did my longing for his touch. I closed my eyes and moaned, declaring my submission. I wanted him to take me, to make me his again and again. Crashing my mouth into his, I let him know I wanted no mercy. He obliged, devouring my mouth with every breath as if my taste was all he needed to live. My body became attuned to the hardness of his muscles as they flexed beneath me, as his hands began to roam over my clothes. I pressed into him, my hip rubbing against his massive erection. I gasped, remembering the pleasure of him entering me.

"Baby, I need you," I cried. "It's been too long."

"Here? You're sure?" he asked breathily.

"Fuck. I don't care. I just need you inside me. Please."

He growled, that raw beastly growl that drove me mad. "If you keep talking like that, I'm not going to last very long," he chuckled.

"Just get us naked," I demanded.

"I didn't bring any protection. Or a blanket."

"I went back on the pill. And screw the blanket. We're good."

He cocked his head and smirked. "Well, in that case…" Very unceremoniously, he flipped me over, the harshness of it making me hotter. He sat back on his heels as he pulled off his gray cashmere sweater, followed by a white undershirt. In the candlelit room, his muscled chest glimmered. He was still sculpted to perfection, but clearly more ripped from the recent rigorous workouts that were part of his physical therapy. But what truly caught my eye, was the newly inked tattoo fully covering his left pectoral muscle, intricately branching out over his shoulder and down the length of his left arm.

I sat up, enraptured by the beauty of the roses adorning his skin. "Tom, when did you get this," I asked as I leaned closer, placing my hand over his heart, and tracing the inked flowers scaling up his smooth chest and around his shoulder.

"A guy I know is a tattoo artist," he said. "After I got back from the Cape and was well enough to see him, I asked him to work on me. It's been several weeks of long appointments, but he finished it last week."

"It's stunning," I said, captivated by the detail and rich colors. "Why didn't you tell me?"

"I wanted you to see it first."

"All these roses… do they have a special meaning?"

Taking hold of my hand, he placed it over his heart and held it there. "The rose is considered a symbol of balance. Its beauty represents promise, hope, and new beginnings. It's everything you mean to me, Sara. Everything I want for us."

My gaze lingered over the artistry and loveliness of the inked design. "You did this for me?" I peered up into his eyes, touched at the intensity of his proclamation, yet fearful he might one day regret putting it on his body. "It's beautiful, Tom. But Tattoos…"

He gently placed a finger over my lips. "I know what it means. It's a long-term commitment. I told you, I'm not going anywhere."

My gaze drifted back to his shoulder and arm. Continuing to trace the design with my fingers, I said, "These thorns, they seem so dark and angry. They wrap tightly around your arm as if trying to strangle you."

"Thorns symbolize defense, loss, and thoughtlessness. They are there to remind me of my duty to protect you and guard you. And they are also there as a reminder of the loss we shared. I never want to forget the life you carried inside," he said softly, placing a palm over my belly. "And I never want to forget that my flaws and mistakes nearly destroyed us."

Awed and full of adoration, I stared at him in disbelief. He truly was everything I ever wanted in a man—everything I ever needed. While happiness seemed to always come at a cost, deep in my heart, I knew we'd already paid the ultimate price.

He leaned in for a kiss and slowly lowered me back down

to the floor, cocooning me with his frame. "I love you," he whispered as he pressed his body against mine, the heat of his arousal revving up my own hunger. Tom could read my signs so well, he didn't need me to utter a single word. He reached between us and slid his hand through the waistband of my yoga pants. I gasped the moment his fingers found me.

He moaned as he stroked me. "You're soaked through your panties."

I tried spreading my legs wider, but with my pants still on, and with him on top, maneuvering wasn't easy.

"Is this what you want?" he asked as he moved his hand inside my thong, his fingers gliding through my folds.

The tingles radiating from my groin and up through the rest of my body were bliss. "Yes," I hissed, moving my hips in tune to his fingers.

He lowered his mouth to my ears and jaw, nibbling on my skin while gliding his fingers through my slit. "Tell me how bad you want it, baby," he commanded, his breath hot against the throbbing veins in my neck.

"My clit is so swollen. I might go crazy if you don't make love to me right now."

I felt him smile as his lips parted in a grin.

He pulled off my sneakers, then rolled off my yoga pants and panties, leaving my naked ass flat against the cold hardwood floors. He then lifted my hoodie over my head followed by my t-shirt. Unclasping my braw, he released a small gasp as he took in my nakedness. "I've imagined this moment a million times over. The feel of your skin, the warmth of your body. Each time I wanted to take my time, kissing every inch, worshiping you like the goddess you are."

He lowered his mouth to my perked-up nipples and began to swirl his tongue over them until they were so hard they hurt. Arching my back, my body pleaded for more attention. "I love watching you get aroused," he said as he feathered kisses down my abdomen, each kiss bringing his mouth closer to my sex. "I've missed the taste of you, Sara. Sweet, salty. And all mine. Only. Mine." He annunciated those last two words with hard conviction.

He guided my thighs open with his hands, and then, using his fingers, he parted my folds. I inhaled sharply as his wet tongue brushed against my clit. "Fuck," I mewled, feeling heat rise to the surface of my skin, my whole body becoming inflamed.

"You like that?" he asked as he licked my slit in one slow and precise stroke up its length.

"Mm, yes."

The next stroke was harder and deeper, stopping at my clit for a fast flick before he brushed his tongue over my entire opening. My hips rose up from the floor, my body begging for more. "You want me to make you come?" he asked, his voice deep and throaty.

"Please. I need to."

Without hesitation, he inserted one finger, then two, and he began to pump hard against my sex as his tongue flicked at my clit. The electric waves rocking through my body could have incinerated me. I held my legs open as wide as I as could, wanting to give him all of me, needing him to take all of me.

And just as I was about to come, he took my clit between his lips and sucked. I burst into a mind-blowing orgasm that had my screams vibrating off the walls.

"I love watching you come," he said.

Panting, I simply looked up as he rose above me.

"Maybe I need to make you do it again," he said as he stood, his gorgeous chest rising and falling in deep breaths, his eyes drunk with lust as his heated stare made my insides quiver.

What woman wouldn't want to be gazed at like this? He made me feel incredibly female and desired.

Pushing to my feet, I stood on my tippy-toes as I reached

up to kiss him, and said, "I believe you're overdressed for this occasion."

"I was about to take off my jeans, but someone decided to stop and distract me." His lips twitched with bewitchment, and I playfully slapped his butt. Hard. He flinched and grunted out a laugh.

Reaching for his belt, I began to unbuckle his pants. "I'm the one distracted. I mean, have you seen these abs? This ass?" I asked, grabbing it through his pants.

"Are you groping me, Ms. Hart?"

"I most certainly am. This entire body belongs to me." Peering up into his eyes, I reached between his legs and grabbed his large cock. *Everything* belongs to me."

An erotic flicker danced in his eyes. "It's all yours, baby. But what do you plan to do with it?"

A feline smile pulled at the corners of my mouth. And without another word, I simply showed him. Very slowly, I dropped to my knees, lowering his jeans and briefs to his ankles on my way down, his cock springing free. I felt his body tighten as my hands began to scale up his muscled legs. Conscious of the scar on his right thigh, I trailed my fingers very lightly over the hard ridge of the scar, circling where the bullet entered through the back. "How's your leg?" I asked. "Will you be able to…?"

"Sara," he growled. "I'll be fine as long as you continue doing what you were doing."

Right.

I took a second to admire the beauty of his cock. Hard as steel, pink with blood, velvety soft, and hot to the touch. My mouth watered. Looking up at him, I grabbed him by the base and guided him through my lips. We both moaned as I wrapped them around his girth, driving him in and out of my mouth. His jaw slacked and his eyes kindled with a carnal fire so deep, he scorched me. Fisting a hand in my hair, he began to thrust, slow at first then hard and deep. I loved it when he became feral, when his male hunger possessed him to fuck my mouth like he couldn't get enough. Then, I saw it in his eyes, that moment when he was ready for more.

"Stand up," he commanded, his voice a deep rumble. Pulling out of his jeans and briefs, he grabbed me by the thighs and lifted me up as I wrapped my arms around his neck and my legs around his waist. If his leg hurt, he showed no signs of it. He backed me into the wall behind me and began to kiss my neck while the tip of his penis gently pressed against the opening between my thighs.

"You're so wet," he rasped against my skin. Holding me up by the thighs, he spread me wider, and asked, "Are you ready for me?"

I nodded, my body already drowned in erotic delirium.

He claimed my lips while he pushed through my walls, and I cried in ecstasy as he began to grind. "Feels so good to be inside you, baby."

I had no words. All I could do was hold on to his shoulders. Every muscle of his body flexed as he thrust into me. Sweat gleamed on his brow and chest. It trailed down his back as I held him closer. But he was relentless. He needed to consume me, to claim every inch of my body with his. And when I thought he was about to come, when his body went rigid, and his cock grew harder and bigger inside me, he stopped.

"Why are you stopping?" I objected with a groan.

"Because I want you to climax with me." Still holding on to me, he lowed himself to the floor in a sitting position, giving me the freedom to straddle him and control the pace. Without hesitation, I grabbed his dick and positioned myself over him then glided my center over his cock. It felt sublime as I buried him to the hilt. He raked my nipples with his teeth until my flesh felt hot and raw. Every inch of my body burned with delight as he grabbed my breasts and gently massaged them until they felt so heavy and full, I thought I might rip through my skin.

As I ground my hips around his pelvis, he reached down between my thighs and strummed my clit with his finger. That fiery tingle he'd enslaved me to spread from my groin to my legs and abdomen. "Keep touching me like that," I told him as I moved harder and faster over him. "Oh, fuck… yes. Just like that."

"Christ, Sara. Your clit is like a hard, little pearl. I love how your legs tremble when I rub it."

"I never want you to stop."

"Yeah? Look at me, Sara. I like seeing your face as I touch you."

I did as he asked, and when our eyes locked, the pleasure I was feeling down in my sex radiated throughout my entire body—my legs, my chest, even my scalp tingled. "Oh, Tom…" I moaned as I bit my bottom lip.

"That's it, you're almost there," he said with a feral smile, the hot coals in his eyes flaring with the heat of his passion.

I closed my lids, struggling to hold on to the pleasure any longer.

"Open those eyes," he commanded as his thumb circled my throbbing center. "I feel how badly you want to let go, baby. Hold it a bit longer."

"Tom, I can't."

"You can."

As I dug my nails into his flesh, he nodded, finally giving me permission to come. And with one final cry, I gave him all of me, my moans making him growl out my name as he reached his own orgasm, his muscles tightening as he filled me with his warmth. Our bodies trembled, our chests rising and falling. He reached for my neck, and bringing my lips to his, he hotly whispered, "I love you, Sara. More than you will ever know."

Thirty-Nine

SARA AND TOM

SARA

Located in the heart of Paris, across from the River Seine and the Eiffel Tower, the Shangri-La hotel greeted us with an elegant façade reminding me of the impressive architecture of the end of the nineteenth century. Tom mentioned this had been the home of Napoleon's grandnephew, Prince Roland Bonaparte, and from the moment we stepped out of our car, the staff made sure we felt like royalty.

When our personally assigned butler opened the door to our top floor suite, I fell into a spell. With its golden-rich drapes drawn back, the panoramic glass patio door—which ran the whole length of the suite— displayed one of the world's most famous landmarks. Barely able to breathe, I remained rooted by the entrance, stunned by the majesty of the Eifel Tower looming outside our private terrace. The unobstructed bird's eye view of the tower, the River Seine, and the city of Paris was unlike anything I had ever seen.

The suite itself was opulently decorated in a French-meets-Asian style, which offered a delightful art deco compilation of textures and colors of ecru, gold, and cream that adorned the large and luxurious accommodations. Unblinking, I continued to scan everything from the exquisitely paneled walls to the artistry of the furniture in the living-room and dining area made of natural wood and marquetry, to the teak and glass terrace, to the softly carpeted passageway leading to the master bedroom. This was a Parisian fairytale come to life. Quarters fit for a princess, not an ordinary girl like me.

"Mademoiselle," our young butler said, "are you all right? Is something not to your liking?"

His beautifully accented voice woke me from my mystified state. I blinked and smiled at him. "Everything is magnificent, Auguste."

He bowed his head, his short smile and twinkling eyes a sign he was satisfied with my reply.

Our luggage was brought up, and Auguste dedicated his time to showing us all the amenities, including the immense marble bathroom with double vanities, soaking tub, and a stand-in shower bigger than my bedroom back home. Tom and Auguste left me in the bedroom as they walked back out to the main living space. Overwhelmed by the lavish surroundings, I sauntered toward the king size bed and flung myself onto the featherlike mattress, laughing as I landed on my back, grinning so wide my face hurt.

"Are you enjoying yourself?" Tom asked as he walked back into our master bedroom. I flipped over on my side and my eyes feasted on the sight of him. Dressed in dark designer jeans, an open-at-the-collar fitted white button-down shirt, and his leather jacket, his body oozed of masculinity. Peering up at his face, my insides turned to mush. He'd shaven off the scruffy beard the day before, and now sporting a day-old stubble, he looked not only a bit rugged and sexy, but also dark and mysterious. Add his shimmery olive eyes and the golden brown mussed up hair…

Oh, yeah. The fantasy was complete.

"You know this is ridiculous, right?" I asked.

"What is?"

"This place!" I sprung up, sitting on my knees on top of the bed. "Have you looked around?" I said gesturing with my hands. "Have you seen outside?" I said pointing at the glass wall. "That's the Eifel Tower, literally right outside our room."

"I know. It's why I picked this hotel."

"This must have cost you a fortune."

He walked toward the bed until he was inches from where I sat on my knees by the edge. He gently grabbed my chin and lifted my gaze to his. Narrowing his eyes into a fiery smolder, he rubbed the pad of his thumb over my lips, and said, "You know this beautiful smile? The one that melts my heart every time I see your face?"

I nodded, enchanted by the rumble of his voice.

"I'd pay a king's ransom to see it every day."

Heat spread from where he touched my lips to the rest of my face. "Will it always be like this?"

"What?" he asked.

"The way you look at me. The things you say. Like I'm the only woman you'll ever love."

His lips twitched at the corners as he bent down to kiss me. "Always, baby."

"Mm," I moaned into his mouth. "Your lips are so yummy."

"Keep moaning like that and I may have to rip that blouse and jeans off you."

"I'm okay with that," I replied with a smirk.

"Hmm. I thought you said you wanted to see Paris. I have your printed itinerary right here in my back pocket." He pulled out the piece of paper I had shared with him of all the places I wanted to see. "First stop, the Eifel Tower."

"It's literally right outside our terrace. So, check."

"Notre-Dame, Sacré-Cœur, Arc de Triomphe…"

"Did I say I wanted to see all those today?"

He chortled. "You booked us pretty much until dinner."

"What time is dinner?"

"I made reservations for seven."

"And where exactly are you taking me for my birthday dinner?

"That's a surprise."

"Can I have a clue?"

"Your clue is in the closet."

"The closet?" Heart fluttering, I leapt off the bed and ran to the double doors of our walk-in closet. As I flung them open, a rush of adrenaline flooded my veins. About twenty designer dresses hung on the racks lining the inner walls. I gasped. Sitting on two rows of shelves were an equal of amount of strappy, sparkly, mile-high shoes. I continued to gasp as I walked inside and ran my fingers over them, fascinated at the textures and colors.

"I take it you approve?" Tom asked.

I whirled around, still reeling with elation. Tom stood by the entrance of the closet, leaning his shoulder against the frame.

"You're insane," I said, laughing. "This is… unfreaking-believable. Thank you. But why so many?"

"I couldn't decide on one, so I had them bring an assortment. Seems they did a great job."

"Whoever *they* are did an amazing job. These dresses are out of this world. I mean, where the heck are you taking me for dinner, the king's palace?"

He smirked.

My breath caught in my chest as my eyes widened. "Shut. Up."

He walked deeper into the closet and gently took my face in his palms. "And this, this brilliant smile of yours, this innocent childlike joy flashing in your eyes, this… is why I love you so much. Why I'd do anything. Why I'd give anything to make you happy, Sara."

"Tom, all this. The trip, the hotel, the dresses… this is not why I love you."

"I know material things are not important to you, that you don't care about all the money, but why shouldn't I lavish you and make this trip feel like a dream when you mean the world to me."

"Well, when you put it that way…" I turned around and gazed at all the beautiful gowns. "Baby, you can lavish me all you want." Bursting into laughter, I twirled in the middle of the closet, giddy and unable to contain my delight.

TOM

We spent the rest of the morning in the hotel room. After trying on all her gown and shoe combinations, she changed into a pair of ridiculously pink pajama bottoms and a white tank top. She looked adorable parading around the suite in comfortable PJs and her hair up in a bun. Her laid-back attire and quirky personality was a refreshing contrast to the over the top extravagance of the hotel. I was in awe of her, but as happy as I was, a deep pang of regret settled in my chest. Regret for how I'd treated her, for having doubted her, for having been such an asshole and almost losing her.

Having Sara back in my life was a gift I planned to treasure forever. I would spend my life making up for my mistakes and making sure she would never regret taking me back.

Around noon, Auguste brought us a French and Asian inspired lunch spread. Although it was October and the temperature a little cool, it was a beautiful sunny day, not a cloud in the sky, and with the outside heaters on, we were able to enjoy our lunch out on the terrace. With the Eifel tower and the River Seine as our backdrop, the afternoon couldn't have been more perfect.

"This avocado salad is killer," she said, taking a mouthful. "It's got little chunks of mango, pineapple, and papaya mixed in there." She savored every morsel as if she hadn't eaten in days. "How's your poached egg?" she asked.

I speared another bite and shoveled it into my mouth. "It's good. But judging from the orgasmic look on your face, not nearly as good as your avocado salad."

She offered me a bite, and the sweet citrusy flavors exploded in my mouth.

"Definitely better than my poached egg."

Sara was silent as she ate her main dish, which was unusual for her typical bubbly self.

"Is the shrimp Pad Thai not great?" I asked.

Snapping her gaze up from her plate, she smiled and said, "Oh, no. This is delicious."

"Why so quiet, then?"

"Look around, Tom," she said. "We're eating out on our own private terrace overlooking *that*," she pointed to the Eifel Tower. "How many people get to experience this? I guess, what I'm trying to say is, I'm extremely grateful for everything you've done to make my birthday memorable. I don't think thank you can begin to even cover it."

Taking a bite of my seared scallop and washing it down with a gulp of water, I smiled and said, "You're more than welcome, baby. Enjoy it."

After lunch, stuffed from all the delicious food and tired from the jetlag, we decided to skip all the site seeing and take a nap. I stayed awake for a while, holding her in my arms, enjoying the sound of her breath, the smell of her hair, the warmth of her body nestled into mine. My heart began to beat fast as I thought about how perfect we fit together, how I never wanted to be with anyone else but her. I had one more surprise for her tonight—the biggest and most important of them all. Thinking about her reaction and her reply had my nervous system going haywire. Closing my eyes and taking a few deep breaths, I calmed the nerves and eventually—ages later—faded to sleep.

Around five-thirty, I awoke to an empty bed. The skies had darkened and the only light in the room came from the tower's lights illuminating the penthouse through the wall of windows running the length of the suite. Still a bit dazed, I rolled out of bed, rubbing my eyes, and trying to shake the sleep off my shoulders.

The sound of running water caught my attention. I knocked on the bathroom door, but when Sara didn't answer, I cracked the door open and smiled the instant I caught sight of her in the shower. Standing behind the steamed-up glass, her naked silhouette was paralyzing. My body instantly shook off the remaining sleepy haze. I began to undress and was about to pull down my boxers when the water shut off.

She yelped the second she saw me. "Geez, Tom! You scared me."

Approaching the stall, and eyeing her wet body up and down, I asked, "Don't tell me you're done with your shower."

"Stop it with those eyes, Mister," she said smirking. "We have dinner reservations at seven, remember? I don't want to miss my birthday dinner. Especially if you're taking me to the king's palace."

"What makes you so sure that's where I'm taking you?"

"I'm not, but guessing from the dress you picked for me, it is definitely someplace uberly fancy schmancy."

"Still using that made up term, huh?"

She huffed in defiance. "It's a real term."

I couldn't hold back the snort that escaped from me. "Anything you say."

She walked out of the stall, strutting her naked body before my lustful eyes. "Your freshly pressed tuxedo arrived, by the way," she said, draping a towel over her delicious skin.

"Yeah?"

"Auguste delivered it earlier."

"Can you lay it out for me?"

"Your James Bond get up?" she asked looking over her shoulder, an amused look simmering in her eyes.

"Is the tux overkill?"

Her lips pulled at the corners in a wolfish smile. "No baby, it's sexy as fuck."

Shit, she'd just used a move out of my own playbook. With that, she left me in the bathroom, needing a cold ass shower.

A few minutes later, with a towel wrapped around my waist, I walked out into the bedroom to fetch my electric razor out of my toiletry bag when I heard a song pipe through the area speakers. Sara was out in the living room, messing with the sound system. She'd taken my phone and had apparently found my ultra-secret playlist. I laughed to myself. Well, apparently not so secret if she was able to find it.

Her beautiful emerald gown lay next to my tuxedo on the bed. I chuckled, remembering her James Bond comment. We would be undoubtedly dressed to kill. Walking back to the bathroom, I rushed to shave and get ready, all while listening to the series of songs which saw me through the start of my recovery and my fresh start with the woman who would soon become my…

I paused and stared at the man in the mirror. Would she say yes? Did I even deserve her? Was this the right time or would asking her now scare her away? I didn't know, and the prospect she could say no frightened the shit out of me. A cold sweat ran down the middle of my back, and I had to crack my neck to help alleviate the tension. I was ready to lay it all out on the line for her. To offer her my name. To pledge my heart and soul to her. To give her my life. To be her everything.

After applying aftershave, brushing my teeth, and making sure my hair looked presentable, I exited back out into the bedroom. Sara was still nowhere to be found, and her gown was still sprawled on the bed next to my tux. Noting the time, I hurried and dressed. Suit fit like a glove. Checking myself over in the mirror one last time, I wiped the sweat off my brow, adjusted my bow tie, and buttoned my jacket.

Show time.

My heart began to beat a mile a minute as I reached into my leather duffle. Tucked inside was the promise I planned to make. I peeked inside the small black box one last time before tucking it into the inside pocket of my tuxedo jacket. As if on cue, a new song began to play. This one was a throwback to when I first met her. It was the song she'd dance to when I found her dancing with Alexei. While that incident had turned into one of our uglier fights, she'd looked magnificent, nonetheless. But the reason the song had made it into my ultra-secret playlist was because I'd broken my promise.

And now I wanted to make sure I'd never forget that promise ever again.

Walking out to the common area, hoping to find her so I could tell her to hurry her fine ass up and get ready, I turned to stone when my eyes found her out on the terrace.

Dancing.

What she was born to do.

What her body was *meant* to do.

She'd turned off the lights and had lit all the lanterns out on the terrace instead, leaving the rest of the suite covered in shadows. The luminance coming from the tower made the scene surreal. Barefoot and dressed in a white nightie, she glided across the terrace, leaping and twirling. My heart grew heavy. Seeing her out there, encased in her element—pouring her soul out in a way unique to her—made me realize how deeply in love I truly was with this woman.

My head spun, dizzy from the overwhelming rush of adrenaline.

In that instant, I knew the moment was right.

As the song neared its end, I stepped out onto the deck.

She was in another universe and didn't even see me standing there, awed. When she finally stopped spinning, she faced me, her eyes slowly opening, her lips tracing a small gentle smile.

Satisfaction. Peace. Fulfillment. It all reflected on her face.

Panting, she placed a hand over her heart. "Oh, my. I'm so sorry. I didn't see you there."

"No apologies needed. I thoroughly enjoyed it."

"How long were you watching me?"

"Long enough to know you're the most beautiful dancer I've ever seen."

She laughed. "I'm sure you're just saying that."

"I'm not."

She blushed. The bashful look in her eyes and her reddened cheeks were my undoing.

Tucking loose hair behind her ears, she said, "Thank you."

"I meant it."

Compliments made her uncomfortable, and she shifted on her feet, unable to meet my eyes. I drew nearer and took her into my arms as a new song began to play. It chimed in the background as we swayed in rhythm to the music.

She finally looked up at me. "I didn't realize how long I'd been out here. Once I heard the music, *those* songs…"

"You found my ultra-secret playlist."

She shrugged. "Well, with that title, who wouldn't want to play it?"

As we continued to dance, I peered down into her deep chocolate eyes and saw my life reflected in them. I knew deep in my soul I couldn't wait any longer. "I want to always remember you like this," I said.

"Like how?"

I briefly closed my eyes before gazing at her and saying all the words jammed inside my head for the last month. "Sara, ever since I first saw your face… when you spilled your coffee, and your eyes met mine, I knew in that instant you were going to be in my life forever. Don't ask me how, but I knew I already loved you." Taking her hand and placing it over my heart, I continued, "I just never guessed how much."

Her eyes began to shimmer, but she remained quiet.

"You are the best thing to ever happen to me. You know that?" I asked, my voice trembling as I placed my forehead against hers, not expecting an answer, simply wanting her to know I knew how lucky I was. "I can't imagine my life without you, baby. You are everything to me, and I want to spend the rest of my life being everything to you, too." Gently pulling away from her, I lowered myself to one knee.

She gasped, bringing her hands to her mouth, the hint of tears I'd seen shining in her eyes earlier began to bubble at the corner of her eyes. "Tom…" she cried softly.

Taking the black box from my pocket, and presenting her with the diamond ring inside, I said, "Sara Angelina Hart, I've loved you since before time began and will love you long after the stars have fallen. Will you honor me and be my wife?"

SARA

We were on a terrace overlooking the River Seine and the Eifel Tower. And he was in a tailored tuxedo, on bended knee, holding a box with a diamond ring shinning more brilliantly than the stars above. It was a dream. It had to be. My body trembled, not sure if from the cold night air or from the electric wave running up and down my spine, but I could not stop my bones from rattling. But it was real. I heard it in his emotional voice, in the tender words he'd spoken to me. I felt it in his embrace, the kind that wrapped me in delicious warmth and made me feel like I was in the safest place I could ever be.

The second he looked at me with eyes so full of longing, I knew he was going to propose.

Yet, I stood cemented to the floor, unable to speak, unable to conjure a coherent thought.

Then the tears began, and I lost it. My chest literally hurt from the onslaught of happiness and joy welling inside me. I sobbed. And I laughed. And every single muscle in my body screamed with desire to break into a number—the final number—because this was the end. This was the culmination of all the heartache and sorrow. This was the universe telling me there was more to life than pain and regret. That all my tears had not been in vain. That all along what she'd had in store for me had been bigger and grander and more beautiful than anything I could have ever imagined.

I looked at my lion as he offered me forever, and I knew all of this had to be true. I'd known from the moment my eyes froze over his. From the instant his breath brushed my skin. From the second his lips kissed mine. It had always been him. And now it would always be us.

I nodded yes to his question. Emphatically. Laughing and crying, my body rippling with euphoria.

He raised a brow. "Is… that a *yes*?" he asked with caution.

Bouncing on the balls of my feet, and finally releasing the burning excitement I'd trapped inside, I said, "Yes. Yes. Yes. A million times yes!"

He grinned, his megawatt smile obliterating the world around us. He pulled the ring out of the box and asked for my hand, "May I?"

Trembling, I extend it out to him as he slid the solitaire onto my finger. He stood up, and still holding my hand in his, kissed me. "You just made me the happiest man on the planet."

"And you just made me the happiest woman in the universe."

Neither one of us could stop smiling.

"Well?" he asked. "Do you like it?"

Extending my fingers and marveling at the way my hand looked wearing the engagement ring, I said, "II..." But I couldn't find the words that could capture the classic beauty of the ring. Sitting on a platinum band encrusted with diamonds, the large oval solitaire was stunningly brilliant. It gleamed, capturing the city lights from every angle in a prism of sparkles. "Tom, it's so gorgeous, I don't know what to say. It's more beautiful than anything I could have dreamed."

"Jen helped me with the design. I wanted to make sure it was perfect, that—"

I gasped. "Wait. Jen knew you were going to propose?"

He sighed with relief. "That means she kept her promise."

"That little witch," I bristled with fake anger. "I can't believe she was able to keep this secret."

Chuckling, Tom said, "She takes her blood oaths seriously."

"I can't believe you two. Bunch of schemers," I playfully chided, winking at him.

He shrugged, unapologetically. "We try."

I shook my head and continued to stare at my hand. Could this be happening? Was I really engaged to Tom?

To the only man I would truly one million percent ever love?

I ran to the edge of the terrace and taking a full breath of air, I screamed at the top of lungs so the whole city of Paris could hear, "I'm going to marry Mr. Thomas Alexander Wright! Woo-hoo!"

Tom cackled as he joined me, cocooning me with his body as he rested his hands on the glass railing. As we stared out at the shimmering river and glittering tower, I nestled my back closer into him, letting his warm body shield me from the cool wind blowing widely around us. "I love seeing you this happy," he said.

"This has been the best birthday ever," I replied, my voice calm and content.

Wrapping his arms around me and kissing the spot right below my right earlobe, he said, "We need to properly celebrate. I'll call down to the concierge desk and will have them bring up a bottle of their best champagne. And some sparkling juice for me."

I whirled around to face him. "Hold up. What about our dinner reservations?"

"Dinner was at seven." He looked at his watch. "By the time we get there… I doubt they'll serve us."

"Where were you taking me?"

With an air of disappointment, he uttered, "Guy Savoy."

I blinked. "Guy Savoy? Are you kidding me?

"I'm so sorry."

My heart sank. Who wouldn't love dinner at a top celebrity restaurant in Paris? Truth was, as disappointed as I was, we wouldn't make it, nothing could cloud the utter joy radiating from me. I had just gotten engaged in front of the Eifel tower to the man of my dreams. Screw the fancy dinner. Room service was fine too.

Suddenly, there was a knock at the door.

"Are we expecting someone?" I asked.

Tom looked as puzzled as I was. "Let's go see."

When we opened the door, my eyes widened. Auguste stood at the entrance holding a large bouquet of helium-filled birthday balloons while also wheeling a catering table with a birthday cake sitting on top and a sparkling bottle of juice.

"For the record," Tom said, before I even uttered a single word. "I had nothing to do with this."

If it hadn't been Tom, I had a pretty good idea who was behind all this. Auguste handed me a card as we invited him in. He bid us goodnight and left.

Opening the card, I realized my suspicions were correct.

To my best friend in the whole wide world on one of the happiest days of her life.

Happy Birthday and Congratulations on your engagement. (Yes, I already knew and I'm not sorry for keeping this a secret. I wanted it to be as magical and special as Tom had planned. You can kill me when you get back home).

Honey, you deserve all the happiness in the world and then some. I'm so excited for you, and I can't wait to help you plan your wedding, and pick out a dress, and go venue shopping. All the things we grew up dreaming about. (Wait, you did say yes, right?)

Anyway… Now, go have yummy cake, drink some of that not-so-yummy non-alcoholic champagne (you're welcome, Tom) and then go have the best birthday/engagement sex of your life!

Hugs and Kisses,

Jen

I was going to kill them both for making me cry so much today. I shook my head, and wiped my happy, soggy eyes. Tom's breath sent a shiver down my back. I'd been so focused on her note, I didn't realize he'd been standing behind me the whole time, reading over my shoulder.

"I think we should listen to her," he whispered near my ear, his breath tickling my neck.

"This cake does look yummy."

"I was referring to the last line of her note," he uttered, his voice dropping an octave, his hands gently climbing up my arms. He pulled my loose hair to the side, and as he feathered his lips across the back of my naked neck, he said, "I've been craving you since we walked off the plane today."

Dear heavens. He was aroused and the rumbling sound in his chest made me wet just thinking about his hard body pushing against mine.

"I've thought of nothing else but making love to you," he said, nipping at the spaghetti straps of my nightie.

"As your fiancée?" I said.

"As my future wife." He turned me around and arrowed

his gaze into mine. There it was, the flame I knew would always burn for me. He picked me up in his arms and carried me to our room where he kissed me as he laid me down on the bed.

Hi lips claimed me as his before he even took me. And we made love. All night. The stars and the moon and the sparkling silver lights of the Eifel Tower looming outside our bedroom window.

Forty

SARA

Several months later...

The morning air carried the scent of pine and fresh water as I stepped onto the back porch of Tom's childhood home. My floral robe billowed in the gentle breeze, the lake stretching out before me, smooth as glass, reflecting the sky in soft pastel hues. A few birds skimmed the surface, their calls echoing through the towering trees that framed the property. The house itself stood behind me like a guardian of memories, the place that had shaped the man I was about to marry.

The day of James' and Penny's wedding, I'd known that if Tom and I ever got married, I wanted it to be here, too. Tom and I couldn't have been more thrilled when Adeline offered to host our intimate affair. Now, I couldn't believe the moment had finally arrived.

The backyard had been transformed overnight into a vision straight out of a dream. Lanterns hung from the boughs of the trees, their glass catching the early sunlight, waiting to glow like fireflies once the evening set in. Wild-flowers and roses wove through the wooden trellises, their petals spilling over in cascades of white and blush pink. The scent of peonies and lavender mingled with the fresh lake air, creating an intoxicating blend that made my heart flutter.

Everything looked perfect.

Tom had stayed at his brother's place overnight, and anxiety bubbled up inside me at the anticipation of seeing him later. I'd fought the urge to text him. We'd promised ourselves to go dark until the ceremony, but the need to talk to him was driving me nuts.

Inside, Jen, my sister Megan—who had flown in the night before—Penny, and Martha were in the living room getting ready, their bridesmaid dresses crisply ironed and laid out for them to get dressed once the makeup artist was done.

"Sara!" Jen called out from the porch door. "It's your turn to get ready."

My heart drummed as I met her gaze. Seeing the nervousness in my eyes, she came outside onto the porch and took me into her arms. "This is going to be the most beautiful wedding ever, and you're going to be the most beautiful bride."

"I'm sweating like a hog," I told her, squeezing her tight.

"It is the middle of July. Who told you to get married in the summer?"

I yanked on one of her curls. "You're lucky I love you."

"Look around, Sara. This place couldn't look more perfect if you tried. Now, let's go. You have a man to marry!"

Loads of makeup and hairspray later, I stood in front of the tall antique mirror that had been hidden in the garage but that Adeline had refinished for the event. I smoothed my hands over my dress, taking in the delicate lace, the way it hugged my figure before flowing into a soft, ethereal train. I'd decided to forgo a veil and instead adorned my hair delicately with pink flowers. I smiled at my reflection.

"You're glowing, Sis," Megan said, her own eyes shimmering.

I let out a breathy laugh. "I feel like I might float away."

Jen, adjusting a flower in my hair, grinned. "You're about to marry the man of your dreams, Sara. It's okay if your feet don't touch the ground today."

One of the event staff hurried over. "Showtime!"

Jen and Megan walked ahead of me, their soft dresses blending seamlessly with the wildflower arrangements lining the aisle. The wooden chairs were draped in soft linen, their backs adorned with sprigs of baby's breath and lavender. The guests—all our closest friends and family—rose as I stepped onto the aisle. My heart pounded, my breath catching as I lifted my gaze and found Tom waiting for me.

He was breathtaking. Dressed in a tailored navy suit, his golden-brown hair just slightly tousled by the lake breeze, he watched me with an intensity that made my chest tighten. His green eyes held a softness I had only ever seen when he looked at me, and in that moment, I knew—without a shadow of a doubt—that this was where I was meant to be.

James stood beside him as best man, his expression joyful as ever. Tom's mother, Adeline, sat in the front row, dabbing at her eyes with a handkerchief. My heart ached for all the years Tom had spent away from them, but today, he was home. *He* was exactly where he was meant to be.

I walked toward him, each step bringing me closer to the life we planned to build together, to the love that had weathered every storm. When I reached him, he took my hands in his, squeezing them gently as if grounding himself in me.

"You're stunning," he whispered, his voice barely above a breath.

My lips trembled into a smile. "You're not so bad yourself."

When the time to say our vows finally arrived, my body couldn't stop shaking as Tom pulled out a piece of paper from inside his suit jacket. His voice was steady, his words laced with emotion. "Sara, from the moment I met you, my world shifted. You are my anchor, my safe place, my greatest adventure. Today, in front of the people we love, I promise to be your partner, your protector, and your best friend. I vow to love you through every high and every low, to laugh with you, to dream with you, and to always remind you how deeply you are cherished."

Tears threatened my vision as Jen handed me my vows. "Tom, you are my home. The place I never knew I needed, the love I never thought I'd find. You see me, truly see me, and love me for all that I am. Today, I vow to stand beside you, to support your dreams as if they were my own, to hold you through every storm, and to love you more with every passing day."

"You may kiss your bride," the officiant announced after we exchanged rings, and before I could take another breath, Tom's hands were on my waist, pulling me into him. His lips found mine, and as our guests erupted into cheers, the world around us melted away.

That evening, the lanterns glowed like tiny stars strung between the trees, their golden light casting a dreamy haze over the reception. We dined under the open sky, long wooden tables adorned with garlands of ivy and flickering candles. Music filled the air, and laughter spilled across the lawn as James twirled Penny in a dance, as Jen clinked glasses with Marko, as Megan laughed with another male guest.

Then, the opening notes of Tyrone Wells' Arms Around Me floated through the speakers. Tom turned to me, a knowing smile playing at his lips. "Dance with me, Mrs. Wright?"

I giggled, slipping my hand into his. "I thought you'd never ask."

He pulled me into his arms, our bodies moving as if we had danced this way for a lifetime. The world faded, leaving only us, wrapped in the warmth of our love. His lips brushed my ear. "Happy?"

I tilted my head up to him, love swelling in my chest. "Beyond."

He grinned, dipping me backward into a slow, deep kiss. "Good. Because this is just the beginning."

Forty-One

SARA

One Year Later

As I sat on the Santa Monica white sandy beach, sipping my now-warm French vanilla iced latte, I allowed the waves to lap at my feet. It was July, and the late afternoon sun was still exceptionally warm, but I reveled in the coolness of the ocean. Wiggling my toes, my hot pink nail polish gleamed under the water.

I'd plopped my beach chair at the edge of the water in the back of Tom's beach house—well, our beach house now—hours ago and hadn't moved since, unable to put down KG Fletcher's latest release. She'd been my favorite romance author for years, and I hadn't been able to stop swooning over my new book-boyfriend.

I placed the finished paperback against my chest and sighed with delight. *Happily-Ever-After satisfaction achieved.*

The salty breeze whipped through my hair and the briny scent of the sea filled me with peace.

Closing my eyes, I took in another deep breath. Ah, yes. *This.*

This moment right here—sitting on the sand, in the back of the beach house where Tom first confessed not only his darkest demons, but also his love for me—reminded me that every day, I experienced my very own happily ever after.

We lived in New York City but had come to the Santa Monica beach house for a much-needed mini getaway, but also to celebrate our anniversary. Tomorrow, Tom and I would be married for a year. I could honestly say it had been the best year of my entire life. Mr. Iced Double—what I'd dubbed him when we first met—was the epitome of masculine perfection, and he'd spent every second of every minute since we'd said 'I Do' worshipping me. Adoring me. Making sure he made me the happiest woman alive.

Sure, every marriage has its ups and downs, and our road to happiness was certainly paved with a hearty dose of twists and turns, but our love had surpassed all of that. And now, I couldn't wait to get started on the next leg of our journey as husband and wife.

Ever since he'd gifted me the dance studio in Soho, making my dream of giving others the gift of dance, the place had been filled with little girls and boys dreaming of becoming principal dancers one day.

And I couldn't deny that shortly after getting married, and after several months of teaching at the studio, a new desire began to kindle inside my heart—the desire of motherhood. Seeing all those little smiling faces made me want to start a family with Tom. We'd agreed to give ourselves a year to explore each other deeper, to truly enjoy being newlyweds, blissfully in love.

And we had been. But the anticipation of finally trying for a baby had me bubbling with new-found excitement and wonder. I closed my eyes and let a smile tug at the corners of my lips, imagining Tom playing on this beach with a little version of himself or perhaps one of me, being the amazing father I knew he would become. Our lion. Our protector. Our hero.

My phone buzzed inside my beach bag, popping my lovely

daydream, but the personalized tone announced my husband's summon, which was perfect timing. I'd forgive him this little intrusion into my bubble.

Reaching for the phone, I pressed talk and placed it to my ear as the smile plastered on my face refused to fade. "Hi, my love," I answered.

"Hey, beautiful," he drawled. "Picking you up in fifteen minutes. Be ready." His voice was languid and tainted with a touch of grim darkness, sending a sharp claw scaling down my back. Suddenly, it felt like the sun had been eclipsed by a cluster of ashen clouds.

I sat up straighter. "Is everything okay? Did something happen at the office?"

There was silence on the other end, followed by a deep exhale.

Yeah, my lion was riled. "Tom, what is going on?"

"Just a shit day at work and…"

That pause sent my heart scrambling up my throat. "Babe, what happened?"

"My brother, he called and… and things are not good back home."

Now it made sense why he was in a foul mood.

He had managed to patch up his relationship with his mom and brother, but he still seldom visited home. Except, his mom had been recently diagnosed with dementia, and he and James took turns taking care of all her medical needs. James still lived in the Lake George area, which made it easier for him to look in on their mother, but in the last month, he and Penny, had decided to move in with Adeline.

Tom could easily afford a top-notch assisted living program, and he even had aides living in the home with his mother around the clock, but Adeline had worsened in the last few weeks. She refused to leave her home, not to mention the aides recently quit the job due to Adeline's violent outbursts. Needless to say, he had a ton on his plate right now and unfortunately, he wasn't always the best at communicating when he was feeling off. He was better at brooding and walking around like a grumpy lion.

"You want to talk?"

He grunted. "I just need to go for a drive. And I need you," he uttered, that last word coming off almost as a growl.

"Where to?"

"I don't know yet. I'll be home in a few minutes. Meet me outside."

"Okay."

"And Sara...?"

"Yeah."

"Wear a short skirt and nothing underneath."

Heat flared throughout my entire body. That was his love language. Right now, all he needed to help him forget what troubled him was me. I was his solace, his salve, his home. And I couldn't deny that I loved being that escape—I indulged it. I'd let him consume me if that was what he needed. I'd get on my knees for him and let him fuck my mouth until oblivion if that's what he wanted. And the mere thought of what he had planned for me right now, of how he intended to use my body, had me quivering.

I ran back inside the house, my bare feet leaving a trail of grainy sand all over the back entrance. I hadn't packed a skirt for this trip to Santa Monica, but I did have a couple of short summery dresses stashed in the closet from previous visits. Dropping my book onto the bed, I pulled off my clothes and searched through the closet until I found something that met his qualifications. Sliding into a soft pink, flowery dress, I made sure to leave the bra and panties—just as he'd instructed.

A little shiver skittled over my back. No matter how many times I made love to this man, the anticipation of being with him, of having him own me, always filled me with tingly bubbles.

As I took a quick glance at myself in the floor-length mirror inside our walk-in-closet, I finger-combed my chestnut hair and took in a hearty gulp of air. After smoothing out my dress, I pressed a palm to my cheek. My skin still felt flushed, and I doubted it was from spending the afternoon in the California sun. Sweet warmth pooled low in my belly, making my nether regions clench.

Heavens, would this feeling ever end? The butterflies and the lustful desire we had for each other, even after a year of being married? God, I hoped not.

Still, as much as I loved our sexy encounters, I hated it when he got like this—all stormy clouds and rough seas. His past was a shadow that would always lurk in the corners, but I was determined to be his beacon tonight. I could be his kitten or his lioness. Whatever version of me he desired, I'd give him exactly what he needed.

The rumble of his new Maserati luxury sports car vibrated through the house, announcing his arrival. Grabbing my wristlet off our dresser and a pair of sparkly flip-flops from the shoe rack, I hurried downstairs and out the front door.

Still dressed in his signature gray bespoke suit, he leaned against the passenger door of the idling silvery-blue car, arms crossed over his chest, the chorded muscle of his biceps visible through his suit jacket.

I paused for half a second at the top of the staircase and tried to mask the little gasp that escaped my lips, because quite frankly, sometimes it was humorously infuriating how attractive he was. To think that *this* man was all freaking mine had me literally pinching myself. I could not believe little-old me, dressed in a cheap-ass summer dress and flip-flops, had scored the billionaire businessman decked-out in an Armani suit. But he didn't need to be reminded of how much I lusted after him; he'd guess it soon enough.

A sudden breeze brushed against my bare legs and up my dress, lifting the skirt enough that my husband probably got a tiny glimpse of my naked hoo-ha. Goosebumps erupted all over my body from the cool breeze, and I fumbled with the fabric to keep the dress from totally flipping over my waist and showcasing my naked ass to our neighbors.

"Hi," I said, smiling as I climbed down the rest of the steps, pulling my wind-swept hair from my face and pretending I didn't know why he'd asked me to meet him outside sans undies.

He smirked devilishly as he eyed me from head to toe, his golden-brown mussed-up hair swirling in the breeze. "Hi," he crooned, those olive-green eyes sparkling with mischief, his intent to devour me shamelessly broadcasting through his gaze. There was no hint of the hurricane that must have been churning in those eyes just minutes before.

"Where are you taking me?" I asked, a coy smile tracing across my lips.

He pushed away from the car until he stood at his full six-foot-four height, his chest inches from mine, the scent of his heady cologne engulfing all of my senses. Lifting my chin up with a finger, he eyed me intently, his brow furrowed into that broody, yet smoldering, manner that never failed to disarm me.

Damn, he'd come fully prepared to play the part. Commanding. Dominant. Exuding that confidence that demanded the utmost respect. Leaning down, he whispered in my ear, his hot breath brushing against my skin, sending a ripple of desire straight to my core, "You're driving."

Two simple words, yet they held so much power, so much promise. My mind had teased me with a myriad of fantasies, but none had included me driving his Maserati. The man owned several automotive toys, but this was his favorite. Sleek, sexy, powerful. Utterly intimidating.

My eyes widened. "Excuse me?"

"You heard me, Sara. Get in the driver seat." His lips

twitched as he lifted the passenger door, took a seat, and lowered the door back down.

Holy fuck. I'd never driven any of his cars. I was a city girl, and I preferred public transportation. Aside from my Jeep—which I no longer owned—I seldom drove. And now he wanted me to drive his favorite car, which cost more than a small house? Would I even remember how to drive stick? My dad had taught me, but that had been ages ago. And the fact Tom hadn't even bothered opening the door for me told me he fully expected me to take control of his car, as if *I* owned it.

Still stunned, I slowly walked around the front of the car, trailing a hand over the sculpted hood, letting the engine's soft purr vibrate through me. How the hell was I supposed to tame *this* beast?

After a deep breath, I gripped the door handle and lifted the door, nearly losing my footing in the process. I still wasn't accustomed to the strange way the doors opened in these fancy sports cars. The interior was definitely all masculine by design, with white stitched leather bucket seats, wood veneer-framed interior, and all the high-tech controls.

My stomach tumbled. This was such a bad idea, and certainly not the sexy encounter I'd imagined. Now I was freaking out inside my head that I might pee myself on his beautiful leather seats. My face flushed with heat for a different reason.

"Sara?" He peered over at me, an eyebrow hiked.

"I don't know, Tom... I've not driven stick since high school. Your car intimidates the shit out of me."

"First, stop with the whole *your* car bullshit; it's *our* car. Second, driving stick is like riding a bike."

Yeah, I seriously doubted that. Gulping hard, I lowered into the bucket seat and even though I'd been a passenger countless times, being in the driver's seat felt like getting swallowed up inside some spacecraft. The engine's purr could be felt inside, which at least was one of my favorite parts about this car—that little rumble tickled all of my sensitive areas.

I buckled up in silence and gently tilted my head toward him. He leaned back with confidence, his suit jacket unbuttoned, displaying his snug suit vest and crisp, white dress shirt. He'd taken off his tie and undone the top two buttons of his shirt, exposing the tanned skin of his thick, veiny neck.

His long, muscular legs were definitely too big for this car, and the way his pants bunched up and stretched across his groin—his hard length clearly outlined—made my heart race a little. I'd seen this man's glorious naked body a million times before—I knew every intimate detail about his impressive cock—but there was still something intoxicating and damn arousing about seeing him in his suit.

Shaking a lock of hair from my brow, I tried to pretend I wasn't salivating just thinking about how good my gorgeous CEO would taste right now if I unzipped him, pulled out his dick, and took every inch of him inside my mouth. Instead, clearing my throat, I asked, "Well, where to?"

His gaze narrowed over me. "Remember that lookout I took you to a little while back?"

How could I forget? It was one of the most romantic spots I'd ever seen in my entire life. It was about two miles down Highway 1, then up a winding back road, surrounded by trees that opened up to a clearing near a cliff that faced the Pacific. At the time, the area had been packed with other lovers looking for a semi-private place to fuck.

The heat in those eyes made my insides melt as if we'd just had the same image play out in our heads. Back then, all we did was make out, but the feral look on his face right now had me wondering if he truly intended to fuck me this time.

"Um, what if it's like last time? With lots of other people—"

"Drive, Sara," he ordered, a hint of playfulness softening his deep voice.

Okay. We were doing this. Puffing out a shaky breath, I shifted the car into a drive, and just as he'd said, it all came back to me.

"Looks like you followed my instructions," he said as I pulled out onto the road, his voice a caress that brushed over my skin. The warmth of his hand startled me as he gently traced his fingers up my thigh. "I've had a hard-on for the last fifteen minutes just thinking about this moment."

I swallowed hard as his touch ignited a flame in my center. Instinctively, I turned to look at him, but he reached his other hand and took my chin in his fingers, making me face forward. "Eyes on the road, baby. I need you to stay focused."

I glanced down at my lap. "Kinda hard to do when your hand keeps doing *that.*"

He chuckled. "Do you *like* what my hand is doing?" His fingers found the apex between my legs, and I gasped in shock, yet I spread my thighs a little wider, enough to grant him further access.

An access he exploited.

As his fingers parted my folds, my body tensed and the air locked in my chest. I could not believe I was allowing him to do this while I was driving. Nerves raked over my body. What if he made me jerk my leg and I sent us flying over a cliff on Big Sur?

"Don't forget to breathe, baby," he mused.

"This is not a fun game, Tom."

"You sure about that? Because I'm thoroughly enjoying it." He moved in closer, enough so he could reach my ear with his lips, bathing me in his masculine scent. "You look so good right now. Sitting there, handling my car in that cute pink dress, looking all sweet and innocent to anyone driving by… yet, down here…" he slowly inserted a finger inside me, and I couldn't help the moan that slipped past my lips, "you're anything but innocent."

His breath hitched as his fingers stroked my clit. "Positive you're not enjoying this game? Because your body is telling me otherwise." Then he pulled his fingers from me and licked them clean. "Yeah, I think your body likes this game very much."

As always, my body was an utter traitor. The battle raging inside me was overwhelming. Tom was an expert at seduction and pleasure, and pretending I wasn't enjoying his game was pointless. I was so wet, yet I still couldn't chase away the fear rooting in my core.

"No one can see inside the car," he said, as if he could read my thoughts.

"It's not just that... I don't want to drive us off a cliff."

He chuckled. "You're doing fine, baby."

I spread my legs as much as I could without taking my foot off the peddle.

"Atta girl." He accepted the invitation and drove one finger inside me again, fucking me with slow strokes. The intense pleasure was too much, and I unintentionally closed my eyes, making us swerve. I jerked forward, but Tom had already taken control of the wheel.

"This is dangerous. I can't drive while you do that."

He withdrew his fingers. "I got us. Just focus on the road and let me do the rest."

"I'm trying."

"Try harder. Think about the beautiful sunset painting the sky in purples and red right now. It's your favorite time of day." His hand slowly dove for the inside of my thigh yet again, causing me to jolt. "Easy now..." He parted my thighs, trying not to interfere with my driving as he reached between my legs. "There we go," he breathed against my ear as he parted me. "So smooth and so fucking wet." As he continued to rub my clit, I shifted in my seat to give him better access without letting go of the gas or swerving too much.

"You got the feel of it now," he praised.

"Tom..." I panted, my body aching for more. I gyrated

slowly in my seat, urging him to fuck me harder with his finger. He obliged, and my body turned into a furnace, my breaths growing shallow the closer he got me to the finish line.

The sun finally set completely, and the purples and reds turned to a deep violet and navy blue. Now that the night sky had taken over, when we wound around the road, the head-lights from incoming traffic bathed the inside of our car in a silvery light, and I was so glad for the tinted windows.

Near to climaxing, my nipples tingled. "Fuck. I can't drive like this."

"Yes, you can." He licked my ear, then my neck, sprouting little tremors throughout my body. I couldn't believe he was making me do this, but I also couldn't make him stop.

Just as I was about to come, he retrieved his hand and I shot him a nasty look, growling my displeasure.

"A bit impatient, aren't you?" he taunted.

With my eyes back on the road, I white-knuckled the steering wheel. "You're enjoying this little torturous game of yours, aren't you?"

"How could I not?" He slid a hand down the front of my dress and pulled one of my breasts free. My jaw tightened, anxiety surging through my veins along with something else— something richer, darker. The thought of possibly being exposed to anyone driving beside us thrilled me, and I sank deeper into his touch. He exposed my second breast and just left me there, practically naked, with my chest aching for more of his delicious torture.

"You look so fucking hot right now, Sara."

"Tom..." I moaned.

"Yeah?"

"I need—"

"This?" He reached over and massaged my breasts, rubbing and gently pinching my nipples. The sting was the most delicious pain I'd ever experienced as it sent a jolt of electricity to my clit, making it swell and throb harder.

"How's your pussy feel?" he asked as he leaned in, palming a breast and sucking on my nipple.

I couldn't speak; I couldn't even breathe.

"This is what my tongue wants to do to it," he added as his tongue swirled around my nipple, fast, then slow, before he did the same thing to the other breast.

I was going to come without him even touching my pussy. He must have read my mind because he immediately lowered his hand and dipped two fingers inside me, pumping hard as I moaned his name like he was pure nectar pouring down my throat.

"That feels so fucking good," I intoned, drunk with pleasure.

"How good?"

I moved my hips in rhythm with his fingers, but it caused me to swerve again. "Fuck."

"Careful, baby."

"I want out of this seat."

"Get us to that overlook," he said, pulling out of me and moving back to his seat. He tugged at his pants and from the corner of my eye, I watched him unzip his trousers, take out his cock, and reach for my hand.

Holy shit. Now he wanted me to give him a hand job while I drove? Everything about this was so crazy, yet I couldn't stop. I didn't know how to say no—probably because I didn't *want* to say no. The danger of it all had my heart pumping with adrenaline, and I wanted to keep chasing that high no matter what. I wrapped my fingers around his warm, hard girth, and I literally felt myself salivate.

His deep breaths fanned my ego as I gripped him harder. "I love how you do that, baby."

A smug smirk twisted my lips. Yeah, I had my own bag of seductive tricks.

Thankfully, the exit ramp to the overlook was only a few yards ahead. We wound around several narrow roads until we were completely surrounded by tall trees, the moon peeking through the thick canopy.

He waved a finger toward the right. "Forget the overlook; turn here instead. It's more secluded. I think I've tortured us enough, and I don't feel like flinging anyone over the cliff if the overlook is crowded."

Dirt crunched under the tires as I made the turn. "You sure driving this car off-road without four-wheel is a good idea? Not to mention, it's dark as coal out here."

"Are you scared I might do something sinister to you?"

I shot him a sideways glance as I slowly drove the car down the path. "Depends what you mean by sinister."

He nodded toward what looked like a man-made parking spot under a tree. "Pull over right there, and I'll show you."

My lips twitched with a suppressed smile, but I did as he asked. The moment I pulled into the spot under the tall oak, he jumped out of the car. "Climb over the console into the passenger seat," he instructed in a rush.

Well then. He was earnest, and I was more than happy to oblige.

Shutting off the engine, we were quickly engulfed not only by darkness, but by the eerie silence of the brush. Once my vision adjusted, the platinum light of the moon was all I needed in order to see what mattered.

Tom stood right outside the passenger door, his legs shoulder-width apart. He'd taken off his suit jacket and had flung it God only knew where. He rolled up his shirt's sleeves, and Heaven help me, as if watching him do that didn't make me almost lose my sanity as I climbed over the console. Unfortunately, he'd tucked his cock back into his pants. Once I'd situated myself on the passenger seat, he leaned down and rubbed the pad of his thumb over my bottom lip. "Turn toward me. I want you to lift that dress and show me exactly how ready your pussy is for me."

Eyes wide, I gulped hard and nodded. Leaning my back

against the console, I lifted my dress and shamelessly spread my legs for my husband.

He unzipped his pants and pulled out his steel-hard cock, stroking his erection and making his dick swell larger. "Touch yourself," he said, his eyes heavy-lidded and lips slack.

Watching him stroke himself made me wild, so I gently parted my pussy and flicked my clit, moaning at the sweet tingle that radiated from my center and up my belly.

"Just like that, baby. Get yourself right to the edge, then stop."

"I don't want to stop," I panted, massaging my clit harder, watching as he stroked himself faster, wanting to see him come undone as well.

He reached over and grabbed my hand, taking it away from my pussy. "I said no."

My clit was so swollen and ready to burst, it hurt not to be able to finish. He used both his palms to keep my thighs spread and just stared down at me, gorging on my exposed body. I breathed deep and heavy as he slowly caressed my thighs, his hands migrating to my center where he began to finger-fuck me with one hand and thrummed my clit with the thumb of his other. I struggled to spread my legs wider in the tight bucket seat.

"You're dripping wet, Sara. And your clit is so swollen."

Moaning and trembling, I prepared to let go, but he pulled his hands away again. This time I was ready to kill him for being such a fucking tease, but his tongue was lapping at my cleft before I had a chance to utter a single complaint. I watched his tongue brush over my tingling clit, and I nearly lost my mind just thinking about being out here in the open where anyone could drive down this dirt path and see us on the side of the road—with Tom's tongue deep inside me, fucking me with his mouth.

The pleasure was too much, and I wasn't able to hold on any longer. This time I didn't hesitate or give him a warning; I came in his mouth as he sucked on my clit and finger-fucked me for added pleasure.

"Good?" he asked, licking his lips and his eyes twinkling with satisfaction. A wolfish grin curled the corners of his mouth as he watched me come down from my post-orgasm aftershocks.

My head was so dizzy from the adrenaline, I could barely see straight.

His grin widened.

"My turn," I said, getting out of the car and straightening my mini dress.

Tom sat back down in the seat, shimming his pants and boxers down to his ankles. Without a moment to waste, I bent down to take him into my mouth. The velvety hardness of his dick felt amazing against my tongue. He tasted even better tonight. I gorged on him, taking him so deep I gagged, but I wanted him fully inside me, filling me to the hilt. I *needed* him to. As I sucked and licked, he pulled my dress over my ass and slapped me, hard. The sting was painful and delightful. Caressing my throbbing skin, he leaned further back until his fingers could reach my entrance and he could finger-fuck me as I worshiped his cock.

"Mmm," I moaned, the vibration of my vocal chords as I held him in my mouth made him shudder. He grew larger and I knew he was ready to come, so I pulled him out of my mouth and was about to ask him for a condom when he said, "Not tonight."

"What do you mean, not tonight?"

"I mean, I don't want to use a condom."

"But I'm no longer on the pill..."

He grinned at me. "*Exactly.*"

"Wait... Are you saying what I think you're saying?"

He nodded, a crooked smile carving across his cheeks. "I want this as badly as you do, Sara. Nothing would make me happier than to make a baby with you."

With a gigantic smile plastered on my face, I sat on him before he could blink. I took his lips in mine while I slid my wet pussy over his hard dick. "Those might be the sexiest words you've ever said to me, husband," I murmured with a chuckle as I struggled to comfortably straddle him. This car was definitely not designed with fucking in mind, but the cramped space kinda added to the excitement. We made it work, even if we had to keep the door open.

Tom moaned and gripped me tighter, his hands riding up my thighs. Then, in one swift move, I seated myself completely over of his shaft, rocking back and forth until I felt a little jab of pain deep in my core. God, how I'd missed the feel of his warm skin inside me.

"Is this what you wanted?" I asked, riding him slowly, keeping his eyes locked on mine.

"Yes," he hissed, grabbing my breasts and bringing my nipples to his mouth.

"You wanted to fuck me in your car?"

"Ever since the night at the club back when we first met."

I drove into him deeper, circling my hips, making sure he felt all of me.

"You drive me crazy when you do that," he uttered, his voice raw and carnal.

"How crazy?"

He took my hips and began beating hard into me.

"People are gonna see us," I cried.

"Let them." His hands spread my cheeks so wide, my ass was completely exposed. I had no doubt anyone driving or walking down this road would catch the show. But the crudeness of it all made me wetter.

"Tom, when you spread me like that... you make me want you in my ass."

"You rouse the beast inside me when you say shit like that," he growled.

"I want you to claim my body—*all of it*—if that's what you need tonight."

He slowed and peered deep into my eyes, sensing I was offering him more than just my body. I wanted him to take everything from me, because deep down, I hoped it would heal him from the pain he was trying to numb. "I will claim every inch of your body and will take you there if that's what you want. But only because you want it, and not because you're doing it for me. And definitely not here. This is not going to be the place where we first do that."

I nodded, my cheeks flushing with heat. I hated that I'd even mentioned it.

He smiled warmly. "Don't feel embarrassed, baby. I like that you want me there, but that's going to take practice. And I want to make sure when we do it for the first time, we do it right. That you enjoy it. Is this..." he motioned with his pelvis as he thrust inside me, "not enough?"

"It's more than enough," I moaned.

"Then let me make you come again." He brought his lips to mine and kissed me feverishly, bringing the both of us to a shuddering release. The car shook, and our screams must have been heard from down the road, but we didn't care. In this universe—our universe—we were the only ones who existed, and nothing else mattered... except, maybe the little person our love might have created tonight.

Tom drove us back home at a leisurely pace, my arm hooked around his as he worked the stick shift. When we got to the beach house, a prickle ran down the length of my spine. I didn't recall leaving the lights on inside.

Suddenly, my body tightened, recalling what had happened to me a little over a year ago when I was attacked by a home intruder. Noticing the panic in my eyes, Tom took my hand in his.

"Sara, look at me. What's wrong?"

"I... I didn't leave the lights on." My breath shook as I turned to look at him. "What if someone's inside?"

He caressed my cheek, a soft smile tugging at his lips. "Aw, baby, I'm so sorry. I wanted to surprise you, but I guess I didn't think this through..."

"Think what through?"

"There *is* someone inside... well, *was*, if she did as I asked."

"Who are you talking about?"

"Given tomorrow is our anniversary, I wanted to do something a little extra special for you, so I enlisted the help of your BFF."

I gasped, "Jen's here?"

"Hopefully not anymore."

"What's the surprise?"

"Go inside and find out."

I couldn't have leapt out of the car and ran up the staircase to the front entrance any faster if I'd tried. When I pushed through the door, my heart plummeted. The entire first floor was lit by lanterns that seemed to light a path to the back deck facing the ocean. Tyron Wells piped through the sound system, crooning my favorite song, *Sea Breeze*. With the glass doors to the deck opened, you could hear the waves crashing against the shore.

The salty current in the air brushed against my skin as I followed the lanterns out to the deck. Perched on our patio table was a sparkling pastry tower in the shape of the Eiffel Tower, displaying a rainbow array of my favorite French treat, macaroons.

Tom's arms snaked around my waist, my hair whipping in the wind. "What is all this about?" I asked, wondering why he'd gone through all this trouble to give me macaroons.

"Did you open the note?"

Note? I'd completely missed the envelope sitting next to the tower. Hurrying to rip it open, I read:

Dear bestie,

It was brought to my attention that last time you visited Paris with your then-boyfriend, soon-to-be-fiancé, you didn't get to visit any of the sight-seeing sites you'd planned your entire life to see because apparently, after he proposed, you spent the entire trip fucking in your palatial suite instead of following your carefully crafted itinerary.

I paused, a hand covering the nervous laugh that bubbled from my lips. "Oh my God. Jen has no filter."

"I love that about her," Tom said.

Shaking my head, I continued:

To remedy that, Tom asked me to help him come up with the perfect gift. So, for your one-year anniversary, your husband is taking you back to Paris to visit all your favorite sites, eat at that fancy celebrity restaurant you missed last time, and still have time to do all the fucking you desire.

Jen (you can thank me later)

I turned to Tom, my mouth agape. "Are you kidding me? *Paris? Again?*"

"Unless you prefer to go somewhere else?"

Throwing my arms around him, he lifted me up into his chest as I planted a kiss on his lips. "I've been dreaming of going back ever since you took me for my birthday."

He set me back down. "Fantastic, because we leave first thing tomorrow morning."

"Oh my God! I can't believe this. I thought we were just going to spend a quiet little anniversary here at the house, and now we're flying out tomorrow!"

"Is the timing not right?"

"Everything is perfect. I'm just in shock. Wait, so the whole thing with your brother and mom, and having a shitty day at work... That was all fake?"

"I wish. I mean, the job part was, but things with my family are... Well, let's not ruin the mood with family troubles, yeah?" Taking me back into his arms, he said, "Right now, I just want to enjoy my wife."

He took me by the hand and guided me up to our

bedroom. "Jen even took the liberty of packing our bags, so we have the night free. What do you say, Mrs. Wright? Should we go for round two and keep trying to make that baby?"

I grinned so wide my face hurt. "Have I told you how much I love you?"

"No, but I know about a million and one ways you can show me."

I already knew what he had planned for me, and I couldn't wait to spend the rest of the night and the wee hours of the morning showing him *exactly* how much I did, in fact, love him.

Epilogue

SARA

Seven Years Later...

"Charlotte Elizabeth Wright!" I shouted after my five-year-old darling daughter as she ran away from me. "Charlie, get back here. We're going to be late for your holiday recital!"

Feet thumping against the hardwood floors, she ran barefoot down the hall of our SoHo apartment, wearing her pink tutu, and her long golden-brown hair swooshing down her back. "I don't want my hair up, Mommy," she snapped, her voice trailing.

With a labored breath, I stood up from the chair of the vanity set in her room. Placing a hand on my lower back, and another on my bulbous belly, I looked around her pale-pink and cream-colored bedroom and sighed. I'd been so stressed about this day. Wanting it to be perfect—fussing about her clothes, her shoes, her solo—I may have stressed her out, too. I'd promised myself I wouldn't push her. That I would let her bloom at her own pace. And she had. To my delight, after spending countless days and nights with me at the dance studio, she had decided entirely on her own she wanted to become a ballet dancer.

Continuing to look around her room, searching for her

ballet slippers, I thought back to the day we found out we were pregnant with our second child. With Charlotte, we got pregnant shortly after deciding we were ready to start a family. It had been an easy pregnancy and birth. And for almost three years, the three of us were inseparable, traveling and doing everything together. But when we decided we wanted to add to our family, the second time around getting pregnant was not so easy. We had been trying for a little over a year to have another baby with zero luck, and right when we thought maybe it was not in our cards, I felt the signs.

As part of our announcement to Charlotte, we converted her toddler room into a big girl's room fit for a young princess. She'd been ecstatic to finally have a full-sized bed. To be honest, it looked more like a throne than a bed. I may have gone a bit over the top when I decorated her room, but she was my first baby—and my daughter—and it filled me with such joy to see her face light up as soon as we revealed it to her. She'd been thrilled to know she was going to be a big sister. And up until recently, she couldn't stop talking about how helpful she was going to be, and how she couldn't wait to be like a second mommy to the baby.

In the last couple of weeks though, her attitude had changed slightly. Watching me prepare for the arrival of her baby brother had affected her. Up until now, she'd been the center of our attention, and with the realization the baby would be arriving home soon, her thrill had turned to a bit of sibling jealousy.

It broke my heart to think she could believe I wouldn't love her anymore because we were going to have another baby. Today was one of those days where for some reason, she felt frustrated with me, and I knew it had to do with the pregnancy. I was two weeks from my due date and had already felt the baby drop lower a few days ago. She must have heard me talking about it, and it stirred up those uncomfortable feelings inside her. This was her way of letting me know.

Broody. Just like her father.

After finding her ballet slippers, I wobbled down the long hallway from her room to the living area, the hardwood floors gleaming from the late afternoon sun shining through the large, ten-foot windows of our eighth-floor apartment. I would have run after her— picked up my pace since we were running so late—but it may have sent me into labor. The last thing she needed was Mommy ruining her recital because the baby was coming early.

As I rounded the corner, relief washed over me. Sitting on our gray sectional by the windows, Tom had a comb between his lips while he worked to slick and tighten Charlotte's ponytail. Once done, he braided it then twisted it into a perfect knot. Mr. Wright was a Pro at ballerina buns. Could he possibly get any sexier? Seriously.

I realized then it wasn't that she didn't want to wear a bun, she just wanted her daddy to be the one who tied it for her. I shook my head, and whispered to myself, "Pick your battles, Sara. Pick your battles. She's a daddy's girl. That's all."

As I continued to wobble toward them, they both turned to face me at the same time. I took in a small gasp. The same gasp I took every time I gazed at them together. He stood up, picking her up in his muscled arms, and said, "What do you think, Mommy? Did I do a good job?"

Charlotte smiled, the biggest and gushiest smile a five-year-old could ever give. It took my breath away.

She was her father's spitting image—the charming smile, golden-brown hair, pouty lips, and the same olive-colored eyes that had stolen my heart when I'd first met her father.

"You did an amazing job, Daddy," I replied, smiling. "And you, my little darling," I said to Charlie, "Look positively beautiful."

"Daddy says I look like a prima ballerina," she uttered proudly, turning to face him. When their eyes met, they smiled at each other like they were sharing a very special secret. They were so in love with each other. She was without a doubt, daddy's little princess. In his eyes, she could never do any wrong, and she had him wrapped around her little finger so tight, Tom was screwed for the rest of his life. And any would-be boyfriends were screwed, too. Tom still owned a gun and was still an expert shooter.

"Okay, baby," I said to Charlotte, "we can still make it to the show on time. Go grab your tiara from your dresser. I'll grab your second outfit."

Grunting, she pouted and wrapped her arms tightly around her father's neck.

"Charlie," Tom said in a very soothing tone, rubbing her back as he held her up with his other arm. "You have to do what Mommy's telling you, okay?" She clung to him tighter. "C'mon, baby. I don't want to miss your big solo. I'm so excited to see what you and Mommy have been working on these past couple of months."

She let go of his neck and perked up, pursing her lips to the side as if contemplating her reply. "Fine. But only if you promise to buy me ice-cream after the show."

"Deal."

With that, he lowered her, and she skipped away to her bedroom.

I whirled on him, my eyes wide and chiding. "Deal?"

"You want to get to the recital or not?" he asked, shrugging.

Letting out a deflated breath, I sagged into his chest. The baby bump making it extremely difficult to put my arms around him. "She hates me," I uttered on the verge of tears.

Damn hormones.

Gently taking my face in his palms, he said, "She doesn't hate you. She's five and she's going through a thing. She'll outgrow it. I promise."

"But what if she doesn't? She will hate the baby and me for ruining the perfect little world we created for her."

He smirked.

Hiking a brow, I asked, "What's so funny?"

Shooting me a sidelong glance, he said, "Nothing. It's just… well, she's a lot like you."

"No. She's exactly like you."

Gliding his index finger down my nose in a tender gesture, he said, "Why do you think she's got me wrapped around her little finger? Because she got that from you. Her smart mouth. The pouty lips when she doesn't get her way, the twinkle in her eye when she knows she's got me eating out of the palm of her hand. She's exactly like her mommy. And the reason I love you and her so much."

"Mommy, Daddy. I'm ready." Charlotte's tiny voice pulled our attention.

She stood a few paces from us, her big eyes staring up at us, her tiara neatly placed on her head, and her ballet slippers in her hands. "Will you help me with these, Mommy?" She held them up for me and smiled.

That smile got me every time. Tom kissed me and said, "See." Then he hurried to the entrance, and taking his keys off the kitchen counter, he grabbed his jacket off the coatrack, and said, "I'll get the car. Meet you girls downstairs."

"Okay, Daddy," Charlotte shouted after her father.

Although difficult to do with a ripe belly, I kneeled to be at eye level with her. "We'll put these on once we get to the studio, okay?" Right now, you can wear your boots."

She nodded. As I grabbed her hand and led her to the entrance so we could grab our coats, a little jab hit me from inside my abdomen. "Ow," I yelped.

"What is it, Mommy?"

"The baby. He just kicked. Hard."

"Can I feel it?"

"Of course, honey. Here." Placing her hand over my belly, her face lit up as soon as she felt the baby push against her hand. "You felt it?" I asked.

She giggled. "Yeah."

"That was him telling you he loves you."

"I love him too," she replied, turning from me, and rushing to get her boots.

Perhaps Tom was right.

Things were going to be all right.

MY PRIMA BALLERINA WAS MAGNIFICENT. Misty-eyed, I watched from the audience, awed and fascinated. I knew she was five and that at this age she was still learning technique, but it was her heart I saw out there—the sparkle in her eyes when the audience applauded, the smile stretching for miles. This must have been how my mother felt when she watched me dance. I was so proud of my little girl. I couldn't wait to tell her.

After the show, we presented her with a big bouquet of flowers and took her to dinner at our usual Italian restaurant. Spaghetti and meatballs were her favorite. And as Daddy promised, after dinner he took us to get ice cream at the best homemade ice cream parlor in the city. Charlotte fell asleep in the backseat of Tom's new Rover as we drove back home. I couldn't stop looking at her. Her hair now loose from the bun, it cascaded down her shoulders in wavy curls. She was so perfect, my heart ached. I peered over at Tom and watched him handle the wheel. He was still so stunningly beautiful. Reaching over and raking the back of his neck with my nails, I said, "Thank you."

"For what?"

"For giving me her. For keeping your promise and making me the happiest woman in the world."

"We gave her to each other. And I think it's the other way

around. I'm the happiest and luckiest man to ever walk this earth."

"Are we just going to keep swapping corny comments with each other? See who can say the cheesiest thing ever?"

"Always. And I'm keeping score, by the way. I have a spreadsheet."

Playfully nudging his arm, I said, "Stop it. No, you don't."

We both burst out laughing and that's when it happened.

Speechless and stunned, I froze in my seat.

"What is it, Sara? Are you okay?" Tom asked, his voice edged with concern.

"My water just broke."

NICHOLAS ALEXANDER WRIGHT was born at 9:53 p.m. When the nurses placed him on my chest, skin to skin, my heart instantly doubled in size. I had fallen in love all over again. He was the most beautiful baby boy I had ever seen. And he was hungry from the moment he came out, latching on immediately without a problem.

"You did amazing, Mama," Tom said, kissing me on the forehead. "He's… perfect." Stroking his son's cheek as he nursed, Tom looked transfixed.

"He looks like you," I told him.

"Nah, he's all you, baby." He kissed me again. "Welcome to the world, little buddy," he said to Nicholas. "Thanks to you, our family is now complete."

A few days later, after being back home from the hospital, I was breastfeeding Nicholas while sitting on my bed. It was 2:00 a.m. and Tom and Charlotte were both passed out next to me. She'd come in around midnight complaining about a bad dream. Tom let her climb in with us and I didn't object. I loved watching them sleep. They looked even more alike when their features were at rest.

Smiling, I looked down at my baby. After gorging himself on milk, he'd finally fallen asleep. His pudgy cheeks were soft and warm, and his perfectly rosy lips were still moving as if he was still suckling. I could not believe how much I already loved him. Looking back over at Charlotte cradled in Tom's arms, her head resting on his chest, rising and falling along with his breaths, I could not believe how it was possible for your heart to be so full of love and happiness.

I glanced over to the floor and found Bax and Skiddles also nestled next to each other on Bax's huge bed. They'd become best buds from the moment they met. Go figure. Kissing Nicholas on the forehead, I placed him down beside me on his co-sleeper then shut off the light. I snuggled next to Charlotte, sandwiching her between Tom and me, and slowly began to drift off to sleep.

And this, right here, was my true happily ever after.

Acknowledgments

Thank you to my family and friends for supporting me during the relaunch of my billionaire duet. I'm also grateful for all my readers, old and new. So happy to have you on this journey. Lots more is yet to come.

Love always,
Liv

Available on
Kindle
&
Audio
Duet Narration performed by
Megan Carver and James Clements

Available on Kindle

REAL LOVE AS IT IS. MESSY. COMPLICATED. AND SINFULLY ADDICTIVE.

Olivia Boothe is a contemporary romance and fantasy author.

Born in Colombia and raised in New Jersey since the age of eight, Olivia always dreamed of becoming a storyteller. Now, she enjoys crafting novels with deep, layered plots because romance is not just about the first kiss and the happily ever after, it's about everything in between.

In addition to writing, Olivia loves reading across all genres, binge watching her favorite TV shows, and hanging out on Tuesday nights with her girlfriends for wine, snacks, and junk-TV therapy. Olivia lives in Northern New Jersey with her hubby, three boys, and a mini Aussie named Rosie.

To read more from Olivia, visit her website and follow her on social media:

https://www.oliviaboothe.com